Antoine Laurent was born in 1᾽ cated in Paris, and later at Ha School of Fine Art. He has tau scripts. He is now a full-time wri *Novella* is his first novel.

ANTOINE LAURENT

Cuisine Novella

PALADIN
GRAFTON BOOKS
A Division of the Collins Publishing Group

LONDON GLASGOW
TORONTO SYDNEY AUCKLAND

Grafton Books
A Division of the Collins Publishing Group
8 Grafton Street, London W1X 3LA

Published in Paladin Books 1989

First published in Great Britain by
Martin Secker & Warburg Ltd 1987

ISBN 0-586-08736-2

Printed and bound in Great Britain by
Collins, Glasgow

Set in Palatino

CHAPTER ONE

With his long black cloak swirling about him and his fedora set at a rakish angle, the Marquis de St Lyre stops before the Place St Sulpice and surveys its windswept acreage. Its stone-flagged square, the vermilion-worn statue at its centre, and the peace that exudes from the church's twin towers hold him for a few moments. But once a burst of pigeons' wings has shattered the unnatural city silence and has altered the square's otherwise equable mood, he resumes his journey and turns down a side street in the opposite corner. Barely glancing at its shop windows filled to bursting with reproduction antiques, he soon issues on to one of the Quartier-Latin's bustling concourses.

Much as the former colonies of once great empires haunt them by clogging their memories with the deed of their shame, so the *cuisines* of the conquests of the French can be found strung along that petulant and often meretricious channel of consumerist chic, the Boulevard St Germain. Could it be because among so many dispensing foreign food it is the only one to serve French fare that the first restaurant to attract the Marquis' attention is La Chaumière?

In adopting the country cottage's most common features, La Chaumière has unashamedly exploited the lodes of nostalgia. It is with amusement that the Marquis gazes at the artful sham of its decor: its fake thatched roof, narrow cross-mullioned panes, rust-coloured wooden shutters, and the petunia-filled flower-pots which have been prettily arranged in a row along its windows. He is just about to move on when, through its spangled panes, he catches sight of a woman in her mid-twenties, garbed rather anachronistically for a rural inhabitant in a tight-fitting leopard skin costume complete with fishnet stockings. Hardly has she crossed the restaurant's threshold and started to sweep dust into the street when she too notices him and tosses him the kind of glance that makes men bar-boast that, if only they'd had the time, they'd have bagged their pleasure's worth there and then.

The Boulevard's flow of feuding traffic, the lazy disportment of foreigners, and the insouciance of Parisians all combine to render it that early afternoon even more tawdry than usual, its commercial bluster clashing with the confident bourgeois self-esteem it was once designed to flaunt. The Marquis, who long ago ceased to expect romance from the Rive-Gauche, continues to saunter down the street until, a little further down, his attention is caught by yet another restaurant.

As its name suggests, Les Pyramides proposes to its clients a variety of Middle Eastern fare, priding itself particularly on its shish kebabs, boiled spiced sheep's eyes, and, the cook's speciality, goat's steak served with couscous. On its front it has smeared the decorations the naive imagination usually associates with that Nile-bisected land: pyramids (of papier-mâché), palm trees (made of some unknown material), a Sphinx's head (that leers), while, at the right hand edge of its plate glass window, there sits the coiled figure of a (plastic) asp. Behind this collection of overworked images, the Marquis is delighted to glimpse the silhouette of a fine-featured young man, his hair ebony, his skin sand, his manner diffusing a rare form of animal charm. Having quickly feasted on this sight, and with a perhaps over self-conscious swish of his cape, he pushes his exploration further on.

Ignoring the thousand and one pleas which the Boulevard's bounteous boutiques and florid pharmacies keep aiming at his pocket and sensibility, the Marquis stops for a moment to peer at L'Escurial which, in contrast to its resplendent eponym, is little more than a garishly decorated corridor boasting Hispanic regional specialities.

In front of this restaurant there stands a mobile menu in the shape of a goateed grandee, a cardboard figure set up no doubt to seduce casual passers-by into tasting paellas, rough Catalan wines and crayfish slowly cooked in clear reduced sauces. In the centre of the grandee's stomach is a small glass flap, with, behind it, a scrolled menu written in elaborate longhand. Precariously balanced on the chair which he has placed next to the cutout, a bearded dwarf, draped in an oversized striped apron, is busy unfastening the flap. In his hand he holds another scroll, presumably the day's menu which he means to exchange for the old. He is in such a hurry, however, and his gestures are so staccato that the chair soon starts to topple over, and only just in time does he prevent himself falling over by hanging on to the figure. When it too starts to collapse, he deftly jumps back on to the stabilized chair. Extracting the old menu from the belly of the cutout, he flings it to the ground and, with the new menu fast in the gap and the glass flap closed, he climbs down as if he had never had the slightest brush with danger. Hands on hips, he takes a few steps back and scrutinizes the change which he has made. Seemingly satisfied, he then strides through the open door of the restaurant and disappears into its depths. The Marquis, who, together with an elderly pensioner promenading his mangy dog, has admired the dwarf's stunt from its danger-ous beginnings through to its triumphant finale, now that the performance has come to an end salutes his fellow spectator and jauntily moves on.

A little way past the shelter of St Germain-des-Prés' limestone square, which a group of Japanese tourists are fast immortaliz-ing with their beautifully tooled black boxes, the Marquis stops outside the imposing and ornate façade of a *belle époque* Brasserie, La Fortune. He looks through its ample glass frontage then, without further hesitation, goes into it. Choosing a table in a far corner, he unfurls his cape, takes off his fedora, and, discreetly looking around him, takes a seat.

The Brasserie's walls are hung with wide mirrors slightly speckled at their edges, testimony either to clever refurbishment or to the discoloration which attends glass anciently electrolyzed with silver oxide. As soon as he has settled beneath this infinity of reflecting surfaces, the Marquis nods at the venerable blue-spectacled matron who, from behind the walnut veneer of her cash desk, dominates her establishment. Distracted from her sums by his greetings, she nods back before swiftly returning to her methodical pursuits. The Marquis next beckons to an angular-faced waiter who is sliding across the black and white check of the floor tiles and who in his arrogance resembles the type Toulouse-Lautrec caught so pointedly in the posters of his *Moulin Rouge* period. The waiter acknowledges the request with a side glance, then heads off in the opposite direction, his gestures finely attuned to the fact that long before a customer's temper is likely to snap, he can first be made to run a humiliating gauntlet of the functionary's own choosing. Taking his time to collect tips from nearby tables, the waiter spills their meagre harvest into a pouch of marsupial proportions before finally ambling over to the Marquis' table. Well accustomed to such mischievous behaviour, indeed apparently inured to it, the Marquis makes no comment but simply gives the waiter his order.

"A glass of calvados and a black coffee and, *garçon*, make it strong."

"At once, *m'sieur*."

While the waiter proceeds to the counter, the Marquis casts his eye over the hunting scenes handpainted on the Brasserie's colourful tiled walls.

Lunch time has long since passed and consequently the Brasserie is almost completely deserted. As the streets are sunny, people are out and about, neither walking with any very definite purpose nor, for that matter, wandering about aimlessly but rather putting themselves through the paces of that proto-typical Parisian activity *flâner*, in the hope perhaps of being blessed by the goddess Fortune.

Bent behind the curved prow of the counter, the waiter manoeuvres the espresso machine's cups and levers, disburses a pulse of steam into the readied grounds, pours a decent measure of spirit into a bulbous glass, and brings the Marquis his drinks on a tray. The latter lets both stand awhile on the table's marble circle – as if movement were somehow inimical to calvados, and coffee should first part-settle its sediment before being drunk – then sips each in turn.

The apple essence and double-roasted *arabica* coffee are pleasantly slipping down the Marquis' throat when the waiter pushes past the kitchen swing doors with a plate of food balanced on his right hand and places it before a female customer. This young lady, sitting only two tables away from the Marquis, has already made some impact on him. It could be the way she nonchalantly flicks through a woman's magazine, making margin notes on a pad whenever something attracts or displeases her in its carousel of fashion. Or her blonde hair, cut in a style which frames her delicately chiselled face. Or her

4

aloofness, the kind which makes fanciers of the secrets of female psychology insist that what the lady behind the frigid façade really hankers after is an amorous encounter. Or it may be that, apart from a nearby drunk slouched over his table, there is no one else in the Brasserie the Marquis might usefully accost.

As soon as the waiter has set the plate down, his customer looks up from her magazine and shifts from her formerly relaxed position, in so doing offering the Marquis a greatly improved view of her profile. Attractive, of that there is no doubt. Probably in her mid-twenties, he also guesses. As for her dress sense – blue gaberdine trousers, a grey, dimpled maritime sweater, leather jacket – while studiedly casual, it is also, he recognizes, at the very height of fashion. Not an uncommon sartorial image and one which she has heightened with a wide-brimmed black felt hat now perched on the table before her.

Placing the magazine to one side she begins to eat. After only one mouthful, however, she winces and puts her fork down.

As soon as the dish's aroma has keened towards him, the Marquis has to concede that the young lady's reaction is well-founded: the food indeed smells vile. He cannot prevent himself betraying a wry smile. Although why her culinary misfortune should have afforded him such immediate satisfaction is far from clear.

Long before we can divine any explanation for this surprising response, the Marquis has risen from his table and has walked over to the young lady's. For a second he stands in silence over her and scrutinizes the dish. "Mademoiselle!" he at last exclaims. "You're not seriously considering eating any more of this?"

At a loss to explain the sudden and wholly unsolicited appearance at her side of this tall, middle-aged customer, the young lady replies: "Er . . . well, no."

"I hope not. I've never come across anything so disgraceful!"

"What . . . what I don't understand," stammers the young lady, trying to come to grips with the somewhat awkward situation, "is that this Brasserie's supposed to have a good reputation."

"Perhaps it did – once!" the Marquis answers, pointing at the dish in which a mix of vegetables is drowning in an oily sauce, "although this is the kind of performance which could put paid to it overnight."

She examines the stranger's unsmiling face and the grey ardour in his eyes. "Do you think I should send it back?"

"Indeed, Mademoiselle, and right away."

For what could be simpler? Has a standard not been debased, a recipe spoiled if not raped? Should every ounce of civic sense, when confronted by a dish of such dismal quality, not be roused to a pitch of outrage? Yet there is also the risk of ridicule. Might the restaurateur, master in his own locale, not put the accuser through a series of humiliating paces? A threat to which, the Marquis surmises, the young lady seems particularly sensitive.

"Perhaps you'd allow me to be of some assistance?" he suggests, pointing to the disgraced dish.

An invitation which surprises her. After a second's hesitation, she accepts it even though, tainted with the notion that she is not wholly capable of handling her own affairs, she comes close to rejecting it. Checking her overly touchy nature, however, she decides that as his offer seems to be genuine, it would be churlish to refuse it.

The Marquis beckons to the waiter who, lacking any task behind which to hide, has to shuffle over from the counter. "*Garçon!*" The Marquis' voice has become coldly authoritative. "What do you mean by this?"

Plainly put out by being cross-examined in his own territory, the waiter shifts his eyes across the room as if trying to avoid the question. Fixed without respite by the Marquis' unwavering manner, he is forced however to glance at the dish. "Monsieur?" he enquires innocently to gain time, fast becoming aware that something unpleasant is in store for him.

"How dare you serve this disaster to the lady!" the Marquis exclaims. "It's a disgrace to the profession. Take it away this instant!"

Not so much shamed by the appalling evidence on the plate but by his inability to counter it with his usual brand of arrogance, the waiter silently clears the plate away. "*Je vous demande pardon*, Mademoiselle. But, you see, the chef is ill today. And as his *commis* hasn't been with us long, he has not cooked everything we offer." Then, parading a solicitude quite at odds with his former haughtiness, he adds: "Perhaps I can bring you the menu? You will choose something else, on the house, *bien sûr* . . ."

6

"I really don't advise it," says the Marquis, interrupting the waiter's plaintive tone and scotching his pacificatory pose. "This mess, let's face it, is a loud and salutary warning." He once again dismisses the dish with a wave of his hand. "No, Mademoiselle, the last thing you should do is venture further into this risk-filled menu. What you need is something that'll wash the foul taste away. I suggest a glass of calva."

"A calva? Yes, why not?"

"Waiter," orders the Marquis, "bring us two calvas. And make sure it's the house's best!"

Her lips pursed, the Brasserie's patroness looks up from her accounts, decides that the storm has abated, and rapidly returns to the refuge of her books. His unusually terse step betraying his anger at being publicly upbraided in his fiefdom, the waiter heads for the kitchens where, a second later, the loud clatter of plates and the clamour of a raised voice suggest that he has lost no time sharpening his wits on the guilty apprentice.

"Allow me to introduce myself," says the Marquis, putting his hand forward. "Jean-Loup, Marquis de St Lyre. Delighted to meet you, even under such strained circumstances, Mademoiselle . . .?"

"Fleury. Annabelle Fleury." She takes his dry firm hand and shakes it.

The Marquis points to the empty chair at her table. "Might I join you, Mademoiselle Fleury?"

"Why, yes, do." She takes her magazine, her open notepad and her hat and, gathering them towards her on the table, makes room for her unexpected guest.

"It's a sad fact that culinary standards are particularly fragile and that they can collapse literally in a matter of days," says the Marquis sitting down. "In this case, of course, I lay the blame fair and square on the chef's shoulders. The idea of entrusting his kitchen – his laboratory, his sanctuary, his haven! – to such a dim-witted apprentice, is beyond belief. And I meant what I said: I don't recall having ever come across such a disgusting smell. By the way, Mademoiselle," the Marquis asks with calculated disingenuity, having already identified the name of the abortive dish, "what was it you ordered exactly?"

"*Champignons à la provençale.*"

"Ah, yes! A dish whose modest ingredients, when properly prepared, can exude the most memorable *parfum*." He leans towards the young woman as if he had some ancestral secret he wished to share with her. "Shall I tell you what makes me particularly angry?"

Annabelle Fleury looks suitably intrigued.

"Do you know why that idiot in there failed?" he asks her, pointing to the now quiescent kitchens. Before she can hazard a reply, he says, "By trying to be too clever! Yes, that's how he ruined what's surely one of the classical dishes in the culinary canon. I hate to think what he did to it. If only he had checked his untutored imagination and cooked the mushrooms simply! Mind you, Mademoiselle, it's a common enough occurrence. And I should know. I've come across it more than once in all the years I've run my restaurant."

"Your restaurant?" Annabelle exclaims, surprised that the genial gentleman whose acquaintance she has just made and whom she has already categorized as belonging to one of the liberal professions – teacher, lawyer, perhaps even man of letters – should reveal himself in so different a light. Doing her best to modify her tone of surprise, she adds: "So you're a restaurateur, are you?"

"Yes, indeed! In fact I own a place in Provence, La Fantaisie, set in the hills behind Nice. You find that strange? Can't you imagine me, my toque stiffly starched, at work in a kitchen?"

"It's not that!" interjects Annabelle, irritated to have had her reactions pinned down quite so accurately.

"And what about you, Mademoiselle Fleury?" the Marquis asks, raising his eyebrows. "Are you at all interested in *haute cuisine*?"

"I love good food, of course. Though, to be honest, in my line of work you have to be careful: it's more what you don't eat that counts. Anyway, as I tend to dine out a lot, I don't have that many opportunities to cook."

"I see."

While the Marquis' manner clearly demonstrates that he would like to explore her attitudes further, Annabelle nonetheless pauses, unsure whether to carry on with this unusual conversation. Yet something inexpressible – could it be an element of trustworthiness in his features? – compels her to

8

continue. Before she has censored her words and passed her thoughts in judicious review, she is surprised to hear herself say: "Actually, that's not altogether true."

"No?" the Marquis remarks, delighted to hear her confessing so soon the presence of a flaw in her story.

"No. You could say I've been put off. You see, my mother is a very good cook. The kitchen's her world, and it's one in which she shines. I suppose that must have intimidated me because I now never turn my hand to cooking at all."

"I assure you, Mademoiselle, I quite sympathize. The kitchen's no place for competition." The Marquis takes a silver case from the inside pocket of his jacket and offers her a cigarette. She shakes her head. "I wonder if it has ever struck you," he adds, curling a blue ring of smoke from the side of his mouth, "that since gastronomy is in your blood, not only do you have a predisposition towards the art but you could even become proficient in a short time?"

"I doubt that! Cooking's much too practical and I don't have the right temperament. I'd never get the hang of it." She smiles. "Mind you, if I ever get that keen on eating well at home, I'll just hunt out a *cordon bleu* and march him up the aisle!"

"One answer to the problem undeniably," says the Marquis good-humouredly. "But you mentioned your work, Mademoiselle. What field are you in?"

"Fashion design. I even occasionally," she playfully lifts her eyebrows as if to connote an aspect of glamour to her life, "model my own clothes."

"A creative profession. So you lead a busy life?"

"Rather too busy, I sometimes feel. Though I've learnt to make time. Not much use going hell for leather if you can't enjoy the advantages success brings." She points to the wealth of fine line drawings on her sketchpad. "Actually, I'm a firm believer in the value of relaxation. I've had some of my best ideas sitting around just like this."

"Beautifully executed," says the Marquis, taking the notepad and examining the voluptuous lines of her fashion sketches, appreciating the trenchancy with which she has penned certain textures. "I congratulate you, Mademoiselle. Does that mean that your schedule over the next few days is very full?"

9

How soon does a woman sense the whirr of the mechanism of seduction being cranked up? No doubt the memory of past approaches helps hone the antennae. Annabelle, who has experienced the direct, the sidelong, the subtle and the crude, decides that the Marquis' approach is tentative and, in consequence, stiffens very slightly.

"Pretty much so," she answers. "There's a dress collection I've got to finalize. A mass of details to get right." She shrugs. A melancholy draught sweeps through her and, before she has had a chance to camouflage it, she adds: "Though, I have to admit, I occasionally ask myself whether the effort's worth it."

"Please, Mademoiselle!" the Marquis retorts. "No false modesty. I'm convinced you have a high regard for your work. And justifiably so." He points to the drawings on her notepad. "Of course, if what you're saying is that there's a hierarchy in all things and that activities aren't of equal value, then I agree with you. Why, some have even argued that," his voice adopts a stentorian register, " 'the discovery of a new dish does more for the happiness of mankind than the discovery of a star.' "

"Extraordinary notion! I've never heard it before. Is it your own?"

"Sadly not. Jean-Anthelme Brillat-Savarin, Master Cook, storyteller and the gastronome's patron saint, coined it some two hundred years ago."

"Really?" intones Annabelle who only distantly recalls that name volleying across the various dining rooms she frequents. Patou, Poiret, Worth, Iribe – those are the bright stars in her favoured firmament. Of that particular luminary's achievements she recalls next to nothing. Sidestepping the subject, she adds: "There is something though that I'd like to know, Marquis. You mentioned earlier that when you're in your restaurant in Provence, you work in the kitchens. Does that mean you do the cooking?"

"What a question to put to a Master Chef! I have *commis* to help me naturally, but otherwise, yes, I am in complete control of my own kitchens."

"Master Chef?" Annabelle repeats dully, confronting the enormity of her gaffe. "I'm sorry, I hadn't realized." In an attempt to recapture lost ground, she says: "I imagine your work is very complex."

"Not at source, Mademoiselle. In fact I've often maintained that its principles could be taught in two days."

"Two days! I thought it'd take years."

"Don't misunderstand me. I'm not suggesting gastronomy's easy. You only have to consider the mountain of books that have been written about the subject to accept that it is a demanding science. But, as in all the arts, what counts are its principles. And those, I assure you, can be learnt remarkably quickly. That's," the Marquis adds conspiratorially, "if you're fortunate and happen to come across the right initiation, the right guidance. As for the qualities you need to become a good cook, I'd say that imagination and discipline are by far the most important."

"Frankly," says Annabelle, remembering her own struggles at the Ecole des Beaux-Arts, "there's no field in which they'd be out of place. Though two days I find hard to believe."

"You obviously wouldn't learn everything there is to know in so short a time. But its basics, why not? All the same, Mademoiselle Fleury, I wouldn't be telling you the whole truth if I failed to stress that the world of creative cooking is highly mysterious. And that it's a world with powers all of its own, powers few people have ever confronted. I accept that plenty of people can toy with them and can even come up with quite amusing if somewhat superficial concoctions. Master it however? No! Take herbs and spices for instance. Do you realize that to a Master Chef they're as crucial as colours are to a painter? The sublime effects they can evoke! Why, Mademoiselle, with a dash of tarragon, a *soupçon* of basil, and a hint of paprika, I could create images that'd make your head spin and your palate beg for mercy."

"I'm sure you could," says Annabelle, intrigued by so histrionic an attitude. "Your fervour on the subject is certainly compelling. Puts slaving over a hot stove in a very different light."

"It is vital that you understand," the Marquis adds sententiously, "that to a gourmet the smallest meal is a journey of discovery."

"*Très romantique*, Marquis. You make it sound quite an adventure."

"Romantic? Extremely! As for being an adventure, that too. And yet . . ." The Marquis takes a sip from his calvados then remains silent, as if preferring to discuss the matter no further.

"Yes?" asks Annabelle, taken aback by this abrupt halt in his narration.

"How shall I put it?" asks the Marquis, apparently searching for the right phrase. "Perhaps I should say that gastronomy is not an art anybody can master."

"Wait! You're confusing me," Annabelle exclaims. "First you tell me I'd be a natural just because my mother's a good cook. Now you imply I might not actually have the necessary talent. Isn't that rather contradictory?"

"Not at all. I'm simply stating that the higher reaches of gastronomy aren't easy to scale and that it takes special talents to reach them. I'd be seriously misguiding you if I didn't emphasize that."

"Imagination and discipline – aren't they the qualities you said were needed?" Annabelle gazes at the notes and illustrations with which she has intaglioed her sketchpad. "I happen to think I've a fair share of both."

"I would be the last to argue with that, Mademoiselle," the Marquis interjects. "Let me put it differently. We all talk, don't we? We use words to express ourselves. Yet wouldn't you agree that it's when a poet manipulates language that it resonates to its very highest pitch? Well, the same holds true of food. Anyone with a smattering of common sense can prepare a meal. But only a Master Chef, someone steeped in the principles of creative cooking, can transform everyday ingredients into a special dish. And those talents, as I said, are not given to all." Resting his case, the Marquis nods towards Annabelle's still unfinished glass. "Wasn't the calva to your taste?" he asks her.

Her mouth thinned by the frustration of hearing his obtuse arguments, she looks down at her glass. "Somewhat sharp but otherwise excellent."

"We meet under strange circumstances, Mademoiselle Fleury, don't you think?" asks the Marquis, keen to isolate and to nullify the pique which he has detected in her voice. "Over the ruins of *champignons à la provençale!*"

"Highly original!" she answers, still refusing to transcend her mood.

It is at this point that the Marquis launches into an exposition of the wonders of the regional specialities which abound near his own restaurant. He appears to have investigated each Provençal dish in considerable depth for off his tongue the aromatic compositions of *bouillabaisse, pieds et paquets, capilotade* of squid and of other equally memorable *mets* resonate with all the devoted hours he must have spent elaborating them. Suddenly veering away from his exotic inventory, he asks Annabelle whether she has ever taken the Mistral to Nice. As it so happens, she answers, offset by his question, never. When she heads for the Midi, she takes the 'plane. Why is he so interested anyway?

Because she would then have her own memories of that exquisite experience, he retorts. Of course train travel is slow. And even, at times, inconvenient. Yet there are plenty of compensations. One can meet unusual characters. One has more than enough time to think. And one has the pleasure – so rare in these overbusy days – of letting one's mind roam in search of new perspectives. Not that the food in the *wagon-restaurant* is worth mentioning. Though funnily enough, on the last occasion when . . . The Marquis cuts himself short. "There you are, Mademoiselle! Proof, if you needed it, that a chef never tires of his favourite subject. While you have yet to encounter the mysteries of *haute cuisine*."

"Though I admit that what you said earlier about learning the principles of cooking in two days has intrigued me."

Yes, he insists. Two days would be quite sufficient. And there's no doubt that, once mastered, the arts of creative cooking do confer the most prodigious powers. Can she imagine, the Marquis adds with a fetching smile, 'phoning her mother in a few days and inviting her over to her flat? As soon as the family gastronome arrives, a truly amazing sight greets her eyes. A dazzling panoply of *hors-d'oeuvre*, a judicious selection of main dishes, a finely garnished main course, delicate desserts and – why not? – a few *amuses-gueules* in between. A consummate feast which she, yes, she would have prepared in its minutest detail. What, the Marquis muses, would her mother say to that?

No problem predicting her mother's response, Annabelle answers. She would round on her and demand to be told the exact amount she had paid her caterers.

Over by the counter the waiter, his face twisted by rancour, observes the two customers who have caused him so much trouble. The proprietress, permitting herself a few more seconds' respite from her work, takes off her tinted spectacles, reveals pale blue eyes set in crinkled folds, then bends back towards the rectilinear perfection of her double entry columns.

Intent on assessing the sincerity of her fortuitously-met companion, Annabelle asks him whether he is seriously offering to teach her. Indeed, he retorts, as long as she has the capacity to learn. Confronted by the brazenness of his invitation, Annabelle hedges around. It is an extraordinary proposition; she will have to think it over. In which case, the Marquis adds, she has a little over twenty four hours to make up her mind. Why so little time? she wonders, her pupils narrowing. Because, he answers matter-of-factly, while his restaurant is in the very capable hands of his assistant, Marius de la Garde, other business calls him to the Côte, and he must therefore leave for Provence on the morrow.

The Marquis casts his eyes over the now completely vacated Brasserie. On consideration, he says, his face taking on a look of concern, perhaps he has been a little rash. The last thing he wants to do is mislead her. Mislead her? How? she asks. She might suppose, he points out, that a process which can be achieved in two days must be easy. Yet nothing could be further from the truth. In reality a crash course in creative cooking is the most intense and excruciating work.

A knowing smile spreads across Annabelle's face. He is trying to put her off, isn't he? Certainly not! he retorts. If there's one thing he has learnt in his long life, it's that once a woman has made up her mind . . . If she is determined, he will gladly put his cards on the table and tell her exactly what he requires of her.

Why is it that every invitation whelps a bastard progeny of conditions? muses Annabelle, sighing inwardly. What will they be this time? The sludge at the pit of most propositions: money? Or could the Marquis be after baser depredations?

Annabelle discovers that, to begin with, the Marquis is unusually vague. Fundamentally, he says, what he and she must do is reach an agreement. She looks at him, awaiting to hear his terms. Clearly, he states, someone as busy as she is cannot afford to waste time. Clearly, she agrees. In that case he must insist that she follow his instructions very carefully. Her expression souring, Annabelle wonders what she is letting herself in for. She must, the Marquis continues, swear to keep everything she sees and hears during the two day course absolutely secret. Can his so-called principles of cooking be that extraordinary? she enquires. They can and, he stresses, they are. The quintessence of a lifelong search, he does not intend to scatter them to the four winds. Is there anything else he requires? she asks. Yes, he adds: she should keep her mind open and trust him implicitly.

To banter about a hypothetical journey is harmless enough. To request an open mind is not outlandish. But to demand her trust before he has earned it Annabelle regards as sheer presumption. So much so that she cannot conceal her outrage. Quickly responding to counter her fears, the Marquis says that she need have no cause for worry. None whatsoever. Everything he has outlined has but one aim in mind: to make matters run smoothly. She has informed him that she has never travelled on the Mistral. Then this will provide them with a perfect opportunity to travel by rail to the Côte. The journey will allow them ample time to discuss everything in detail. And, once they arrive in Nice, they will drive over to La Fantaisie and there cap the course in its kitchen. She must leave everything to him, he adds. He will, it goes without saying, take care of all expenses.

Bridling, Annabelle rushes to defend the letter, if not the spirit, of her independence. She thanks him but insists that it is out of the question. She always pays her own way.

Chère Mademoiselle – the Marquis propels his words on a powerful wave of gallantry – if a gentleman invites a lady and she does him the honour of accepting, it is only right that he take charge of all practical arrangements. Perhaps she might look at the situation in this light. If she appreciates the skills which he has accumulated in the course of a long career and can apply them, that will more than reward him for his time and trouble. Surely she does not want to deprive him of that innocent pleasure, and will give in with good grace?

"Oh, very well," says Annabelle, acquiescing with a shrug in spite of herself. "As for these precautions, I don't see the point of them. All for a crash course in cooking?"

"Wrong, Mademoiselle. Not for any course, but for a very special creative course and one which, I assure you, you'll remember all your life. Ah!" he exclaims, "I almost forgot. One final detail: would you please bring with you two objects of which you're particularly fond."

Why his requirements should become increasingly elaborate Annabelle cannot imagine.

The Marquis puts a finger to his mouth. "I shan't tell you why. Let it remain a surprise! As for what you bring along, I leave that entirely to your discretion."

"If I've understood you rightly," summarizes Annabelle, who can hardly believe that a conversation barely ten minutes old has already entangled her in a skein of bizarre conditions, "you're proposing that I travel with you to Provence for a cookery course. And that, on the journey down, you'll teach me arcane gastronomic secrets. To what end? I mean: what will I be when I get back to Paris? A *cordon bleu*? A mistress of hearth and home? Or a restaurateur just like you?"

"On your return to the capital, Mademoiselle?" the Marquis asks. He pauses, smiles sardonically, and answers: "Let's say that you'll be a consummate cook, a superb storyteller, and a lady whose powers of seduction will far exceed their already considerable scope. I do hope that will be temptation enough." He stubs out his cigarette in the ashtray. "So, Mademoiselle Fleury, will you or will you not be joining me?"

"How could I refuse?"

"Then we meet tomorrow evening, at the Gare de Lyon, at ten to six. All you need to bring is an overnight bag. I shall take care of everything else. And don't be late. I'd be sorry to leave without you."

"But . . ."

"No hesitation, young lady. The Mistral tomorrow."

As the waiter is nowhere to be seen, the Marquis rises from the table and goes over to the proprietress' pulpit. He whispers a few words to the matriarch veiled behind her tinted spectacles, pulls out a large denomination note, and pays for all the drinks. Stepping over to his table, he dispenses a few coins on a plate, turns to Annabelle, bows, and with a curt "*A demain*", dons his hat and walks out.

Left to her own devices – after an extraordinary encounter in which she has been offered the highly inflated proposal of becoming a Master Chef more or less overnight – Annabelle is not sure what to think nor what to do with herself. The magazine at her elbow looks lifeless. As for the Brasserie, it appears as pathetic as an overlit set suddenly voided of its cast. The promise and the threat of so strange an assignation make her shiver. To shake off the weight of her reverie, she downs the last of the calva and seizes her various belongings. And once she has left the Brasserie, she heads for the shelter of her Montparnasse flat where she will have to decide whether to accept this rendez-vous with *haute cuisine* or consign it to the wasteland of proferred, but ultimately rejected, opportunities.

CHAPTER TWO

The cord of Paris traffic is snarling and the quays – once the sporting ground of roués, duellists, drunkards, and now of foreigners looking for the reason why the Pont-Neuf is neither the ninth nor the newest but the oldest bridge across the temperamental bank-breaking Seine – are bulging with the home-running flow. The city's streets are inflamed by the fumes of countless engines when a somewhat battered taxi manages to extricate itself from the thickly knotted fibre and comes screeching to a halt at the foot of the Gare de Lyon's monumental clocktower. The passenger door opens and Annabelle Fleury, wearing a beige dress and with a suede jacket draped over her shoulders, rushes out. Avoiding with a handsome note any acidulous request for a *pourboire*, she pays the driver his fare, clutches her small overnight bag, and runs into the station.

A mix of passengers mill around the vast platforms, some carrying the international signs of organized vagrancy – backpacks and unwashed faces – and others clearly commuting to the suburbs so well served by this majestic example of nineteenth-century confidence spun out of iron and glass. A third category, wearing the dour faces of supplicants, await by grimy platforms the arrival of their infidelity-sodden consorts, while caricatures of domestic life from France's southern region – berets, widow's weeds, long-tressed garlic – rush past them, eager to feast on the delights the capital has to offer. Occasionally blasts of well-nigh deafening and wholly incomprehensible sounds burst out of elephant-eared loudspeakers before breaking their strained sibilants on the station's latticework. Through

18

this mass Annabelle, in a great hurry and making the common mistake of confusing main lines with local departures, ricochets from one side of the station to the other searching for where the Mistral, surely about to leave without her, is berthed. The lack of directions reminds her of the books she has read about the Occupation when road signs were dismantled by patriots attempting to confuse the invading forces, a gesture poignant with symbolic significance yet void of almost any practical effect. She eventually locates a worn blue plaque which points her in roughly the right area. Running down the platform, she comes close to colliding with a black-silk-dressed and large-hatted lady who, in a loud foreign voice, dispenses orders to a porter hauling an enormous pile of luggage on a trolley and berates all the while the growlings of the black poodle which she has tucked under one arm.

"Stop it this instant, Cerby!" says the full-bosomed figure in English. "I won't have you make such a fuss!" Disengaging her ticket from her bag, the lady stops outside one of the first-class carriages, and tells the porter in her impeccable, if accented, French to carry her luggage in forthwith.

The creaks from the trolley, the growls from the dog, and the rustling of the lady's silk are making their momentous way down the platform when Annabelle comes panting up to where the first-class carriages are standing. There, waiting for her, impressively turned out in a finely-cut tweed suit, is the Marquis. With a deft and agile move, he seizes her bag and ushers her in.

Doubling in these recessive times as a substitute Station Master, Jules Pinard, the Chief Steward of the Mistral, waves a flag at the head of the train where a figure we shall never meet – yet whose story might well have been fascinating and rank with passion – interprets the familiar sign. With a gesture that must cruelly disappoint the romantic leanings of all steam-age enthusiasts, this unnamed character, far from loosening cocks, pushing levers, and spurting steam into the belly of the station, merely presses a button and releases energy from a diesel-electric dynamo. And as the hydraulically-operated doors swish shut, and the Steward jumps onto the runner board and into a compartment, the shiny, blue-painted, steel-hulled vehicle slides slowly, and with almost effortless grace, out of the station.

The Marquis carries Annabelle's suitcase through the corridor of the first-class carriage, stops outside compartment no. 40, marked reserved, and waves her into it. She discovers that it is luxuriously appointed in the idiom of the *belle époque*, a period when trains borrowed from bourgeois domestic vernacular and covered every metre of their cramped interior with the requisites of comfort and security. This being a refurbished effort, however, the decor is not quite as lavish as the original from which it drew its inspiration.

"I do hope you'll be comfortable here," says the Marquis, placing her bag on the sofa.

Annabelle surveys the train's decorations which, she surmises, have been undertaken in a spirit of nostalgic veneration. Yet far from soothing her, the rich walnut panelling grates against her *beaux-arts* inspired, puristic conviction that only the original is worth keeping, and that copies are fool-flattering devices, fundamentally offensive except to sensibilities lacking the experience of the genuine article. To her mind, if an artefact fails to be true, she prefers to go without. Tactfully reining in her feelings however, she smiles at the Marquis' apparent effusiveness.

"The Compagnie des Wagons-lits recently redecorated its first-class carriages," the Marquis comments. "Although the materials aren't as fine as the original, the effect, I think you'll agree, is still quite pleasing." He lifts her bag from the sofa, places it on the rack, and turns to leave. "I'm just a few doors down the corridor, compartment no. 44. Do join me once you've settled in."

Annabelle casts her eye round her compartment, thanks her host, and tells him that she will be along in a short while.

The door closes and Annabelle, still slightly nauseated by the fakeness of the decor, continues to make an inventory of the compartment. As she is to spend quite a few hours in its surroundings, she decides to show it tolerance. Then, with a sigh, she falls onto the sofa bunk and extracts from her handbag a black lacquer powder-case, a handkerchief, and a little mother-of-pearl hand-mirror. She holds up the latter and lightly touches up her face flushed from her exertions.

When she has finished unpacking, and made the space hers by infinitesimally small reorderings of its arrangements, she takes her handbag, locks the compartment, and wanders down to the Marquis'. His, she observes, after she had knocked on his door and been invited in, is furnished with much the same luxury as hers, except that it is rather more ample, possessing its own bunkroom en suite. On its table she also notices a block of loose-leaf paper on which she can make out a rich vein of notes and drawings. Typically for a scene redolent of the romance of long-distance travel, a bottle of *Dom Perignon* '64 is cooling in an ice bucket; while next to it two fluted glasses stand. The express is already slicing its way through the grimy strata of the capital's suburbs when the Marquis uncorks the bottle, pours Annabelle a glass, and raises his.

"*Santé!*"

"*Santé!*"

"Now that our journey's begun," says the Marquis, inviting Annabelle to sit down on the sofa next to him, "I should like, with your permission, to propose a toast. Yes, Mademoiselle, to the birth of new skills," he declaims in faintly rhetorical tones, "and to the success of the course which will generate them."

Amused by his theatrics, Annabelle sips her champagne and appreciates its maturity.

As the train lurches out of Paris and furrows towards the commuter-infested dormitory towns of the Ile de France, Annabelle gazes as a number of simple sets parade past the window, as if moved by unhurried stagehands. First a dumping ground of piled-up prams and partly buckled cars hemmed within a compass of grey breeze-blocks. A few kilometres hence, she observes concrete-stressed conurbations whose walls daubed with plastic frescoes seem untainted by the slightest trace of decay. Eventually this urban sprawl gives way to valleyed woodlands pockmarked by half-ruined farmsteads. Soon the landscape becomes swathed in a darkness interrupted here and there by hillocks blotched with fluorescently-lit hamlets, their faces, in apparent disdain, turned away from the capital.

Annabelle remains quiet and looks past the sealed windows at the countryside sweeping past her. Her glass is half empty and its surface trembles from the vibration of the carriage wheels. Interrupting a silence that had threatened to become momentous, the Marquis offers his companion a cigarette and, unconcerned by her courteous refusal, lights one up himself.

"In the kitchens of the best restaurants you'll meet an old tradition. You'll hear the apprentice cook addressing his boss as

21

Maître while the *patron* calls his subordinate every name under the sun. Not that I'm suggesting," the Marquis adds, an amused expression on his face, "that you should call me *Maître*. Jean-Loup will do very well. While I, if you don't mind, will address you by your own charming name, Annabelle."

Annabelle wonders when the Marquis will try to slip into the familiar *tu*, and whether she will then want to join or to combat his hurdling of the barriers of linguistic formality. The danger being, she muses, that one thing leads so easily to another.

"You cut your arrival rather fine, didn't you?" the Marquis remarks wistfully. "I was afraid you wouldn't arrive on time."

"So was I. As usual there was a last-minute panic at my office. I hadn't realized just how much I'd have to reschedule to come along. The important thing is that I'm here." God! What a woman! How could she have been so unreasonable about a two-day break? But before the irritation of her thoughts betrays her, Annabelle brushes aside the complexities of her relationship with Melanie Blanchard, avoiding all reference to the crises, the bitcheries, and innuendoes with which she had to cope when she informed her partner and erstwhile lover that she was going to take a short holiday.

"An indispensable quality in a cook, punctuality," says the Marquis, paraphrasing Brillat-Savarin. "You know, don't you," he adds, "that the Mistral travels right through the night?"

She does.

"Good. In which case, as we've a great deal to get through before we get to Nice, I suggest we waste no time but start right away."

"You mean now?" asks Annabelle, who was looking forward to a light collation followed by a burgundy-induced sleep in her well-locked couchette.

"No time like the present."

"Very well," Annabelle answers, forced to file away her expectations.

The Marquis replenishes Annabelle's glass. "At the very heart of gastronomy, Annabelle, you'll find three principles."

"Aha! A culinary trinity!"

Recognizing in Annabelle's remark an attempt to put herself at her ease, the Marquis takes only the slightest exception to it. "Please concentrate! And don't mock what you can't possibly understand. You'll have ample opportunities to search for hidden meanings later. As I was saying, gastronomy is based on three principles. The first concerns ingredients. The golden rule to abide by here is to settle only for the best and to be willing to pay over the odds for the right quality."

"Fair enough," says Annabelle, surprised at the simplicity of his opening remarks.

"Next, methods. Of which you can never have too many. Within the term I include recipes, cooking skills, and so on and so forth."

"Everything you've said so far sounds like common sense."

In theory, he is happy to admit, common sense is exactly what he means to teach her. However, it would be wise of her to reserve judgement until she has had some experience of its practice for she might then have to adopt different views. And the third principle of creative cooking – with which he suspects she will have the greatest difficulties as it is the most demanding task an aspiring Master Chef will ever face – touches on the subtle powers of sympathy.

Sympathy? Annabelle repeats mechanically, failing to have any purchase on the notion. Indeed, he maintains. And to ensure that the subject remains as clear-cut as possible, he will first deal with ingredients and methods and tackle sympathy, that highly delicate topic, last.

Regarding ingredients, the Marquis stresses, the trick is to realize where to locate them, and how to go about it. Personally he knows of only one way to do that, and that is through the use of the imagination. No, he exclaims, taking her obvious bemusement into account, she must not worry herself unduly about the ideas to which he is introducing her, however strange they may seem, as he will in time go into their every detail. To begin with he suggests that she watch him at work and make as much sense as she can from her own observations.

Methods naturally enough, he continues, come with practice. The more skills are exercised, the better the results reaped. Now, when explaining the role which sympathy plays in the principles of creative cooking, he concedes that it represents a much more problematic area. And why should that be? Annabelle enquires, sensing the ground of familiarity swiftly slipping under her. Because it involves so many complex levels, the Marquis insists. Timing – undeniably one of the most crucial facets of sympathy. To take but one example, if food is cooked too long, or, for that matter, not long enough, it will spoil beyond recovery. Can she not remember the numerous occasions on which she has heard her mother curse a soufflé that had collapsed? the Marquis asks with a wry smile.

Never! Annabelle retorts, piqued that her mother should make so unwelcome an appearance in the conversation. She can't recall one such catastrophe. It is infuriating but the fact is that she never gets anything wrong. Of course she does, the Marquis maintains. What's possible is that she may have become quite an expert at hiding it! But that particular setback, he can assure her, has hit every hostess who has ever faced a party of hungry dinner guests. No one, he maintains, not even the best chef, has ever escaped that disaster.

He pours her another glass of champagne. What was he discussing exactly? Ah yes! Timing. It would be impossible to overemphasize, he continues, the critical part which timing plays. She is of course aware that certain foodstuffs have to be consumed soon after they have been picked or slaughtered while others on the contrary need a period to mature. The Marquis raises his glass to the light and admires the liquid's *pétillance*: here is a first-class instance, but there are plenty of others. Has she ever prepared pheasant? No? Well, after the bird is shot, the Marquis explains, it should be left to hang for several days until all the signs are apparent. The signs? Annabelle asks. Why, yes, the bird's head snapping off its rotting body, the Marquis replies. When that happens, one can be certain it is ready for the pot.

So, the Marquis concludes: even when one has managed to locate the necessary ingredients, and has at hand all the right implements and the exact recipe, if one then mismanages timing, all the dish will be good for is the bin.

That's easy enough to grasp, says Annabelle, becoming a little impatient with the Marquis' slow-moving pedagogic manner and astonished that his concepts have not provided her with more of a challenge. Unfortunately, he answers, understanding in this case is not enough. Not for their needs anyway. To master the arts of creative cooking, it is also vital that she develops that rarest of qualities, yes, she must develop sympathy. Sympathy for where she is, for who she's with, and for what's feasible at any time or place. For the ingredients themselves, the people she is cooking for, all play a part. She has, he presumes, heard of the Spirit of Place? But has she, he wonders, ever taken the notion seriously before? The fact of the matter is that places do have atmospheres. One could even say that they have feelings. And these have to be sensed and evaluated before the best results can be reached. Yes, indeed, he stresses, sympathy is the very cornerstone of the art of creative cooking and one with which she will soon have to come to terms.

"Now I'm really lost!" Annabelle exclaims.

"No need to be. It's a simple enough technique," says the Marquis, "and one which I'll be glad to show you."

The Marquis lowers his tone. "Listen! What do you hear?"

"Nothing in particular," Annabelle whispers, entering less than willingly into the Marquis' enquiry.

For what sounds are there apart from the train's unceasing threnody?

"Nothing? Nonsense, Annabelle! We're surrounded with sounds. Pick one out. Any one. Yes, why not? – the noise of the train's wheels."

Overcoming with difficulty her initial resistance, Annabelle agrees to participate and tries to isolate the noise of the wheels from all the other sounds – from the creaking of the carriages, the hum of the air-conditioner, the scuffling of passengers, and the thrashing of the wind – competing for her attention. It is with considerable surprise that she discovers that the wheels are coming to the fore, blanketing all other stimuli and, even more strangely, revealing within their apparent lifelessness nuances as telling as the shadowy, wraith-like faces which she has sometimes glimpsed on a winter's night within the flickering of a hearth.

"Now hold it!" the Marquis exclaims with urgency, clearly conscious of the extraordinary development which has just happened to her. "And concentrate on its rhythm."

"On its rhythm?" Annabelle asks, taken aback by the suggestion.

"Yes, on its rhythm, its beat, its harmonies."

"Then what?"

"Surrender to them."

What is she to make of this? This is not simply bizarre: is it not also way off the point?

"Surrender? To the noise of a train? What has that got to do with cooking?"

As if nothing counted more than this exercise, the Marquis answers her: "Quick! Do as I say! Close your eyes and listen very carefully."

A disgruntled expression on her face, Annabelle submits. To begin with, the sounds of the wheels remain as loud as before. She then realizes that she can in fact distinguish minute changes in their sound patterns. Changes which, she presumes, must stem from their contact with different rail surfaces. Yes, there are indeed a number of distinct sounds: the hum of smooth seamless surfaces; the grind of gritty sections; an increase in friction on whichever side the train happens to be swaying. And was that, she wonders, a muffling of their thrum as they swished over rainsoaked lines?

Her sensitivity to an area of stimuli to which she has never before given a moment's thought is not however the sole sensation to overwhelm her. For could it be the champagne's influence which is making her mind spin, exposing how very melodious the Marquis' voice is, and how subtly he modulates it in the fashion in which she imagines a hypnotist would? Or might the languor which has seized her not be caused by tiredness, by this being the very first opportunity she has had of not rushing around in a day otherwise entirely given over to tidying up what she would normally regard as the organized nature of her life? A life which, now that its habitual rhythm has been interrupted – galling as it is to admit it – appears horribly jagged.

Bathed in this new-found and disturbing clarity, Annabelle is forced to confront the inconsequence of so much of her business life: endless meetings in pursuit of slips of paper guaranteeing her so much for such and such an item. Ceaseless activity, and towards what elevated end? None other than helping her business partner become even richer. And concomitantly demanding.

Meanwhile the charming and authoritative figure from whom, in a moment of weakness and of crazed romanticism, she has accepted a most unlikely invitation, to become a mistress of the kitchens overnight, keeps telling her to listen to, of all things, the murmur, the susurration, the surprisingly complex rustle of steel against steel, of fast-flowing surfaces tensed against ribs of acceptant metal.

"Let it permeate you," the Marquis whispers. "Let it take you over."

It is actually not that unpleasant, Annabelle concedes, her eyes shut, the champagne loosening her limbs, to be, as he would put it, taken over in this way – even if the slightly worrying fragrance of surrender is also hanging over her. Well aware that she is not as guarded as she should be when drunk, Annabelle wonders when she should react against this sly slippage of her moorings in the Marquis' seductive swell.

Yet why deny it? To sit, her eyes shut, in a comfortable first-class carriage with a man who seems to know exactly what he is doing, has about it a remarkably warm, even sensuous quality.

The sounds of the train's wheels are penetrating her with greater and greater thoroughness when Annabelle, although still confused by the Marquis' audial exercise, recognizes that she has now stopped worrying about it. For while she and the sounds do seem to have become fused, an extraordinary event in itself, nothing else, nothing untoward, has happened. No hand has slithered across her knee, no fingers have explored the nape of her neck, nor has any gentle or urgent breathing played across her ear. Instead there have been moments when she could have sworn that she had come to grips with the train's nature, felt with a baffling degree of intimacy its anguine length, shimmered with the creaks of its hard-pressed springs, and sensed the flight of its sleek blue coat through the chilled air. Moments when she pitched with the whirr of its generators, rolled with the smoothness of its bearings, and echoed with the roar of its engines. And there have been other sensations too, like the whine of the train's electric generators, the wear and tear on its couplings, its schedules of stops and starts, and a thousand and one events which she has intuitively apprehended along with others more difficult to articulate, yet all of which have resonated through her within a few seconds. She is busily assessing the value of these experiences and wondering whether she and the train have really reached an all-embracing entente, a unified and resonant harmony, when suddenly there is a tearing separation and she feels herself falling helpless on one side while the sounds become frayed and collapse on the other. Then, with a terrible abruptness, they fade into the same background from which they had so vividly sprung and the hum of normality becomes once again dominant, returning all the sounds to their former dull register.

Startled by the violent interruption of her reverie, Annabelle opens her eyes and stares in a state of minor shock at the Marquis.

"Rather unusual, don't you think?" asks the Marquis, as if to soothe her obvious confusion. "Don't worry: it's just one of the many phenomena to which you'll soon get used," he adds, gratified that powers which he had not recently had a chance to put to the test have performed rather persuasively. "What's really important, after that little interlude, is that you now have a better, yes, an infinitely better understanding of the train's nature. In essence, you communed with it, became one with it. You could say that the train spoke to you or, if you prefer, through you. And considering that you're about to spend a good eight hours riding on its back, taking the trouble to learn something about it is surely the least of courtesies, let alone the fact that it is also intrinsic to the skills which I mean to teach you. For, yes, Annabelle, the ability to get under somebody's or something's skin is an integral aspect of sympathy."

Annabelle cannot hide her bewilderment, a state of affairs with which the Marquis seems to be satisfied, as if her muddled mood were precisely the effect for which he had been striving.

"Confused? Excellent!" He proceeds to confirm her fears. "Nothing quite like a burst of disorientation to shake up a stale attitude. Let me assure you, however, before you give in to a bout of panic, that you're in no danger. None whatsoever. In the end, you'll see," the Marquis adds comfortingly, "everything will fall neatly into place."

Jarred by having just been ripped from the depths of a sensual state of whose existence she had had no previous inkling, irritated that the only explanation which she had been offered for it is the totemic term "sympathy", about whose mechanisms she has still no understanding, Annabelle is about to voice her several reservations concerning her involvement in this escapade when the Marquis asks her whether she has brought along her two objects.

"Er, yes," Annabelle replies, still peeved at being taken in by a trick all the more objectionable for its reasons remaining mysterious. "They're in my bag."

"And what are they?"

"Oh, things I'm rather fond of but which I don't suppose

have much value – except to me, that is. I've had them quite some time."

"Perfect! Couldn't have asked for more. Objects thoroughly imbued with your personality."

"What?"

The Marquis outflanks her question by showing a determined interest in the objects which she has chosen.

"Well, there's a small silver locket I picked up at the *Puces*," Annabelle continues, slaking her companion's curiosity, "which I bought mainly for its beautifully ornamented mother-of-pearl frame. And a hand mirror which my mother gave me, a memento really. I'm told it belonged to a spinster aunt I never knew, Tante Yvonne."

"Superb choices."

Pointing to the overhead rack in his sleeping quarters next door, the Marquis asks Annabelle if she would be kind enough to bring his briefcase over to him.

Why can't he fetch the briefcase himself? Annabelle wonders. While determined not to allow his footing of the bill to become a pretext for her running his errands, she nonetheless submits this once to his request.

The leather briefcase, she soon discovers, is wedged on the rack between a small wicker basket and a larger pigskin suitcase. Reaching out to the rack, she grabs it, almost knocks over the wicker basket, then places it on the table from which the Marquis has cleared the empty champagne bottle.

The Marquis thanks her, turns the briefcase's jaws towards her, and asks her to open it.

Responding to the Marquis' request with the caution anyone capable of conjuring out of the thrum of a train's wheels a semi-hypnotic state deserves, she opens the suitcase very, very slowly.

Beautifully laid out against a background of purple silk, she comes across a number of peculiar objects. Initially there seems to be little sense of unity among them. But after she has examined them rather more carefully, she decides that they could belong to a prestidigitator's stock-in-trade, could be part of his essential paraphernalia. For among the objects she notes the presence of a multicoloured hand-painted pack of cards; a crystal phial, its sides opaque and faded; a fob watch, its cover chased with astrological signs; a monumental golden key which

29

might well breathe life into an ormolu clock or wrest open an oaken door in some hidden palace; and a gold-plated cardboard crown, the kind which always graces the *Galette des Rois*, the traditional marzipan pastry tart, on Twelfth Night.

"What an odd collection!" exclaims Annabelle. "I expected – oh, I don't know – a set of Sabatier knives, a copy of a gastronomic *grimoire*, kitchen ware, that sort of thing. But these, what are they for? To keep us amused on the journey? Don't tell me," she gives the Marquis an ironical smile, "you're not just a chef: you're a conjuror as well!"

"A conjuror?" the Marquis muses. "Perhaps I am, in a manner of speaking. But do have a look at the objects. They're beautiful, aren't they? You've brought along two objects, haven't you? So that means we have to choose two more from this collection. The question is, Annabelle, which ones?"

Quite unable to divine the basis for his simple addition, Annabelle quickly excuses herself. "I'm sorry, Jean-Loup," she says, hazarding the use of his first name, although refraining from using the familiar form of address, "but I don't have the first idea what they're about so asking me to choose one is to expect too much of me. I'll gladly pick you a fabric from a book of samples or design you a suit but, as far as this collection's concerned, I wouldn't know where to start."

"In that case, let me show you how to go about it," the Marquis answers.

He places both hands over the objects and fondles each one in turn. None appears to catch his attention until, hovering over the phial, he betrays a second's hesitation. The Marquis casts a look in Annabelle's direction but as his hands have not yet ceased their sensuous perusal, he shakes his head. Then, as they settle lightly on the large golden key, he nods.

"Mmm . . . I rather think the key possesses the sympathetic qualities we're after. Go on!" he adds, as Annabelle tentatively lets her hands go towards the key imbedded in its silken surroundings. "Experience what it feels like."

No sooner has she touched the key than she takes her hand away. For it is unmistakeably endowed with a strange, sentient quality.

"God! What was that! I felt something . . . Was it hot? Cold? No . . ." She stares at the Marquis, almost afraid to say what has slipped into her mind. Reluctantly she blurts out: "It's incredible, but, just then, I think I felt sad!"

"Very impressive!" exclaims the Marquis, colouring his voice with an appreciative tint. "You're remarkably sensitive, you know, Annabelle. Few people would have sensed that. I must say this bodes very well for the course's success. Sad you said? Well, we'll have to see. Meanwhile the quality of your reaction has clinched it: the key it is!"

The Marquis takes the golden key from the case and, without further explanation, slips it in his pocket. Next he searches among the pieces of paper on the table, yet so discreetly that Annabelle, who had hoped for a clue with which to string together what he has been up to, sees no more than his choosing two among them: one covered in writing, the other bearing some kind of sketch. He peruses them both then also places them in his pocket. "Oh, yes, there's one final thing," he adds, "we have to agree on before we go any further: the recipe for *champignons à la provençale*. Do you happen to know it?"

"Yes," answers Annabelle. "I looked it up in a cookery book yesterday."

"And?"

"And asked my mother," says Annabelle, answering the Marquis' question, if at a slight tangent.

"Really! And what did she suggest?"

"She said, let me remember, she said that she'd use *cèpes* for the mushrooms, preferably young, tender ones."

"Good!" says the Marquis, choosing neither to contradict her mother's practice nor to temper Annabelle's enthusiastic research with the pedant's notation that *girolles* or *lactaires délicieuses* are more commonly used by Provençal hands.

"Then that she'd fry them very gently in a little olive oil. When the mushrooms had turned brown, she'd dice a clove of garlic and, stirring all the while, add it in."

"Y – es," says the Marquis.

"Finally, to garnish the dish, she'd put in a sprig of finely grated parsley."

"Is that it?"

"I think that's what she said."

"*Formidable!* Precisely the way I prepare them!" the Marquis exclaims. "Have you ever, Annabelle, I wonder, considered just how alike recipes and folk stories are? For a start, they're both anonymous. It's impossible to ascribe authorship to either – I exclude of course all recipes recently penned by *grands cuisiniers*. And the same do tend to turn up again and again if, admittedly, in a wide variety of disguises. A state of affairs which, as far as the world of gastronomy is concerned, is not all that hard to explain for, as you may know, every chef worth his salt takes considerable pride in his methods. You'll see him leave out a condiment here while there add in a spice. Not that it matters when a Master chooses to exercise a little leeway though I hardly have to remind you what can happen when an idiot gives free rein to his undisciplined imagination! You wouldn't believe, *ma chère*, the number of local variations of mushrooms *à la provençale* you can come across in the Midi! Why, just about every restaurant has its own recipe and, hot-blooded as they all are down there, each chef swears blind by it."

"Rather reminds me of the fashion world. Thousands of petty rivalries with everyone cutting each other's throat to interpret the same trend."

"Yes, it does sound familiar," says the Marquis, pleased to hear his apprentice seeking out parallels between her world and the one more obscure to which he is introducing her. "Mind you, given the special nature of what we're attempting, it's vital that we stick to simplicity. You'll find tracking down four ingredients quite taxing enough." With the course's aim now outlined, the Marquis gives his young companion a wistful look. "That's settled then! *Cèpes* fried in olive oil to which we add garlic, and garnish with a few sprigs of parsley."

Now that he has laid down guidelines for the success of the course, the Marquis settles back in his chair and puts the finishing touches to his exposé. "So our very first task, Annabelle, will be to seek out the freshest, the most perfect ingredients we can lay our hands on. Fortunately," he adds, "we do have one great advantage."

"Oh? What's that?"

"We know what to avoid."

"We do?"

"You haven't forgotten what landed on your plate yesterday?"

"Good God no!" Her lips register disgust. "You're quite right! Anything'd be an improvement after that."

In short, he continues, they have contracted a mission. A

mission with a single goal: the righting of a serious wrong. To erase the gastronomic scandal which they encountered in the Brasserie the day before, what they must do is endeavour to cook the very best mushrooms *à la provençale* they can. Which means tracking down the right ingredients. And with four to locate, says the Marquis, examining his watch, they'd better get a move on.

What is he suggesting? asks Annabelle. That they pull the emergency cord and hop out of the train? She points towards the window where thickly-wooded pine brushed by a full moon obliterate all signs of civilization. This is commuter land, for Heaven's sake! They're hundreds of kilometres from Nice!

True, the Marquis answers. They are some way from their arrival point. But, he adds mysteriously, almost no distance from their destination. For if they apply the right methods, use their imagination, and react to everything that befalls them with the correct degree of sympathy, he is confident that they will lay their hands on all the ingredients they need.

If she is not careful, the Marquis adds, noting the confusion on Annabelle's face, the wind may change and she will have to wear that ghastly expression for the rest of her life. Which, he guarantees, will not win her friends. Come! he adds, gently touching her right hand. She must learn to relax and to trust him. As for the course's rules and parameters, she need not concern herself unduly about them as he will point them out as they go along.

Rules. Parameters. Conditions. Trust. Objects steeped in feelings. Noises that possess. Annabelle, although becoming used to these facets of the Marquis' fantastic course – and at a speed which amazes her – wonders what his next trick is likely to be.

The Marquis in fact does not keep her waiting long, for, turning to her after a moment's silence in which he has gazed out of the window at the swift passing of the obscured vista, he asks her if she would be kind enough to search in the suitcase for a set of dice. It is with resignation that she delves through the various flaps and vents with which the case seems particularly well endowed, some lying concealed within others which in turn reveal enough space for *bibelots* and jimjams to be priest-holed away; until, her fingers scouting through every visible recess, she runs down in the depths of a particularly artfully covered pit a small and beautifully tooled pigskin holder in which the dice sit snug.

The Marquis snaps open the holder. She must be wondering what they are for, isn't she? How can he best explain? Perhaps by stating that these dice have the power to inject an element of chance in a journey which might otherwise be uneventful. Is she aware that every moment is surrounded by a vast array of potential events, even if, of course, only one can actually occur? Then she should consider some of the alternatives which attended their own encounter. The dish in the Brasserie for instance might not have been ruined. He might not have made his offer to her. And even if he had, she might have turned him down; and so on and so forth. Now, what the dice will do is permit them to sidestep the all-too-predictable, wholly expected rhythm which would normally swamp their journey, and instead allow the unusual, the imaginative, the aleatory potential within reality to come into their lives. They are, after all, searching for unusual ingredients, are they not? And there is, in his experience, only one sure way to secure them – and that is via a most unusual route. A route which the dice – surely one of the most potent symbols of the infinite variations of fortune – will open for them. Every so often, as she will soon discover, they will part company with the train's humdrum nature and head off in their own particular direction. However, the Marquis adds, recognizing the signs of poorly camouflaged trepidation which have broken out on Annabelle's face, as his explanations are rather more likely to baffle than to enlighten her, he prefers to let the dice show her what they are all about.

Up in the air the dice fly. Down on to the table they then spin, rolling and twisting with astonishing grace, keeping Annabelle guessing what numbers will come up until, their energy spent, they at last reveal the tally on their upturned faces.

"A two and a four," says the Marquis. "Not a bad start. That means our first port of call will be compartment number six," he adds, without further explanation. "Are you ready?"

Annabelle has opened her handbag and is taking a handkerchief out of it when, to her surprise, the Marquis takes the bag firmly away from her.

"No! leave it behind," says the Marquis. "You mustn't weigh

34

yourself down with unnecessary props. From now on your principal helpmeets must be your imagination and your sense of adventure."

While acquiescing before this further intrusion into her customary behaviour, Annabelle nonetheless takes the precaution of secreting the linen square up her sleeve.

As they turn right out of the Marquis' compartment and start to pace through the train, Annabelle muses whether the number 6 possesses special significance. After a few moments, during which the limited gamut of her symbological knowledge – the hexagon, the hexagram, the Seal of Solomon, the six-sided crystalline forms within nature and various other patterns perhaps salient, perhaps farfetched – are all passed in review, she decides that she is wasting her time. Which is surely the wisest conclusion as there is no way to tell whether in this puzzle-proliferating story there is any rune, occult connotation, or, indeed, subtext to be divined from a number generated by nothing more than the tumbling of the dice.

Her steps soon take her past compartments in which she glimpses a collection of long-distance commuters. Some are shielding themselves from human contact with newspapers which they hold up like phylacteries. Others are nibbling away at *Petits Lu* or are sniffing garlic-soused *saucissons*. A number are fretting over objects placed in the folds of the deepest luggage while the rest stare with wide-eyed wonder at the shadow-encloaked features cascading past their line of vision. While the Marquis strides purposefully in front of her, Annabelle tries to fathom what she has let herself in for.

Ambling past one particular compartment's glass front and casually glancing into it, Annabelle can hardly believe her eyes. For instead of the velveteen upholstery and Midi-bound passengers which she expected to see in it, what greets her instead is a group of South American *peones*, their white linen tunics draped with multicoloured shawls, sitting on a set of wooden slatted seats. Some clutch hens; others have their laps heaped high with vegetable produce, while through the window the viridian heights of the Andes provide a realistic backdrop to the improbable scene. This would be quite sufficiently astounding in itself were she not to encounter in the very next carriage a band of Russian *kulaks* who, fur-swaddled and leather-enwrapped against the asperities of a snow-bound Siberian winter, confront her, rifles at the ready, with the kind of hostile scrutiny which, she suspects, a female intruding on their patriarchal traditions would arouse.

Thoroughly disoriented, Annabelle does not tarry, as the last thing she wants in the middle of this suddenly enchanted carriage is to lose sight of the Marquis. Yet is it conceivable that he has not noticed these scenes ripped out of some exotic travelogue? Or is his attention so fixed on tracking down the right compartment that he has rigorously excluded all extraneous information? Faced by the Marquis' apparent imperviousness, she has to admit that there is nothing for it but to continue.

And so on and on she trudges through interminable corridors, past compartments which fortunately revert to a more naturalistic decor, past others deserted yet bathed in lights as bright as cinematic floods, and even past one in which there is nothing to be seen except a garish poster of a statistically average family taking the rail route to the Midi and smiling all the while out of its unashamed and slightly nauseating two-dimensionality. Apart from the disturbing possibility that she is undergoing a severe hallucinatory outburst, Annabelle can provide no other explanation for the occurrence of her visions. She is about to call out to the Marquis to slow down and to tell her what is going on when a sharp tingle in her left eye, a grain of dust flying through the compartment, forces her to stop.

With both eyes closed, she is waiting patiently for her tear ducts to wash away the particle when she is startled to see in her mind's eye – and with quite extraordinary clarity – a big, black book of fabric samples, plaids, cashmeres, woollens, all of them flicking back and forth, all showing off their finely-textured plurality. She watches the display for a few seconds in utter disbelief. This really is brilliant! And such a great help too! Annabelle thinks, opening her uninjured eye and taking the opportunity offered by a particularly long corridor down which her companion's form is fast progressing to remain leaning against the wall in the hope that the speck of dust will soon disappear. What on earth is she to make of this rapidly unfurling parade of cloths? Does it offer her the smallest shred of advice? Is it replete with worldly consolation? Or does it not go towards

36

the inexorable conclusion that there is little point carrying a coffer-full of so-called pertinent details about reality in one's head, if, just when one most dearly wishes them to fall into some kind of meaningful shape, the best they can generate is a set of useless images?

As the Marquis is about to round the far corner and to disappear into the bellows of the next compartment, she opens her now somewhat soothed eye and chases after him wearily, fretting over the grotesque and capriciously unhelpful nature of her mental images. She is striding over the vertiginously flowing ribbon of the tracks visible between the two carriages when she suddenly stands stock still, feeling her taut body rocked by the differing rhythms of the two compartments. For, yes, a remarkably novel notion has just pulsed through her mind.

Of course! she gasps, edging over to the next carriage. Now she seizes the connection! Those fabrics, they're items from a range! They're examples of what's in stock! What she has just experienced, walking down the endless labyrinth of corridors and peering into those compartments, does bear some relation to the book of sample patterns, to that catholic selection of cloths which flashed up through her mind. All those strange scenes, those weird apparitions, why, they're the train thumbing through its own book of patterns, through its own stocklist of alternatives! What it has done, surely, is to show off a number of the scenes which have long been associated with it. It has, in other words, proudly paraded its imaginary wealth!

Isn't that astounding? Or is it rather astoundingly unlikely? ponders Annabelle, whose critical sense is warning her that her intuition has just taken a leap in the dark. Still, for all its subtlety, it does make some sort of crazy sense, she decides as she catches up with the Marquis staring straight ahead and devouring the lengths of the corridors one after the other, quite oblivious to anything else. The kind of sense moreover which, she suspects, this enchanted train might well engender. And now that she has dropped – if only momentarily – a number of her own admittedly banal strictures, and confronted a surfeit of unbelievable events, she is willing to accept that anything could happen in this train – and quite probably will! For, she concedes, once the premise that nothing is wholly impossible has been adopted, why shouldn't the train run through a catalogue of the scenes which it might incorporate? Didn't the Marquis stress a few

37

minutes ago that the dice would show up the main alternatives which surround every event?

This far-ranging theory certainly goes some way towards explaining why, in the compartments past which she next walks, Annabelle encounters sequences from films which she vividly remembers. These make no attempt whatsoever to conceal their identity, but openly offer up their factitious nature to her gaze and pretend to be nothing more than clips.

All appear to have one aspect in common: their characters, for some reason or another, find themselves travelling on a train. As for their plots, morbid! In one of the compartments for instance, Annabelle catches sight of a woman staring out of her window and witnessing a slow strangulation taking place on another train running in the same direction if at a slightly different speed. Her stomach turns. She rushes past the gruesome scene only to come across in the next one two men who, discovering that they both lead unhappy domestic lives, decide to rid each other of the unwanted party in what would, in the absence of apparent motive, become perfectly conceived crimes. She does not spend a second longer than necessary with that benighted duo. In a third she stumbles on a group of people at the very instant that they are knifing to death the man who blighted their lives by kidnapping and killing a much-loved child. Expecting further massacre, she is about to avert her eyes from the next set when she is mollified to discover that the compartment is in fact bathed in a deep romantic glow, and that the tall dark officer and his former flame, the courtesan, are making their way through rebel-controlled lands to the open city where, if their luck holds, their former differences may be reconciled once and for ever more.

Relieved that at least one of the scenes which she has most unwillingly witnessed did not lead to mayhem, Annabelle walks further down the corridor. Then, without so much as a flicker of warning, the lights go out and the train slips into the moist folds of a tunnel, an event whose all too obvious metaphoric potential is immediately exploited by her becoming surrounded on all sides by cries of ecstasy, the kind she remembers crackling over the soundtracks of films shown at libertine dinner parties she has on occasion frequented. The moment the light returns, however, these over-explicit notations thankfully disappear, and the train's normal sounds again take over.

Nor are those the only episodes she meets, for the corridors seem bent on delivering a never-ending supply, each one precisely framed within a compartment's glass front. Somewhat sickened by their sheer volume, and by the emotional hold each one has over her, Annabelle quickly heads past them and so fails to recognize from which script or production house they came. Nonetheless, catching sight of their images in the corner of her eyes (some produced in flaky monochrome, some caught in the more lurid photochemical processes by which West Coast fiction factories illumined their less than plausible plots), Annabelle cannot help wondering whether it is not her mind which has derailed. For the only explanation she has so far devised for what she is going through is, to say the least, extraordinary: that she has just traipsed past a series of screens on which, backprojected by some film archivist with a fetish for trains, scenes have been lined up one after the other. But if so – leaving aside questions such as how the fantasy was orchestrated, what palms had to be greased, what official forms typed in triplicate, and by what means such an elaborate performance was made possible – towards what end was it achieved? The conclusion which she eventually reaches is, to say the least, tentative and is also, for some inexplicable reason, couched in her mind in overflowery terms: namely that the remarkable sequence of phenomena which she has just experienced has been orchestrated to induce in her a sense of train-ness so deep that she would thereafter have an unimpeachable apprehension of its savorous essence! Ha!

To add to the general state of chaos – or to the system whose particular logic she has not yet worked out – it is the compartment numbers which next prove to have a life of their own. Far from following a rational sequence, they choose to conform to their own patterns, invaginating, pirouetting, indeed making complete nonsense of the normal progression of numerals. Annabelle would find this utterly bewildering were the Marquis' occasional over-the-shoulder smile of encouragement not sufficiently strong a lifeline for her to prevail – however tired, dismayed and disbelieving she feels – through the corridors' interminable entrails.

After tackling yet another empty compartment, and pressing past the soot-filled accordions which join carriage to carriage, the Marquis stops outside a door and points it out to Annabelle triumphantly. Here it is at last, black on white, its digit plainly visible, the number they have been searching for.

Annabelle, usually fit, is surprised at how out of breath she is.

"You look tired out," the Marquis says. "I must now concentrate so why don't you use the time to get your breath back? Then the moment I'm ready and you feel better, we'll go in."

From his pocket he takes the two pieces of paper which he has brought with him and reads them with care. He then closes his eyes as if committing them to memory. The rapid darting movements which his eyes make against the stretched gossamer of his eyelids attract Annabelle's attention. What is her companion, her guide, up to? Has he fallen into some kind of trance?

Annabelle leans against the sides of the corridor and awaits his return from his somewhat showy performance, adding this bizarre item to the lengthening list of strange events which she has had to suffer since she foolhardily accepted his invitation. Gathering her wits about her, she resolves to continue to take matters as they are, ruefully aware that she has next to no control over them anyway.

"All right?" the Marquis asks, issuing from the manifest torpor into which his concentration had plunged him, and putting the pieces of paper back in his pocket. "In that case, let's discover what fate has in store for us."

And with that ominous statement, he opens the door to compartment no. 6 and ushers Annabelle into it.

CHAPTER THREE

Finding it hard to become acclimatized to the lack of light, Annabelle cannot at first make out where they are. All she can tell is that they are now trekking down a low-ceilinged and musty passageway. A passageway so hermetic that she can even hear her own breathing bouncing back from the close-hugging walls. A few steps ahead she catches the sound of the Marquis pushing against what she presumes must be a door, for there soon follows the unmistakeable dirge of worn hinges. Once its echo has scraped past her, and she has blindly followed in the Marquis' footsteps, she discovers that she has debouched on to a much wider space. As her eyes become progressively used to the penumbra, what lies before her falls into shape. One thing is certain: this is no train compartment. Indeed, nowhere is there the slightest sign of the train. They appear to have landed somewhere completely different. Although Annabelle would like nothing more than to get out as fast as possible, the Marquis, who seems to have taken this abrupt metamorphosis in his stride, and who has retraced his steps, gently takes hold of her hand to still her confusion. Satisfied that she has been comforted, he turns to explore this new space, while she resigns herself with a long sigh to her fate.

She can think of no more apt description for the place in which they have arrived than a seedy theatrical dressing room. While most of it lies in the dark, its barely illumined walls flecked and peeling, she can distinguish at its far end, aureoled in a constellation of grubby light bulbs, a dressing table. On it there sits a catholic collection of creams, lotions and greasepaints, and, next to them, a blonde wig on a stand. But much more

astonishing is the sight, close to the dressing table and somewhat in the shadows, of a woman. She straddles a chair, is busy
applying her make-up, and wears only the skimpiest leopard
skin bikini and fishnet stockings.

Drawn towards the arc of lights, Annabelle notes that the
woman is magnificent: her figure is full, her coiffure leonine,
and her arms are both muscular and sleek. Her age, however, is
difficult to tell as liberal amounts of face powder have obscured
the sagging skin and crow's feet by which time's attrition can
usually be reckoned. Nor is her occupation all that clear. She
could be, Annabelle muses, a vaudeville actress playing the part
of some jungle-stalking feline; or, more prosaically, a stripper
about to go on stage. Certainly the last detail to fall into
Annabelle's line of vision would tend to the latter interpretation;
for, at the woman's feet, big black blotchy striations covering its
yellow lacquered body, there looms the massive and impressively lifelike model of a papier-mâché leopard.

Perhaps to make the point that the artiste is little more than a
demi-mondaine, the Marquis directs Annabelle's attention
towards a ragged poster half hanging on the wall behind the
dressing table where, in a graphic style dripping with drama,
the rubric:

SENSATIONAL!
NEVER TO BE REPEATED!
VISITING YOUR TOWN TONIGHT!
COME AND SEE THE LEOPARD WOMAN!

frames a rough, hand-printed picture of the leopard-skin-
garbed woman.

Sitting at her worktable, surrounded by the deceiving tools of
her trade, her features both veiled and highlighted by the
unguents and oils of masquerade, the so-called Leopard Woman
represents a sight so alluring, and yet so appalling, that Annabelle
cannot take her eyes off her. Not that she has benefited long
from the incognito of her unannounced entrance. Clearly
irritated by the interruption, the artiste turns round and focuses
a cruel and unflinching gaze at her. The worst of it, Annabelle
discovers, is that she has to face this inquisition alone as the
Marquis has wandered off to a part of the dressing room half
encloaked in darkness, where he appears to be assessing some

aspect of the scene. If only to break the awesome silence that surrounds them, Annabelle is about to speak when the Marquis, rapidly returning from his investigation, puts a finger to his mouth and counsels her to be still. He then points to two chairs standing on the far side of the Leopard Woman's dressing table.

"Sit down over there and wait for me. I'll only be a moment. And whatever happens, don't say a word even if spoken to. Let me do the talking."

The Leopard Woman, concentrating on Annabelle rather than on her companion, stares at her in silence and makes her feel distinctly unwelcome. With studied insouciance, Annabelle walks across the dressing room's floor but the weight of her self-consciousness, allied to the woman's open hostility, conspires to drain her gestures of grace. She nonetheless goes over to one of the two designated chairs and repositions it a fraction or so for no better reason than to adopt the air of someone who is in no hurry. She then inches away the creases in her dress, looks around the chamber and finally, as if satisfied, sits down. If only the Marquis would stop his survey and join her, at least this intense scrutiny would then be shared. Fortunately Annabelle's silent plea is soon answered for, seemingly satisfied with his search, the Marquis walks over to her and, showing not the slightest sensitivity towards her embarrassment, takes his seat next to hers.

He crosses his legs, directs his gaze at the still glaring artiste and, with evident good humour, says to her: "And a very good evening to you."

"I don't remember hearing you knock," the Leopard Woman replies in an accent tainted by the granular tones of some Central European language. "I'm surprised fine people like you," she says, rubbing her forefinger and thumb and pointing at the travellers' elegant clothes, "have forgotten your manners."

"You must forgive us interrupting you like this," says the Marquis. "But my assistant and I," he waves in Annabelle's direction, "will only take up a few moments of your precious time. I presume your call must be due any moment."

"As it so happens, I'm not on for another half hour. But that doesn't mean I'm after company."

"Of course not, of course not!" says the Marquis, adopting a tone so obsequious that Annabelle wonders whether he has not mistaken registers for his submissiveness seems quite out of character, loathsome even. "We quite understand. However, as we've come a long way to seek your help, we'd be grateful if you'd at least hear us out. We're in a great deal of trouble. And when we heard that you too had had your fair share, we hoped you'd show our plight some sympathy."

"Ha! So that's your game, is it? You've been snooping! Delving into my private life!"

"We have not! That would have been sheer impertinence. We simply asked around."

About to put back on the dressing table a pot whose creamy contents she was applying to her neck, the Leopard Woman suddenly stops midway. The next instant she discards her cool expression, widens her eyes and – presumably an easy trick for her to turn, a well-rehearsed aspect of her quick-change stock-in-trade – she parts her mouth wide and exposes the coral-white of her vulpine teeth.

"I haven't the first idea what's wrong with you but whatever it is," she cries out, "it's got you into a fine old mess!"

With an intensity bordering on the indecent, the artiste now stares at her two visitors. Desperate to know what the Marquis is making of this violent reaction, Annabelle looks away from the Leopard Woman, turns towards him, and discovers to her horror what it is she has found so compelling.

It is indeed a word-defying sight. But as those loose, slippery and ambiguous generators of sense are our sole medium, we will try to convey the ludicrous, the mesmerizing, the ghastly event which has overtaken the Marquis.

"You're in bloody desperate straits, aren't you?" the Leopard Woman interjects. "No wonder you barged in and didn't bother knocking!"

For the Marquis' features are going through a profound transformation. His face has turned a sickly grey. Where his cheeks were, dark brown gills have grown. And his neck has taken on the hue, texture and shape of a long sinewy stem. Although dumbstruck, Annabelle has enough wits about her to recognize that only one description will do for what is occurring: the Marquis' face is fast turning into a mushroom!

Annabelle steals a glance at her own face in the dressing room mirror. Cold sweat sweeps through her body. Her heart quickens, her legs shiver. Oh no! Not her face as well!

Perhaps because Annabelle is younger, the *cèpe* whose skin, colour and smell she is taking on is fresher than the Marquis'. Otherwise the change – her cheeks wide brown gills, her skin grey and squelchy, a purple ruff irradiating around her neck – is in every other gruesome detail the same. Horrified, yet unable to scream – has her larynx already been muted by a mass of newly-formed fungoid cells? – Annabelle clutches the rubbery substance of her face. Quick! How can she become free of this fearful apparition? She must tear this mask off! But there is no mask. There is only burgeoning, knobbly flesh. And the only sensation which her panicked fingers manage to elicit from the newly-formed mass is a cold and distant pain, as if her flesh had become frozen or dulled. Overcome by a growth as real as an outbreak of pustules on her flesh, Annabelle can conceive neither how such a fate has befallen her and her companion, nor by what radical means she can reverse it.

Paradoxically, the Marquis – whom she can glimpse out of the corner of her painfully-swollen eyes – seems quite unperturbed by the transformation. With his arms neatly folded on his tweed suit, and his hands already exposing a stem's mud-brown consistency, his sole concern seems to be to carry on his conversation with the Leopard Woman. So overwhelming are Annabelle's fear, nausea and disgust at the bulbous growths which have seized her skin that although she does not want to interrupt him, remembering his counsel to let him do all the talking, she is about to grab him and to beg him to help release her when, frantically looking into the mirror again, she discovers that her skin is resuming its former shape, that the mycological nightmare is receding, and that the Marquis' face is also re-emerging out of the folds of its grey, puffed-up appearance.

"You're absolutely right," the Marquis remarks to the Leopard Woman. "There's no better word than desperate for what has befallen us. The worst of it is that this ghastly fungus growth just comes and goes. We never know when we're next going to suffer an attack. In fact sometimes simply talking about it can urge it on. It's a disease for which we haven't managed to find a cure. And that, dear lady, brings me at last to the reason for our visit. We think – no, we're absolutely sure – that you can help us. Because we're after something which you and only you can get us and yet which would make a world of difference to us."

"Fancy that! And, tell me, why should I put myself out for a couple of sickly strangers?"

"I understand your reservations. On the other hand, were you to come to our aid you would, I assure you, not go unrewarded. The fact is that we've found a solution to your problem."

"A solution! To my problem! Ha!" the Leopard Woman exclaims, putting her hand through her resplendent blonde hair, leaning far back on her chair, and eyeing the travellers with a look so long and piercing that Annabelle fails to fathom whether it is amused or disdainful. What next? Will this petulant female throw them out or will she help them? And if so, how? Questions which obscure the central problems plaguing Annabelle's mind before once more giving way to them. For what is she doing in this mysterious dressing room? What has happened to the train? And what is the nature of this scene into whose compelling and frightening texture she and the Marquis appear to be patterned?

Although the artiste's manner seems at first uninterested, her hands caressing the pots and lotions on her boudoir, it gradually dawns on Annabelle that the Marquis' offer must have aimed true. For every so often the artiste interrupts her fidgeting and gazes at her two visitors in a wistful manner. Perhaps it is also the unfeigned perplexity etched on Annabelle's own face which goes to convince the Leopard Woman that the strangers' request is genuine and that there may be something in it for her. Whatever the cause, she casts a sad glance at her tattered poster and strokes the leopard's smooth back with an affection born of some deep experience. Then, turning towards the travellers, her voice low, the Leopard Woman says: "All right. Though what you're suffering from is disgusting and, for all I know, deserved, as you've made an effort to see me, I'll hear you out. I've still a few minutes before my act's on. But before I do, I'm going to put you two straight. Because I'm sure of one thing: whatever you've heard about me is bound to be cockeyed. I'm the only one who can say what happened to me and there are damn good reasons for that! As for you," she adds, singling Annabelle out for her narrow-eyed attention, "you sit there nice and quiet and take in every word of my story."

Annabelle closes her eyes and settles back in her chair just as the Marquis with a rapid, almost impatient gesture has counselled

her. As soon as she has done so, she discovers that she can –
dimly at first then with fast-focusing clarity – distinguish in her
mind's eye the outlines of a vast forest scene. Nor, amazingly, is
her vision limited to sight for she can also sense the general
movement of the trees, smell the coiled mass of vegetation, and
even feel the cold wind thrashing at the grasslands which
surround the forest. It is indeed as if she were joined to the very
lifeblood of the setting. Long spiky ranks of pine stretch to the
horizon at which dark and hazeous point the mountains, a
far-off fortress wall speckled with snow, intercept them. The
outer edge of the forest is encircled by dark swards of leaves. At
its base, in a small clearing, stands a cottage. Its roof is finely
thatched, its narrow windows cross-mullioned, its wooden
shutters display a rich and weather-worn rust-coloured hue,
while its sills are flanked with a neat phalanx of late flowering
pots. Out of its chimney gunmetal spirals of smoke slowly wisp.
With a creak that splices the humid air, the front door of the
cottage swings wide open and an adolescent girl, wearing a
simple grey peasant dress offset by a band of red cloth around
her waist and carrying a small wickerwork basket, wanders into
the forest.

Her voice soft and low, her accent slightly heightened, the
Leopard Woman begins her tale. "Shall I tell you of my earliest
childhood memory?" she asks the two hushed travellers. Then,
without waiting for an answer to a question which was clearly
rhetorical, she continues: "the grumbling in my stomach never
stopping. That's right: I always seemed to be hungry. My father
barely earned enough in the State Forests to make ends meet.
But though we were poor and didn't know where the next meal
would be coming from, thankfully we never starved.

"Late one afternoon, returning home after a day of gathering
wood, my father was caught out in a gale. Was it the violence of
the wind ripping through the foliage or the rain bouncing its fat
drops off the trees' hides which stopped him hearing the loud
firecracker sound? I will never know. What's certain is that
the great fir which fell on top of him took him completely by
surprise.

"Night-time had fallen, the storm had gathered around us,
and we – my mother, brother and I – waited by the dimming
fireplace in our cottage with no idea why my father hadn't come
home. Finally, armed with a lantern to guide us, we trudged

through the heavy downpour until, in the deepest part of the forest, we came across his dreadfully crushed body. I don't remember how we carried him. Perhaps for once my brother helped us. Somehow we brought him back home, put him to bed, then stood by helplessly as the colour slowly drained from his limbs."

A single spluttering candle throws its desultory rays over the woodsman's flourwhite face and onto his wife's ceaselessly wringing hands. The young girl stares at her father while her brother, with remarkable dispassion, whittles a piece of wood on the other side of the bed. Nothing can hide from the family the terrible truth that the woodsman is dying. But while his wounds are deep, and he, poor man, is in torment, those are not the main reasons for his swiftly sapping strength.

"As he lay there my father, the strong woodsman, the manly provider, was forced to face the fact that he would never work again. And so great was his shame that he would not drink the gruel we had made nor would he sip the nettle infusion, but turned his head to the wall and left our entreaties unanswered. However much my mother and I begged him to take food, there was nothing we could do to stop him fading. For it wasn't only his body that had been affected: his spirit had also been crushed. A cruel wound which took two days to kill him."

The Leopard Woman's voice quavers with a sadness so evocative that Annabelle is surprised by the depth of feeling that the story draws from her. It is a truly inexorable force which drags her into the tale. And so insidiously does it act upon her that she cannot resist its subtle process. Is she, she wonders, providing the feelings herself or are they being imposed upon her by the story? Quite unable to provide an answer to a question whose ontology has at one time or other troubled most aestheticians, and aware that she might well lose the story's nuances if she does not stop fretting over the origin of the emotion she is experiencing, she admits her ignorance and once again surrenders to the flow of the narrative.

"There's no doubt," the Leopard Woman briskly resumes her tale, "that with my father's death, and the withdrawal of his State salary, if my mother hadn't been a fine seamstress and taken in work from our neighbours, we would never have survived."

Under a lowering sky dimly perceived through a closely sown

patchwork of leaves, the young girl picks her way through the forest, her fingers foraging for its hidden fruits. Her steps are nimble, her manner sure, and so she soon locates the berry, moss, nut or mushroom which she is seeking.

"No matter the weather, come rain, come shine, my mother'd send me into the woods to root out whatever food I could find. Frequently I'd come home, my fingers torn and swollen and my hands smeared with blood."

From the densest part of the forest, a thickly matted band of firs, the young girl emerges into a sandy clearing. Before her the quicksilver expanse of a broad lake. She stops and gazes at its surface. Tiptoeing to its edge, she looks to left and right then, in a sudden and graceful move, spreadeagles on the bank and stares into its dark waters.

Slowly, from the water's ice-cold depths through to its levels of translucence, there arises a most extraordinary shape. Its form at first misty but soon boldly coloured, a leopard appears. And what a massive creature it is too, its powerful features slightly diffracted by an occasional ripple, its jaws wide open, its tail beating a momentous rhythm. Indeed, were it not for the veil which the gentle lapping of the water interposes, Annabelle is sure its roar would split the funereal calm of the autumn scene and scatter the crows which watch from the high branches of the surrounding trees. But what astounds her most, as she gazes at the leopard in her mind's eye, is that around its neck there hangs a key on a large golden chain. And so close is the creature below the surface of the lake that she can discern that it is a perfect replica of the key which the Marquis slipped into his pocket.

After she has watched the creature for a few instants, the young girl starts to sing. From the sight of its fast swishing tail and of its silently roaring jaw, it is clear to Annabelle that the creature delights in the lulling sounds which its young visitor makes.

Taking for granted her audience's acceptance of the mirabilic vision to which she has just introduced them, the Leopard Woman continues her tale. "There was however one thing I hated," she adds. "I had nobody – nobody at all with whom I could share my friend. For had I spoken of the leopard to anybody, something terrible would have happened."

On that particular night in the people's calendar the cottage is more brightly lit than on any other occasion for the young girl's relatives have assembled around the dinner table to commemorate the Feast of the Workers' Heart. The abode's main room is decorated with red flags and sashes and on the wall, in pride of place, the portrait of the Father of the Nation has been highlighted with a chorus of candles. Once the venison soup, braised pig's trotters and stuffed marrow have been consumed, and the company has fallen with gusto on the cranberry and chestnut pie, the conversation moves on to serious matters. It is with avidity that the young girl listens to her elders discussing what punishment was recently meted out to the zealots who dared champion the outlawed heresy of eternal life. And while naturally none of the company defends the outlandish notion that at every step along man's way his actions are judged by an absent Creator – a concept long ago bleached out of the people by the astringence of their modern orthodoxy – it is nonetheless apparent that some consider that the State has treated the dissidents too harshly. "Let them be with their crazy ideas!" exclaims the eldest uncle, a prosperous smallholder whose marrow has been copiously complimented for its magnificent roundness. "Couldn't have put it better myself!" retorts his brother, Assistant to the Keeper of the Forests, whose venison was skilfully transformed into a finely spiced stew. "Don't forget History vomits those who turn their back on progress!" ripostes the Town Clerk, whose cunning in the marketplace placed pork on the festive table. "Brothers! I beg you. Surely this is not a subject for children?" the young girl's mother remonstrates, her hands still sore from the cranberries she picked and baked so deliciously in the pie.

Were we to have greater ease of access to their rough-hewn language – whose crude gutturals and pungent plosives seem quite untouched by the civilizing polish of Romance influences – we would no doubt intuit what sympathies the eldest uncle harboured for the radicals, in what guilt-ridden awe the Assistant Game Keeper holds them, and might have some inkling of the big black tome in which the Town Clerk lists those he suspects of leaning towards the heresy. Much easier to read fortunately has been the behaviour of the girl's brother. For while the company's parries have exploded across the feastday linen, the rough fruit wines, and the remnants of the meal, he has concentrated with rare appetite on the official brutality dealt out to the believers after the rash publicizing of their creed. In contrast to his bloodlust, as soon as the young girl has heard the catalogue of cruelty which was their sorry lot, now aware of the penalties she would face if she ever betrayed her own guilty secret, she herself falls into a sombre mood.

"It was – I remember it well – May Day. My family had gathered round the dinner table to celebrate the Father of the Nation's unmasking the enemies of the State. During the meal, the subject of what had happened to people who said they had visions came up. My uncles seemed to know all about it. Some, they said, had been arrested; others tortured. As for the ringleaders, they had, naturally, been executed. Perhaps you can now understand," the Leopard Woman stresses, her voice marked by fear, "why I couldn't breathe so much as a word about my friend in the lake. But how I hated keeping it to myself! How I hoped I might one day share the leopard's friendship with others! Yet had I mentioned it to my mother, she'd have beaten me black and blue, not to punish me but to stop me speaking of it to anyone else."

One afternoon, while the sun backlights a low-lying canopy of clouds, the young girl and her brother are browsing through the forest, scouring its mottled marquetry of leaves and moss for food. Breaking through a curtain of prickly fronds, the boy stumbles on the clearing which leads to the lake. He stops wide-eyed before it, picks up a large stone and, with a shout, slings it into the water. His sister holds her breath. What if the stone harms the leopard? But the ripples soon clear and the forest's silence stifles the echo of the splash. Her brother is rooting around for berries at the edges of the forest when the young girl decides that she can bear it no more. She must tell him, yes, she must share her secret with him. Is he not after all her own brother? Of course, like all boys he is rough. Yet, surely, when he sees the leopard with his own eyes, will he not want to play with it, will he too not fall in love with it?

She runs towards the water, stares into its obsidian depths and, in an instant, catches sight of the creature. Out of the shadows of the lake it rises, remaining as always a few feet below the surface yet so close that Annabelle can distinguish its powerful features, the mottled and shiny quality of its coat, and the never wavering splendour of its opalescent eyes. It has once again answered her summons. Overwhelmed with excitement, the young girl turns to her brother and calls to him to come and join her.

He looks up, notices her mooning above the water – her reflection mosaicked by a wind that ruffles the surface of the lake – and, in his usual gruff voice, asks her why on earth should he bother. Her ugly face he can see any day! He hardly needs water for that! In the hope that he will change his mind, and that his curiosity will lead him to discover for himself with what creature of wonder she has been communing, she remains hunched at the water's edge. The opportunity is too good to miss. Dashing towards his sister, the boy falls on top of her and, grabbing her by the neck, plunges her head into the lake. Unnerved by the shock and the speed of his attack, she does not at first react. Then, as instinct seizes her limbs, she tries to wriggle free. Endowed with greater strength than hers, however, he holds her under so long that she is soon flailing about in panic. Only when he notices the damp patch that has soiled her dress does he release her. And once she, speechless and shamed, gasping for breath, tears mingling with the water on her face, rushes home towards the consoling folds of her mother's dress, he falls to the ground and beats it loudly with his fists. And so uproariously does he laugh that his shrieks cut through the ramparts of trees and scatter the crows from the height of their funereal contemplation.

"I now realize," the Leopard Woman adds, "that I was wasting my time. Even if he had looked into the water, the little brute wouldn't have seen anything."

Early one morning, so early that the dawn chorus has not yet struck up its strident song, the young girl wakes up in her tiny bedroom and gasps. She has a terrible pain in her stomach. She pulls back her bedclothes, lifts the veil of her nightdress, and stares at the large red mark which has spread on to the sheets from the gap in the fork of her body. She then slowly runs her fingers along the perimeter of the still damp stain.

Her face wan, she bursts into the kitchen where her mother is sitting by the hearth. Dutifully, just as she does every morning, the peasant woman stares with a devotion once reserved for images far more numinous at the portrait of the Father of the Nation. And what a portrait it is too; his clear-cut features immortalized in a heroic mould, his proportions gigantic, his face unmarked by doubt, his eyes fearlessly levelled at the empyrean of progress, his figure upheld by an unquestioning brand of realism and offered as a retable of truth to his seemingly disabused people. But before we impair the story's drama with an excursus on the contradictions to be found in a materialist philosophy and the idealized representations it never fails to design, we should quickly return to the scene at hand in which an adolescent girl has run to her mother to show her the first signs of her burgeoning fecundity. Disturbed by her daughter's interruption, the peasant woman looks up from her meditation and is about to chide her when she too sees the telltale flecks which have stained the nightdress. As the compassion of her maternal role vaporizes her initial resentment at being disturbed, she rises and embraces her tearful daughter.

"When I told my mother the news, she kissed me and fetched from her bedroom a beautiful scarf which she said she had made for this special occasion and on which she had embroidered my name."

The scarf proudly pinned around her neck, the young girl runs towards her closest friend, the leopard, to tell it what has befallen her. She trips through the forest, hurdles the broken backs of old treetrunks, takes shortcuts through the damp hollows of leaf-sodden dells, until, her heart pounding and quite out of breath, she parts a final net of brambles and reaches the lake.

"At last! It had happened! I was a woman! As you can imagine," she says, reinforcing her hold on her audience with a direct call to identification, "I could not run fast enough to tell my friend the news. But as I lay by the bank of the lake, looked into its cold glassy waters, and called it to me time and again, I couldn't see it anywhere. It was nowhere to be seen! No matter how often I sang the tunes it loved, it did not come! No, it had vanished without a trace!"

The young girl, her fingers tightly clasped, the corners of her mouth shivering, cannot prevent her tears falling into the lake. She is alone. She has been deserted. The leopard has left her! Worse, as if to taunt her, exactly where the leopard used to come, a red plant has grown overnight. Its fat leaves have spread through the dark waters, and its thin pink flower barely protrudes past its roseate petals. As for the plant's shape, the young girl notices with disgust as she stares at it through the frosted screen of her tears, it reminds her of the stain which she discovered only that morning in her bed.

"The next day, hoping I had made a mistake, and that the leopard would this time appear, I ran back to the lake. But it had gone. And however much I have hoped to see it, and stared into a thousand other lonely stretches of water, I have never, no never, met it again."

Sensing that the Leopard Woman, hunched over the phials and potions, is about to cry, Annabelle decides to open her eyes. But the artiste has not lost control and manages, her voice strained, to cap her tale.

"And that, strangers, is my story. How I ended up in this gypsy's outfit isn't something I want to talk about. Though I'll say this much: there aren't many jobs a girl on the run from the forest can find in town."

The Leopard Woman pauses, leans on her chair, fiddles with one of her phials, then continues. "In a moment the curtain'll go up, and I'll be on again, making provincial punters froth into their beers and giving the poor bastards a glimpse of what they'll never get to touch. And if, night in, night out, I ride on the back of my papier-mâché leopard, that's because it's the closest I can ever get to the friendship I once had, but lost."

Annabelle opens her eyes wide, negotiates a more comfortable position on the chair and, forgetting about the handkerchief which she has secreted up her sleeve, hurriedly wipes away with her fingers the tears she has shed. Nor is the Marquis unmoved by the Leopard Woman's story, his face reflecting the apparent sorrow which the tale has evoked in him. Perhaps to console the artiste who has remained still and silent since relating her tale, he turns towards her and says: "I believe that's the saddest story I've ever heard. And you're right: in contrast the rumours which we heard about you were but pale shadows. As for the leopard, you say it disappeared and that you've never seen it since?"

"Not once," she replies. "Though what is it to you and to your pretty companion, eh?" she adds bitterly, twisting the normally complimentary epithet into one whose rancour Annabelle feels coursing right through her.

"A great deal. Especially as the way out of our predicament could well provide you with the key to your happiness."

"And how d'you suppose you'll manage that?" she retorts.

"Very simply, if you'll only let us. But first, if you don't mind, I'd like to tell a little about our own problem." The Marquis points to his face. "You've witnessed our dreadful deformity. It has baffled most of the doctors we've consulted, although the wisest called it a fungus infection and told us that there's only one known cure, an ancient folk remedy. Which means that if we want to be rid of this crop of sores and blisters once and for all, we have to drink an infusion made from the freshest forest mushrooms available. Yes, the kind you could get us. Knowing the forest as intimately as you do, that shouldn't be too difficult, should it? In return for that favour, we'll hand you a solution to your own sad situation. Isn't that so, Annabelle?"

Annabelle, who has followed the Marquis' extravagant explanation with some bewilderment, is jolted from her purely passive position by his direct question. "Er, what?"

The Marquis throws her a dark look.

"Er . . . er. . .yes! Of course we will," she stutters, trying to keep abreast of the constantly shifting situation.

The Leopard Woman looks at the travellers resignedly. "Mushrooms? Is that really what you want? Strange request, I must say." She picks up a bottle of ointment and shakes it so that its sediment, loosed from its bottom, floats upwards and suffuses the glass with a pale ochreous cloud. "Still, what have I to lose? My own dream disappeared long ago." She turns to her uninvited guests and adds: "Very well. Sit here quietly and I'll see what I can do."

The artiste leans back on her stiff chair, cups her hands, and closes her eyes. The next moment the temperature throughout the room lowers, as if a door on to a steppe had suddenly been opened and had let in a glacial draught. Shivering, wishing she had worn more protective clothes, Annabelle looks around. Her companion has also closed his eyes. Unsure of his reasons but unwilling to be left out, she follows suit.

At first the only stimulus to greet her mind's eye is that of a pale swirling grey mist. Then, to her surprise, the mist lifts and reveals in the distance a tiny porthole of light in an otherwise impenetrable darkness. By applying her will to it, she manages to make it come closer and closer, until, peering through it, she discovers that she is once again gazing at the wooded landscape of the Leopard Woman's childhood. One intriguing difference however: all the colours of the scene are faded. Why? Annabelle is not sure. Could the Leopard Woman have had difficulty remembering every shade and intensity of her distant childhood? Apart from that baffling change, everything else is plainly visible: the forest tapering off towards its vanishing point in the far-flung mountains; the clearing, fringed with firs, ringed with tall grasses and thorny bushes. As for the cottage in its clearing, Annabelle realizes with a start that it has fallen into terrible disrepair. On its roof a blight of moss has spread. Its chimney is holed to the sky and the sunken cheeks of its windows have almost buckled in.

While enrapt by the quality of the images she is observing, Annabelle still cannot comprehend why there should be any difference between the first vision of the forestscape which she experienced and this one. And indeed, as the origins of the lack of colour, of the blur in detail, and of the depredation of time and decay on this once idyllic sylvan scene belong fundamentally to the phenomenology of the imagination, they are beyond her immediate reach, deriving principally from the distance between imagined and recreated space, the one existing within the period of its conception, the second being subject to the laws of entropy. Yet it would seem that, lured by the promise of a fair exchange, the Leopard Woman has agreed not only to re-evoke the aromas, flavours and rhythms of the forest which encapsulated her youth, but has also undertaken the much more demanding task of materializing within it. She is about to make a considerable effort to recreate a long gone scene and to act in it too. And could it be because this task demands such concentration and because only so much energy is available at any given moment to mount creative forays that certain aspects of the scene have had to be sacrificed to produce it, aspects which, in this instance, appear to be those of colour and detail?

As she flows with the sequence of images, Annabelle tries to follow the logic of the Leopard Woman's imagination. She soon finds herself taken to the very centre of the clearing where her attention is focused on a small puddle, the probable remains of a recent heavy downpour. It is a dark and muddy puddle which, for no explicable reason, starts to bubble and to become a whirlpool, its sides brimming as if stirred by unknown forces.

Annabelle peers into it and is amazed to come across there, slowly rising out of the water, the image of the young girl with her simple grey dress, now monochrome sash, and her scarf tied round her head. Yes, in no time at all the young girl has risen from the puddle and is standing there, in the humid forest air, on the rain-steeped leaves, against the stark backdrop of the straight-backed pines.

First this undine-like apparition shakes swathes of water off her body. Then, so abruptly that Annabelle does not even get a glimpse of her face, she walks, still dripping, out of the clearing and towards the dark forest. Once again Annabelle is privy to the young girl's sensing of the forest – privy to the mulch of moss beneath her feet, the dankness of the leafy atmosphere, and the buzz of a swarm of insects – and realizes that she must be heading towards one of the special hide-outs which she, and only she, knows. After foraging among the broken branches, the fallen nuts, the hand-staining lichen and the straggling strands, the young girl at last comes across the night flowers that feed on corruption.

Strange, Annabelle muses, that the Leopard Woman's clothes should be so misshapen. And why is her dress tearing at its seams? Bending down to avoid a low-lying bramble bush which had threatened to tear her eyes out, the young girl turns around to reveal to Annabelle that . . . she is young no more! This is not the pubescent youth! No, it is the Leopard Woman, the artiste with her well-shaped legs, menacing pout and muscular thighs who, beneath the overstretched and water-sodden peasant garb, has somehow become incarnate into this sylvan scene.

While this is a fascinating detail and one which throws some light on the difficulties which the self-image faces when attempting to recapture the shape it had yesteryear, it does not advance the travellers' quest one jot. It is therefore with relief that Annabelle notices that, in spite of all the problems which attend her form, the figure in the forestscape parts the rotting leaves around which the *cèpes* have grown, takes from a pocket in her dress a small knife and, one after the other, severs half a dozen mushrooms. And as she slices through them, each releases a few drops of colourless liquid from its stem which she then wipes away onto the rough grey texture of her distended dress.

Her task done, the Leopard Woman returns through the forest's dense undergrowth and, after making her way past lowering fronds and cruel brambles, eventually reaches the glade. Annabelle watches her colourless figure stand stock still next to the churning puddle. Holding the mushrooms in her hands, her shape suddenly liquefies, becoming a long jet, and merges into the water. Next, as if the energy that had upheld this fragile illusion were slowly being switched off, the pastel-shaded landscape loses its definition, blurs, and fades into darkness.

When Annabelle opens her eyes, she discovers that the dressing room's temperature has risen only slightly, and that she is shivering. As for the Leopard Woman, not only is her face stark and wan, as if utterly exhausted by the imaginative journey she has just undertaken, but she is also wet through and through. Slowly uncupping her hands, she reveals within their hollow a number of fragrant yellow *cèpes* glistening with dew, and one by one hands them to the Marquis.

This too clearly stretches credibility to the limit, as it is surely one thing to evoke aspects of the past, another to materialize within it, and a third to carry back objects from its sphere of influence. Certainly to the kind of people who are easily upset by transformations like the thrice-yearly Neapolitan liquefaction of the blood of St January, or St Rita's bread becoming roses, or for that matter St Nicholas bringing back to life children who had been thrown into a pot of "long pig" stew, such an event is bound to be a serious obstacle and one against which their over-keenness on verisimilitude and their poor nourishment on the stuff of fables are bound to rue. But for those who regard the known world as but a paltry reflection of the flux that underlies and motivates every event, the mushrooms' speedy telekinesis will represent no greater conceptual problem than the often-bandied notion that pecuniary profit is man's ultimate goal, or that History and Progress are the twin pathways along which his course must run.

"Superb!" says the Marquis, palpating the *cèpes* and smelling them with enthusiasm. "I've never come across such perfect specimens. Smell this, Annabelle," he passes one of the mushrooms to her. "Now there's an aroma you'll never forget!"

Annabelle has to agree that the mushrooms are rank with an earthy and visceral odour which she has never met before.

"Exquisite!" the Marquis exclaims, turning to the Leopard Woman, "exactly what we wanted. We really are in your debt."

58

"You can say that again!" the artiste retorts, leaning forward on her chair. She points to Annabelle. "Don't think I did this for your pretty eyes, either! You said you had something for me, remember?"

"Indeed we did," says the Marquis, searching through his pockets, fishing out the golden key and handing it to the Leopard Woman. "Both Annabelle and I hope this'll be to your satisfaction."

After a moment's hesitation, during which she stares almost uncomprehendingly at the key, the Leopard Woman suddenly recognizes it. Here it is! Yes, unmistakeably, the key that once hung round her friend's broad neck. Her hands trembling, her eyes fixed on the papier-mâché figure, the Leopard Woman rises from her chair and climbs onto the creature's back. Is the artiste, Annabelle wonders, about to throw away the thinly drawn veil of her spotted bikini?

But the Leopard Woman's act involves no disrobing. Not at first anyway. Instead, in a gesture as precise and as fevered as a woman ripping open a *billet-doux* from her beloved, her fingers feel across the leopard's left flank, a gesture whose desperate fumbling Annabelle again senses with painful clarity. In no time at all her fingers have found in the creature's striated flank a well-concealed flap. She opens it and inserts her index into a small aperture. As if she had located exactly what she had been looking for, a relieved expression courses across her face. Gripping the leopard's back with her thighs and leaning over to the left to ensure that her aim is true, she takes the key and plunges it into the hole. A ghastly crunching sound – bone breaking, flesh being ripped – suddenly resonates throughout the room, and blood, with all the vigour of a severed artery, spurts from the hole, down the leopard's ribbed flanks and onto the floor. Then, with quite unexpected and pronounced violence, an animal roar echoes round the dressing room.

The Leopard Woman's face is ecstatic. She gasps, she holds the creature by the neck, she rubs her face against his. And while the room crackles with an almost phosphorescent intensity, she opens and closes her eyes with increasing rapidity.

The Marquis seizes Annabelle by the shoulder and tries to shake her out of her stupefaction. But she cannot, no, she cannot stop staring. Can this really be happening? Before her very eyes! No tricks. No veils. No conveniently placed curtain or svelte assistants to divert her attention from the legerdemain which she was convinced was at the root of the scene. The papier-mâché leopard is papier-mâché no more! For, stripped both of her bikini and of her stockings which lie like a sun-parched, sloughed-off lizard skin on the floor, the artiste now writhes on the back of a real leopard which, in a series of tight and dangerous circles, stalks around the dressing room. At a safe distance Annabelle, watching the tension on the artiste's face as she cavorts with the feline, can distinguish the pent-up pressure and the years of anticipation which this reunion has unleashed. And when the artiste crouches on the floor and the leopard, its front paws on her back, its pink member un-sheathed, mounts her, to her amazement Annabelle discovers a sensation pulsing through her groin which, although excruciat-ing, she does not want to stop. And at the precise moment that this appallingly intimate sensation overwhelms her, the dres-sing room is pierced through with yet another sound, not the leopard's roar, no, but the artiste's own cry of joy.

Now that the mushrooms are secured, and that the dizzying shapes joined on the floor are caught up in a moment of exquisite intensity, woman and leopard in the throes of redis-covery, the Marquis decides it is high time that they were on their way. He therefore takes Annabelle, still caught up by the luminous display on the floor, by the hand and drags her to the other end of the dressing room. And while she looks over her shoulder in the hope of catching a last glimpse of the scene, he finds the door, pushes her through it, closes it firmly behind him, and guides her through the dark corridor until the moans and cries in the dressing room have finally been muffled.

CHAPTER FOUR

Visible through the panoramic plate glass windows is a languid expanse of wind-worried corn fields, shot through with clumps of ancient oaks. In the distance, parallel to the train, an old viaduct carries nothing more urgent on its badly crumbled back than a savannah of weeds. Annabelle, shivering from the delayed shock of her experiences in the dressing room, finds momentary solace in the orderly procession of the dusk-encloaked landscape. What she would have felt if the train had not resumed its former ordinariness once she had burst into the corridor past the enchanted compartment's door she dares not imagine. Fortunately it did. And although she is still unsure whether it was its blue-liveried and silver body which changed, or whether her own mind provided the illusions, she is nonetheless very relieved to be back within its soothingly familiar shape.

There is however something particularly irritating about the fact that the Marquis, in total contrast to her own state of exhaustion, now seems imbued with new-found vigour. Of course, she realizes, she will need time to assimilate all the baffling events which have just befallen her and to summon the energy necessary to cope with it. Meanwhile, as if aware of her disorientation, and intent on letting her deal with it in her own way, the Marquis leans against the wall of the corridor and gazes through its windows in tactful silence.

Next, however, the travellers' contemplation is shattered by the Doppler effect of a hand bell pealing down the corridor. From one end the Steward of the first-class carriages makes a brusque entry and, with all the delicacy of a town barker, brushes past them, repeatedly calling out: *"Premier service, premier service!"*

For those whose appetites have been whetted by their transitional state, the first sitting of dinner is presently being served in the train's restaurant. Forced to work in a galley the size of a monk's retreat, the restaurant's chef has long ago pawned whatever ideals fuelled him through catering college and is now content if provisions arrive on time, his *commis* do not fight each other, and he can organize a decent rake-off on the back of the uninspired catering concern which won the contract to feed the hungry on the road to Nice. And as during the entirety of the travellers' adventures on the train, the Marquis and Annabelle are not once scheduled to visit the dining car – unless something unpredictable occurs to harm the otherwise orderly procession of events – there is no need to explain the feuds and vendettas which perennially punctuate the cook's life and which make the occasional outbreaks of food poisoning all the more surprising for their rarity.

Among the passengers who, summoned by the bell and obedient to the clamour of the angry acids in their stomach, are making their way down the corridor towards the dining compartment, the Steward cannot help noticing the to-his-taste perfect proportions of an English Memsahib who holds as if it were a dirty bundle a quiescent poodle in her arms. Indeed, the moment she walks past him on her way to the dining room, he is fatally drawn to a bosom which, if no longer in its first bloom, still has the power to draw his eyes towards its ample and well-rounded valley.

The moment the disturbing flow of passengers has ceased, the Marquis asks Annabelle whether she has a clean handkerchief. And indeed she does, for although he stopped her from bringing her handbag with her, unwilling to be taken short in any eventuality she took the precaution of inserting a white handkerchief up her sleeve. She remembers it and hands it to him. One by one he carefully places the mushrooms within its expensive linen folds so as not to harm their soft ventricles, adding that it would be a shame after such a successful expedition to let them lose their flavour. The moment he returns to his compartment, he will put them in the little basket which he has brought specifically for that purpose. He is giving the handkerchief bulging with its strongly-smelling spoils an appraising, almost admiring glance when he notices that Annabelle is being particularly quiet and that her face is wan. Putting his left arm around her shoulders, he enquires how she feels. Rather nauseous, Annabelle replies.

"In that case a stiff drink should soon put you right," says the Marquis bluffly. "Come on, the Bar Buffet can't be very far." And with that comforting gesture he leads her towards the train's refreshments.

The travellers locate the Bar Buffet on the far side of three carriages and enter it. They discover that it is only half full, having probably just been drained of custom by the recent rush towards the dining car. Choosing an alcove table on which a small redshaded lamp is flickering, they settle down and stay silent for a few seconds before ordering.

Over by the counter two youthful and surprisingly slim waiters, their short white jackets and the deep black of their uniform trousers knife-edge creased, are standing talking to each other in hushed tones while a barman, perfectly kitted out in a purple dinner jacket, contemplates the semi-deserted scene with a coolness which could betray pathos or, equally, indifference. A long thin menu colourfully informs the travellers that, although catering mostly for quick-fill snacks such as *croque-monsieurs* and savoury *baguette* sandwiches, at which it cannot be bettered at any of the stations along the route, the Bar Buffet also offers a variety of *hors-d'oeuvres* and, as a *pièce de résistance*, possesses an organ of aperitifs whose proudly arrayed pipes of well over a hundred bottles the barman could in an instant make flute, keen or roar a gamut of pleasing tunes. But as the travellers feel that this is hardly the moment to put their palates through a journey almost as demanding as the extraordinary one which their other senses have just experienced, they put in a modest order to the waiter who has lounged over to them, a double cognac for Annabelle and an aromatic cooked wine for the Marquis, an order which the clearly unimpressed, and even perhaps disappointed, barman prepares in an instant, places on the counter, and dispatches to them via the same waiter.

"There, drink that down!" says the Marquis, watching Annabelle cup her drink in her slightly shivering hands and mist the glass before taking a first sip. "I can't have you losing energy like that, not when the course is only just beginning and the night's still young. I'm surprised at you tiring so easily."

"I'm not tired!" says Annabelle, stirring herself from the depths of her headache. "I'm shattered! For Heaven's sake! What was all that about?"

Faced by Annabelle still shaking from the trauma which has unsettled her nervous system, the Marquis takes off his evening scarf and hands it to her. She thanks him and, proving how easy it is to pick up others' habits, ties the scarf in much the same way in which the young girl did hers.

"I knew you'd be affected by that little encounter but I didn't envisage you'd feel it to this extent."

"A little encounter! Is that what you call it? What happened in there was, frankly, unbelievable."

"Taxing, yes. Unbelievable, no."

"Well, I've never experienced anything remotely like it. And I doubt if anyone else on this train has either. That weird woman, where did she spring from?"

"I'll come to that in a moment, Annabelle. All in good time. Meanwhile why don't you drink up? Let some colour back into your cheeks. I can't have you looking like a ghost all evening."

Annabelle takes another sip from her double brandy and feels it rasp her throat.

"Mmm," murmurs the Marquis, mulling over his drink, as if trying to identify the various herbs suffused through the wine. "I presume you'd like me to cast some light on what happened back there?" He pauses as if marshalling the well-drilled troops of his thoughts into an experimental formation. "In which case, if you don't mind, I'd like you to imagine that you're visiting an art gallery."

"What now!" Annabelle exclaimed, her headache hardly improved by what appear to be evasion tactics.

"Patience! It'll soon become evident. So there you are, standing in front of a painting you've never seen before. Now, what kind of reaction do you suppose you might have? Do you see yourself taking a knife out of your handbag and scraping the pigment off the canvas? Or slashing it to bits to discover how it was put together? Unless you happened to be in a particularly destructive frame of mind, that hardly seems likely. No, I prefer to think of you studying its composition, gauging the effect it is having on you and, if a narrative painting rather than some abstract daub, admiring the skill with which it told its story."

"Is this analogy leading somewhere?" Annabelle queries.

"I'm suggesting that you adopt the same attitude. Don't try to fathom on what strong or slender foundations the illusion you've just experienced is predicated. That won't do any good, not, that is, until you've grasped its nature, its possibilities, and its overall plan. The question you should ask yourself is this: is the iconoclast any the richer for the ruins that lie smouldering at his feet? Or wouldn't it have been wiser to have appropriated the work of art and to have subsumed it to his own possibly enlightened, possibly devious, plans rather than to have wantonly destroyed it? Before you can dissect a scene, you must be able to generate one for your own purposes. The best critic should always be able to turn his hand, however amateurly, to the art he is analysing. And at the moment, let's face it, Annabelle, even if you wanted to – and I take it you're here because that's exactly what you do want – you couldn't begin to lay bare the mechanics of what occurred in the compartment. You have neither the tools nor the know-how. So why don't you regard the story of the Leopard Woman as an introduction to the course? Then leave it at that – at least for the time being."

Annabelle fiddles with her half-filled glass.

"And yet, in spite of my advice, you're still itching to discover what that episode had to do with cooking, aren't you?" asks the Marquis, noticing her fingers fretfully sidling up and down the side of her glass. "Who the Leopard Woman was? And how come a compartment turned into a dressing room?"

"That certainly – and a whole lot more!"

"In which case, Annabelle, I'm sorry to have to disappoint you, because it's irrelevant. Totally irrelevant. It's all over. We can't go back to it. Please don't think though that I'm keeping answers from you. I'm not! I honestly don't know who the Leopard Woman is. More to the point, I don't care. What she had to achieve, she did. And, as far as I'm concerned, that's the end of it." The Marquis leans over the table, an avuncular expression on his face. "And don't look so glum. You've every reason to be happy. After all, didn't the story get you what you were after?"

"If you mean a headache and a confused mind, then, yes, it did!"

The Marquis points to the mushrooms which he has placed on the table, their sumptuous aroma suffusing through Annabelle's handkerchief.

"Oh, those!" she shrugs, casually dismissing what she did not strive for. "What about the compartment, the train, they just . . . disappeared!"

"Did they? Are you sure? We're still here, aren't we?"

Blocked from making any headway, Annabelle buries her head in her hands. Then suddenly she looks up. "For Heaven's sake!" A tremor of hesitation crosses her face only to be submerged by her querulousness. "That's not all! Something else happened. You remember when I touched the key I said that I had felt sad? Well, I got the same sensation when she was telling her story." She shivers and censors the details of the other infinitely more intimate sensations which she also experienced. "It was uncanny!"

"Those sensations, you'll be pleased to learn, Annabelle, were the first stirrings of sympathy. Excellent! The course is getting to you. And so it should! You don't want to stand on the sidelines all your life, do you?" He pauses, takes another sip from his drink, examines her strained features, then adds: "Let's leave it at that. We've done quite enough analysing for now." He glances at her glass. "Drink up. The brandy'll do you a power of good."

The Marquis offers Annabelle a cigarette which she surprises herself by accepting. The narrow flame spurts from a nozzle deeply imbedded in black lacquer and, in a swift and seamless dive, lights her cigarette.

The Bar Buffet has slowly been filling with people, diners perhaps put off by the dismal fare on offer in the restaurant car. And it is certainly wondrous, how, after inventing an unnamed chef in a place unlikely to be visited, we can now flush people through the Bar Buffet on the unproven pretext that they are escaping from the lowpoints of a menu about which we have said and, in truth, know nothing.

"In all the years I've travelled around the world," says the Marquis, settling down to discourse on his favourite subject, "preparing meals, collecting exotic ingredients, and tracking down unusual recipes, I've never ceased being amazed at the sheer extravagance of the things people will put into their mouths. I mean: can you picture yourself braving a rhinoceros' charge for the supposed aphrodisiac powers of its horn? Or murdering a foe to feast on his virility? And yet those, I assure you, are but two of the more comprehensible concoctions I've come across. I could relate other stories about the delights of coprophagy, for instance, which I suspect, Annabelle, would make your stomach turn. *Et je t'en passe et des meilleurs!"* the Marquis adds, slipping into the familiar form by way of a jocular remark. "However, if you seriously intend to master the arts of creative cooking, then you must have a fair idea what people eat, not just locally but right across the globe. Turning your back on outlandish tastes simply because they don't suit your palate is not only pointless but self-defeating. Limit your horizons to what's the *plat du jour* in your neighbourhood *routier* and, frankly, *ma chère*, you'll never get very far."

Two tables away there sits a solitary traveller. His neck, Annabelle notices, is little more than a tensed cord, his face has been excoriated of all fat, and his hands issue from the pendulous tunnels of a dirt-brown suit. Having piled his plate high, this wafer-thin apparition is now fast stoking up on all available energy. What he is shovelling into himself, she cannot quite make out from where she is sitting although, from an examination of the multicoloured mound of food on his plate, she suspects that he has helped himself to the *hors-d'oeuvres variés* which, for a fixed price, a customer is at liberty to debauch. Never once ceasing to feed his famished furnace, when pearls of sweat pour off his face he quickly wipes them away with the back of his hand.

"You wouldn't believe some of the recipes far-flung people have come up with! Mind you, the way in which societies prepare food can often provide a privileged insight into how they think. Although, even then, it isn't all that clear what that is. You try working out what crazy combination of magic, taste and chance went into a concoction like sago-nurtured grubs, one of the dishes that's all the rage in Papua New Guinea!" the Marquis exclaims, clearly relishing his self-elected role as encyclopaedist of the bizarre culinary fact.

Annabelle shrugs. How could she have the first idea? Her cigarette is disappearing into thin streaks of grey-blue smoke, her head keeps spinning, and she is finding it increasingly hard to concentrate on the modalities of the Marquis' baffling course. "I really couldn't tell you. Though, if you ask me, Jean-Loup," adds Annabelle, "as far as exotic notions go, we're not doing too badly. I'd say that getting a stripper in the middle of a train to unearth us mushrooms takes some beating."

"Quite!" answers the Marquis, glad to hear Annabelle parading her pique. "The fact is, Annabelle, that on this course you and I must be willing to go anywhere and do anything to procure the best ingredients. Anywhere and anything. That's crucial. All through history people have been willing to pay a king's ransom to lay their hands on extraordinary flavours. Yes, they've made massive efforts," adds the Marquis, "to feast on the ecstasy of untried essences. And to get what we're after, we may have to outdo their endeavours."

On the other side of the room, Annabelle observes, quite as touching as a mother bird parrying the rapacious volley of its young's beaks, a pair of lovers are feeding each other. Caught in a close-knit ritual, each in turn a submissive communicant offers the tremulous pit of a mouth to the morsel which the other has tenderly cut up.

"If you go globetrotting," the Marquis continues, after calling over the waiter and, without asking Annabelle's opinion, ordering them both a second glass, "you'll discover that each country possesses its own gastronomic delights. Take the Chinese. There's one dish Mandarins were said to adore. They'd apparently do anything for it. Thought it such a delicacy they even had a table specially built to eat it. Funnily enough I came across one – oh, years ago – in a private museum in Bordeaux. A simple enough design. Two hinged semi-circles made of the finest rosewood. In the centre a hole. Now, what they'd do was place a macaque monkey so that its head stuck out of the hole. The creature was alive but couldn't move at all as its paws were tied under the table." The Marquis takes an appreciative sip from his drink. "Anyway, from all accounts, the Mandarin would tie a silk napkin round his chin and would slice off the top of the monkey's head with a knife, leaving the soft mass of its brain exposed. Then he'd dip in his spoon as if into a soft-boiled egg, scoop out the living cells, and eat them raw."

"I don't believe it!" Annabelle's stomach reacts violently to this page torn out of a barbarian's cookery book.

"I grant you – an unusual delicacy. I've often wondered what essence those over-refined palates were after. Simian agility? Monkey wile? The lasting ardour of macaque love-making? Or maybe," says the Marquis, rounding off his anecdote with a chuckle, "its brains tasted exquisite and that's all there was to it!"

If only to seek out some distraction from her companion's increasingly rebarbative tales, Annabelle again casts her eye around the room. At the next table soberly-suited, serious-miened, two businessmen are entrenched in conversation. At considerable risk to the bottle of wine their expense accounts have chosen, the younger of the two, she notes, is illustrating some anecdote with gestures of a quite fatuous brio. Curiously she remembers the vintage very well – a pleasant enough *cru* graced by some highly desirable form of *pourriture noble* – from having once had it at dinner with a man fool enough to imagine that the way to her body was to lavish it on her when he could as easily have satisfied his lust by pickling her in a vulgar local *pinot*. What's his gestural bombast all about? Annabelle wonders, staring malevolently in the man's direction. Isn't it to cover the fact that he is a mean little liar? Doesn't one look at his face prove it? Periphrases, over-embroidered words, meretricious quips, don't they just keep dripping off his tongue? She can just see him rehearsing his social act in front of a mirror late at night . . . While Annabelle displaces her spleen on a subject who might, yet who equally well might not, deserve it, the Marquis continues to limn in the background to his description of creative cooking.

"Being squeamish is a luxury no chef can afford. Have you ever heard the lobster sing as it hits boiling water? Seen the fish's *danse macabre* under the steel gutting it live? Gazed at the bloody brush strokes the ox's slit throat applies round the slaughter house? You haven't? Then, *ma chère*, you haven't begun to explore the ins and outs of cooking. You have to know these things, relish them even as part and parcel of a noble craft. For how can you create a meat dish if you won't cut up a carcass?" The Marquis examines his apprentice's reactions which have pulsed and waned at each revelation, and presses on: "Don't tell me you've never eaten anything raw, still alive?"

"Damn right I haven't! What do you take me for?"

"A budding gourmet, Annabelle. Are you sure?"

"Of course I'm sure!"

The dress . . . yes, the dress. Sidling into the side alley of a reverie, Annabelle recalls her dress with particular intensity. It is delightful. Pale green moiré, cut low on the shoulders, spreading out in a blazon of silk. Her design, her choice of cloth, naturally. She is however taking rather less pleasure in her closest friend getting married before her. Although, to be fair, this mean and envious thought is fast becoming blurred in the copious amounts of champagne which she has already consumed under the billowing baldaquin in whose shade a spattering of *tout-Paris* spaniels has gathered to drink her friend's health. On her fifth glass, well aware that she has not yet eaten anything and that if she continues to quaff on an empty stomach she is likely to end up with decidedly the wrong partner, she accepts the first passing tray which a black-uniformed maid offers her. Without giving the matter a moment's thought, she downs three of the little beshelled creatures, enjoying their canny saline taste which, having once dared to make a practical comparison, remind her of the piquancy of her own intimate secretions. After they have wriggled under the lance of the lemon with which she squirts them, she further subjects them to the prodding of her tongue.

God! Raw and alive! So she has! Years back! Would have sworn! Not that the Marquis, eyeing her intently, can possibly be aware of it. Best suppress the whole incident. Pretend it never happened. Deny it if needs be. Ridiculous! Why, she hates oysters, can't bear their clammy texture, their slithery feel, their abominable deliquescence, they remind you of, you know . . . As these rapidly rehearsed rationalizations course through her, Annabelle does her best to keep her composure calm, unashamed, unruffled. Unfortunately a plentiful blush irradiates across her cheeks and only the glass she quickly puts to her mouth helps to conceal her embarrassment.

"Strange," says the Marquis in an infuriatingly knowing fashion. "I somehow thought you had, Annabelle, and more than once."

Next, as if it were not enough to be thought a liar, another startling series of images screen past Annabelle's mind's eye. In the first of what would appear to be a set of eighteenth-century lithographs, a young lady in a state of almost complete undress, apart from the garters which hold up her fine silk stockings, is being held at arm's length above the half-naked body of her much older lover. The boudoir background reminds Annabelle of Boucher and of the scenes he so admirably portrays – ladies in the process of making-up, or adulterously waiting for the arrival of a lover, or bent over *billets-doux* their indiscreet maids have already perused.

In the second print, the tender young lady is being held firmly by the head and is brought slowly to the point of contact with the roué who has found a way, if not to her heart, then at least to her still puppy-fat enfleshed body. At first she exhibits a wave of resistance. No, please! She really doesn't want to. By the third print, overwhelmed by the desire to please her lover, she allows the shaft into her mouth. The taste, Annabelle remembers, is faintly saline; and the fullness of his engorged masculinity almost makes her choke. In the fourth Annabelle notices that her lover has forced her to take more than she had bargained for. Although she puts up an initial struggle, she soon surrenders to the act which, with a violence and a suddenness for which she was not at all prepared, delivers a warm charge. However hard she tries to escape, his hands hold her fast, and there is no choice but to let the stuff slide down her throat. Then, and only then, while his hands follow the rhythmical movements of her swallowing, does he let her withdraw, a satisfied smile on his face, while she, pleased yet anguished by the speed of her initiation, looks at him enquiringly. What will he inflict on her next? But the tale of this eighteenth-century rake, with his wide-sleeved shirt, and his fine white wig, and the slightly effeminate tone of a skin never exposed to the sun, cannot be pursued. For Annabelle, somewhat sickened to have come across such a pointed and animated coda, observes that the Marquis, who has been staring at her as if he could read her mind, is lighting a cigarette and is clearly about to embark on another story.

"Fairy tales, Annabelle. Do you enjoy them?"

She is about to answer that she feels that she has become trapped in one when she stifles her quip and says: "I suppose so. I used to read a lot of them when I was young."

71

"There's one I'm particularly fond of. I wonder if you know it. It concerns a handsome Prince."

"Don't they all?" says Annabelle, hiding behind a veil of nonchalance the still throbbing irritation of the last images.

"Quite a few, true. In this one anyway a handsome Prince, journeying on the deck of the Royal Barge, and admiring the beautiful pearl which his mother had given him that very afternoon to present to the lady who would one day share his dreams, with almost unbelievable clumsiness lets it fall into the sea. Disconsolate, he immediately orders the Captain to cut the pleasure trip short and to turn back home. Now, it so happens that when the Barge has docked in the harbour, the moody Prince comes across a group of fishermen laying out their haul on the quay. One of them is loading his catch into a big wicker basket beside which his daughter is standing. And, yes, you've guessed it, she is a magnificent girl. The moment the Prince sees her, he forgets all about the pearl and, spurred by the arrogance of his noble birth, strides up to her, aims a few well-chosen words at her, and there and then arranges a secret assignation. Amazingly, after the maiden has met him in the back room of a local inn and surrendered her virtue to him, far from discarding her as his *droit de seigneur* would normally suggest he would, the young Prince discovers that he has fallen in love with her. But as the daughter of a fisherman is hardly a suitable match for a Prince, when his parents' spies inform them of the illicit affair they send a purse of gold coins to the fisherman, tell him to control his besotted daughter, and, brooking no rebellion, pack the Prince off to a foreign land to get some sense into his silly young head."

Although she has always had a shameless passion for pearls, Annabelle, fatigued by the surfeit of adventures which have tumbled on to her in such a short space of time, is only loosely following the drift of the Marquis' story when her attention is further distracted by two people at a nearby table. A dark-haired, weasel-faced man wearing a blue blazer, grey flannels, a yellow shirt and a tartan tie, is busy seducing a young, prettily got up in tulle, if rather dim-looking blonde. And while he narrates the story of his life to her, no doubt editing it to keep in frame the master shots of his flair and acumen, she ceaselessly directs the glaucous gullibility of her fish-eyes at him. He wheedles; his hands caress her arm; his eyes feint and toil for hers; his mouth puckers into an exhaustive glossary of romance-filled gestures. And just as a now overworked phrase must have once been thought daringly original to survive the sedimentation of time and to end up fossilized in the common weal, so it would seem that to her blanket admiration his every hackneyed move is freshly forged, wonderfully inspired, and worthy of belief. As if on cue, she too parades her own limited repertoire of responses: her pupils dilate, her lips tremble, and her glance aims by turn coyly at the table then rather more flirtatiously at him. Although at too great a distance to overhear the tenor of his rodomontade, Annabelle cannot help but be faintly nauseated by his quarry's all-accepting credulity.

"Well," says the Marquis, pursuing his folk story to its conclusion, and seemingly impervious to Annabelle's slowly closing eyes and wandering concentration, "one afternoon, while the Prince is still far away, the fisherman's daughter is sitting by the quay gutting fish when, wonder of wonders, what does she come across in one of the bellies she has just slit but the pearl."

Annabelle, rousing herself before the inevitability of the Marquis' story line, retorts: "Who'd have believed it?"

"As you say, who indeed. Anyway, the big day on which the Prince is to return to his native land arrives. Naturally, a feastday is officially proclaimed, a procession is laid on to greet him, and everybody turns out to see the King, Queen and handsome Prince ride past in their golden carriage. That morning the fisherman's daughter – the flame of her forbidden love still burning in her heart – puts on her best clothes and sets the pearl which the sea had cast before her on her breast. Now, it so happens that at the precise moment that the Royal Carriage clatters past her, the sun glints off the pearl and strikes the Prince in the eye. Distracted, he looks into the amorphous mass come to greet him and catches sight of the fisherman's daughter. Rushing out of the carriage, he calls the procession to a halt and, before the eyes of his consternated parents, the amazed retinue of courtiers, and the baffled populace, he falls on his bended knee and announces to the world that here she is, his true love, and that nothing can now stop him marrying her."

"Very touching!" says Annabelle softly, her eyes half closed.

"Exactly. A tiny object bridges two apparently alien worlds and lets the spell of love run its course."

"I presume there's a point to this story?" asks Annabelle wearily, hoping that if she delivers her cues on time, the conversation will end and she can retire to the warm oblivion of her bunk.

"*Naturellement!*" the Marquis answers. "Though what, it's up to you to work out. While it's the cook's task to prepare the meat, it's the customer's to digest it." Choosing to pay some attention to Annabelle's inability to keep her eyes open, he leans over and gently touches her right hand. Her expression is so distant that she seems out of touch. Nor does she make the slightest effort to avoid his contact. "You haven't quite recovered yet, have you?" the Marquis adds. "Then the best thing for you is to lie down for a while in your compartment and get some rest."

Annabelle nods. The Marquis takes a banknote out of his wallet and places it on the table. He rises, helps her out of her chair, and with a nod to the distant waiters and their dispassionate boss, leads her out of the Bar Buffet.

The trek back to the traveller's compartment is long and arduous but is thankfully unmarked by any exorbitant phenomena. Standing before Annabelle's compartment, the Marquis says to his companion: "After a siesta, you'll find you'll be able to concentrate properly. Don't worry if everything seems jumbled up at the moment: that's perfectly normal. The imagination is a very powerful tonic. Until you get used to it, it'll make you feel sick. Meanwhile trust me: sooner or later everything'll fall into place. And get your strength back. It's crucial that you're fit and alert for the next episode." He examines his watch. "I'll come and get you in an hour."

"You mean there's more to come?"

"A great deal, *chère* Annabelle. We've only just begun," the Marquis adds, parading before her the mushroom-filled handkerchief. "Don't forget we've still three ingredients to locate. I accept that the first episode was hard on your nerves. But the next, I assure you, will be much easier."

The Marquis waits for Annabelle to unlock her compartment then, as she quietly lies down on her bunk, he places a blanket over her and pulls her blinds down, caring gestures which she accepts without a fuss. Wishing her a good rest, he closes the door behind him, walks down the corridor, and goes into his own compartment.

It takes Annabelle but a second to rise, to slip the safety catch on, and then to retire to her bunk, safe in the knowledge that her haven is now secure.

CHAPTER FIVE

With his feet up and his long lanky body cutting diagonally across his minuscule cubicle, Jules Pinard slowly recovers from announcing the first sitting of dinner, a duty he has always maintained should be undertaken by the catering staff for why should he carry out something for which he has not the slightest sympathy? Nor is that the sole source of his irritation for above his head there hovers a wooden panel in which all first-class compartment numbers are framed; a panel on which, whenever a passenger calls for service, a small flag infuriatingly bobs down. These calls Jules considers a dastardly interruption of the time which he should devote to the discussion of his quandary. And so, safely bastioned behind the heights of this unshakeable policy, he tends to ignore them.

At this precise moment he is busy scrutinizing an unusual railway map of France which a quaternity of pins secures to the cubicle's wooden panelling. Unusual not for its colourful spider grid of the primary and secondary rail routes which crisscross the Gallic hexagon but rather more for the poppy field of snapshots which has sprouted next to many of the main towns through which the Mistral runs. All depicting women.

We have just mentioned how Jules hates the interruptions which take away his concentration from discussing his quandary. Although how a man can discuss a topic when he is by himself is far from evident. Could it be that the burden of years – during which he has been shunted back and forth along the tracks like some obedient shuttlecock – has exerted so great a pressure on his mind that it has now cracked in two, one half arguing for, the other against whatever issue currently exercises what is left of his identity? A mental scission which, while permitting him to proceed along the first two levels of the dialectic, thesis and antithesis battling out their positions in his head, prevents him ever reaching the ecstasy of a synthesis? Or could it be that the energy born of this *Spaltung* has given birth to some familiar which, when Jules is not at his other functions, he can berate for the downturn his life has taken?

Although it might have raised the narrative's tension by a few degrees to ponder the nature of Jules' psychology, this line of enquiry is abruptly interrupted by the at first shy then increasingly confident appearance of a small and furry face from the depths of the Steward's blue standard issue gaberdine jacket. Moreover the term familiar appears to be exact. For while the Steward studies the women perched on his map in various monochrome, amateurishly snapped, much faded, and occasionally coloured representations, and nods his head in despair, the furry face gazes around the cubicle and exposes a further hairy section of its small and sleek body. Then, steering across the Steward's trousers, it moves to a corner of the table, where, without further ado, it curls up with catlike efficiency in a small wicker basket. The creature's name? Anatole. Its status in the scene about to start its intrigue? Jules' confidant. And now that the ferret has deigned to peep out of its hiding place, Jules, addressing him in tones condescending if despairing, relates to him, presumably for the nth time, the greatest problem to affect his life.

"You'd think, Anatole, when they got to see me, uncommon as that is, that they'd look after me properly and cater for my needs. In which case, *mon vieux*, you'd be right and wrong! Because in some ways I get so much I can't cope, while in others so little I'm in a dreadful state about it. Take Fifi for instance."

No sooner has Jules pronounced this lady's name than he points to a colour photograph which is pinned with a lepidopterist's precision on Bordeaux's supine body. Fifi, as the ring to her name, the blue bow in her hair, and the heavy application of make-up suggest, possesses many of the caricatural attributes of the coquette. However, as the photograph also makes quite clear, the striped and flounced apron which she has donned over her gaily-printed summer skirt proves that she, unlike decorous but impractical *grandes horizontales*, delights in the disciplines of the stove. And, indeed, how she fusses over Jules seated at her kitchen table, while he, seemingly untouched by her solicitude, does nothing to dispel the grumpy expression that has grown on his gaunt face.

"*Mon p'tit* Jules," says Fifi in the reanimation to which the Steward subjects this small sliver of an event which took place at some undisclosed time, and whose photographic record is now gathering dust and bad cess on his cubicle's wooden panelling. "What do you get up to on that train? Why, you're all skin and bones!" she apparently adds, feeling the thinness of his arms. "You should be ashamed, not looking after yourself properly. Don't worry though: your Fifi'll soon fatten you up. Come on: napkin round your neck! There's a good boy! Do it up tight or sauce'll spill all over your uniform. And the SNCF wouldn't like a sloppy Steward, would they?"

Whether Fifi's true character is even a close approximation of the manner in which Jules has portrayed her in that somewhat threadbare cameo is not something we mean to investigate as there are limits to the research we are willing to do into the backgrounds of secondary characters. There have already been more than a few temptations during the unfurling of this story to build up, to put flesh on, indeed to follow through a wide variety of simple, commonly-met types. Yet a line has to be drawn somewhere for otherwise, in order to keep tabs on the relationships which secondary figures engender with each other – they being as promiscuous and as keen on their own development as the flora in the gut of any animal – we would have to erect the kind of genealogical map which adorns the frontispieces of thousand-page historical romances in which the resolutions of moral dilemmas are daringly set against the *dégringolade* of dynasties and the life and death of nations. And as the scope of this tale is merely to depict, like any other *Lehrlingsroman*, the development of an initiatory relationship – its tentative beginnings, its inevitable conflicts, its unexpected end – to make use of a broader canvas, or, to be more precise, the whole stretch of a tempera-prepared wall, would only obstruct the modest dimensions of this enterprise. In the name of brevity therefore we will not explore Jules' *affaires* with the same diligence which we will, wherever possible, apply to more seminal details. Instead we will take at face value the veracity of the stories which the Steward chooses to inflict on his ferret in the belief that one, to do so limits the cautionary statements we might otherwise periodically have had to issue about their nature; and that two, as their path hardly ever crosses the main plot, eruptions of gross improbabilities can be contained, quarterized and perhaps even nullified. What cannot be denied, however, is that next to Bordeaux, the land of the *entrecôte bordelaise*, of *crépinettes*, of *confit d'oie*, and of other memorable delicacies, a colour photograph of a young lady is pinned. And that if Jules maintains to his ferret that her name is Fifi, and that he has developed a close rapport with her, little can be adduced to gainsay him.

Before interrupting this scene, we were listening to Jules telling Anatole how he sat at Fifi's table while she promised to fatten him up. Unfortunately for the Steward, Fifi's total immersion in her gastronomic rigmarole suggests to him that his fondest hopes have once again no chance of being met with success.

"Guess what I've made for you tonight?" chants Fifi, wiping her hands on her apron. "Yes, Jules, your favourite! *Foie gras de canard à la bordelaise.*"

And what a delicious spectacle Fifi's speciality offers to the eyes as she brings it out of the oven – the unripened, unpeeled grapes delicately macerated in Armagnac surrounding the over-ripe duck's liver – and proudly shows it to Jules before placing it on the table! Yet strangely, Jules shows not the slightest sensitivity to the exquisite savours about to erupt on his palate.

"Then, Anatole," adds Jules, shifting his gaze from what he clearly regards as a culinary cul-de-sac to another photograph set above Lyons, "there's Laurette."

A woman of commodious proportions, Laurette the *lyonnaise* has deflected much of the energy she might otherwise have lavished on the cosmetic appearance of her pleasing person – now sadly engulfed in folds of fat – towards the arts of her table. But while the state of her dress may leave much to be desired – the stigmata of previous creative stove sessions still staining her apron – no criticism of any kind, only the highest praise, can be levelled at the altar on which she daily offers up her fastidious fare. For how superbly starched is its linen! How appropriate for her monogram to be inscribed on its *limoges*! As for the cutlery reflecting the elaborately barley-sticked candles placed at the heads of the table, how memorably it disports its well-polished and antique patina! And so finely honed is her sense of occasion that when she takes the *poularde en demi-deuil* out of the oven, she even heralds its arrival with highlights from a recorded requiem.

As we have already agreed not to subject Jules' story to too close a scrutiny, we will leave unanswered how a humble functionary from France's railway system ever came to meet a woman so dedicated to the culinary arts that she went to the lengths of commissioning her own crockery. We will instead relay his interpretation of events without a hint of criticism and portray him just as he chooses to tell his ferret he is, ensconced, that is, with a large napkin round his neck at Laurette's magnificently laid dining table. And yet, as if it were not difficult enough to take that much on trust, is it conceivable that, faced by this supremely imaginative event from the kitchens of the Lyonnais, Jules can remain untouched, unthrilled? Are we to believe that he can snub with his boorish melancholia that exquisite mushroom, the reclusive truffle deeply nurtured beneath the black soil of the Périgord which Laurette has artfully concealed under the chicken's skin in order to achieve that sublime gastronomic conceit, the fowl displaying, as it were, widow's weeds for its own passing? Where lies the root cause of a morbidity recurrently evoked by the good things of the table?

"There, Jules!" says Laurette sweetly, about to serve the dour Steward with a generous helping. "Get a whiff of that! Go on, tuck in! Don't look so sad! After all, the little *poularde* did die for you."

"Yes," Jules says to Anatole, cutting back from this montage of cameos, each syncopated in disappointment, "they've all got their own speciality. And I have to eat everything they put before me if I'm to keep them happy. But do you suppose they ever give me what I want, Anatole? No, never!"

Jules' digit now strays towards Strasbourg where Berthe's sepia-tinted photograph hangs like a trophy. If her likeness is to be believed, Berthe, her broad face dispensing a full smile, is a massive lady who in this hastily focused snapshot has been captured standing next to a stove which belches forth steam. "D'you remember, Anatole, the last time we were in Strasbourg we stopped overnight? Something had gone wrong with the engine and it had to be overhauled in the workshops. Well, after I left you here in your basket, I said to myself: I know what I'll do. I'll go and see how Berthe's getting on."

Anatole does not, however, react to his name. His head he has tucked into his coat, his eyes are glazed, and his fur lacks its usual proprietary shine. What is wrong? Is he off colour? Not that his master displays any interest, let alone sympathy, for the ferret's suffering, being more interested in his perverse views of France's gastronomy. "When I get to her little stork's nest, what do I find there, eh, steaming as usual? That's right, Anatole, you guessed it!" Jules adds, projecting onto the ferret's lack of movement an empathy quite at odds with the creature's actual mood.

Berthe's kitchen has been done up in the pompous rustic style much favoured by Teutonic Alsatians, who, borrowing from the Wilhelmine idiom, have transported it to the divided province and have thus cleverly disguised their dislike of French republicanism under the safe form of ornate imperial decorations. Heavy oak panelling further darkens the room, while the stove itself, a finely wrought iron monument on which a pageant of duck shoots, boar hunts, bird traps and other netting devices have been hand-painted on blue Delft tiles, is the centrally-set furnace whose ritual fire Berthe always keeps at a great pitch of activity. And she is just about to ladle a generous helping of the finely-hashed cumin-vinegar-salt-and-elderberry-soaked cabbage surmounted by a few fat sausages onto Jules' plate when he gives her a look of studied sweetness.

"My little canary," says Jules, trying his best to look conciliatory. "I've a confession to make. Promise you won't mind? You see, *mon choux*, I'm not very hungry tonight, so I don't think I can do your *choucroute* justice."

When everything is ready, at the very moment when steam is conveying the nonpareil aroma of pork and vegetables around the room, just when this the zenith of Alsatian magic is about to be degusted, what happens but Jules confesses his loss of appetite! The appalling timing of it all! Visibly taken aback, hurt indeed to the depths of her pride, Berthe puts the dish back into the oven, wipes away the honest sweat from her face, and stares with disbelief at the wisp of a man who has dared reject her.

Quite unaware of the tremors which his behaviour has generated in the well-enveloped lady's form, Jules walks over to a chesterfield set in a corner of Berthe's vast laboratory and cajolingly beckons her to join him there.

"Don't look at me like that, my little *millefeuille*! Appetites are funny things, you know, they come and go. But my feelings for you stay the same. Eh! Don't take it so! Here, I'll cheer you up."

But Berthe has not moved from her position by the stove, her true state of mind betrayed by her fiddling with her pony tail. Then, without so much as a word, she turns round and leaves the room. Jules, who has been watching her with some concern, decides that this is a good sign. Beaming with contentment, he kicks off his shoes, pours himself a glass of Sylvaner, settles back into the sofa's resilient and crackling hide, and undoes his tie. Matters for once are going right. The little lady has gone to freshen up, to add maybe a discreet drop of cologne to her perspiring brow. At least she understands that Jules is a man possessed of more than one appetite!

Relaxing in expectation of the pleasures to come, Jules closes his eyes. At last! In the secret theatre of the flesh into which his failed hopes have frequently forced him to take refuge, there is a catalogue of positions, a taxonomy of states, and a pharma-copeia of applications via which the female form can be subjected to a thousand and one preparations. A space where balms and lubricants, stimulants and opiates, yes, even gags and whips are ever at the ready to help the baffled Steward rise to the Olympus of his aim and spill his frenetic seed in solitary sessions. Yet surely there is now no need to raise the curtain over the proscenium of that fantastic stage nor to expend further energy on onanistic reveries, for is the reality after which he so hankers not about to be delivered in his lap?

His eyes deliciously closed, Jules has reclined into the sofa's lush expanse when, with quite vicious suddenness, a hand grabs him round the throat. No question of escape: his neck is held far too tightly for that. Indeed, try as he might, Jules cannot fight Berthe off for her face is twisted in a dreadful grimace, part justice, part fury, and not only does she have a full plate of sauerkraut in her hand but also one aim in mind – to force its heaped contents down his throat. Borrowing from peasant practice in which the struggling goose is fed grain till its liver is bloated and its pea-sized brain demented, Berthe holds Jules' nose tight while her foot, sagaciously shoved into his groin, is ready to devastate him if resistance be met. With Jules thoroughly immobilized beneath her weight, she proceeds to ram the sauerkraut into his mouth with the efficacy of a veteran gun loader.

"Ach! So we have lost our appetite! We shall see about that! Open wide. Good! One for Berthe," she says, forcing down a full dollop of cabbage. "One for Jules." A sausage makes its enforced and somewhat suggestive entry into his mouth. "Another one for Berthe." The charge is rammed down the forcibly held breach. "Keep it open I said!" And as the meal starts to journey down the extended tract of Jules' gustatory snake, the Bürgerin adds with a chuckle: "You like it, eh? It's good, *mein Liebchen?*"

Once Berthe has made her crude if effective point, she allows the winded yet belching Jules to rise from the sofa. With the maddened gestures of a cornered ox, he angrily pushes aside the half-filled dish which, with a crack and a dispersal of its various fragments, spills all over the floor. As if he had nothing left to lose, he grabs his hostess by the shoulders and tries to manoeuvre her onto the sofa. It is a short-lasting embrace. Endowed with redoubtable muscles, Berthe's fists batter the off-duty Steward with such force that to parry her blows the thoroughly routed Jules has no choice but to cover his head.

"They're all the same, Anatole! Food, food, food! All they give me is food! Love, never! Can't they see that a man who's always on the tracks needs affection? But no, Anatole, they deny me that simple pleasure. The minute the meal's over – I can't even have a *digestif* in peace – I get given the most horrible looks and get pushed out of the door."

Which is exactly what Fanny, the red-headed *marseillaise*, does once Jules has put away the final simmering richness of her *bouillabaisse* and begun his usual pathetic advances. "That's it! *Allez ouste!* You men," she mouths the repelling formula with a shameless lack of imagination, "are all the same!"

A tale of frustration whose unending saga Jules could trace across the map. For it would appear that, even after staring defeat so many times in the face, the Steward has still not grasped the rudiments of the mechanics of exchange. Never a word of thanks for a *sauce bien mijotée*, for a *petit plat digne d'un ange*, for a *dessert exquis*, never the kind of sweet word with which the world is made to run more smoothly. Such polities seem to have quite passed him by. Which no doubt explains why, while the women in his life exercise their basic maternal sentiments by feeding his meagre frame, they will take no steps to satisfy his cruder cravings. A cautionary tale whose moral Jules, with his fondness for casting himself in the role of the innocent victim, seems quite incapable of digesting.

"Then boom! They tell me not to come back till I've developed a more healthy appetite. Heartless creatures, that's what they are! Utterly heartless!" Jules, addressing his companion who has not stirred once throughout this narrative, asks him: "So, tell me, Anatole: what am I supposed to do?"

Fortunately, before the ferret can make any reply and reveal whether he is endowed with the powers of speech and animal wisdom, or whether he is like the rest of his genus, rapaciously acquiring energy to maintain his place in the race, this catalogue of despair is interrupted by the ringing of the service bell and by a little flag popping down on the panel.

"Now what! Some stupid passenger wants his back scratched . . . *Merde!* That's what I say!" Jules opens the door to his cubicle and shouts down the corridor angrily. "Go to hell!" He refastens it and puts his hands to his stomach. "What's more, *mon vieux*, I don't feel that well. My stomach's rumbling. My gut's inflamed. Must have been the meal last night. Trekked all the way to Montmartre to taste a *fricassé* of hare in a heavy cream and wine sauce. Did me no good. Not a drop of compassion from that beanpole Odile! Out on my ear by ten o'clock. What a life, eh?"

Why does the ferret still not stir? Could it be because, unlike those fables in which the hero and his enchanted creature develop an empathic relationship which is then held up as a model from which humans could learn much, the ferret has never had the first inkling what his master is going on about? Whatever the reason, annoyed by Anatole's lack of response, Jules, mumbling to himself, opens a small cupboard, finds an open tin, and tries to entice his little companion with a chicken bone. He offers it to the little animal who, however, will have no truck with it.

"Anatole! What's the matter?" asks Jules. If only to escape from the dismal prognosis of his various *affaires*, Jules puts his jacket back on and heads out of his cubicle to answer the passenger's call. "Don't be difficult. I'll have to go now but there's a good boy: you eat up your chow before I get back, all right?"

The door shuts and the Steward's faint footfalls echo down the corridor. In spite of his master's exhortations, Anatole makes not the slightest attempt to tackle the food which has been left out for him. Curled in his little wicker basket, he remains what he has been throughout the ins and outs of Jules' belief-stretching narrative, a forlorn and pitiful sight.

CHAPTER SIX

The main light in Annabelle's compartment is off. Only the night light's red eye suffuses her half-naked body prone on the bunk. The narcotic of the train's wheels has had the required effect, as has indeed an overdose of events impossible to place within the comforting categories of logic and sense. Such a totally undramatic situation – the all too regular swaying of the express on its metallic hips, the occasional turbulence felt as it is buffeted by some ill wind, the emphysemic wheezing of its air-conditioning – might have lasted all through the night and denied us further adventures, leaving the narrative short on the leaps and starts it requires to keep the reader from falling into a sleep as deep as our young and confused heroine's, had it not been for a sudden series of woodpecker raps on the door.

The noise penetrates Annabelle through and through. Stirring, she identifies the source of the sound and calls out that she is coming. She rises from the bunk, turns on the main light, and puts her dress back on. Damn! Not even enough time to re-anoint her face although it needs blusher, and a hint of lipstick would certainly pep up morale. But as the raps renew, once she has looked at herself in her small mother-of-pearl hand mirror, and administered a vigorous brush to her hair, she releases the safety catch.

The Marquis, conscious that it was Annabelle's sense of insecurity which made her lock her door after he had tucked her in, also notes the ruffled surface of her bunk. "So you got some sleep. Good. Do you feel better now?"

"Much, thank you," she answers, trying to exercise the languor out of her still lazy limbs.

The Marquis takes a seat by the window and seems about to make some comment on the dark-shrouded landscape when he instead bangs his fist on the table and mutters irritably: "How silly of me! I've quite forgotten it." He gazes at his companion and, with a smile as broad as it is manipulative, asks her: "I wonder if you'd do me a favour? You remember the little leather suitcase, the one in which I keep those objects I showed you?"

She does.

"You'll find it on the table in my compartment. In it you'll see a small glass phial. About this size," he shows her its dimensions with the play between his finger and thumb. "Would you bring it back? That would be very kind. Here's the key to the compartment."

She takes it without any enthusiasm.

"I . . . yes, I suppose so. But . . ." How should she explain that she objects to leaving him alone in her compartment? To begin with, her personal belongings are in her overnight bag and a cursory examination of her vanity case would generate a résumé, however flawed and incomplete, of her intimate life. In a train which appears to set no store by barriers, where nothing is off limits, and which seems all too well equipped to break down her defences, the Marquis may now have an opportunity to invade her last enclave. Why should she hand it to him? At a loss to find valid grounds on which to deny him this request – without drawing attention to matters which, however private, she admits, are hardly secret – she reluctantly acquiesces.

"Don't concern yourself about me," says the Marquis disingenuously, fully aware of her apprehension. "I'll be all right. In fact I've a few things I should get on with." He points to the notepad which he has brought with him.

An expression of displeasure stretched tightly across her face, Annabelle leaves her compartment.

The Marquis listens to the sounds of her footsteps moving down the corridor, opens the pad, leans on the table, and starts to draw in it with a felt-tip pen. A few trenchant strokes and the profile sketch of a young man is done. The style is unmistakeable. Not the full-face, voluminous and representational mode produced by perspective. Rather the deeply symbolic figuration, the hieratic style proper to Ancient Egypt. With care the Marquis recaptures the young man's sultry eyes, his sandy skin, and those unforgettably sharp features. A drawing which not only makes far higher demands on a viewer's imagination than would any Renaissance illusionist's but which also remains vague in the extreme, at best a generalized experience which cannot be pinned down to specifics. The Marquis next doodles two motifs next to the profile: one of an obelisk, the other of a geometrical compass.

Once he has executed his sketches to his satisfaction, the Marquis reaches for his wallet, locates within its lizard-skinned folds a small silver needle and, again exercising the smooth mechanism of his black lacquer lighter, heats its tip. That done, he spreads the sketches before him, and contemplating the landscape's passing silhouettes, awaits the return of his apprentice.

She is back in a few minutes.

"No trouble?"

Annabelle shows him the phial and, discreetly eyeing her baggage to check whether he has disturbed it, says somewhat acidly: "None. Here it is."

She hands him the phial.

It is with a devastating swiftness surely honed by practice that the Marquis grabs Annabelle's right hand, holds it tight and, before she has had time to react, jabs the sterilized needle into her little finger.

"Ow!" A monosyllable which cannot conjure Annabelle's shock at the Marquis' unwarranted assault, but whose curtness in the absence of more cogent sounds will just have to do.

And what fine fruit the Marquis' operation has borne forth, rich, ruby red droplets which he swiftly collects in the little glass phial his apprentice so conveniently fetched for the task.

Annabelle tries to wrest her hand away from him. But the Marquis, holding her fast, his voice unmarked by the slightest doubt in the validity of his actions, says: "Do be still, Annabelle, or blood will spill on the table." Not until the phial has become filled does he at last set her free.

"Have you gone mad?" Annabelle interjects, retreating in horror and falling on the bunk. Her wounded finger in her mouth, she stares at the Marquis, dismayed at her inability to produce an adequate response to his attack. But as quicksilver responses depend on untrammelled instinct or on repeated training, as her inbuilt mechanism has been dulled by surprise, and as she has never – thank God! – encountered any situation remotely like this one, she is at a loss. Should she slap him? Yet the time for that is already over. Scream? What would that achieve except attract interfering attention? Storm out? Although doubtless the most dramatic action she could take, as she is in her own compartment the response would be half-cocked. Choked by outrage, she realizes how cunningly she has been outflanked, and on her own ground as well.

The Marquis examines the bright liquid by the flood of the wall lights then, brushing her anger aside, comments with equanimity: "Isn't *'Il faut souffrir pour être belle'* a commonplace of your profession, Annabelle? I can imagine you saying it to your long-suffering models all the time, although I wouldn't be at all surprised if you had never before experienced it quite so graphically! The fact is, *ma chère*, that the pursuit of the rare always entails a certain amount of suffering. And the more precious the goal, the more one has to strive for it. A situation which is equally true of creative cooking for which, as I've already told you, you must be willing to make all kinds of sacrifices." He generates a sly smile. "Anyway, what's a little blood to a healthy young lady like you? A few drops for a good cause can't possibly harm you."

Annabelle takes her finger out of her mouth. An insubordinate muscle in her upper lip twitches. Her voice shrill, she cries out: "You call this . . . this masquerade a good cause!" She nurses her finger. "What the hell do you take me for? Some little floozy you picked up and can do whatever you want with? I could have you arrested for assault!" She pauses, surprised by the power of her own temper. Then realizing that a pinprick to her finger, however humiliating, hardly constitutes an overwhelming case for a charge of bodily harm, she changes her tactics. "I really don't understand you! I came along on this so-called course in good faith. Yet all you've done is attack and mystify me! When will you tell me what's going on?"

As coolly as would an internist the cries of a chronically disturbed patient, the Marquis answers her. "Please don't work yourself up, Annabelle. That you haven't yet found your feet is quite normal. But I assure you that if you watch everything that happens and take matters on trust, you'll begin to make sense of it soon enough." He pauses and takes out a cigarette from his silver case, as if to fill the interval with a predictable action. Then, after a long and languid puff, he continues. "By the way, I wouldn't want you to think that I can do whatever I please. I can't. There's nothing arbitrary about my various preparations. I too have to abide by strict rules. As for this blood," he adds, pointing to the phial, "I'm sorry for the minor inconvenience but, believe me, I had no choice. I really had to take it. You'll see why in a moment."

"Oh, I will, will I?" Annabelle retorts pugnaciously. "Isn't that reassuring? And what particular treat do you next have in store for me, I wonder? Rape?"

His face suddenly set in an expression of grim determination, the Marquis rises and opens the door. Before Annabelle has any idea what is happening, he has seized her by the hand and is dragging her down the corridor. "If that sums up your attitude," he says, pacing furiously, "it's high time you took a good look at the alternatives!"

Down the corridor, past a junction, then down another corridor, his hand holding hers so firmly that she stumbles along behind him. A humiliating experience yet enacted so rapidly that she has no opportunity to resist before they reach, three carriages along, the Marquis' destination.

In front of them the closed half-glass door of a second-class compartment, full of the most ordinary, indeed as Annabelle, still flustered, cannot fail to see, depressingly ordinary travellers. A couple of middle-aged men in suits worn, like tired minds, at the point of least resistance; a strait-laced young woman, her mouth misshapen by the real or imaginary events that have outraged her; a mother and suckling child composed so like a *Maesta* that the very essence of reverence seems to have attached itself to them. And could it be because she exudes vapours as sulphurous as those of sanctity are said to be sweet that the seat next to the young woman has remained empty?

Annabelle tries to wriggle free. When she becomes aware that the Marquis is not about to release her, like an animal surrendering to forces tyrannizing it she slumps against the walls of the corridor and waits for her ordeal to be over.

"Would you prefer being in there?" the Marquis asks Annabelle, nodding towards the occupants of the compartment.

Desperate to keep their disagreement between themselves, she silently implores him to keep his voice down. He, however, takes no notice of the plea which, in spite of being delivered discreetly, he clearly registered. "These the travelling companions you'd rather have instead of me? In which case join them! Don't let me stop you. If that's where you belong, by all means go in."

He pauses and watches her acutely. "But before we go our separate ways, there's something I have to confess: I'm afraid I made a serious mistake. I quite misjudged your character. Because when I saw you in the Brasserie, I could have sworn you had potential. Instead of which the experiment has turned out to be a disappointment." The Marquis shrugs. "However, it doesn't matter any more," he adds. "Take your seat, Annabelle. I'll tell the Steward to bring your bags."

He slides open the door of the compartment. Genially, and quite at odds with the resentful, almost recriminatory tone which he had adopted only a second ago, he exclaims: "Look, Annabelle! You're in luck. An empty seat." Noting the prude's fingers unfettered by any sign of connubiality, he turns to her and addresses her. "Excuse me, Mademoiselle," he says. "Is this seat taken? No?" he asks before she has made any objection. "Excellent! There you are," he turns triumphantly towards Annabelle. "You'll fit in here famously! *Bonne fin de voyage!*"

Secure in the space which they have conquered, most of the passengers have paid little attention to Annabelle. Perhaps because the young woman regards Annabelle as a rival for the opportunities which her role as the sole unattached female has so far afforded her, she stares at her with unfeigned hostility. Either oblivious to this unpleasant ray or, on the contrary, taking pleasure in exacerbating it, the Marquis pushes Annabelle into the compartment and directs her towards the empty seat.

She immediately discovers how excruciating it is to be caught between pretending to be at her ease while trying simultaneously – and without appearing to do so – to prevent the Marquis from forcing her any further into the compartment. Next, without any warning, he releases her so fast that to counter her own resistance and to keep herself from falling over she has to hang on to the door of the compartment, a gesture perfectly in keeping with the movements of a wildly jerking train but inexplicable on a run as smooth as this. Trembling with irritation, Annabelle assesses the simple truth of her situation:

the Marquis has just abandoned her to her fate and has left her surrounded by people who, she can sense, already resent her untimely appearance.

Almost in tears, Annabelle, half in, half out of the compartment, watches the Marquis' figure disappearing down the corridor, then pivots round to confront the passengers. Her status in their eyes, she realizes, is at worst low, at best undefined. The men have glanced her up and down, have noted her fractious rapport with a now vanished male, suspect some kind of amorous tiff, and have concluded that there is nothing to be gained from interfering. The young mother hugs her sleeping child whose beatific smile suggests that nothing short of an epiphany will rouse him. As for Annabelle's rival, her stare is unequivocal: she'd better decamp or else! Conscious that her position has become untenable, Annabelle mumbles an apology, something about a mistake being made, she's sorry, she'll shut the door behind her, good day to everybody; and, finding herself back in the corridor, she curses the speed with which the Master of Ceremonies has defused her anger and brought her face to face not with a succession of available alternatives but with a single and wholly unappetising option.

What now? To her own compartment? To the Marquis'? Followed by . . . ? Admitting that she was wrong? Yet wrong about what? It is with a particularly heavy and frustrated tread that Annabelle heads back towards the compartment from which her indignation has, in an uncanny resemblance to a Japanese hand trick, turned her energy against her and expelled her.

The Marquis, who is standing by his compartment door gazing out of the corridor window at what look like aircraft warning lights winking from the top of a distant water tower, betrays no sign of victory as Annabelle, downcast and angry with herself, comes up to him. Courteously, though not without a touch of irony, he waves her towards his compartment, an invitation which she mutely, and with a continued sense of impotency, accepts.

He waits for her to settle down before taking a seat. He pulls a cigar out of a leather humidor, asks her permission to light up, makes sure that the air-conditioning is full on, and finally, puffing contentedly, says: "Thank goodness we surmounted that crisis of confidence. It'd have been a shame to have given up the course so soon." He sighs. "Now, if you don't mind, I'd like us to get back to the matter in hand. You recall that I've asked you to trust me."

"You've gone on about it often enough! Although, as far as I'm concerned, I regard trust as something that has to be earned," Annabelle answers, her lips clenched against another burst of anger which might lead her God knows where. "It's a particularly fragile quality, the kind an unwarranted attack can kill stone dead."

"Yet you're still here?"

"Yes," Annabelle answers, "stupidly, I am."

"In which case I'm going to ask you to trust me a little further because there's an important attitude you need to adopt from now on. Namely that of being on your guard."

"Really? Against what?"

"False expectations."

Every so often, thinks Annabelle, the Marquis' arguments become more slippery than a slime-smeared causeway.

"That's right. Ditch them."

Biting her lower lip, Annabelle shakes her head in disbelief.

"They serve no purpose," the Marquis continues. "None at all. You realize we're about to set off for another compartment?"

Cattily: "I expected as much."

He leaves her facetiousness unanswered. "And that we've three more ingredients to find?"

"So?"

"My point exactly. So nothing. Don't load yourself with useless expectations. Whatever you thought might occur next, put out of your mind. For the imagination to operate efficiently, what it needs is a definite context, not hazy hopes and vaguely formulated suppositions."

"You're becoming quite a tyrant. Now you're telling me what to think."

"To be precise, Annabelle: what not to think. Because if you imagine that you've guessed what'll happen in the next episode, all you'll do is interfere with the course's rhythm."

"Sorry, Jean-Loup," says Annabelle, "you're not making sense. I've already been to one of your enchanted compartments and seen what it was like. Nothing can undo that. What's more, if the next episode's anything like the last, I already know I've no stomach for it."

"So like a woman to be perverse!" the Marquis exclaims, apparently pained by her obtuseness. "I never told you not to analyse the stories. On the contrary. I've expressly counselled you to keep an open mind and to watch what occurs with care. For if the course is to succeed, it's essential you discover just how stories are put together. What I am saying is that you shouldn't flesh them out before they occur. That can't possibly help. At this stage, you should concentrate on methods and consider what recipes are involved. And let the stories surprise you. Remember: we're after fresh ingredients, not yesterday's turgid leftovers. Believe me, Annabelle, when your turn comes, you'll feel exactly the same about it."

"What do you mean, my turn?"

The Marquis stares at her as if she were beyond redemption. "To create scenes, of course. *Dieu!* Haven't you grasped anything? The little mirror, the locket you've brought along, don't you see? They're your starting points, they're the ingredients you need to effect an exchange." He again shakes his head as if it were inconceivable that she could have made so little progress. Then, portraying a rather more solicitous attitude, he asks her: "By the way, do you still have a headache?"

She says that she has.

He goes over to her, seizes the back of her neck in a strong grip, and starts to massage it. She shivers. The contact is unwelcome, frightens her, the prelude to what she has always suspected he has had in mind all along. She is about to brush him off when a powerful and soothing sensation makes her reconsider. For the pressure he is applying to her shoulders is expert and his touch deft. And it is with quite uncanny prescience that his fingers locate the knot that has formed, the strain in the sinew, and the muscle bruised by the macerations of stress. Perhaps after all, Annabelle thinks, as she eases into the rhythm of his pliant fingers, she does not really want the Marquis to stop, not quite yet anyway.

"Good! That's it," he counsels as her tension starts to drain away. "Relax."

In a few minutes Annabelle's pains have been soothed and the Marquis, walking round to face her, asks her to show him her wounded finger. The pinprick has caused no swelling, he comments, so she can forget all about it. As he settles back on his chair, he fishes around in his waistcoat pocket for the dice. He darts his hands through his jacket and, a second later, judiciously takes them out. What will they add up to this time round? he wonders, throwing them on the table.

The vanity spots on their otherwise glabrous ivory faces bob and roll across the polished walnut of the table. A one and a three. Fine. Compartment number four it is! he exclaims. Quick! he urges Annabelle, or they'll be late. She should never underestimate the importance of correct timing! The potential for a creative period does not last for ever. It has to be exploited within limits, on either side of which lies only the sterile soil of wasted opportunity.

The compartment numbers are again jumbled up. So much for trying to rid oneself of expectations – false or otherwise! – thinks Annabelle, dismissing the Marquis' constant exhortation. If there are important differences between all the unpredictable events which keep peppering their walks through the train and the occurrences she thought would take place in the compartments, well, she has not discerned them. And what about those persistent harsh scraping sounds she can sense shuddering through the corridor as if the wind were out to tear the train off its tracks, roll it down an incline, and flatten it at the bottom of some rock-sharp gully? Perhaps on impulse, perhaps to alleviate the tedium of her own obedient pacing down a series of anonymous corridors behind her determined guide, or perhaps to do something on her own initiative for once rather than being limited to a set of simple responses, Annabelle decides to peer into a compartment. An unmarked door opposite her appearing as good a candidate as any, she reaches out and pushes it wide open.

A gouged-out, red-soiled vastness unfolds before her and an intense desert heat reaches out and sears her skin. The light is intoxicating. It bounces off the rocks and echoes off the sheer walls of the valleys, sliding down to where a red, mud-engorged river snakes its way through the raw remains of the soil it has devoured over millennia. Unable to clutch at anything around her, and about to be devoured by the red immensity, Annabelle screams. She has already started to tumble when the Marquis, who must have sensed the gust of wind tearing down the corridor and seen her helplessly hovering, rushes to the edge of the entrance and, with one hand around her waist and the other seizing her dress, drags her back from the gaping void.

Slamming the compartment door shut on the fragmented boulders and on the fast flowing rapids into which she had seemed doomed to fall, he turns towards her and reacts with vigour.

A resounding double crack. First her face flicks to the left then to the right. Her hands run to her red-burnished cheeks. The Marquis' eyes are cold yet furious. Annabelle staggers against the wall of the corridor, stares at him, bewildered, gasping, shocked.

"Never do that again!" the Marquis exclaims in a tone of voice all the more authoritative for being glacial. He pauses and watches Annabelle's reactions. Shock, pain, resentment, each one as distinct as the rainbow irradiations a drop of ink yields to a blotter. "You amaze me! Don't you have any conception of the danger you just put us in? Why do you think I urged you to follow my instructions? For your protection, that's why!"

"I . . . I was curious," says Annabelle lamely, "I just had to do it."

"Incredible! You almost kill yourself, damn near drag me down with you – and what's your excuse? That you were curious! Listen," the Marquis adds in his most patronizing manner, "from now on you stay close by my side. We're dealing with forces which can only be handled with skill. I've repeatedly told you that the course is arduous so don't go treating it like a game! If you act without consulting me again, I can guarantee you only one outcome – catastrophe!"

After that brutal encounter, there is nothing left for them but to renew their pursuit of their particular chimera down the length of the corridors. On consideration Annabelle realizes that the disorientation which she has consistently experienced in the train's surroundings hardly reflects the confusion which she feels within. Nor is it of any help to know that the image which almost proved her undoing, and which caused her humiliation, is hackneyed through and through. Indeed that it must have been culled from some cheap travelogue and can be found, what's more, the world over where it usually denotes the exoticism of travel and suggests the leaps of imagination which its vast hollowed-out landscape should evoke. Nor does it matter that she has no idea why the canyon should have emerged out of that unmarked compartment. For, in a strange way, it and the continuing jumbling of compartment numbers, the unending procession of corridors, and the shrill sounds that every so often erupt to disappear a few seconds later seem to console her, perhaps as a psychotic welcomes carnage for the echo it provides of the turmoil in his soul.

Without so much as a word passing between them, the travellers continue to walk through so many carriages that Annabelle soon loses count. Then, in the middle of a quite nondescript corridor, the Marquis stops and points to a compartment numbered 4, a compartment which, she notes is, at least in appearance, similar to all the other doors past which they have just wandered.

As if forced to pay tribute to some technique which always insists that familiar gestures should be enacted before characters are thrust into novel experiences, thus providing the mind with a temporary haven of safety before confronting it with its next brutal buffeting, the Marquis takes two pieces of paper from his pocket and studies them with care. He then closes his eyes. So speedily does he read them and fold them over that Annabelle, who had a great and renewed desire to discover what they referred to, is once again disappointed.

What is he up to? she wonders. Memorizing something relevant to the next episode? Saying a prayer to protect himself from the kind of destructive forces which she witnessed a few minutes before? Or is this some kind of amulet to prevent them tearing like harpies at his flesh?

The Marquis opens his eyes, places the pieces of paper back into his trouser pocket, and invites Annabelle to open the door. But as stepping into the unknown is no longer her favourite occupation, she politely declines. It is therefore with a marked show of gallantry, a reverence in her direction, a slow and ceremonial unlatching of the compartment door, and a final wave of the hand to usher her in that the Marquis inaugurates the second exploratory phase of their quest for the perfect gastronomic ingredients.

CHAPTER SEVEN

They once again find themselves in the dark. Impossible to make out where they are. All Annabelle can hear is the dull echo of their shoes against what seems to be a sand-encrusted floor. The Marquis searches through his pockets and finds his lighter. Once lit, like a will o' the wisp flitting across marshes, the flame illumines a space so vast its limits can barely be defined. And as it dances, it generates looming shadows from objects lying pell-mell across the floor. Here a mass of wooden, bejewelled furniture; there statues whose stretched-out arms, under the flame's wavering investigation, appear both welcoming and forbidding. On the distant walls paintings of vultures in full flight over a sandy land whose every detail is depicted in perfectly drawn lines. Ambling around the chamber, Annabelle soon comes to the startled conclusion that the colours in this overwhelming space, unlike the museums in which she has come across similar figures, have not been touched by the hand of decay, and that the atmosphere is imbued with a hint of musk. She takes in a deep breath to settle herself. And once she has surveyed the scene under the lighter's fast diminishing vigour, she concludes that the Marquis' magic seems to have landed them this time – incredible as it may sound – deep within the *sanctum sanctorum* of an Egyptian mausoleum.

Leading the way, the Marquis continues to throw his flickering beam on to wonders of heaped artefacts. He approaches a three-headed wooden candlestick standing on a cedarwood table enriched with gilt. The flame from his lighter immediately enlivens the candles as if their wicks had been readied but a few days before. Holding his luminous trident high, he pierces deeper into the space that lies before him. He closes in on one of the painted walls and casts the now fuller light on to a most unusual sight. A tall, apron-bound man, his member superbly erect, is flanked by a diminutive servant who is collecting his seed drop by drop in a golden bowl. For what purpose? asks Annabelle who has crept up behind the Marquis and is staring at the ithyphallic theme. Is it for some kind of rite? Rounding on her, her companion brushes her question aside and tells her in a low yet trenchant tone to keep quiet.

Next the Marquis goes over to the most prominent feature in the chamber: a massive, luxuriantly painted wooden sarcophagus. Presumably the chamber's main *raison d'être*, it is set at its nub. Pleased to find the sarcophagus secure, its numerous sheaths and covers untouched by grave robbers, the Marquis walks round the chamber until he comes to a halt before an alcove. Within it another sarcophagus is set on a wooden plinth.

Annabelle has trailed a little way back in order to admire a range of pastes radiantly intaglioed in a cosmetics caisson. She has looked over their aquamarine and opalescent splendour, each hand-carved and filled with beautifying substances when, out of the corner of her eye, she observes that the object over which the Marquis is presently poring is a much more modest and not so elaborately painted sarcophagus. A sarcophagus which, given its position in the order of the room, she presumes must have belonged to some senior official or friend of the family.

With a wave of the hand the Marquis summons Annabelle to join him.

When she reaches his side, she can see that this final resting place, unlike its companion, has been breached. Whether by grave robbers or by some other cause she cannot tell. She stares into the open sarcophagus and cannot prevent herself exclaiming: "What on earth . . . !"

"Be quiet!" says the Marquis agitatedly. "Can't you see he's asleep?"

For his candlestick has revealed within the wooden frame the awesome figure of a heavily bandaged and unmistakeably male Mummy.

"He? Who's he?" Annabelle whispers, unable in spite of his interdict to smother her curiosity.

"The Mummy of course," the Marquis answers, his use of the

definite article stressing his familiarity with the faintly reeking corpse in the painted coffin, his curtness cutting her off from further knowledge. "It may be quite some time before he wakes. So while we're waiting, I suggest you take a look around the mausoleum. But don't make any noise!"

He takes one of the candles from the candlestick, hands it to her, and picks up two wooden chairs conveniently lying nearby, setting them close to the sarcophagus. Then, with the warning that she should not go wandering too far, he places the candlestick on the floor and sits down to await a development which his pose suggests he is confident will eventually occur.

Although Annabelle – whose initial unrest has been replaced by an almost tangible curiosity – would dearly like to ask the Marquis what this might be, she settles for his offer and walks away, holding the candle at arm's length to prevent it spitting on her dress, to explore the tomb.

She has examined a number of the period objects which are stacked in loose jumbles around the chamber when she senses something distinctly awkward, even irksome, about their nature. Although they are perfect in appearance, they lack something, something indefinable. She picks up a sculpted lotus-leaved alabaster vase. A frayed name tag flutters loose from its base. She bends to retrieve it and is amazed to read on it:

Lot no. 320
On loan to: "The Curse of the Mummy's Tomb."
If found please return to the Property Master.

A prop from a film set? What is going on? Does that mean that everything here is artificial, make-believe, no more than an illusion? Not only is this startling, it is also utterly at odds with the otherwise stunning consistency of the decor. Trying to make sense of the conflicting evidence before her, and repressing as best she can her revulsion before the fake, Annabelle reaches for another object, a jewel box carved out of lapis lazuli. She scrutinizes it and can hardly stifle a gasp. For written on its underside in a most unruly script she sees:

Lot. no. 321
On loan to: "The Risen Mummy."
Fragile: do not damage. Property of Isis Studios.

Unsure what to make of this, she decides to pursue her exploration alone rather than ask the Marquis – whose all-knowingness is at times overwhelming, if not downright patronizing – for help. For she hopes that if she roots around, she might develop her own theory on the nature of the place.

To credit Annabelle's intelligence and the sagacity which often springs to woman's aid under stress, while she might indeed have put together the pieces of the mystery in roughly the right order and come up with a fascinating conjecture as to how, why and to what purpose the objects seem to be sham, her meditation is suddenly interrupted by a snarling, rasping sound which travels right round the mausoleum before finally cutting into her nerves.

Where did the sound come from? She swivels round. Surely not from over there? She stares in the Marquis' direction, picks out the glow of the candelabra reflected in the sarcophagus' side in the distant alcove, and cannot believe her eyes. For next to the apparently unflappable Marquis, the Mummy, now apparently resuscitated, has raised his heavily-bandaged torso from the sarcophagus and is looking at her from the depths of his dark orbits.

The Mummy points an equally bandaged finger in her direction and calls out in the same rasping voice which she has just heard: "How dare you violate the sleep of ages and break into this most sacred chamber?"

Without waiting for a reply which Annabelle, dumbstruck, would have found hard to provide, the Mummy, like a hound on the scent, sniffs the air and turns his head this way and that as if he had just detected a repulsive smell. Finally, in a gesture so grotesque that it momentarily distracts her, he puts his bandaged hand to his nose.

"By the jaws of Anubis!" His voice crepitates around the chamber. "What is that vile smell?"

Annabelle adds to the many surprises which the course has so far spawned the fact that, in spite of the Mummy's strained tone, she can make sense of his language.

"I recognize it!" the Mummy exclaims, his neck swivelling in a strained and mechanical manner. "Garlic! Yet how could the forbidden bulb have been brought here?" He casts his moribund eye around the mausoleum with its scattered funerary furniture, its sacks of dried victuals, its mummified cats, and the sacred bric-a-brac which has been assembled there to comfort the *ka* during its aeons of anticipation. It takes him only an instant to conclude that the smell of garlic can have but one origin. Levelling a long accusatory finger at the intruders, he cries out: "Wretches! Not only have you stolen your way into this venerable chamber but have also desecrated its atmosphere. I order you: stand back! For I cannot suffer the stink of your base origins!"

It would appear that the ingredient which the travellers are pursuing has once again taken its toll, and that the Marquis and Annabelle are becoming as densely aromatic as a crushed clove.

Whoever the eviscerated body behind the enswaddling linen belongs to, masquerader, thespian, or genuine Egyptian, his knowledge of dietary custom cannot be faulted. For garlic is indeed taboo in the Land of the Two Kingdoms. While the slave hordes may feed on it, it must never degrade the palates of the higher estates.

Are you responsible? Annabelle gestures to the Marquis, unable to smell anything dubious on her breath and almost sure that nothing malodorous is emanating from her body. It's not just me, he replies with an equally telling gesture: both of us are guilty. To settle the matter Annabelle walks up to the Marquis and discharges a blast of air into his face, an intimate act which immediately makes him step back.

Forced to bow to the evidence, the travellers tactfully retreat and move their chairs away from the Mummy.

"Neither my tomb nor the other one has been attacked, I see. Are you not grave robbers then?" the Mummy asks, addressing in a somewhat kinder manner the strangers who, now that they have backed off, have spared him the unbearable odour of the bulb.

"No, Your Excellency, we are honourable people, not pillagers," the Marquis replies in tones even more obsequious than Annabelle remembers him using in the first episode. "We are here for one reason, and one reason only. To entreat you to help us."

"You would have me listen to a request?" the Mummy enquires.

"If you would, Your Excellency. For not only would you then save us from a terrible fate – the ghastly smell to which you so rightly objected is a disease that unchecked will eventually kill us – but in helping us you may also be able to relieve your own age-long suffering," the Marquis says, and waves a hand at the desolate space in which the Mummy must lie until the Underworld cracks and his soul can return to his Ur-ancestors' resting place.

"It is true, strangers, that the hours here are endless," says the Mummy in an almost contemplative voice. "And that listening to your tale might provide me with a welcome diversion."

Annabelle stares at the Mummy and searches for some flaw in his behaviour which would reveal this awkward and ridiculous apparition for the fake which she is convinced he is. For surely it is just a clever mechanical device intoning a recording in some hastily if at first convincingly mocked-up set? A tomb on a train! Really! The idea is preposterous! How can a corpse become animated? Anyway, were the Mummy real, wouldn't it speak Egyptian? And wouldn't it have made some comment about their clothes, so different from the apron it once wore? So this is the inconsistent world, Annabelle complains, which the Marquis would like her to take seriously.

But before Annabelle can adduce further evidence for the props' fakeness, the Mummy – apparently unaware of her attempt to expose him and insensitive to her refusal to submit to the illusion – returns her inquisitorial glare with a force equal to hers and continues: "Very well, I shall listen to your request. But not before I have told you how I, a simple courtier, came to be granted the rare honour of being buried in a Princess' tomb." His hands point to the regal decor and the domestic implements which have been brought here to soothe his and the occupant of the other tomb's limboed souls. Then, in a voice tremulous with misery, the Mummy adds, "An honour that has been my bane and my torment ever since."

The Mummy begins his tale and Annabelle, although determined to pierce through the thin defences of this absurd apparition, nonetheless closes her eyes the better to expose the charlatanry which she is sure underpins the set. As soon as she has done so, her scepticism is not so much overcome as suppressed. For in a moment her mind is drawn past the mists of her inner vision towards the panorama of a sandy land. A land which, she notes from the vantage of a high vision, is bisected by a river whose seasonal moods, she senses, has for aeons disbursed silt on hard-baked banks and brought life to its sun-parched people.

Narrowing down from this bird's flight view, her attention soon focuses on the fine mansions which line the river in the more opulent quarters of the Holy City. From there, it settles on a window on the first floor of the largest mansion to overlook the Palace walls. It then flies through that window into a rectangular, low-ceilinged and simply furnished room.

In one corner she glimpses a large wall map on which are traced the curlicued paths of all ascendant stars. In the other a large work table strewn with precision tools, among which a wooden ruler and a compass are splayed on papyri in states of varying disorder. On a rug-covered pallet she also makes out the sleeping figure of a small grey cat, its paws white, a star on its breast.

Moving over to the window, a young man stands and stares at the silvered carapace of the sluggish Nile. His features are fine, his hair ebony, his skin sand, his whole expression suffused with animal charm. Walking back towards his work desk, he bends over plans of the greatest intricacy. Then, as if urging the afternoon to bring on a consolatory breeze, he seizes a small plumed fan from a side table with which he attempts to chase away the sun's intensity.

"The day I came into this world," Annabelle hears the Mummy overlay with his voice the images which have just so fluently swept through her mind, "my father, the Pharaoh's Master Builder, cried with joy. A son! At last! I, Amonhotep, the fruit of his loins, would become the harvest of his hopes . . . Poor man! How could he have divined the depths to which he was mistaken?"

The Mummy's voice is fast becoming lighter and is losing its archness, although it still carries within it a deeper, rasping sound.

"Perhaps you have heard how Pharaohs used to blind their Master Builders so that the secrets of their tombs could never be divulged. Happily by the time my father was appointed to his noble post, those cruel days were long past. Not only had he

104

survived the construction of the necropolis whose sacred confines you have just breached, but he had been further honoured with many a royal commission throughout the land. But you need not concern yourselves. I shall not ask how you broke into this sacred chamber for I know only too well, and to my eternal cost, that there are no walls strong enough to stop those who mean to breach them.

"I had been an apprentice in my father's firm for a number of years when one day I received my very first commission. And what a commission it was too! To design new fountains for the Palace Gardens."

The Palace Gardens are protected from the eyes of the curious by a high wall which also gives cover to the fronds and grasses fed by the neighbouring Nilotic waters. It is early evening. The summer's shadows have lengthened although the light is still stark and resplendent. Sitting on a low wooden bench next to a pond, Amonhotep is busy drawing on a length of papyrus which he has firmly secured to a small portable desk. In these his final and nearly completed designs, he has incorporated the heads of crocodiles, along with some of the rare flowers which he has discovered the length and breadth of this most secret garden. His workmen have already downed their tools and departed. And so, indeed, should he, for the hour has come when the Ladies of the Inner Court are wont to wander in the cool of the evening and lie by the fragrance of the lily ponds.

"I should have remembered that I was trespassing for I had been warned often enough that the Gardens were out of bounds after sundown. But on this my last day of designing, I could not leave until my drawings were fully to my liking."

Amonhotep is here adding in a few lines and there rubbing out others which have lost their meaning, and is even occasionally cursing an art which so easily loses it savour with each addition when he suddenly looks up. Are those people he hears approaching? Yes, those are indeed the sounds of footsteps, laughter and chatter. Aware of the terrible danger that he is now running, his expression darkens.

"I only stopped working just in time. For had I been discovered at that late hour in the Palace Gardens, I'd have surely been arrested – and perhaps executed – for my transgression."

Rounding the corner of the Gardens in which the pond lies in the shelter of a semicircle of sycamores, a small and joyful retinue of young ladies, dressed in short white skirts, surround the justly famous beauty of the Pharaoh's youngest daughter, the Lady Nephtys. Apart from the distinguishing mark of a small golden crown floating on a curled mass of ebony hair, the Princess is dressed very simply. It is with undimmed horror that Amonhotep perceives that the party is heading directly towards him and that, unless he is to die, he must hide immediately. He seizes his quills and portable apparatus, dives behind a nearby row of reeds, and falls face down on to the powder dry ground.

So violently is his heart beating that he is sure it will give him away. A minute elapses and he has still not been apprehended. He raises his head a few inches off the ground, parts the curtains of reeds, and, with great caution, looks out.

All is well. Solely concerned with the delicious rhythm of their own chatter, the young ladies have noticed nothing. Some have already set cushions and sweetmeats by the side of the pond, while others have enticed little monkeys with titbits, and are affectionately stroking their sparsely covered heads. The more intrepid among the women disrobe, offering to his eyes a feast of lank and well-fed limbs, breasts which have lost nothing of their pubescence, and loins whose curved promise almost makes the fortune-blessed architect swoon with ardour. Finally, with all the naturalness of her young grace, the Lady Nephtys herself throws off her garments and reveals to Amonhotep the sight from which he will never recover.

"Then," Amonhotep says, "I confronted what none of my humble estate should have ever witnessed. A Princess in her private hour bathing in the Palace ponds and a Royal Lady unaware of the stranger's eyes devouring her."

As if torn by a terrible pain, the Mummy interrupts his narrative and staunches the flow of images which he has been feeding through Annabelle's mind. Forced out of her reverie, she opens her eyes and stares at him, half dazed. What is wrong? Why has he stopped? And why is the Marquis – who has also opened his eyes – looking at her in that curiously detached way?

"O eternal misfortune!" the Mummy cries, his linen-wrapped body taut, "that I should have come upon the entrancing figure of the Pharaoh's youngest daughter! If only I had left the Gardens earlier! If only I had never seen her! For once the veils of Isis were ripped away, and the loveliness of the Princess had been revealed to me, I was cursed, yes, I was cursed for ever." He gazes at the two travellers then points towards the massive sarcophagus in the centre of the mausoleum.

"Look, look over there!" the Mummy continues in the same searing tone. "Do you see the other tomb in this dusty room? Do you realize who lies there, cold and still? Yes, my love, the Lady Nephtys."

What of Amonhotep still lying low among the reeds? It is not until the Marquis has calmed the Mummy down with a few soothing words and reminded him that if they are to understand him, he must return to his narrative; and it is not until the travellers have again submitted to the required protocol, closed their eyes and concentrated, that the scene in the Palace Gardens is recaptured.

Taking advantage of the ladies enjoying the cool of the evening air, feeding on the delicacies they have brought, and exchanging gossip with each other, Amonhotep crawls painfully through the bed of reeds. Fortunately he issues on the other side of his hiding place without having made a sound and is able to leave the Gardens by a side door where lax sentinels who recognize him wave him on without enquiring as to his tardy departure.

That evening Amonhotep sits hunched over his desk, his stylus scratching the soft surface of a papyrus. If only he could surrender to the temptations of his imagination! If only he could depict what he had experienced in the Palace Gardens with the colour of his emotions! Sadly, as he is well aware, the rules and restrictions of his time's artistic codes will not permit it. Yet does the Lady Nephtys' beauty not put all descriptions to shame? Is she not the soothing bed on which the weary soldier might lay his head? (muses Amonhotep who has never seen a field of battle). The bank against which the Nile of his love might flow? (he wonders, quick to adapt an image from his engineering studies). The pillar on which the temple of his hopes might depend? (he adds, pressing his knowledge of masonry into metaphoric service). However mediocre his literary attempts may be – and he is the first to admit it – do they not show how poetry, in contrast to the poverty of the pictorial codes which he must use to convey his inspiration, can kindle the fire of love in the heart of even the poorest fellaheen? Yet he has no choice but to resort to those free-form, loose-leaved stone fragments on which wall painters thumbnail-sketch before they buckle down to paint the traditional lines of hieratic representation. No choice but to dilute his unique erotic vision and make it conform to every drawing he has ever studied. Short and shameful as the Heretic's phase may have been – for Akhenaton ordered his artists to depict him as a long-limbed and pot-bellied king – at least his style had life! At least it bore some relation to truth! But the dull priesthood has eradicated almost all traces of that bizarre style along with every public mention of the Mad Monarch. Which means that, no matter the intensity of his own desire, Amonhotep has to admit that his personal interpretation cannot be indulged.

So, when at the end of an hour Amonhotep sits back to admire his labours, he concedes that his modest effort is indistinguishable from any other drawing of any other Princess. Bowing to the inexorable conventions of his era, he consoles himself with the notion that for him at least the drawing will always symbolize his Princess, the lady with whom he has fallen in love, the lady who, even if unawares, paraded before him the nakedness none but her husband should pleasure. With that in mind, the young architect next considers how he should contact this creature of beauty and how he should tell her that she has not only conquered a distant admirer but that his life is now hers to do as she wishes.

"No sooner had I drawn what I had seen by the lily ponds than I realized that if this sign of my trespass were ever to fall into the wrong hands, it would constitute a proof of guilt for which I would be executed. Not that I was afraid to die. No! In my fervour I would have happily embraced death a thousand times rather than keep from the Princess the effect she had had on me."

The shadowy side street is flanked with tall houses leaning towards each other with the reckless abandon of drunks or destitutes. Amonhotep would have preferred a more salubrious place; but it was only by chance, and after a three day search, that he chanced upon one of the Princess' maidservants decked out in the familiar livery of royalty. And rather than lose her, as she frisked past kiosks dispensing fried fish, jellied snakes and fruit in spiced wines, he decided that he must catch her eye and tell her of his quest. Now she stares at him, her pointed face half in, half out of the shade, while he explains what it is he wants and how much he is willing to pay for it. As his speech is in demotic only a rough transliteration is possible. Yet the gist of his words can be surmised from the fact that, having met with little resistance from the maid – who is perhaps rather more used to rough types trying to take her in side streets than to being accosted by a young and elegant gentleman wearing the insignia of the Master Builder's workshop – he brings out two papyri from under the folds of his garment. The first he hands to her still rolled up. The second he surprisingly unfurls before the maidservant's fascinated eyes, revealing a representation whose adjacent cartouche identifies it as a self-portrait. If her mistress asks her why he sent it, he tells the little maidservant, this is what she should answer: so that she may ponder at her leisure the features of her fervent if distant lover.

"Fortunately," the Mummy adds, "a handsome bribe convinced Lady Nephtys' maidservant to bear to the Princess the drawings which I had made."

Accepting the golden coin which gleams in the half light, the maidservant nods her agreement. Amonhotep refastens the self-portrait and gives it to her. She tucks the two papyri into her small wicker provision-filled basket, gazes at the young architect's drawn features, bows, and hastily leaves.

Doubt projects Amonhotep from one side of his study to the other and back again. Despair makes him curse and pummel his pallet with terse energies. Hope leads him to stare at the Palace behind whose walls lives the woman he loves. And a truly corrosive longing renders him incapable of working, unwilling to hunt, indifferent to his horses, and fretful before the massed papers of his studies. In short the Lady Nephtys' brief apparition has quite unbalanced the young architect's senses.

"And so I waited. My mind was on fire. I could not work, could not eat, could not sleep. A succession of moons went by and still there was no reply. As I stared night after night at the Palace bathed in the palest starlight, my heart seemed close to breaking."

A few days later, along with the inevitable ebbing of fever that comes not with a lessening of the illness but with a weakening of the body, Amonhotep lapses into a kind of calm. This period of unexpected quietude he uses to rough out a number of drawings which his father has commissioned from him. He has just put the finishing touches to them when there is a knock at the door. His own servant walks in, bows low, announces the arrival of a Royal Messenger, and ushers the latter in. Showing the son of the Pharaoh's Master Builder all due reverence, the Messenger, a Nubian of powerful muscular appearance, his thighs hams of astounding thickness, hands the architect a parcel. Hardly able to disguise his excitement, Amonhotep nonetheless takes the parcel with decorous nonchalance, then, with a wave of the hand, dismisses both functionaries.

With its wrapping lying on the floor, Amonhotep stares at the parcel's contents in horror. No! It cannot be! His own drawing returned! The Princess has rejected it! Distraught, he throws himself on to the bed while the dam of his reserve shatters and releases a flood of tears.

Little by little his sobs become less violent. Dragging himself to his desk, he spreads the drawing across his paper-strewn desk.

"Mortified by the rejection I had just received, I stared at the image of loveliness I was certain I would now never possess."

Amonhotep contemplates his own handiwork. After an instant's contemplation, he leans over the drawing and examines it with a fierce, almost disbelieving intensity. Extraordinary! This detail, where does it come from? He does not remember drawing it in. And surely he would have noticed it if he had. Yet there it lies, unmistakeably, on the stretched papyrus.

"Suddenly I came across something I had never seen, something I was sure I had not drawn. A detail had been added to the drawing, a detail so small I could not have noticed it as I lay behind the reeds. A detail so intimate only one person could have put it in. It was in appearance like a tiny birth mark which Nature, with her infinite reserve of invention, had lodged on the Princess' left thigh. Yes, there it lay on the papyrus, inked in a delicate hand, in the shape of a snake's head."

Amonhotep leans by the window, his eyes on the horizon, a vacant expression on his face. He returns to his work table and scrutinizes the drawing once again.

"The more I examined it, the more I could hear it whispering to me: come! it seemed to say: come and see for yourself! If I dared make my way into the Palace, I would discover whether the mark was where it had been drawn in. From that moment," adds the Mummy, his voice faltering, "my life changed. I had but one thought in mind: how to gain access to the Royal Palace. And while I hoped for the far-off moment when I might embrace her, I also imagined the Princess swaying in the heat of her heretical desire."

Surprised that there should have been no mention of the other drawing, the self-portrait which Amonhotep had sent to the Princess but which had not been sent back, Annabelle wonders whether this is a telling detail which will later have a role to play, or whether, perhaps like the fake objects which alerted her to the sham of the mausoleum set, it is an oversight which has momentarily fractured the fluidity and consistency of the story.

In a corner of the inner courtyard the old bull stands. On its back a green ceremonial robe. It is tired. Gladly would it have rejoined its ancestors long ago had its successor been born sooner. But it was only a few weeks ago that, to the jubilation of the people and the relief of the priests, the infertile piebald calf was found, marked with all the signs of its noble calling: the square spot on its forehead, the figure of an eagle on its back, the tail with its double hairs, and the mark of the beetle on its tongue. Amonhotep, who has taken his place with the rest of his father's retinue, waits as the silence in the courtyard becomes momentous.

The intensity of the noonday sun has transfigured the sand in the courtyard into a mirror throwing the fire of its rays back into the faces of the audience. Casting his eye round the audience, the young architect admires the parabolas of the silk fans which slaves hold high above the Ladies of the Court. And now that the sun is hovering directly above the courtyard, and that the sundial's golden gnomon leaves no trace on the newly-raked ground, aware that the hour has indeed arrived, a murmur courses through the crowd.

From one of the courtyard's cardinal entrances, a group of slender neophytes from the temple school enter, headed by a shaven-headed priest, their master. At his behest, they surround the old bull and lead it to a large water-filled cistern set in the centre of the courtyard. Once it has been tethered to a bronze ring in its side, the priest raises his hands to the sky, addresses a last prayer for the soul of Apis, and the drums begin to beat.

The priest makes a sign. As if conscious of its fate, the bull rips sand from under its hoofs. The neophytes, with a violence which belies their ascetic demeanour, take the bull's head, and thrust it under the water. The beast struggles, its tail beats wildly against its tensed back, its legs hammer the ground. Momentarily overpowering its executioners, it raises its head out of the water and bellows a loud call. In vain. For with renewed vigour the neophytes again force its head under. With a shudder which the silent crowd sympathetically senses, the spirit of surrender suddenly seizes it, and its horns slip meekly into the water's cobalt. Aware that the ceremony is not yet at an end, the shadow-flecked throng makes not a sound.

As his father's retinue has long enjoyed the privilege of sitting on the same side of the cloisters as the Royal Family, Amonhotep cannot make out which members of the Household are in attendance. Crane as he might, a thick lotus-leaved pillar keeps blocking his view. Cursing this circumstantial blindness, he turns back to the ceremony's age-old procedure.

Now that the old bull's body is motionless, the neophytes haul it out of the water, take its robe from its back and, in a corner of the courtyard, proceed to cut strips from its flanks with their long knives. A chorus of official mourners march towards the flayed corpse, lamenting its noble death, smearing their faces with its still steaming blood, and consuming a fragment of its flesh. A second group of monks, their ponderous pace and weatherworn features marking them out as temple elders, make their orderly way from the opposite entrance and lead in a young bull, the new Apis, by a thin white cord. The arena immediately shakes under a burst of acclamation. Throwing palm fronds before it, the Ladies of the Court welcome it as the once dismembered, now resuscitated Osiris, the Great God himself. And as the old bull is dragged away by temple servants, the new is blessed by the priests, draped with its predecessor's green robe and loudly hailed by the people.

It takes an hour for the courtyard to clear and for the members of the Court to reassemble in one of the Palace's inner chambers. Its atmosphere is thick with the fumes of incense. The High Priest kneels before a flame and intones an intricate prayer. In the background, tambourine players punctuate the ceremony with shimmers of high-pitched bells. Amonhotep stands in a line of courtiers, his head bowed, his hands stretched out before the Pharaoh's throne. On his embroidered shirt he displays the symbols of his father's profession, the splayed compass and the obelisk. While his fellow courtiers listen to the prayers, he glances with longing at the far side of the chamber where, behind a tall, elaborately carved cedar screen, the Ladies of the Inner Court also attend the service.

"Both the Princess and I took part in all court ceremonies," says the Mummy from the resonating cavern of his hollow frame, "I before the Pharaoh, bearing the arms of my father, she assembled with the other Ladies of the Royal Household, well hidden from view. The incense choked me, the singing confused me, and the tambourines clawed at my brain. Nor could I stop wondering whether, aided by my drawing, she had identified me behind her cedarwood screen when all I had to remind me of her was a fleeting vision by a lily pond and a few lines drawn on papyrus."

From the midst of the seething crowd, a nod tells the little maid that it will be to her advantage to join him in the alleyway in which they spoke before. A few minutes later, she discreetly sidles into it and stares at the fevered architect, her eyes occasionally wavering away as a sign of respect. First the golden coin scintillates in the dark before disappearing in the hollow of her hand; then, once she has listened to his new request, the little maid bows and rapidly leaves to discharge her secret duties.

"I could eventually bear it no longer. No matter the danger, I would bridge the distance which the Princess' elevated estate and the high walls of the Palace had placed between us. I therefore sent my love another message, telling her I would do all in my power to be with her as soon as it could be achieved."

If his plan is to succeed, Amonhotep must, among other acts of daring, climb the steep walls of the Palace. He therefore needs to be sure of the day which will be blessed with the gods' good fortune. It is to that end that he sends for his soothsayer.

Everyone in his father's household is asleep. Only the

sporadic baying of roaming dogs and the crackling of ritual fires on the other side of the river disturb the calm that suffocates the shrouded city. In his study, at a table lit with candles, the young architect sits opposite his soothsayer. Rice wine fills cups of amber, sweetmeats adorn a blue glaze bowl, and a glowing mound of incense fast disperses throughout the room.

An outcast of the temple schools, the soothsayer now makes a living from the throwing of bones and other divinatory arts which he picked up before the priesthood ruled that he lacked the qualities requisite for the high calling. Since his expulsion his hands have been soiled a thousand times with blood of dubious origin with which he has tried, and, it should be said, not without success, to cast into the future. Amonhotep finds this bejewelled, over-fed, oily-complexioned and feminine-mannered creature irksome, but his expertise undeniable. Offering him yet another candied fruit, which the divine eagerly devours, he informs him what he is after: a propitious occasion and a moonless night.

A moonless night presents no very great difficulty. The soothsayer consults a big black tome, isolates a celestial chart, applies his intuitive skills, and conjures up a few. What of the propitious occasion? Hardly has he cast his ragged collection of bones when he suddenly starts for his subtle arts have revealed more than he expected. Yes, the portents are sinister, the danger imminent, even if the signs are not as clear as they might be. His bloated face pearled with sweat, he fidgets with his empty cup. Amonhotep notices his consultant's unease and asks him if something is the matter. The pythoner, pleading sickness, points to his stomach: he is not feeling that well. He must have eaten something that disagreed with him. Satisfied with the answer, the young architect rises from the table, walks over to the window, and stares at the walls of the Palace. Mopping his brow with a broad handkerchief, the soothsayer stares at the young man with trepidation. But business being business, to satisfy Amonhotep's love-hungry look and to earn his fee, he suggests an evening propitious as far as the moon is concerned, and leaves unmentioned the shadow which he glimpsed falling across the ultimate source of his client's light.

"As soon as I had been informed on what night I might risk entry into the Palace, I put the rest of my plan into action."

His clothes black, his manner furtive, his limbs tensed for the climb, Amonhotep stands at the feet of the outer walls of the Palace. No one about. The sentinels have either completed their rounds or are tarrying over other matters. Amonhotep's first throw is unsuccessful and the hooked rope clatters next to him on to the ground. On his second attempt the hold fortunately becomes secure. He strains, heaves and, a moment later, reaches the top of the wall. In a far corner of the Gardens, he espies his own now finished fountains. He notes that while the masons have deviated from the purity of his designs and their waters seem dull in the shade, their song, as they cascade from one level to the next, remains, as he had hoped they would be, enchanting. Hitching the rope up, he throws it into the garden side and follows it down. Silently and with measured tread, he makes his way towards the Palace, watching out for guards all the while.

"I scaled the outer walls and headed for the wing of the Palace in which I knew the Princess slept. Now you may wonder," the Mummy says, interrupting the flow of the narrative to interject a personal note, "how I, who in the course of my normal duties only had access to the Palace Gardens, could make my way around the interior of that walled and marbled space? The answer is simple. I had been fortunate. Aware that no man in the Two Kingdoms had built as much for the Pharaoh as my own father, I searched through the plans of his past commissions. To my delight I discovered that he had some years previously renovated the very quarters in which the young Princess lived. When I had located his drawings, and memorized each contour, each curve, each gallery, I realized that I was well and truly ready."

Amonhotep nears the Palace walls and can soon make out by its silhouette the quarters in which the Lady lives. He grapples with the creeper which hangs there in thick clusters and after considerable effort succeeds in scaling the walls. He reaches the first floor, slides past an open window, and lands in a long corridor. Once he has ensured that no one is standing guard within it, he treads down its poorly lit extent. Its silence, he observes, is occasionally punctured by guffaws which issue from a nearby guard room. He sidles up to its open entrance and sees by the light of a brazier two sentinels playing cards while a third pores over his dinner of dried fish and bread. It is no small

115

feat to glide past them unnoticed but the young architect, seizing the right moment, achieves it. A few yards down the same corridor, taking care not to wake them, he steps over a huddle of young maidservants, each lying on a straw pallet, each the guardian of her mistress' chamber. At its end, he confronts a wide arch surrounded by hand-painted tiles which depict herons netted in the marshes. At its base, asleep on her own pallet, he recognizes the little maid's face. He walks over her stilled body as quietly as possible and opens the door to the Princess' bedchamber.

"At last! I had arrived! My father's drawings had brought me to the place of my desire."

The Lady Nephtys' bedchamber is furnished in a simple style. Silken embroideries illustrating the Solar Barque's passage over the horizon hang on the wall. In a corner a wooden shrine to Isis on which are placed a set of golden incense bowls. By the window, where veils waft gently in a complaisant breeze, a boudoir of cedar over which the sheen of a copper disc dimly reflects the phials and lotions with which the Lady heightens her beauty. In the centre of the room, squat and finely carved, a narrow sandalwood bed. Amonhotep tiptoes over to it and is overjoyed to see on a small bedside table the now framed self-portrait which he sent her. And on the surface of the bed, on top of a thin linen sheet, the naked Princess deep in sleep.

"Overcome by tiredness, the Princess lay on her bed. Her beauty and her resplendent nakedness did not fail to lure me."

Annabelle is now convinced that the self-portrait has played out its role and that it was an oversight on the Mummy's part to omit that it had not been sent back rather than a carefully inserted detail to be exploited at a later juncture.

Could it be the fear that when he rouses her he will discover not the Lady of his dreams but a petulant and troublesome Princess making much of her high position and of his lowly status which keeps Amonhotep lingering for a few seconds, breathing in the perfect composition of the scene, his prey vulnerable, her surrender so complete, her femininity ideally prone? Nervous yet unashamed of his powerful priapic state, the young architect approaches the Princess' body.

"My agitation, my love, the sap that rose could no longer be denied. And so I came close to the bed, so close that I could smell the amber with which the Princess clothed her nakedness, so close that I could view with my own eyes the intimate detail with which she had tempted me."

Yes, it is here! The snake's head, the birthmark, set sensuously – precisely where the drawing had shown it would be – on the Lady Nephtys' left thigh. Enthralled by his great good fortune, by the beauty of his lover, and by the supreme felicity of having arrived at her bedside, Amonhotep lets his robe slide to the floor.

The next moment, however, a terrible shadow falls across the young Egyptian's face. The thrill of erotic expectation gives way to amazement then to absolute horror. Putting his hand to his mouth to stifle a scream, Amonhotep falls onto the floor, writhing and clasping his left leg.

"A searing pain coursed up my leg, tore the cells in my body, and froze my blood," the Mummy cries, his voice almost breaking under the strain of the memory of the fate that befell him. "And so extreme was this new pain that the other pain, the passionate torment I had nursed in my loins, was dispensed on the floor, leaving me empty and in despair."

No sooner has the seed with which he had hoped to found a secret dynasty in the folds of a royal womb spilled onto the floor than Amonhotep, his eyes glazing, his limbs shivering, catches sight of his foe. There, fast slithering towards a wickerwork basket under the Princess' bed, is none other than a grey-green asp.

The venom takes immediate effect. Close to the tiny wound Amonhotep's leg has already started to swell. In a vain attempt to staunch the mounting pain and to apply a makeshift tourniquet, he grips his leg.

"How I yearned to scream yet dared not! For the slightest sound would have roused the sentinels, dishonoured the Princess, and dispatched my father into exile for having sired a criminal."

His thoughts muddled, his breathing cramped by the poison coursing through his chest, Amonhotep stoops to seize his fallen robe. With no regard for safety, but solely to evade detection, he clambers out of the Princess' bedchamber window and falls heavily on the grass below. With an effort born of panic, he then drags himself up the awaiting rope and out of the Palace Gardens.

The door of his bedroom opens with a crash. His face blue from asphyxia, his leg grotesquely puffed out, the young Egyptian collapses at the foot of his bed, his flailing limbs striking his work table. Jolted by the shock, the drawing of the Lady Nephtys slides off it and, in a graceful pirouette, lands on his blackening groin, covering his nakedness. There it balances most precariously until Amonhotep, seized by a great convulsion which arches then drops him like the curve of an arrow's flight, is extinguished by the snake's bite.

"Back in my father's house, twisted by the poison that had inched its cold hands round my heart, I fell down and died. When my body was found in the morning by my servant, my father, fatally damaged by the loss of his only son, did not know where to turn. Counselled by my soothsayer who, on hearing the news, had hurried to his side to console him, he informed the world that I had been stricken by a rogue snake which had entered my bedroom at night, and that he would henceforward retire from his practice to pray for my soul."

A crazed solemnity hovers over the young architect's features. As if intent on haunting his corpse through the long sleep of the soul, a rictus has spread at the corners of his mouth. This is not to be, however, for the morticians have already laid him out on the cold alabaster slab and their art has begun its complex involutions. A copper needle inserted into his jaw soon relaxes the recalcitrant muscles, placing a most becoming smile across his face. There follows a neat incision. The flaps of his stomach are folded back and, applying their expert procedure, the functionaries of the dead extract his vital organs one by one.

Heavy shadows born of flickering lights dance across the morticians' high chamber as the embalming ceremony progresses. Among the many sounds which fill the marbled vaults are those of metal scraping against bone, sounds so familiar that Annabelle is sure she has heard them somewhere else. But long before she has had the time to pinpoint the association, the Mummy has begun to discuss the seminal operations of this long-lost art.

"My mortal remains were embalmed with due pomp. Hardly had the morticians scraped out my brains through the hollows of my nose, and placed my heart, lungs, liver and viscera each in its own canopic jar, and soaked my body in natron's decay-thwarting crystals, than the Pharaoh, as a mark of his respect for my mourning father, and keen to woo him back into royal service, decreed that my body would be buried in the mausoleum which his Master Builder had built."

The sarcophagus is carried into the mausoleum by an escort of half-naked slaves accompanied by the loud wailing of official mourners wholly inured to the solemnity of the moment through the repetitiousness of their daily office. So newly appointed is the chamber into which Amonhotep's stiff and eviscerated carcass has been brought that its walls have not yet been painted, nor has its space been cluttered with the rich baggage of death. In a small corner alcove a space has been prepared for the young architect. Sent by royal command, one of the High Priest's deputies begins to officiate at the ceremony. Calling on the gods who attend the Weighing of the Heart and prepare the souls of the deceased for their last journey, the priest blesses the coffin, then, his prayers at an end, he orders the neophytes to set it in its final resting place.

"Which is how, in a chamber reserved for the Pharaoh's children, I was placed in a sarcophagus to await the Final Day of Judgement."

With the fading of that ceremony, the next scene to confront Annabelle is set in a bedchamber at night. Although this is another deathwatch scene, however much can be said for economy of means and ingenuity of redeployment the props used for the last hour of the felled woodsman will not do as, apart from the need for verisimilitude, whose high and exacting standards might have been duped as long as rustic upholstery and threadbare furnishings had been kept out of the light, the decor of an Egyptian palace is too far removed from that of a country cottage to serve a dual function. So the candles which here adorn the chamber are made of desert goat's rather than of sheep's fat, and the space, though dimmed and almost crepuscular, is still recognizably set in the Land of the Two Kingdoms. It is the Princess, not the broken-backed forester, who, her face drained of all colour, surrounded by her weeping servants, lies in bed. And it is the little maid, not the peasant woman and her two children, who tenderly wipes the Princess' perspiring brow.

"Ten years later," says the Mummy, "while on a tour of

recently reconquered territories, the Lady Nephtys fell gravely ill. After a short fever, whose symptoms closely resembled the intensity of my own, she too closed her eyes on the Land of the Two Kingdoms for evermore."

On this particular occasion the mausoleum is very brightly lit, while the mourners, who have been more handsomely paid than for a simple courtier's funeral, exhibit a truly telling style of misery. The High Priest himself has come to recite the prayers. Borne by a train of slaves burnished by the implacability of the noonday sun, the Lady Nephtys' remains are finally laid to rest in a richly adorned sarcophagus, its many-sheathed splendour dominating the funerary chamber.

"When the period of mourning was over," says the Mummy, his words duplicating the visual splendour of the scene, "the Princess was buried in the very chamber in which I had myself lain for a multitude of moons." In a low, sad voice the Mummy adds: "And it has been my fate ever since to be close to the woman I loved yet separated by the cruel distance which death places between all of us mortals." Raising himself on the edge of his sarcophagus, he then turns towards the travellers and cries: "There! You have now heard the details of my story!"

"And what a tragic story it is too," says the Marquis with considerable emphasis though, Annabelle feels, with perhaps not quite the sincerity required. "I must say that, now that you have done us the supreme honour of sharing it with us, Your Excellency, I'm convinced that we can help you."

"You!" cries the Mummy, beside himself with anger at the Marquis' insolence. "Help me! Isn't it evident I'm beyond your feeble efforts?"

"And yet, Your Excellency, if I may point out a seminal fact, we are alive while you are not."

"Alive!" the Mummy again exclaims, as if shocked by this seemingly startling reality. "You say you're alive?"

"We are indeed. Which is why, if you'd fulfil our request and procure us a few cloves of garlic, we'd be only too happy to provide . . ."

"What! You'd have me, the son of the Pharaoh's Chief Architect, fetch you the food of slaves!" the Mummy splutters with rage. "Apart from the lowliness of the task, haven't I made it plain its smell would befoul me?"

"Surely a small price to pay for your dearest wish to come true?"

"You . . . you lowborn blackmailer!" the Mummy roars, as if unsure what to call the bizarrely dressed stranger who has made him a tempting if surely impossible offer. Forced by the steadfast intensity of the Marquis' clear-eyed gaze to accept that his bargain is not negotiable, he adds: "However, as I can see I've no choice, no choice at all . . ." Languorously stretching out the length of the sarcophagus, he closes his eyes, and, with due solemnity, cups his hands.

Aware that if she too wants to witness the episode's finale, she must follow suit, Annabelle leans back in her chair. And such is the speed with which fantasy can be assimilated into a realistic format that she is not surprised when her mind harmonizes with the Egyptian's vision and is swept along towards another unknown scene.

As if held in the grip of a formula which requires scenes to begin with a period of darkness, Annabelle's mind's eye is guided along a dark corridor, illumined sporadically, and then somewhat ineffectually, by solitary spluttering candles. This lack of definition is soon interrupted when she is made to focus on a strange pyramidal arrangement in the centre of the corridor around which there gravitates a mass of blue flames. Nor is it with any great surprise, remembering the events of the last episode, that she catches sight within this ardent hive, dimly at first then more and more clearly, of the figure of Amonhotep wearing the very robe in which he expired. After a little while the flames die down, abandoning the wraith-like Egyptian, steaming from the heat, alone in the corridor. His body, Annabelle notes, is in a sorry state: his limbs are black, his bitten leg is swollen, and his contorted face has turned into a cruel caricature of his own. Recalling how the Leopard Woman had failed to recapture her adolescent self when propelling her imagination to the sylvan setting, Annabelle realizes that the Egyptian must have had the same problem: he has been unable to recall his healthy body and has had to materialize within his poison-corrupted carcass.

Down a series of corridors Amonhotep now shuffles, tiny blue tongues of flame licking at his side. The massive blocks of stone which line the corridors, the heavy iron rings notched in the walls, the dark cells past which they wander, and the mass of dejected humanity incarcerated there all suggest to Annabelle that the Mummy has pitched himself into the bowels of the deliquescent den in which slaves while away the hours during which their gaolers let them rest from their labour.

This set, Annabelle observes, unlike the woodland scene, has not been wholly deprived of colour. Perhaps because it is a prison, it does not possess such a wealth of background details and so requires less energy to be constructed than a forest. Perhaps. But in one respect at least, she suspects, travelling in the mind must be a more gruelling process than the construction of imaginative scenes for the Egyptian's figure, like a badly eroding statue, is visibly fragmenting.

Amonhotep, oblivious to the progressive breakdown of his foul, swollen features, brushes aside the salamanders that pursue him, shuffles past the slaves' cells, and peers through the heavy iron bars at the captives. Untouched by the cries which they utter in a babel of foreign tongues, he shuffles on. And although it would no doubt show compassion to pore over these victims' fate and to consider the circumstances in which they have been forcefully expatriated, cut from their homesoil, and cruelly patchworked on to another, this seminal scene is hardly the occasion to try to do these sad castoffs of history the justice their plight deserves. So, rather than flaunt an inevitably shallow if still commiserative glance in their direction, and perhaps induce in them a hope that would only be later baffled, we should leave them free to relive the moments of their capture and to conceive the countless cunning routes by which they might have escaped from their now lacklustre and senseless fate. Thus released from devoting attention to secondary characters, we can quickly catch up with the hobbling figure of Amonhotep apparently decaying at ever greater speed.

The Mummy eventually reaches the corridor in which the stores are kept and there confronts a guard. It takes only a few seconds for this functionary to be dealt with for the sight of Amonhotep's decrepit face so overwhelms the poor uniformed peasant that, reeling back, retching, and clutching his stomach, he immediately flees. With the path now clear, Amonhotep pushes open the surprisingly unlocked door to the stores. On the floor, in mounds, lies the slaves' staple food, garlic.

Groaning from the pain, the exhaustion, and the infestation of flames which have seared his clothes, he bends down and seizes a handful. The moment he touches the pile, however, it squirms while from its depths there issues a loud and angry moan. It is not until he has torn at the bulbs resisting him with the full strength of their vegetable fury that he manages to prise a few away. Holding them by their tendrils, he limps past the pleading prisoners, and comes to a halt in the corridor in which he had originally appeared. At first only a few tentative flames approach him but then more and more come to attack him, until they finally engulf him in a bright magnesium flare.

Annabelle rises from her chair, walks over to the sarcophagus, and leans over it. The Mummy's swaddled body is hot to the touch while his hands have cupped within them three cloves of garlic, their powerful essence fast spreading throughout the chamber. The Marquis, who has followed Annabelle, carefully prises out of the Mummy's hands the second of the ingredients which he has told his companion are vital for the preparation of the course's dish. And, turning towards her, he says: "Do something useful, will you, Annabelle? Take this," he hands her the blood-filled phial from his jacket pocket, "and pour its contents into His Excellency's mouth. Quick! Don't keep him waiting!"

It is hardly surprising that Annabelle should be nauseated by the idea of pouring what flowed not so long ago through her own veins into the dried-out, yet magically mobile, carcass of the Ancient Egyptian.

"No!" she cries. "Not that!"

"Do it, I tell you! And do it immediately!"

Her disgust overcome by an inexplicable compulsion to obey the Marquis, Annabelle stands over the Mummy, who has thrown his head back in anguine anticipation, and pours the blood into the gaping slit of his bandaged mouth. Once the last drop has trickled in, thoroughly soaking the bandage, the Mummy's body shakes violently, and a monstrous shiver courses through the mausoleum. Its walls shake, expose gaping cracks, and the whole chamber convulses so violently it seems about to collapse.

His limbs creaking, his performance unsubtly mechanical, the Mummy rises out of his coffin and, with tread unsteady yet determined, stumbles across the sandy floor towards the central sarcophagus. In an astonishing display of strength – his bandages, parodying the climactic scenes of gothic movies, fast unwinding – he lifts the many wooden painted covers of the Princess' sarcophagus as if they were little more than papier-mâché. And after scattering them across the floor, his legs tensed, his groin bulging, the Mummy climbs onto the sarcophagus, straddles the Lady Nephtys, and kisses her.

Red around his mouth. Drops of blood on her lips. It takes no more for the pulse of life to stir miraculously once again through the Princess' desiccated body. She slowly opens her eyes and gazes for the very first time on the commoner who dared to brave the Palace's high walls and sentinels, only to be poisoned at her sleeping feet. Writhing in the heat of his long delayed passion, the Mummy embraces the Princess and, at last, possesses her.

Strangely, Annabelle muses, picking out just one facet from a scene filled with unlikely details, this act of passion leaves her cold. Unlike the previous incident, when the sensations which ran through her were, to say the least, highly provocative. She has no single explanation for why this should be so. All she can muster is a constellation of unprovable theories. But to which should she subscribe, she wonders? What about that being a woman, she cannot empathize with a male character? Or that as man's sexual rhythm is generally held to be a thrust with woman's a wave, the two can neither know, nor blend, with each other? Or might it be because she has never suspended her disbelief, regarding this episode as little more than a mechanical charade, a charade she was willing to observe but to whose influence she has never once submitted? As the last is the most seductive – even if it obscures the fact that after resisting and almost refusing to pour her own blood into the Mummy, she can hardly regard herself a detached observer – Annabelle, in a moment of self-delusion, settles for that explanation.

Making no mention of the physiological problems likely to attend an act achieved by creatures without central nervous systems; leaving in the dark how in a few well-documented, if outlandish, cases men have been known to perform co-ordinated acts with less than half their brains intact; preferring not to discuss the scene's total denial of the material considerations commonly held as central to the consensual experience of reality, the Marquis takes Annabelle by the hand and wisely leaves unchallenged, and therefore whole, the mechanics of an illusion which, for all its defiance of nature, has still generated enough narrative power to motivate its themes. And while the travellers quickly retreat with their booty from the mausoleum, now inflamed with sounds and pulsed with seisms, the Marquis draws a tactful veil over a scene which no longer concerns them.

Her face ashen, her gait clumsy, Annabelle traipses behind the Marquis down a multitude of corridors. Not until she has returned to the Marquis' compartment, shut the door, and collapsed into a chair does she at last speak. "I can tell I'm not going to survive this course."

"Of course you are," says the Marquis, once again bursting with vitality as if he had just had another shot of some reviving substance in the arm. "I appreciate it's all very new to you but don't let it bowl you over."

"You remember before we went into that last compartment, you asked me to concentrate on methods? Well, I've only worked one out so far, although it does go some way towards explaining what I've been through." She wipes her brow. "I think you spiked the champagne."

"Are you really accusing me of resorting to such crude techniques?" the Marquis asks her, adopting a frown of outrage. "I'm disappointed, yes, very disappointed at the level of your perception. Don't you realize that everything has been orchestrated by one force, and one force only – the imagination?"

"That's what you'd have me believe."

"It is. As for your explanation, I'm sorry but it doesn't stand up to a second's scrutiny. Consider for a moment: you've now experienced the process twice and have had a rest in between. Now, what drug could have such an intermittent effect? No, *ma chère*, the extraordinary ground we've covered could never have been prospected by such a simple method."

"Fine ground we've covered!" Annabelle exclaims. "In the first compartment we visited a papier-mâché leopard turned into flesh and blood. While in the second a three-thousand-year-old corpse made love to another."

"Details, all of them, secondary details. How often must I stress that what's at stake is not a few surprising effects but a question of profound understanding? I'm trying to make you understand that cooking and storytelling are part of the same process, that both are subject to the same principles and that they are ultimately ruled by the imagination. And that if you work hard to master the one, you can have power over the other. That's if you allow the process to occur unimpeded, and stop putting up petty objections every time something new occurs."

Exasperated by the Marquis' highhanded manner, Annabelle explodes. That's it! She has had quite enough. She's sorry but when nothing makes any sense, her instinct's not to wonder what clever connections she may have missed: it's to get the hell out.

Did he not warn her, the Marquis reminds Annabelle, that this would be a demanding course? The truth is that, although she may not have realized it, she has already made considerable progress. And that, give or take the odd bruise to her pride, she has come out of what might have been a set of highly unpleasant situations unscathed.

Unscathed! she retorts, holding up her wounded finger. How dare he brush aside his disgusting act of vampirism?

Nothing, he replies, but absolutely nothing in this world is achieved without some form of barter. She should make an effort to apprehend the situation from a standpoint broader than her own. To take but one instance, from the start of the last episode, he was aware that the Mummy could provide them with the ingredient they wanted. It was therefore only proper to offer him something in return. They could hardly have gone to Egypt empty-handed, could they?

"Of course not!" answers Annabelle, reaching for sarcasm. "So what do you do? Grab the nearest donor – which happens to be me, conveniently at hand – make a quick transfusion and presto! the trick's done! Now we've got a phial-full of blood, we can look the Mummy in the face and beg him to procure us what? A chestful of treasure? A golden necklace? No! Of all the unbelievably worthless things, a few cloves of garlic! Quite a coup, I must say!"

"While I sympathize with your anger, Annabelle," answers the Marquis in a remarkably soothing manner, refusing to take the slightest umbrage, "unfortunately we don't have the time to indulge it. We've two more ingredients to locate and only half the night left to get them in. And before that, there are one or two points I'd like to discuss with you."

"Let me guess. The same tedious subject?"

"Your petulance is irrelevant. I really shouldn't have to remind you that you came on this course of your own free will." He pauses, letting the truth and severity of his words check her, then continues in a gentler tone. "To begin with, I'd appreciate it if you would tell me what sense – if any – you have made of the course."

"That's easily done," she answers, riled. "It seems to me that we're involved in an elaborate fantasy – and one from which I haven't unfortunately yet found a way out." Realizing, however, that she is no longer in the first throes of anger, and that she is moreover avoiding the issue, she adds: "All right. I'll tell you. A throw of the dice somehow – I know you've explained it but don't ask me how – leads us to the compartment of some bizarre character. Once there, we strike a deal on the lines of 'you get us such and such an ingredient and we'll hand you whatever it is you're after'. A *quid prod quo*, fundamentally." She surveys the Marquis' face. "Frankly, that's all I've pieced together."

"And you're not struck by a coincidence: that we always have exactly the object the characters are after?"

"To be precise, Jean-Loup, it's not me who has what they want – it's you. As for being struck, yes, I have been, and not just by that either. By quite a few other things too. Not the least of which is: when do you intend to reveal what I'm doing here and what this crazy journey has to do with cooking?"

"A perfectly reasonable request and one I'll fulfil as best I can," answers the Marquis, in his most pedagogic manner, eyeing her with an almost protective gaze. "You agree that both cook and storyteller are out to make a success of their art? Good. The guests assembled around the dinner table and the tribe huddled around the camp fire are all waiting to be fed, aren't they? Physical food on the one hand, spiritual sustenance on the other, right? Their aims may seem worlds apart but both in fact have to rely on practical, well-tried and reliable methods to reach their desired ends." The Marquis looks at Annabelle as if she might have some comment to make. She however merely shrugs.

"You're not sure what those are? In which case, would you please listen carefully because you'll soon have to apply the information which I'm about to give you. First," he says, lifting up one finger, "they must plan everything well in advance. Next," he continues, lifting a second, "they must make do with whatever's close at hand – never sacrificing quality, yet showing as much craft and ingenuity as possible. As far as cooking goes, that's quite simple. You look in the larder, you investigate the refrigerator, and if the necessary ingredients aren't in the house, you just go out and buy them. When dealing with storytelling, the kind we're involved in, the kind in which you have to produce a story from scratch, on your feet as it were, it comes down to what you've laid in store." The Marquis taps the side of his head. "That's right! What's in there. Your experience, taste, and temperament."

"You mean," says Annabelle, transfigured by the picture which he has just presented to her, "that those stories – you planned them?" She pauses. "Of course! That would explain how come you had the objects the characters needed. You planted them there in the first place!"

"Precisely! The role which each ingredient was to play I had firmly in mind before we went into the compartment. However," the Marquis says, making a disclaiming gesture of the hand, "while planning beforehand's important, you mustn't suppose it guarantees results. Far from it. Each time a cook puts a concoction in the oven, there's a risk. No telling how it'll come out. Similarly only a fool'll boast that the story he's narrating will end up just how he thought it would. I'm afraid, Annabelle, that things rarely work out that neatly."

Annabelle nods as certain aspects of his at first confusing course coalesce into a more comprehensible shape. "You know, I'm beginning to recognize a pattern."

"And not a minute too soon!" the Marquis exclaims, as if on the verge of giving up. "Another aspect which is worth bearing in mind is to keep your methods simple. You haven't forgotten what started us off, have you? The needless sophistication to which that Brasserie dish was subjected. You'll find that simple fare done the simple way usually gets the best results. Which is why, as you're bound to have noticed," the Marquis adds, "the stories I related all had obvious settings, yes, and unashamedly made use of stock characters. As for attempting to inject a new lease of life into old materials, that's a particularly fascinating challenge. Nor should you ever waste anything. Whatever you come across that you find interesting, store it for future use. Just as vegetable peelings and offal give body to broths, so the odds and ends which occur all around you can be transmuted into the stuff of art."

"So that's what you've been up to!" Annabelle says, her earlier resentment turning to admiration. "You amaze me!"

"Thank you, *ma chère*. But my aim is not to dazzle you, rather to help you develop the skills with which you can amaze yourself."

"And how do you intend to go about it?"

"All in good time. Now that I've elaborated on key aspects of the course's process, it's up to you to meditate on the stories so that when we meet the next one, you'll have a fair idea how scenes fit together and ingredients combine. No, I haven't overlooked the third principle of creative cooking but I realize that you haven't yet come to terms with how sympathy works. Not that it need concern you unduly at the moment. Master the first two and sympathy will soon enough become second nature to you." The Marquis puffs contentedly on his cigar and looks up at the ceiling. "First though, Annabelle, I've got a task for you."

What is it to be now? she wonders, her stomach muscles tightening.

"I want you to choose the object for the next episode."

"Not that!"

"No shirking! You have to become responsible for the success of this venture sooner or later. I shan't always be by your side, telling you where to search for this ingredient or what method to use. Eventually you'll only have yourself to rely on to organize your creative cooking." The Marquis pushes the leather-bound suitcase over to her. "Here! Take it to your compartment. If, on the other hand, you feel that the course has become too much to cope with and you prefer to back out, then, Annabelle, I prefer to say farewell now. I'm sorry but as I can't bear to look failure in the face there'd be no point us meeting again." In a voice matter-of-fact and void of feeling, he adds: "If that's your decision, just call the Steward and ask him to bring the suitcase back to me. Otherwise" . . . He consults his watch. "Let's meet back here in, shall we say, half an hour?"

Having discovered more of the infrastructural processes of the course, and relieved that she can undergo this latest test of her talent in privacy far from the Marquis' unrelenting scrutiny, Annabelle grabs the suitcase, says goodbye to her companion, and heads for the quiet and safety of her own compartment.

CHAPTER EIGHT

The Steward crouches over his ferret. No escaping the fact that something mysterious ails the little creature. Unsure of its cause, Jules can hardly ignore the effect: Anatole has still not regained his appetite. Curled in his basket, he has left untouched every morsel of food which his master has put out for him. And no matter with what teasing, seductive, alluring, cajoling and even, in the end, irritated tone of voice Jules has tried to tempt him to fall on titbits, his furry companion has made not the slightest response.

"*Allez*, Anatole! Don't be so difficult," exclaims Jules. "Go on, have a nibble. That's all I bloody well need," he adds, *sotto voce*. "A ferret with a weak stomach!" He strokes the creature laid low, then, to cheer him up, decides to tell him what happened on his last foray through the train. "Listen to this, Anatole. This'll amuse you. You know I got a call. From number twenty-four, it was. Guess who I met there? A Milady! Yes, *mon vieux*, a real English Milady!"

To lend an objective base to Jules Pinard's story, as it is not in our interest to have doubts cast over the Steward's version of reality, we will momentarily break the narrative framework, borrow from the omniscient mode, and throw a retrospective glance at what the English Milady was doing instants before Jules knocked at her door.

Surrounded by the panoply of her pigskin baggage which, placed on the overhead racks, encircles her well-appointed suite, the English Milady reclines fully dressed on her bunk. Around her washstand she has placed a phalanx of toiletries, presumably so that these items of domestic colour will render her journey that much more homely. While apparently perusing an English fashion magazine, she still looks up every so often from some article to gaze at a small wooden box placed on the rack, an object which unfailingly evokes from her a series of deep long sighs. She is just giving in to a renewed burst of melancholia when the knock which she has been expecting comes. She smooths down her dress, puffs up her hair, repositions herself in the bunk to adopt her most regal manner, then, confident of her appearance, orders the caller to come in. When she casts her eye on the newly-arrived Steward who, with his fawning gestures and wheedling ways, has all the makings of a monument to continental obsequiousness, it is with the focus of utter disdain.

"What a woman!" says Jules, who survived the withering cruelty of Milady's stare by the simple expedient of being unaware of it. "Rich, dressed beautifully, and – just my luck – travelling alone. Everywhere I look I see diamonds, jewellery, furs. Oh!" Jules interjects, suddenly aware that in referring to that part of Anatole's anatomy which might end up shimmering around some admittedly cheap female's shoulders he has made the one faux pas the raconteur should always avoid, namely that he has attacked one of his audience's key fears and has thus weakened the trust that binds the bard to his customers. "Er, *pardon, mon vieux*," he adds lamely. "As I was saying, I go in, notice her baggage and the labels with her name on it – that's right! Your Jules never misses a trick – and ask her in my best voice: 'How can I, Milady, be of help?'

" 'So there you are, Steward,' she says. Her French, by the way, is *im-pecc-able*. 'And about time too,' she adds very tetchily. 'Didn't you hear the bell?'

" 'Surely Milady realizes,' I point out – rather pertly, I confess, yes, rather pertly – 'that if I had not heard the bell, I would not be here.'

" 'Humph!' she snorts. 'And not a minute too soon. See this window?' She points her finger at the carriage window. 'It is stuck.'

" 'Forgive me, Milady,' I say, 'you are mistaken. It is not stuck. It simply will not open. We may look old-fashioned here but we are actually very modern. This carriage, Milady,' I tell her, 'is fully air-conditioned.' "

There are occasions when the notion which the Marquis

revealed to Annabelle concerning the alternatives that surround every event makes us seriously reconsider how sound it was to grant the Steward such a prominent role in secondary scenes. For, to state it quite crudely, unless the conversation between Jules and the English Milady soon peps up, we will rue our decision to leave unprospected the Mistral's engine driver's potentially racy adventures. If only we had taken the trouble to visit his cockpit, what rich seams might we have exploited! If only . . . Might he, for instance, have revealed the changes that come over him when driving the express through a full moonlit landscape? How he and the train sometimes merge into a vast priapus pumping its fervent seed into the belly of every tunnel? Might he also have touched on how his intimate life lies in ruins because he, poor man, cannot approximate between the sheets the sensations which so deliciously pulse through him when at the train's controls? Might we have extracted these and a thousand other equally thrilling stories from him if we had only staked the right territory? But as we chose to dig elsewhere, we really must stop mourning the loss of this hoped-for and quite unassayed eldorado, and return to the duller soil of the scene at hand, a scene in which the Steward of the first-class carriages of the Mistral attempts to cheer his malingering ferret with his account of how he met a wealthy English Milady.

"'Pfaa! How dare you address me in that tone, Steward?' the Lady spits. 'I said I want it open, and that means now!'

"'I am sorry, Milady,' I answer, as courteously as I can, 'but it cannot be done. Not for you, not for anybody.'"

The Steward is about to produce another reason why the Lady's desires cannot become reality when there is a violent interruption. A swift, curly-headed, manic blur darts from under the bouffant canopy of the English Milady's dress and, in a cacophony of incessant and strident barks, attacks Jules.

"Then, Anatole, from nowhere up jumps this ugly little cur and, yap-yap-yapping, comes damn close to biting me. The next thing is that she joins in. What a racket! 'Down, Cerby, down, girl!' she screams. As if the bitch cared! Because, Anatole, it's of course a bitch! Round and round she goes while the Lady screeches: 'Stop it this instant!' and her pooch just keeps on running. In the end, you'll be glad to hear, it makes a mistake. A serious mistake. It sinks its teeth into my trousers and won't let go. So I take its ears and . . ."

After numberless encounters with creatures illegally sneaked on to trains under coat or hat or within basket by their brazen owners, so that on requesting a ticket, or leaning over to help some passenger, he has been bitten or bled, Jules has over the years perfected an effective, if brutal, method of dealing with such assaults. With a sweep of his left hand he grabs Cerby's right ear and gives it a twist so sharp and adroit that the bitch squeals and cowers away.

"Just a twist to her ear," says Jules, very pleased with his strategy, "that's all it takes and the fight is over."

Was it his deftness that appealed? Or the chivalry with which he bowed to the Milady after disposing of her beast? Or was it the fear of the legal pursuit which might have followed so obstreperous an attack which made the English Milady's spun steel turn so sweetly to gossamer? Whatever the causes for the change, she has indeed become, in the wake of her dog's behaviour, remarkably amenable, cajoling even.

" 'I am sure, Monsieur le Steward, that at heart you are a kind man. You will forgive the poor little thing, won't you? If I have said it once, I have said it a thousand times: that dog has no manners. But do not blame her. A dog is the sum of its master's training. And what a master Cerby had! Oh, yes, tonight you see her with me but, please, do not conclude because of that that she is mine. No, it was not I but my late husband who moulded her. Cerby was his doing, and look what he made of her.' Well, Anatole, while she has been speaking, her tone has become very soft. I tell you, that woman is a devil! Her eyes . . . ! Ah! What her eyes did to me! 'And since he died,' she carries on, 'she has gone from bad to worse. It is understandable. They were inseparable, my husband and Cerby, they loved each other. Why should I hide it from you, Monsieur le Steward? I am no substitute. I am not a good mother. What is more,' she points to the dog which has tucked itself behind her robes and is steadily if cautiously growling, 'travelling doesn't suit her either. Ah! The difficulties of being a widow! The strain of being alone! And now you tell me I cannot have fresh air in here. Very well, Monsieur le Steward, I shall take your word for it. Perhaps you would be kind and fetch me a bottle of *eau minérale*. The heat has made me quite faint.' 'Of course, Milady,' I say, delighted that she has offered me an opportunity to visit her again.

"Anyway, Anatole, when I return with her water, what do I see? The Lady has changed. She has made herself comfortable. Has put away her er . . . her . . ." – Jules narrowly avoids the pitfall – "things. And there she is, stretched out on the bunk. Even better, to prevent another incident, she has locked the bitch in the washroom. 'Monsieur le Steward,' she says, as I pour her a glass of water, 'it is such a comfort to know you'll be close by if anything happens.' 'Anything happens?' I answer her. 'Why, Milady! Nothing ever happens on the Mistral. Everything here is as smooth as crystal, as precise as clockwork. But, if you need me at any hour of the night, press the little button and I, Jules Pinard, will be there at your service.'"

Well aware that she has nothing to fear from this little lickspittle with his spindle frame, eager eyes and hangdog expression, the English Milady puts her right hand forward and allows Jules to cover it with kisses.

"Then, you know what, Anatole? I gave her the most delicate *baise-main* she has ever had. You should have seen how pleased she was. As for her perfume! Why, smell how it lingers on me. Here! What do you think of it?" asks Jules, pushing his right hand under Anatole's nose.

Still visibly off colour, the ferret refuses to appreciate Milady's perfume and turns sharply away. A response hardly surprising as the scent with which the Lady has anointed herself, while admittedly made from the secretions of rabbits' anal glands, is also laced with chemicals simulating the essence of natural oils, a performance which, hovering in alcohol and fixed in amber-gris, may do wonders to attract the bruter to the fairer sex but does nothing whatsoever for the polecat's nose. What does hold Anatole in instant thrall however is the odour subtly emanating from his master's other hand.

So little sensitivity shown to his amorous hopes makes the Steward particularly irritable.

"Not that hand, Anatole! That reeks of that disgusting dog." He wrests his hand away, then notices that the ferret has still not touched his food. "Eh! *mon vieux camarade*! Come on. Why are you so down in the mouth? Shall I get you something tasty from the kitchens? A slice of pork? A bit of *bifteck*? Please, Anatole, whatever you do, don't fall sick on me."

As Jules' visit to the Milady has endowed him with new-found enthusiasm for life, he is able to summon a certain amount of energy with which to try to console his little companion. Unfortunately his attempts fail to have any effect for the ferret, quite unimpressed by the Steward's inept ministrations, remains coiled in the same seemingly despondent and semi-lethargic state.

CHAPTER NINE

The borders of the landscape are blurred as the moon is being strangled by a thin scarf of fog. Tongues of fire leap from the engine at the fast-flowing fields and illumine them in an instant's light. Wherever railway workers have perished, victims of wartime raids, landslides, or carelessness, tiny reliquaries, their flickering candles an open chancre in the flesh of the night, can be seen at the side of the track. These details Annabelle devours with an appetite whetted not by some vague yearning for naturalistic objectivity but rather to fill in time before tackling the task which the Marquis has set her. For haunted by the fear of failing, she cannot make up her mind which object to choose. Indeed, as if each carried a deadly virus, she keeps them all at a safe distance, quite unable to distinguish among them a prime candidate.

A silver watch, a pack of cards, an amulet, a golden crown. Eventually deciding to brave the objects, she runs her fingers across them, using the same method which she remembers the Marquis applying. With the immediacy with which sound rises from a needle in a groove, each one produces its own sensation. All, however, are unpleasant. Repelled by their uncanny power to evoke episodes which she was certain she had sealed in the strongrooms of her memory, she decides that if these are the linchpins of future episodes, she prefers to have nothing to do with them. And yet something indefinable – could it be her curiosity? – makes her try her luck once more. On this occasion, as her fingers graze the gilded cardboard crown, she comes across a feeling which does not disgust her but which recaptures a dimly remembered episode from her distant childhood.

Two silver candleholders stand on the pale linen which covers the dining room table. The heavy velvet curtains are drawn tight against the winter's cold. It is dinner time. The members of her family have already taken their allotted places around the table. Who is present on that particular evening? Her mother and father, of course; Omer, her bewhiskered uncle, and Geneviève, her lace-trimmed aunt; and yes, her three cousins, Paul, Frédéric and Gaston. Paul, the eldest, his upper lip a light shade of grey, has been pressganged into a brand new brown suit; while the twins, Frédéric and Gaston, appear equally grotesque in their over-starched sailor outfits. Her parents sit at each end. What is her mother wearing? Could it be the dress she reserved for special occasions, a full blown, faintly roseate silk that trailed down, as if she hankered for an age when corsets were worn and white gloves were essential evening wear? As for the dress Annabelle had on that night, she has no precise memory of it, only of the pain its tight-fitting party-time starchiness produced round her waist.

Once the main course, a *gibelotte de lapin*, has been savoured, and the wine-sauce-smeared plates have been taken away, as it is Twelfth Night the *Galette des Rois*, with its fragrant golden pastry and the succulent aroma of its marzipan filling, flanked by two gilded cardboard crowns, is brought into the dining room on a large white plate by Olive, the maid. Olive, a stout Breton peasant who fled the harsh routine of agrarian life to end up pinafored, properly turned out and subserved to the duties of a bourgeois household; Olive who, Annabelle recalls with a shiver, stripped one afternoon in her tiny room, and showed the fascinated child the shapes she said would one day swell on her own body, sets the dish down in the centre of the table, takes a step back, and breathes in the festive spirit from which her function excludes her. Everyone greets the circular pastry with "oohs" and "aahs". Chanting the self-evident refrain: "*C'est la galette, c'est la galette!*", the twins repeatedly clatter their forks on their plates until a brace of resounding slaps, Uncle Omer the boy on his left, Aunt Geneviève the child on her right, swiftly puts paid to their frolic.

Awed by the event, Annabelle stares as her father slices through the pastry, serves his sister, his wife and his brother-in-law. Then at last it is the children's turn.

"You all know the rules, now, don't you?" her father asks them.

"Of course we do!" Annabelle's cousins cry, while she, bashful, simply nods.

"So don't forget: whoever finds the bean must say so straightaway," he adds, keen to avoid a tense period during which the bean might lie impudently concealed in a child's mouth.

"Yes, yes!" they repeat and quickly dive onto the splendour of the pastry, cutting through it in search of the bean whose magical power might turn the tables on their usual subservient state and confer on one of them, if only for a few hours, the dizzy title of Monarch.

"As for you, Geneviève, don't go breaking your dentures on the bean, will you?" Annabelle's father teases his sister, who, as is her wont, takes the jibe with complete equanimity. Meanwhile, in their grating sopranos, her twins intone: *"Qui sera le Roi? Qui sera la Reine?"*

Volumes to be read off the faces of the company: apparent indifference, longing, expectations, even bonhomie. For her part Annabelle's mother savours the pastry, which she herself cooked, with the gourmet's readiness to find fault. Her husband, in the meantime, eagle-eyes his guests in case anyone dares to dissimulate the bean. Aunt Geneviève, usually a paragon of the bland response, momentarily lets her guard down and makes no secret of the pleasure things sweet bring her. Annabelle has just taken her third bite of the rich flaky mix when her face splits with joy. She rolls the little object in her mouth, licking it free of marzipan and of pastry. Here it is! She cups her hand, her tongue sets the bean in her palm and proudly presents it to the company.

Grand Vizir, Chamberlain, Janissary and paterfamilias all rolled into one, with a solemnity for which he is justly famous, her father rises from his place at the head of the table, takes one of the crowns, and places it on his daughter's head. Abashed yet delighted, Annabelle stares round the family circle. Her moment has arrived. Who is to be her consort?

There is Paul, but his dark eyes frighten her. The twins, but the yank they gave her hair before dinner and their general meanness rule them out. Her father, yet somehow he, like Uncle Omer, about to tuck into a second helping, does not seem eligible. No, there has only ever been one choice. Slowly, decisively, Annabelle points to her mother and says softly: *"Je choisis Maman."*

A medley of reactions bursts across the table. A chortle from Uncle Omer, an expression of bemusement from Aunt Geneviève, a salvo of ridicule from Gaston and Frédéric, while their brother, who had secretly hoped his young cousin would consecrate him, casts a look of utter contempt at her. Hasn't she understood? asks her father, taking on the additional role of judge and attempting to silence the clamour of outrage. She has to crown a King, not a Queen. Although flushed, the little girl does not change her mind but repeats: *"Je choisis Maman."*

Such stubbornness incites the twins to attack with redoubled vigour a target which, generally reproved, they are sure they can wound with impunity. "Don't be so stupid, stupid! Don't you see? You have to choose a King, a King!"

Annabelle, isolated on all sides, fails to prevent the formation of tears. Amazed at her child's vehemence, her mother for a few seconds does not react.

"Come here, child," she eventually says softly, "come to Mummy." Touched by the strength of her daughter's sentiment, she quells the baying company with a curt wave of the hand. Annabelle, her face fixed in a grim stare, walks round to the other side of the table, removes her own crown, and gently places it on her mother's head. Then, racked by the re-eruption of tears, she buries herself among the cool folds of her mother's dress.

Reaching for her handbag, Annabelle opens it and finds a handkerchief in it. She dabs her eyes, extracts the cardboard crown from the Marquis' suitcase and folds it along its crease. Once she has shut the suitcase, she leaves the compartment with it.

Bathed in the pallor of a gibbous moon, the countryside parades a panorama in which a patchwork of smallholdings vies for attention with vestigial clumps of woods, sanctuaries for the rare game which has survived wintertime's massacre. All around hundreds of inefficient fiefdoms, the shards of former estates cut up by the legislative knife, provide classic illustrations of the misguided foundations of the French laws of inheritance. Occasionally a farm which has not yet been hacked to bits by its inheritors flaunts its intactness as if it were somehow immune to the rapacity of progeny waiting to destroy it. Turning away from the window, the Marquis sets aside his arguments for primogeniture and nods to his apprentice as she comes in.

Numerous pieces of paper, all covered in the Marquis' handwriting, are spread across the table. He makes no move to hide them. Each sheet, Annabelle logs, bears a title. A rather crumpled one is named "The Golden Key"; another, clean and intact, "The Silver Watch"; on a third the soubriquet "The Pack of Cards" appears. There is even one that bears the title "The Silk Scarves". It is with a shudder of recognition that Annabelle comes across the one most appropriate of all: "The Crown". Fresh from having consulted the suitcase, she needs no prompting to recognize that these one-page memos refer to the objects which she saw in it.

"Welcome back, Annabelle," says the Marquis.

"Seems I'm still in the running."

"I never doubted you'd stick with it." The Marquis points to the cardboard crown which she is holding in her hand. "Mmmm. Interesting."

"It took me quite a while to make up my mind."

"Really? And what made you decide? A pleasant feeling?"

Annabelle nods.

"Feelings are the rhythms of the mind. The fact that you're beginning to trust yours is a sure sign of progress." He once again points to the cardboard crown. "So that's what's going to solve the next story, is it?"

"I'm not sure. It made an impression on me, that's all I can say." Annabelle frowns. "I'm surprised you didn't guess which one I'd come up with."

"It's quite true that I chose the first object with which we traded. As for the second, if you remember, it was a combined effort: my phial, your blood. But even if I did provide the objects, that doesn't alter the situation: the crown is still your choice." The Marquis flicks through the papers on the table and takes the one entitled "The Crown" from the pile.

"Any idea what this is?"

Annabelle shrugs.

"A list of relevant ingredients." He hands her the piece of paper. She reads it.

"You'll see there that I've jotted down notes. Reference points you could call them. In the case of 'The Crown', it designates where we'll be heading to next and what we're likely to find when we get there. It's a list of characters and of locations. Generating those is easy."

"Is it? How do you go about it?" asks Annabelle.

"If you're interested in a historical period, it's no problem recreating it in your mind. You have to pay close attention to details but, apart from that, it's a simple enough imaginative process. The period existed so there's no shortage of books illustrating it. All you have to do is concentrate, tune into its frequency, and let it seep into you. Sometimes you can slip up. I must say, Annabelle, that I found the speed with which you caught me out in the last episode very impressive. A silly mistake really."

Annabelle cannot recall what the Marquis is referring to.

"Remember when you wandered around the mausoleum, you came across a number of fake objects?"

"Oh those! Yes! They were particularly disconcerting. I couldn't work them out at all," she replies, choosing to make no mention of the aesthetic revulsion she felt when confronting fakes in an otherwise sumptuously convincing decor.

"Call it inadvertence on my part, coupled with a certain fascination for trivia. I should have done better research and not used details which I had glimpsed in the backgrounds of cheap films. Which goes to prove how essential it is that you envision everything in your mind's eye down to the last detail before you set an episode in motion. Not that you're out to pass a historical exam. No. What you're after is to evoke a convincing atmosphere, an atmosphere within which your aims – whatever they happen to be – can be reached. The crucial question now, Annabelle, is: what role will this vital ingredient, this little cardboard crown, play in the elaboration of the general recipe?" The Marquis smiles wrily. "It may surprise you to hear that I don't know. I haven't even begun to concoct these notes in my head. And, to be honest, I'm not that concerned about it either, because – and this is central to creative cooking – I trust my creative abilities completely." The Marquis shakes his head. "Although you've confessed to me that you don't trust others (a sad fact), trusting your own creative powers must become a priority. Because as soon as you do, you'll find that they'll respond automatically and that they'll give you the results you seek."

Annabelle hands the piece of paper back. Her companion folds it, places it in his jacket, and takes the dice out of his fob pocket. As her interest in the mechanics of the illusions which he has sprung on her has been renewed, she weighs them and looks them over as if she expected them to be loaded. But, as far as she can tell, there is nothing extraordinary about them: no flawed corners, no smoothed edges, no carefully weighted facets. Resigning herself to their apparent innocence, and obeying his silent instruction, she casts them.

Across the table they bounce. They have almost settled when, as if imbued with a last gasp of energy, they skittle about for a few more seconds before displaying a two and a six.

Annabelle glances up at the Marquis. Seemingly signalling his approval of the results, he nods. Finally, without so much as a word being spoken, proof surely of the regularity of the routine which has developed between them, they leave the Marquis' compartment and wander down the corridor.

The search for compartment no 8 turns out to be very tiring. Every so often Annabelle slows down to wipe her brow with her handkerchief. She is about to sigh with relief at how little has distracted her attention in the perfectly ordinary corridors down which they have wandered when, pushing past the dusty bellows which lead from one carriage to another, and entering the next one, she notices a series of shiny copper portholes built into the walls half way down on the compartment side. As these are at head height, her curiosity gets the better of her and she peers into the first.

In it she sees a man of about fifty, dressed in a dark formless suit and wearing thin clerical glasses. He is sitting at a desk in what seems to be a finely furnished, wainscoted library and he is busy reading a book. In comparison with some of the scenes she has experienced, she might have regarded this one as only slightly strange were it not for the fact that the studious figure keeps repeating the same gestures. From the jerky movements of his head she realizes that as soon as he has reached the bottom of the right hand page and has started to turn it over, he is forced by some unknown impulse to return to the top of the left hand page and to read it all over again. A scene all the more pathetic for the surprise it appears to deal him each and every time. Unable to make any sense of this cameo, Annabelle moves over to the second porthole.

This particular exhibit is either out of order or has nothing to show, being completely blacked out. However, the moment that Annabelle leans on the polished copper porthole, perhaps triggered off by her weight, it suddenly bursts into life, revealing a scene in which another clearly cultured individual, whose clothes and heavily bewhiskered, middle-aged face place him somewhere in the *fin-de-siècle*, squats in what seems to be a richly endowed museum. Before him, a vast wooden frame set on the floor. In it ceramic fragments have been arranged in neat piles. Neat the piles may be, but it is evident that their ultimate reconstruction has eluded the scholar. For try as he might, no piece will fit any other so that, as he attempts to latch on to judicious combinations yet fails to find any fragment which might match up with another, he becomes more and more angry, throwing pieces over his shoulders, until in the end – this melodrama takes only a few seconds to reach its dramatic finale – in a fit of pique Annabelle sees him jump up and down on the glazed remains of civilizations which have refused to unfold their secrets to him. The moment that this scene has played itself out, the lights once again go out, and remind Annabelle of those little ten-centimes seaside kiosks which used to line the parade and which, just as they were supposed to reveal some ribald scene, would instead with a cruel click cut out the hoped-for payoff.

Only one more porthole in the corridor. It is with a fascination magnetic in its intensity that Annabelle stares through it. Its set is lit like a courtesan's parlour. In it a tall, dark-haired and unusually beautiful Creole, her eyes opalescent and fiery, seems enrapt in the whirlwind of a musically unaccompanied dance. A strange dance and one whose main motion consists in her tearing manically at her ample bouffant dress – a dress which, Annabelle notes, is made up of large strips of manuscripts sewn in a ragged yet at the same time remarkably graceful gypsy garment. Why is she doing this? Annabelle wonders. Does it hurt her? Is she in a trance? Or is she stripping to get at some terrible itch? Whatever the reason, the more she tears at it, the more she discovers that it can never be torn to shreds, and that even though her lace shift is occasionally visible under the dress, there are more garments underneath, each covered with quotations and literary excerpts, influences from which it would appear she would dearly like to but cannot escape.

This scene is so entrancing that Annabelle could have continued to watch it, and might indeed have been held forever in the thrall of those mad gestures had the Marquis not seen her immobilized before the porthole and quickly walked across to her. He shakes her and tells her that she should only spend long enough with the images for their basic message to filter through. Their message? asks Annabelle dully. Their basic message? Yes, surely it is obvious that they are all saying the same thing, the Marquis adds. That nothing is more pathetic than ignoring one's origins, failing to finish anything, or indeed lacking control over the forces that have shaped you.

Dragged away from the scenes about whose nature the Marquis seems to have complete knowledge without having even glanced into them, Annabelle, who had wondered whether they were part of a set or were totally unrelated, and particularly irritated to have been fed their apparent *raison d'être* before having had a chance to work it out for herself, decides to ascribe only marginal significance to his explanations and, in a moment of pique, puts them out of her mind.

Beyond them, thank goodness, there is not much to look at, for she and the Marquis are now walking through carriages which boast neither windows nor passenger compartments, let alone further portholes. No, there is really not much to look at – or at least there wasn't at first! For, true to its aim of keeping her forever challenged, yet also able to recognize the repetitions within its flux, the train is presently proposing a bold new feature, one which it takes Annabelle a few seconds to assimilate but which she then takes into her stride.

For, amazingly, the train is changing shape. God knows why but it seems to have taken a sudden fancy to the maritime and to have consequently sprouted – in a fit of imitativeness – all the layers and decks proper to a ship. With the result that the travellers are forced to negotiate steep ladders, leap manholes, and even, for a short but highly unpleasant moment, to wade along a corridor inch-deep in bilge. The worst part of this transformation, Annabelle perceives with dismay, is that the accompanying atmospherics are also those of a sea-going vessel heaving and falling amid the tumult of a rapidly rising swell. She soon feels queasy and has to hold on to the corridor rail to steady herself.

Leading the way, the Marquis notices her difficulties and

shouts at her above the roar of the wind and the waves to cheer up. This won't last much longer! True, *rites de passage* are excruciating, but, he adds, they've a part to play in undermining the enemy of their eventual success. Yes, in no time at all they'll put expectations to flight.

Annabelle, her head spinning, her mouth acrid with the early warning signs of vomit, quite out of phase with his philosophical soundings, tries to keep moving but has to stop as her stomach is once again heaving. She stares stoically at the brine-soaked flooring, retches, and waits for her nausea to dissipate. She has taken three deep breaths in the battle against faintness when she hears the Marquis' voice rallying her, shouting that he has found compartment no 8. It's here! Come on! Just a few more steps! *Courage!*

Although the exacerbated pitch and yawing of the whole carriage have blurred her vision, she can make out the compartment's number plainly enough.

While the noise of the storm-racked sea rages about him, and the vessel upon which they have seamlessly embarked pitches and rolls frenetically, the Marquis runs through his notes, closes his eyes and concentrates. Presumably, Annabelle guesses, images are now welling up in his mind's eye and he is constructing a period, putting everything in its place. Resorting to base caricature, perhaps to amuse her, the Marquis suddenly gives Annabelle a seadog's smile, accompanies it with a roar of enthusiasm, pushes the door open, and ushers her in.

The instant they walk in, however, both travellers are shaken about so violently that they immediately spin out of control and are thrown to the floor. Panicked, helpless and bruised, Annabelle tries to pick herself up. But the rough cement floor is coursed by a jolt so strong that she cannot gain a safe foothold. She quickly looks around her, endeavouring to discover where they are and what has happened to them.

It appears that she and the Marquis have stumbled into, then been tossed around, an unknown space whose tall black walls curve towards a distant, dark horizon. For yes, he too has fallen onto the ground a few feet away. Above her, only the chasm of a starless sky. No marks anywhere, nothing remotely related to the train, not even to the sounds and movements of the sea which only a moment before had almost made her faint. She strains her eyes, becoming accustomed to the surroundings' lack of definition. Apart from an occasional and faint iridescence, and distant booming sounds, the world into which she has been thrown is completely black.

Her companion, as if shielding himself against some vicious sound, has placed his hands around his head. Annabelle has to admit that to witness him, usually in such complete control, so powerless is unnerving. What can have gone wrong? She has just asked herself that question when a mass of coloured whorls rises up before her, as if some hidden projectionist had started his scrotal-shaped reels a-whirring and sent a shimmering and continuous montage of images crackling before her eyes. And what a baffling variety of shapes they are! Ball lightning spinning in slow motion; waves flurrying like a miniature aurora borealis; even a lacework of white fibres no sooner espied than disintegrating. She next distinguishes faces coming out of the darkness, faces which, like half-whispered truths, appear all the more ominous for being hazeous and vague. As for the Marquis, she can make out his shadowy form a few yards off, crawling on his hands and knees, searching, she hopes, for the way out of this confounded place.

Against the indistinct yet occasionally intensely luminescent background, Annabelle, squatting on a surface as mobile and as slippery as a whale's back, is confronted by a succession of incorporeal beings. At first they evoke no clear-cut emotion in her except for slight unease as they loom out of nothing and almost immediately return to their void. Some, she realizes, noting their periwigs, powdered hair and pancaked faces, seem to hark back to the *ancien régime*. Others on the other hand issue from an indeterminate period: their clothes are not recognizable and neither their jewellery nor their make-up gives them away. They sidle to and fro yet seem curiously oblivious to her presence. A number, she senses, scrutinizing their flaccid faces, seem vice-ridden. Others look horrifyingly virtuous, their eyes filled with a knowing intensity, as if they had long ago discovered how to avoid the decay of sensuality. Faced by these images, Annabelle is overwhelmed and closes her eyes. How is she to escape? How is she to conquer the fear that has made her throat so dry? Nor is it any consolation to discern that the Marquis is

147

having as bad a time of it as she is. Clearly she cannot rely on him to help her out for he too seems quite out of control.

Nor is that all. She soon discovers that there is worse, far worse to come. For what assails her next are images of her own self. These to begin with have no fixed shape but are rather more like echoes of unpleasant memories, requiring only the briefest sensation to remind her of the episode to which they refer, each harping on some embarrassing incident all the more loathsome for being part of her most carefully-closeted store of secrets. Nor, she recognizes with a start, is this her first confrontation with them. For only a few minutes before, while she was fondling the other objects in the Marquis' little suitcase, did the same sensations not ripple through her, yes, the same irksome sensations?

She has grown, if not used to, at least less mortified by their cruel assault on her sensitivity when, a few yards to the side, perfect in every external detail, she catches sight of another vision: her own reflection. No mistaking it. There she is, crouching on the floor, her dress hitched up, her legs wide apart, a lewd expression on her face, her fingers visibly inserted into her moist crescent. Hardly has this obscene sight made its appearance then curtseyed away when more apparitions arise, yes, other moments of abandon. Flagrantly catwalking before her, a *catalogue raisonné* of shame. All this occurring before her eyes and – oh no! she thinks, staring in the direction in which she last saw her companion – before her once confident and all-knowing guide!

But at that particular moment the Marquis is neither confident, authoritative, nor immune to the torsions and pressures of the chamber. Still unable to keep his balance or to stand up because of the pulses that keep throbbing through the floor, he has crawled backwards and forwards and looked for an issue to this damnable chamber. With no success. Why, O why, did he open this of all doors? he berates himself. Why did he land them in this limbo area? And with what terrible results! For he has now been stripped of his carefully-constructed poise and revealed quite as helpless as his apprentice.

What if, he considers, biting his lips in anticipation of further shock, what if, in this ghastly dispersing room, Annabelle were to find out something, were indeed to find out everything, about his plans? How can he prevent it? How can he keep his wits about him when everything is in flux and so disorienting? How can he check the plot when in this constantly fracturing space nauseating notions are rushing through his mind, are being given shape, may even try – God forbid! – to address Annabelle directly? There is nothing, nothing at all, that he dreads more. Before that appalling possibility befalls him, he must get her out of here, and quickly!

Could it be because he dreads it most that his fear in no time at all produces the perfect illusion? Slight, svelte, white teeth gleaming in the darkness, the Marquis catches sight of the construction, is astounded at how very meticulous it is, then shakes with anger. For, in the near distance, the boy – the bait which lured him to his pitiful state – is standing there, stripped to the waist, and his excruciatingly alluring eyes are trained on him the way they were in Marseilles, the way they were in that dingy back room. There he is, teasing, amused, ready to tell Annabelle everything if the Marquis does not behave, does not pay his dues, does not lure her on towards her doom. God! Will he ever get those gestures, those expert hands, out of his mind? Will he ever forget how they took him apart, releasing him from a sordid dream, only to cast him into a nightmare that has still not ceased?

The boy is smiling. He points towards Annabelle who, her back to him, has not yet seen him. Is he about to talk to her? Pinned to the ground, lost in the shadows, the Marquis watches helplessly as the figure makes his confident and insolent path towards her.

He tries to call out to her. He, Jean-Loup, her companion, is over here! She must not be taken in by what the boy tells her! But Annabelle no longer knows where the Marquis is and, anyway, his voice refuses to carry that far. He waves his arms again, calls out to her louder. Don't listen! I can explain! Don't trust him! He's just a phantom! A shabby trick! But no matter how much he gesticulates and how loud he cries, it makes no difference: she remains out of reach. Meanwhile the boy is nearing her. The bastard! moans the Marquis. In a few seconds the boy could well reveal everything he has been planning, everything he has in store for her.

Thank God for that! thinks Annabelle, attempting to combat the noise and the stench, both of which are sporadically erupting features of this nameless place. For there, before her, is the Marquis. He has at last pulled himself together and is coming towards her. So he is going to lead her out of this infernal mess after all.

The Marquis, aware that if he does not immediately stop the boy, his tormentor, everything he has so far achieved could be ruined, somehow finds the energy necessary to pull himself up and to thrust himself at the phantasmagorical being.

To Annabelle, what happens next is totally inexplicable. From one angle she notices the now poised, confident Marquis leaning towards her, no doubt about to lead her out of this limbo. Then, just as she is about to take his hand, from another angle, another Marquis, looking wild and frenetic, jumps on the first and throws him to the ground.

The Marquis strikes the boy. Annabelle watches as the two men wrestle on the ground. While the Marquis batters his antagonist, Annabelle stares in disbelief at the sight of the grotesque duplication: her companion split into two, locked in combat against himself.

Impaled on a violent and pulsating burst of light, the boy reels back and collapses on the floor. Before Annabelle's eyes, one of the Marquises falls to the ground, arcs upon himself and disintegrates, leaving behind only a smell reminiscent of sulphur.

Had it not then been for the survivor of this fantastic struggle coming over to her, holding her in his arms, and helping her to her feet, Annabelle is sure that she would have fainted. With no other means of support, she accepts his hand and leans on him.

The Marquis, seizing Annabelle, half blinded by the glare, drags her to one side of the space. The floor once again shakes. He retains his balance. She, however, taken aback and unsteady, slips and falls down. He helps her to her feet and, his hand buttressing her against further shock, reaches the rough edge of a wall.

While rugous, the wall is otherwise seamless apart from a tall rusticated arch which dominates it. The entrance to the arch is blocked by a large slab of rough masonry. The Marquis examines the space around him and concludes that, for all the wall's unbroken exterior, they cannot have come into the chamber via any other route. But how is he to dislodge so monumental a slab? He will just have to apply pressure to it.

Once he has pushed against the slab, he is gratified to feel it heave to and reveal behind its bluff and grainy exterior a narrow wooden door. He walks up to it and wrenches it open. In front of him a dark corridor. Now that he has found the way ahead, he returns to Annabelle, puts his arms around her, and helps her out of the chamber. A few more steps, one more door this time effortlessly opened, and they are back in the familiar corridor of the train. He then slams the door shut on the shifting forms which had almost swamped him.

Thankful that the ordeal is over, the Marquis stands against the side of the shiplike corridor still shaking under the buffeting of the storm. To have had his stratagem so nearly uncovered – and by the very demon who seduced him so many months ago! To calm himself, he brushes his suit down with both hands, ridding himself of dust marks. He can see that Annabelle has sufficiently recovered from her own difficulties to go through the same perfunctory grooming process. Unfortunately, even after he has dusted himself, he feels no calmer, for the same question keeps whirling in his head. How could this disaster have happened? Did he not apply the right methods? Or did the dice lie and send them to the wrong compartment?

He stares at the number on the door, fingers its copper plate, examines its worn surface, then curses: "What the hell! I could have sworn . . ."

It has only taken the Marquis a second to understand what has gone wrong: the copperplate-engraved number has its left hand screw missing. It has slipped! He turns the plate round to its proper position. No, this is not – nor ever has been – the number 8. The now righted sign on the door displays a completely different symbol. How could he have been so stupid? For plainly inscribed on the copperplate is not the number 8 but the symbol of infinity.

So that is where they landed! he exclaims. In the centrifuge of infinity within which their every turbulent thought and the objects of their most unavowed desire were expelled from their hiding place and were then granted a dream life. Under the influence of that sudden illumination, the Marquis starts to pray. He prays that Annabelle did not see, did not hear anything which might have ruined his plans. For she must remain in the dark and the reality of his stratagem must also remain unknown. What he cannot deny is that the disaster was caused by his own failure to check procedure properly. The very notion he has been drumming into her is the one of which he has fallen foul. If only he had not been so confident. If only he had not expected the number to be what it had seemed but had checked it out, this would not have happened.

He glances at his apprentice. She is still in a daze. How should he handle his quandary? Dupe her? Make up some excuse explaining away the whole ghastly experience as some clever teaching device? All for her own good, he might say. Now she can appreciate the dangers that lurk in every corner of the course. Surely she didn't think he had lost control? What an idea! . . . and so on and so forth. After only a moment's contemplation, and aware that his apprentice is just as dependent on him as before and could not even make her way back to the compartment alone, he decides not to pretend, not to lie, but to admit his mistake.

He calls Annabelle over to look at the door, points out the wrongly positioned copper plate to her, and swivels it round so that she can understand how the mistake occurred. Then, in spite of his initial desire to be honest, unable to prevent himself bluffing, he bursts into laughter.

No, Annabelle is sorry but she can neither understand how a slip in a digit could have overturned the logic of the course nor does she find the Marquis' laughter comprehensible. For her thoughts are embroiled in fears and her mind is concentrated on a single topic: she hopes he did not glimpse her self-images, the appalling ones which paraded themselves before her. She hopes he did not see her crouching down, her naked legs splayed, her fingers inserted . . . However hard she tries to convince herself that he could not have witnessed anything, that he wasn't even near her at the time, and that, anyway, he does not come out of this disorienting incident in a particularly good light, she still feels exposed. And it is with that self-absorbed, self-punishing notion whirling in her mind that she leans against the sides of the corridor and stares out of the window, sickened, angry and vulnerable.

Immersed in their own thoughts the travellers do not exchange so much as a word. Annabelle yearns to turn back to the safety of her couchette and sink into the oblivion of those thin, crisply starched sheets. The Marquis meanwhile prays that she will not become a liability but will remain completely captivated by the course.

As there is no point remaining before the scene of their

failure, the travellers press on down the corridors, searching for the correct compartment. Somewhat comforted by their shared bout of muteness, they tread through passageways which gradually lose their shiplike nature, becoming as neutral as the corridors of institutions, high-ceilinged, dim and spotlessly clean. It is in one of these, unendingly long and with an easily roused echo, that they come to a halt. Here, unmistakeably – its copperplate firm, its symbol utterly unambiguous – is the compartment they have been seeking.

"Bearing up?" the Marquis asks Annabelle, parading surface tenderness to screen his dismay at having fallen so far short of his designs.

"Just about," Annabelle answers, still unsure whether he did or did not witness her shame. "Is it this one?"

"Yes, this time it is," answers the Marquis.

Recognizing that, if he is to rekindle the trust which the last whirlwind experience must have almost snuffed out, he must be at the peak of his form for the coming episode, he does not rifle through the pieces of paper but confidently leads the way into the compartment which it has already cost them so dear to find.

CHAPTER TEN

Complete darkness. On either side of her Annabelle senses the chill walls of a low corridor. The surefooted Marquis has already marched on so far ahead that she is no longer sure where he is. Catching sight of a silver light seeping from an uneven crack at floor level, she guesses from the breaks in its razor-edged silhouette that he is standing in front of it. Next she hears a series of scratching sounds: the Marquis seems to be fumbling for something on the wall's surface. Something elusive, for she hears him curse under his breath then administer a sharp blow which echoes down the cramped corridor. His efforts fortunately are not in vain: a creak of ancient wood ripples past her and, sensing the slow movement of a massive block swinging away from her, she realizes that her companion must have located the trigger to a secret door. Once the block has come to a halt, and the Marquis has walked past the breach, she herself follows.

What confronts her is a large and dimly lit bedchamber. A bedchamber filled with a wealth of oaken pieces. There are buffets, sidetables and wardrobes and, most imposingly, a monumental four-poster with curtains of green brocade which hang limply from beams whorled like barleysticks. An aristocrat's room, Annabelle, standing on its threshold, decides. She steps into the room and pursues her inventory of the scene. In a corner, erect, a silver coat of arms; hanging from a wall a rack heavy with bejewelled swords; on a massive chest carved out of mahogany, a set of gilt-framed maps on which South American conquests are illumined in gilt. These and other details she manages to make out by the meagre candlelight which coruscates from a crystal chandelier.

She immediately warms to the room, appreciating the sparkle that descants off the heavy silver goblets, the sumptuous colours of an oriental carpet lying on a table, and the sideboard on which fruit vie for attention with an indecorous haunch of venison bleeding on a pewter plate. And so perfect, so retinal, is the scene that for a second she dares not move in case its surfaces turn to ice and its objects revert to two dimensions.

The Marquis glances in his apprentice's direction, clearly seeking her opinion of the scene. She nods to prove to him that the decor's imaginative richness has indeed impressed her. That he has spared no expense is obvious. But there is something else: his attitude has changed. Yes, he has dropped his supercilious manner and is treating her with what might well pass as complicity. Why? she wonders. On account of the danger they have just shared? Because she witnessed his vulnerability? Or is his surely devious mind planning something to her disadvantage, a bitter pill for which his recent affability is no more than the sugaring? However pleasant his change in attitude might be, unable to discern its cause she decides not to lower her guard.

Nor are those the only changes which she has detected: she has to admit that she also feels different, no longer an ignorant bystander wide-eyed before a total mystery but well able to appreciate that everything surrounding her is not some easily put together arrangement, but rather results from the care that the Marquis has expended on it. And it is a very appealing set. She admires the silken, embroidered coverlet on the bed, the trefoiled design of the chimney's dog irons, and the ceiling's finely drawn stucco of fruit-and-flower motifs. Then, perhaps strangest of all, there is the excitement which has sprung within her, an excitement all the more baffling when she recalls that only a few moments before she was shivering from the turmoil encountered in the infinity room. After examining this feeling rather more closely, she isolates within it a sense of belonging, the kind which she recognizes with embarrassment she might experience inspecting her fiancé's home for the very first time. An irksome discovery, to say the least. Struck by its incongruous nature, she considers it for a few seconds before coming up with an idea of how it might have arisen.

She is in the Marquis' room – that much is undeniable. His creation. His effort. His world. Nor is it any exaggeration, as he makes his usual survey around the set, picking up objects, gauging the quality of the props, and assessing every detail, to imagine that he is parading it all off to her, asking her with the looks he keeps throwing at her whether she could be happy here. And although to equate the exhibition of a fictional room with the sensations that commonly attend matrimonial engagement seems farfetched, it does go some way towards illustrating how experience need not be contained within strictly defined categories but can blur at its edges and seep from one context to another, influencing areas which might otherwise seem distinct. So why not confess it? She is flattered to what lengths he has gone to build a highly decorated set for her. Flattered and not a little worried for she is aware that this elaborate scene is not simply for show but is also designed to make her come to grips with the mysteries of the creative process.

Annabelle wanders deeper into the cavernous and poorly-lit room. Behind her, the Marquis continues to examine everything to make sure it is the way he has planned it. She meanwhile tries to grasp what her Master has intimated: namely that everything before her is a construct, an artifice as craftily assembled as any dress held together by invisible seams, scalloped hems, and double yokes. Yet the curlicued four-poster and its fabric of mock foliage, the monumental furniture and its broad-faced marquetry are so well designed that she cannot conceive how they can have been put together in a hurry. Nowhere can she detect the slightest flaw which might betray how Jean-Loup has produced so consummate a set. And no doubt Annabelle, walking wide-eyed around the room, would have mulled a little longer on the advantages that attend modernism's foregrounding of materiality, had her thoughts not been interrupted by a very poignant sound, that of a grown man crying.

She turns and glances around the room's dim interior. Then she notices him. In a far-off corner of the room, clothed in a diminutive doublet and draped in a servant's apron, a bearded dwarf. Even stranger, not only does the little man seem sunk in his thoughts but he also has a feather duster in his hand and is absentmindedly dabbing furniture. And yes, the sounds of crying do come from him.

Annabelle's first reaction is to look around for the Marquis. Typically he has again left her to face the situation on her own. She cannot see him anywhere. Her next reaction is one of extreme embarrassment. She should not be here. She is intruding. She should leave the unfortunate to his sorrows. But it is too late. For the dwarf, sensing that his privacy has been flouted, pivots round and, tears running down his bearded cheeks, stops dusting the furniture to stare at Annabelle with unfeigned amazement.

In a safely shadowed segment of the room, the Marquis, surveying a scene he had previously only encoded on paper, is gratified to see how well the transfer has worked. The dwarf has been transplanted from his early afternoon menu-changing to a setting suited to his role. And although Annabelle is not privy to this information, and so might seem at a disadvantage in relation to the sources and dynamics of artistic creation, she is in truth no more disenfranchized than a theatrical audience which, enchanted by a protagonist's monologue, will never be told that the sentiments portrayed are a crude reworking of the playwright's hatred for his mother. For nothing else matters but that Annabelle appreciate the diminutive figure's dramatic worth. But what is his worth? And who, and what, is he? A servant about his domestic duties? Perhaps. A member of a noble family? Could be. But then, why stoop to such base activity? The cut of his clothes anyway suggests a better class than that of a menial. Yet the apron and the fact that before being interrupted he was dusting the furniture do add up to a contradiction.

Well-versed in the arts of stage managing, the Marquis tracks down the two chairs on which the travellers always sit while listening to the character's tale, and places them conveniently near the centre of the room. Satisfied with the arrangements, he beckons Annabelle to join him.

The dwarf does not move from his stance but watches the two strangers take their seats. Once the Marquis has made sure that he is comfortable, that Annabelle is at her ease, and that his sense of timing is as good as it will ever be, he begins his narrative.

"Our apologies. We hope we haven't interrupted your duties."

The dwarf, whose tears have disappeared without leaving the slightest trace on his cheeks, reacts as if he had been struck full in the face. "Urggh! Don't say that word!"

Annabelle is startled to hear that his voice is deep and melodious, contradicting the commonly held notion that dwarfs always speak in squeaky tones.

"What do you mean? What word?" The Marquis asks, as if taken aback.

"Hope, hope! That's what! Didn't you say hope?"

"Yes. And what of it?"

"Don't you know that he who hopes is damned?"

"On the contrary. The scriptures teach us that he who hopes is saved."

The dwarf seizes the tenor of the Marquis' argument and, in a voice obsequious yet unconvincingly humble, cries: "O wisest of scholars! O most cunning of orators!" Slipping into the register of contempt with which he is obviously more at ease, he continues his lament: "But don't you try to trap me in your sophist's web! I know what hope did to me! Took me to the very gates of hell, that's what! And left me there," he exclaims, pointing to his apron, "in this pathetic state!" Swiftly remodulating his voice, he adopts a truculent tone: "Who are you two anyway dressed in those strange costumes? Some po-faced doctor and his fair amanuensis?" He scrutinizes Annabelle then, with a wave of the hand, asks: "How did you gain access to the Duchess' hacienda?"

"That's simple," the Marquis answers, pointing to the sliding panel in the wall. "We found a way in."

An expression of profound amazement runs across the dwarf's features. Yet it is not the mouth of the secret passage which has mesmerized him for his eyes are fixed on the two travellers. Striding up to them he cries: "By all the Saints' holy bones! What is this filth? I thought Court life had shown me every vice, every obscenity! Yet I never met there anything which prepared me for a sight as vile as this. Look at you," he aims his diminutive index at them, "glistening like fatted pigs made ready for the ovens!"

Certain perspicacious researchers have stated that there are only so many paths a story can take. It is therefore inevitable that a tale as heavily determined by formula as this one will reveal its mechanics more than most. This explains, perhaps even excuses, the fact that it has happened again. Obedient to the sympathetic process by which the object which the travellers seek is somehow lent a material form, the Marquis' and Annabelle's faces are now covered in olive oil. Yes, Annabelle can feel the bright yellow liquid exuding through her pores. Nauseated by its acrid smell, she reaches for the second

158

handkerchief which she has tucked in her sleeve and wipes her face in the hope of staunching the flow. Nor is the Marquis coping any better with the mess for his shirt is already sticky with the slowly seeping fluid.

"You mean the oil, of course!" the Marquis answers the dwarf. "I shan't hide from you that that's the reason why we're here. My companion and I have travelled a very long way to seek a cure. And believe me: we've tried everything, absolutely everything, though so far, sadly, without any success. I quite realize," he adds, scraping a few drops of oil from his face and spattering them on the floor, "how horrible all of this must seem. But don't, in God's mercy, turn us away! We desperately need your help!" he calls out, glancing at Annabelle and silently urging her to add her plea to his.

Annabelle, ready for her one-liner, this time delivers it on cue. "Yes, we really do need you!"

"But please don't think that because we're asking for your help," the Marquis says, standing on his dignity, "we've come empty handed. Far from it. We're not beggars. In fact we've brought you something which should make you very happy. Yes, the answer to your problem."

"What!" the dwarf explodes. "You burst in on me like thieves in the night! Drip oil on the floor I've just swept! Beg me to help you! Then have the audacity to tell me you've the answer to my problems! Ha!" He defiantly places his hands on his hips. "And by what devious means have you gathered so much about my life, eh? Go on, confess! You're magicians, aren't you? Worshippers of the Evil One!"

"We are not magicians!" says the Marquis, quick to scotch a slur which, in the superstitious epoch in which he has placed the story, might lead them all too soon, and without a decent defence, to an inquisitor's scrutiny. "As for the story of your life, the few elements which we know we heard at Court."

"So, who are you?"

"We are merchants. And like merchants the world over, all we seek is fair trade. Help us and I promise you that we'll do our best for you."

"Fair trade? And what rare and precious commodity might you be after?" snaps the dwarf, his voice brimming with suspicion.

"A gourd of your finest oil."

Uncertain whether to regard this statement as a joke or as an insult to his intelligence, the dwarf waves his hand at the oil still running off the strangers' faces. "Oil! Are you mad? Haven't you had your fill?"

"Indeed we have. However, to apply the ancient and well-proven principle of fighting fire with fire, it is vital that we lay our hands on some of yours. If our efforts are rewarded, with it we'll make a tincture which should – with God's help – rid us once and for all of this terrifying pestilence."

The dwarf scratches his head. "And how am I to profit from this extraordinary exchange?"

"We'll show you how you can escape from your unhappy situation," the Marquis answers, his arm encompassing in one broad movement the bedchamber, the apron and the dwarf's dejected state.

A broad lecherous grin smeared across his face, the dwarf stares at Annabelle. "So that's what's in the balance, eh? Your health against my freedom." He rubs his chin. "Very well. If only for the sake of your fair companion, I'll listen to your request."

Unless I have failed to grasp the procedure, thinks Annabelle, the dwarf is now going to insist that we listen to his story, then he'll embark on some credibility-stretching exercise which will somehow involve the crown. In the meantime, what should I do? Piece together the Marquis' storytelling methods? But what confounded methods? Settling back in her chair, she decides that no matter what happens, she will not let herself be seduced by the dwarf's tale but will instead investigate its pattern and its textures as detachedly as if she were watching a master cloth cutter to determine the secrets of his craft.

It would appear that Annabelle has predicted the substance and the rhythm of the procedure with accuracy for next the dwarf discards his duster, puts aside his apron and jumps on to the chest, the better to dominate his audience.

"Before I hear of your woes and travails," says the dwarf, examining his captive audience from the height of his makeshift dais, "I will first relate to you how I, Alonzo, once the King's most trusted courtier, fell from grace. And why it is that you see me reduced to this sad and servile state."

Having just introduced himself as a courtier and revealed the trust invested in him at Court, Alonzo now initiates the

160

imaginative process on whose wings Annabelle hopes to explore the intricacies of his past and the mechanisms of his storytelling technique.

"I was born the child of a misalliance."

Carried by the dwarf's introductory words, Annabelle hovers past the swirlings fogs which once again greet her in her mind's eye, until little by little she is drawn towards a clearing which appears out of the depths of the hazeous atmosphere. There she comes across a sparingly lit, baroque-furnished set, the finely appointed bedroom with which Alonzo has decided to begin his tale. For dispensing with all expository details, the dwarf has inserted her directly into the fabric of his tale.

As the structure of the storytelling process has become rather more familiar to her, Annabelle realizes that she can now cope quite adequately with its various strands. She can for instance appreciate the echoes and differences within the voices which the Marquis has set up. Among those the easiest to place is, of course, the dwarf's own voice which, from its very first provocative statement, has guided her along, and will no doubt continue to do so. She decides to name it the puppet. Then there is the apparently neutral narrative which organizes the story, which makes it flow. Presumably the Marquis', so, yes, why not call it the puppetmaster's, doing? Finally there is her ability to interrupt the story with her own comments and observations: the audience's reaction before the puppet theatre. It is with pleasure in the subtlety of her achievements that Annabelle considers that she has distinguished at least three important strands to the storytelling.

The bedroom slowly comes into focus. Warning herself against taking too much notice of its decorative riches, Annabelle instead gives herself more time to assess the methods which are propelling these images through her mind's eye. One question in particular irks her: is she picking up the method's warp and woof accurately? Or is she imposing meaning on them quite arbitrarily? Hard to say, except that her analysis of the situation has a logic to it which, even if not correct, does make sense. Unfortunately, she concludes with sorrow, she cannot maintain this structural level of analysis any longer, for the pace of the story is fast taking her over and is demanding all her concentration. And however hard she tries to react against its sensuous pull, she cannot prevent herself surrendering to it.

For its central image the scene eventually settles on the chamber's ample double bed. At its foot, Annabelle notices, there stands a large linen-draped table on which what appear to be the kind of tokens two families might bestow on the union of their newly-wed children have been placed: an embroidered coverlet, a doll in child's clothing, a bouquet of posies, its stalks tied with red ribbon, and a handpainted maiolica tile embossed with the likeness of St Margaret of Antioch, patron saint of expectancy. Most becoming in her bridal nightdress, a young lady is sitting upright on the bed's distaff side, her hands neatly bordering the sheets, her eyes filled with tears. Overwhelmed by the ignominy of the empty place next to hers, she suddenly buries her face in her hands and gives in to an inconsolable sob. Well might her dark features and sharp eagle silhouette have destined her to pose for Velasquez had her life not been so tragically curtailed. But rather than give the story away, we should explain why this maid, on her wedding night, is all alone, and to where her bridegroom has intemperately disappeared.

"It was not until her bridal night," comments Alonzo in a tone of voice lightly laced with shame, "that my mother discovered that the man she had wed was not what she had thought him to be."

At the same time that the young lady's tears are soiling her virginal wear, in one of the many corridors that cuts across the ground plan of the Escurial, reasonably well lit along its length with a series of spluttering torches, an effete young man is lounging against the rough masonry of the wall. Such an unprepossessing locale must have special significance as a place of nocturnal rendez-vous for there soon appears at its other end a typical product of Court life, an over-rarefied, whippet-featured, dark-haired, goateed nobleman, his small and foppish frame encased in lavish material and his plumed hat set at a rakish angle. This character visibly on the hunt is none other than the absent bridegroom, Alonzo's legal father. Half way down the corridor, he sidles up to the young man and embraces him while his hands explore how pleased the catamite is to see him.

Some months later the young lady herself, her well-proportioned features encased in a full black dress, a lace mantilla over her head, wanders down a corridor startlingly similar to the one in the last scene except for being somewhat better lit and for having rather more commodious rooms leading off it. A courtier, no longer young yet making up in finesse what his salt-and-pepper beard shows he has lost in vitality, gallantly awaits her arrival by the side of a half open door. As she approaches, he rises, puts his arms round her waist, and takes her into an adjoining room which, with candles, a light collation, and a fine Andalusian wine, he has made most welcoming.

"Consolation, I am glad to say, my mother soon found elsewhere. For her beauty and discretion, allied to the abundance of spare rooms in the Palace, provided her with plenty of opportunities to pearl a rosary of lovers."

Guards shiver in the face of the cold winds which drive off the plains of La Mancha. At the foot of the tall, decoratively crenellated walls, a horse-drawn carriage slowly rolls out of the Palace courtyard. Her face covered with a veil, the darkly-dressed figure of Alonzo's mother stares out of one of its windows.

Might Alonzo's tone, Annabelle muses, the rhetorical formality with which he is mediating his narrative, be an attempt to lift his mother's base behaviour on to a higher moral plane? Certainly the facts which he is conveying – aristocratic adultery – are unequivocally sordid, and it can be no easy matter endowing them with a semblance of dignity.

"I am sure that my mother," Alonzo continues, "showing caution at all times, put the methods of prevention to proper use. One day, however, she discovered that they had failed her. Already three months with child, she visited her husband in his rooms and informed him that in due course there would be an addition to his family. She added that, mindful of her reputation and refusing to become one more rumour in a Court rank with gossip, she would journey down to her country estates where she would ensure that all necessary arrangements for the child's safe arrival would be made. Delighted at being offered the fruits of union without having had to stoop to the distasteful act of sowing, her husband accepted her terms with alacrity, asking only to be informed of the happy event."

The bedroom is in the grip of a mood of controlled urgency.

Tightly garbed in her white costume, the midwife orders about the various chambermaids and servants, sending them scurrying for steaming water, more linen, and balm to rub into their Lady's swollen stomach. Soon the moans from the bed redouble and the birth process begins. As the light outside grows dim, new candles are placed at three corners of the room, the last being left in the dark to ease the escape of bad spirits. And it is on the stroke of midnight that the child at last emerges into the tense and expectant audience.

Then comes the longed-for moment. Cleansed of blood, the child is presented to his mother. No amount of scrubbing, however, can conceal from the Lady that her child is dreadfully stunted. For his face is as wizened as a homunculus', his limbs are as crooked as if accursed, and his body is covered in a thin down of reddish hair. The Lady reacts with uncharacteristic violence, utters a loud and strident scream, and refuses to be calmed. Nor will she heed the midwife's soothing words that babes are sometimes born looking wild, but manages in between spasmodic bouts to cry out that the disgusting creature be taken from her, she cannot bear to see it, ah! this seed of Satan, this broken form, how cruelly she has been punished! Once the midwife has staunched her shouts with a well-administered slap, and her heaving frame has been stilled, and the frightened servants have crept away, and the Lady's maid has been told to have a peasant woman fetched from the estate, quiet begins to reign once more over the severely disturbed household.

In a small antechamber adjoining the bedroom, the Lady's maid closely questions the peasant woman. Will she take the child and raise it as her own? The peasant woman nods. Does she understand that she is never to speak of this to a living soul? She mumbles her agreement. Does she realize that she is fortunate to be offered such favourable terms? Her rough garb reeking from the livestock she keeps, her face hidden in the shadows, awed by decorations of a quality she has only seen in churches, the woman meekly submits. Satisfied with her answers, the Lady's maid takes the child from the wicker basket in which he has been lying, hands him to the rustic, and gives her a handful of gold coins which shimmer in the light of a candle.

The sun's first rays have only just pierced the clouds and the red earth is still veneered with hoar frost when the head groom, rounding from the stables on to the courtyard of the hacienda and leading his mistress' favourite brood mare for a walk, is greeted by a terrible sight. For directly below her bedroom window, on the dusty paving stones, her head bloodied, the Lady's silk-gowned body lies in a curiously crouched position.

"Cursed with shame, convinced that my misshapen body had been a punishment which God had visited on her, my mother took the sole path which she could see before her."

Years pass. The noble Lady's death has long ago become part of local lore, a thousand stories haunting her untimely end, some whispering of the midnight visit of the Evil One come to collect his promised son; his rage on discovering that she has given him away; and how, his eyes avid embers, his tail forked and fiery, he finally flings her out of the window with his own hands. Now a small, sturdy lad of eighteen, Alonzo is standing against the barren and sunparched background of his adoptive mother's smallholding. How very unsuited he is to the monotony of farm life is evident for while the peasant woman scurries back and forth across the farmyard with feed for the hens, he stares at the sky, recites the verses of a song he has just composed, and seems quite unaware that the earthenware pot in his hand is spilling its contents on the dusty ground.

"She had of course been sworn to secrecy. But the woman I had called mother all my life could not keep quiet for ever. One day . . ."

Alonzo stands in the middle of the courtyard in a daydream. Eh! Good for nothing! the peasant woman shouts at him. If he doesn't get a move on and start to earn his living, it'll be no supper for him! But the only sounds to reach the dwarf are the chords of a melody playing in his head. Well, is he going to get on with it? she bawls at him. How many years is she to feed a mouth that does nothing but sing? Exasperated by his self-absorbed immobility and unable to control herself any longer, she at last gives full vent to her anger.

"She screamed that I was a little bastard, a child of shame. That my mother was a whore, a noblewoman who had disgraced herself. Let no one say that she had been responsible for a monster like me! No! She had not given birth to the Devil's spawn."

Is it the stridency of the peasant woman's voice or its message which resonates through Alonzo's being? And indeed what child, stifled by its dependence on dreary parents, has not sometimes dreamt that he is the son of a Princess, that his grandfather, the King, has never ceased looking for him, and that the whole Court still mourns his mysterious disappearance from his cradle? And now here it is, from the foul woman's own mouth, a close kin of that great myth revealed as God's solemn truth! As soon as Alonzo has digested the peasant's words and realized that he does not belong to her humdrum world after all, he drops the feed he has been carrying and speeds towards the farmhouse.

"It was so clear! If the old witch wasn't my mother, then this dirty, dreary hovel wasn't my home either. I was free, yes, I was free at last to go my own way!"

The dwarf rushes round his tiny quarters, gathers his clothes and his guitar, and places them on a sheet he has spread out on the floor. Glancing round the room, he suddenly grabs a pot and, with a great shout of joy, flings it against the wall. Hardly have its fragments scattered about the floor when he ties the sheet into a bundle, grabs it, and flies out of his room. "Eh! You God-forsaken fool! What do you think you're up to?" the peasant woman screams as he races past her. "Get back to work immediately! You aren't done with your tasks yet, scum that you are!" But as he becomes a smaller and smaller speck on the horizon, there is nothing left for her but to curse the disappearance of her one and only help.

Intoxicated with his new-found freedom, Alonzo ambles along a dirt track cracked by the unyielding intensity of the summer sun. He has barely journeyed for an hour when he reaches a crossroad and is there confronted by an unfamiliar yet heartening sound, the strumming and ululations of a band. For, just beyond the crossroads, taking refuge from the noonday glare under a grove of cypresses, a troupe of Strolling Players is sprawled around the semi-circle of their three gaily painted caravans. It takes the dwarf only a few seconds to realize that they are a rough, tumbledown lot, rich in native cunning and no doubt adept at surviving on their wits.

The Strolling Players catch sight of Alonzo and can hardly believe what the wind has blown their way. Fancy that! A little man all on his own! What's he doing here then? Hey, cripple, they shout, come on! show us a trick! Pull out your thing! Can it fill a girl's gob or make her hunger for more? And it is with that initial burst of good cheer that the company sparks itself off.

Facing the menace of the chanting crowd, Alonzo wonders what he should do. After a second's hesitation, he sets his object-swollen sheet down on the hard dusty ground and performs a pirouette. As soon as he has completed a cartwheel and a handstand, he arches his back to show the company the bizarre articulation of his double-jointed body. His simple grey clothes have become tinged with the dust of the track and his face is covered in sweat when he strides over to the sheet, parts its greyish folds, takes out his guitar and, strumming loudly, starts to declaim verses from one of his own songs. His impromptu show at an end, he turns to the ragged company and honours it with a deep and ceremonious bow.

Astounded by the vivacity of the dwarf's performance erupting like a dust cloud out of the heat of the midday sun, the Strolling Players fall silent. Then one of them, a gaunt fellow with a straw hat, throws the little man a gourd of wine. Catching it in full flight, the dwarf uncaps it and squirts a jet of scarlet into his mouth. Next a red-headed young hoyden saunters up to him, kneels by his side, takes his sweaty brow in her hands, and gives it a kiss. A cry of delight runs around the camp fire. The senior Player, impressed by Alonzo's skill, spreads his cutlass-scarred face into a grin, strides up to him, and offers his hand in friendship. He then looks at his companions, who are now better disposed towards the wanderer, and formally invites him, surely as much a child of fortune as they are themselves, to share God's fate with them. Alonzo looks round the toothy faces, the dirt-encrusted clothes, the children in their brightly-coloured hand-me-downs, and smiles. Bowing to the senior Player, he gratefully accepts the invitation. Hardly has the sound of the company's cheering died down when the band strikes up its interrupted tune and soon has everyone dancing.

"The moment they realized that my size and skills could work to their advantage, the Strolling Players invited me to join them. How right they were! For I had played with them in the open spaces of only a few market towns when the troupe, on the strength of its growing reputation, received a summons to play before the Court."

The Jester's costume, variegated, spiralled, and whorled with colourful textures, is symbolic of the myriad attitudes and roles

167

which this most misunderstood of figures, envied, despised yet held in awe, must adopt to soothe and balance an audience's mood. An ancient costume which fits Alonzo perfectly as he sings against the finely furnished background of the Court's Great Hall.

On that particular occasion the King is himself in attendance and has taken his customary seat in the centre of a large oaken dining table at which a mixed company of courtiers, clerics and noblemen have also gathered. So loud is the general carousing, however, that neither Alonzo's song nor the Strolling Players' accompaniment can hope to rival it.

It is on the King's frame, wholly attired in black apart from a bold white ruff, that Alonzo feasts as he tries to counter the assembly's indifference with his best songs. An attempt that at first meets with no success. The dwarf has just finished his repertoire when, to the courtiers' amazement, the King applauds the performance and thus imposes an awed silence on the revelling company. Astounding! one courtier mutters to another. Our own dear Monarch, usually so dour, actually clapping! Well, well! Hasn't the little man charmed his way to our King's heart? If heart he has! answers the more cynical of the two, sipping at his wine.

In the small hours of that same night, troubled by some over-rich food which he has had, the King wakes up, sweat copiously dripping off his brow. O cruel longings! O base desires! How he has tried but failed to dispel the temptations those wicked dream women flaunted before him! He must immediately send word to the Palace Prioress to have her novices say a mass for the peace of his soul.

Once his flowing white robes have absorbed his sweat, and his heartbeat has resumed a more natural pace, torn between the tedium of telling all to his Father Confessor or the threat of slipping back into the sensual depths which had been torment-ing him, the King suddenly settles for a third option. He therefore pulls the cord next to his bed and when his page arrives, he orders him to have the dwarf who sang at supper, and his instrument, brought to him forthwith.

Rudely roused from his straw pallet in the stables which he shares with his fellow Players, Alonzo follows the page to the royal bedchamber. And there, at the foot of the bed, his guitar quietly fretting, he performs for the King and lulls him into the now demon-exorcized abyss of sleep.

"So very sweetly did I sing that night," says Alonzo, "that the King saw fit to name me first among all his minstrels."

In the oppressive trough of a hot afternoon the Monarch summons Alonzo for a private audience in one of his smaller chambers. His face marked by a mournful look, as if he could never for a moment forget the corruption at the heart of Creation, the King, bold upright on his throne, his hands set in a tall thin arch, his eyes half closed, questions the minstrel on his deformity.

"Now although it had always been my Master's keenest wish to spy on his courtiers, he knew well that were he to loosen them from their leash, his guards' mastiff manners would rouse everybody's suspicions. And so one day, as I sat at his feet, the King asked me if someone as small as I could go anywhere and hear everything. I told His Majesty that that was indeed one of the few gifts with which God had blessed me. When he heard this, he seemed very pleased. As you can imagine I needed no further encouragement. If it were the King's command that I go everywhere and hear everything, then so be it. Gladly would I serve him in that modest capacity. And that is how, you see," says Alonzo, aiming a rare comment at Annabelle, now quite rapt, in spite of her analytical self, before his tale, "I became the Monarch's eyes and ears."

How does Alonzo spy for the King? With the finesse of a butcher's knife, separating the offal of rumour from the carcass of fact. And is it not with guise innate that he peeps through keyholes, laces maids' drinks, unbuttons mercenaries' tongues, gathers the venom of rejected favourites, and even, on occasion, extracts a pungent secret from an overfilled commode? Yes, and his bag of intrigue has soon grown so big that it is high time that he spills his rich pickings before the King.

Alonzo saunters into the King's antechamber and there requests the privilege of an immediate audience. He is promptly informed by the officer on duty, a moustachioed and bluff-mannered Captain of the Royal Guards, that he cannot go in. But he is expected! he insists, he has an important message for the King. To the Captain, veteran of a thousand bloody skirmishes, the sight of this only recently promoted entertainer demanding to be allowed before the Monarch is laughable. And he has just picked him up by the scruff of the neck and is about to send him on his way when the King's Secretary, whose history

169

of the Mozarabic period has won him great esteem and whose angular and ascetic mien would have made a perfect study for El Greco's pastelled yet fiery palette, enters, having overheard the commotion in his adjacent study. Seeing the dwarf hanging like some ragged war trophy at the end of the soldier's fists, he orders the Captain to release him, and tells Alonzo to wait and to be still for the King has asked that a letter be given to him. He enters his study and returns a few seconds later bearing a document marked with the Royal Seal. With a bow he hands the document to the red-faced and somewhat less cocky dwarf whose outrage has been slightly doused by this outer mark of respect. Informed that it is the King's express wish that he peruse the document in his own rooms, the dwarf leaves the antechamber, though not before he has waved an irate fist at the Captain who dismisses the gesture with a burst of barrack-room laughter.

"As I went up to my rooms, I kept asking myself why the King had refused me an audience."

Once the Strolling Players have fulfilled their role as the vehicle through which Alonzo's talent could be conveyed from a rural retreat to a place of great opportunity, void of further *raison d'être*, they are sent on their vagrant way. Which makes good sense, thinks Annabelle. Characters take up space, consume energy, need looking after. No point carrying dead wood. The moment they have enacted their potential, best be rid of them so as to be free to deal with more important issues. Not that this new recruit to the academy of minstrels has been treated with especial generosity. True, he has been granted quarters but they are cramped, poorly-furnished, and huddle directly under the Palace's rafters, a prey to the screeching of the wind, open to the worst downpours, and a broiling house at the height of summer. It is in that small space that Alonzo, cross-legged on his grubby bed, now sits, an incredulous expression on his face, reading and rereading the King's letter.

He begins by reciting the preamble in which the glorious nave of His Majesty is upheld by the thousand and one pillars of his titles, each paraded in proper order. Unlike more experienced officials who rapidly weave past these architectonics of nobility, Alonzo peruses them all very carefully. After passing in review the decorative devices which invoke the Monarch's origins, he discovers that the body of the letter stresses that he should never forget that he is first and foremost the Monarch's favourite minstrel and that the King will consequently search for truth in the words of his songs.

Perplexed by the missive, the dwarf puts the manuscript on to the bed and stares abstractedly at the numerous and nameless maculations which have spattered the ceiling. He has twisted the King's written words through every possible combination, ferreted through them for the most unlikely revelations and is indeed about to shatter his guitar against the wall and run down to the kitchens to vent his frustration on the pleasing proportions of a little serving maid who has a delightful way with her tongue when he suddenly understands what it is his Master has been conveying. Favourite minstrel! Search for truth! The words of his songs! Of course! It is so obvious. Why had he not thought earlier of the squalls that periodically whip his Master's imagination into a jealous froth? Now that he has snapped the neck of the mystery and can suck on the warm marrow of the King's hidden meaning, Alonzo jumps on his pallet in such excitement that it soon disgorges tufts of straw on to the floor from its poorly stitched seams.

Having survived the first of the King's tests and shown his ability to read between the lines, the time has come to write between them too. The first song whose words he chooses to rework possesses a traditional melody so that its familiar tempo fails to rouse the courtiers from their customary indifference. In contrast to his lazy retinue, however, the King pays the song the keenest attention. And as he harvests the clues which his minstrel has planted, ears of treachery, spoors of slander, and gathers them in the barn of his rancour, his eyes narrow and his expression becomes colder than the most bitter winter wind.

"Of course all who attended the banquets heard the songs which I performed. Yet none but the King listened to them and recognized what I had placed in them."

Hemmed in by stern-faced guards, his feet manacled, his clothes ripped, a man kneels on the stone floor of a dark chamber and begs for mercy from his impassive King. For here, uprooted from his own foul-mouthed anonymity by the dwarf's covert methods, is a courtier accused of slander.

"Armed with the knowledge which I secreted in my songs, the King dealt traitors blows of the utmost ferocity. Yet no one at

Court could fathom how he was able again and again to rip the mask from the face of deceit.''

With care Alonzo clambers on to a recess at the top of one of the Palace's circular staircases. From there he moves to its cobwebbed end where a loophole opens on the early evening sky. He squeezes past it and delicately manoeuvres on to an outside ledge. The wind lashes the Palace gables, whipping sand and dust into fast flowing whirlpools, half blinding him as he edges towards a window along a narrow way. By holding on to a jutting drainpipe, he manages to swing through a window before falling into the antechamber of the one apartment which he has long wanted to search.

"Curious to know what guilty secrets the Chamberlain's life might yield, I decided that I would one evening pay his chambers a visit.''

As befits his high estate, Duke Ferdinand lives in considerable luxury. The furniture is gilt along its edges, the decorations are inlaid with mother-of-pearl, and the crucifix that hangs over the marital bed is a masterwork in porphyry. Driven by the single-minded aim of uncovering damning evidence, Alonzo sets about his tasks. With relentless efficiency he swoops round the room, darts into drawers, fingers through furniture, and leaves almost no object untouched. Although deeply engrossed in his work, the rattle of a key in a nearby lock does not fail to rouse him to the proximity of danger. Quick-wittedly he rushes to a wicker basket standing in a corner of the salon, removes its cover, makes space among the soiled linen it contains, and dives into it. And as he slowly sinks to its malodorous depths, he peers through the slats of its weave to discover who is about to enter the chamber.

In spite of the wickerwork's interposing screen, Alonzo recognizes the sturdy build, the face bruised by warfare, and the close-set eyes famous for having once seen the enemy in countryside which scouts had reported deserted. The Duke's heavy tread resounds around the room. Taking a small key from around his neck, he stops next to a desk and unlocks the one drawer which Alonzo had failed to rifle through. From it he extracts a leather purse, its load of coins betrayed by a high-pitched jangle.

"My visit, I am glad to say, was not to be,'' Alonzo adds, ''a disappointment.''

Duke Ferdinand has only just sat down on a chair by his desk when there is a knock at the door. He orders the caller to come in. Enters a sinister creature. A three-days' growth of beard softens features otherwise as sharp as a kriss yet cannot palliate the small unfeeling eyes. Nor can his obsequious manner obscure hands whose sinewy length look as if they have throttled many a throat. The Chamberlain remains seated and gives the lanky character his instructions. These are few and precise. On the Feast of the Assumption. Once the meal has ended. A sharp knife in the heart. Escape via the high windows. A horse will be waiting. Ride to the frontier. Here, he adds, showing the felon the purse, is half the amount. The rest to be paid when the act is done.

Alonzo, imbued with the gravity of the situation, lifts the lid of the basket a fraction and gazes with fascination at the face of a rogue vile enough to contemplate assassinating his Master, the King.

The Duke opens the leather pouch and places a number of gold coins in the palm of his own hand. Without further ado, he then replaces the coins in the pouch, gives it to the cutthroat, adds a few words invoking God's fortune upon the project, and bids him leave. The door creaks closed and the assassin's footsteps recede. The Duke is left alone to ponder the reforms which his hoped-for reign will bring his downtrodden country and the love his future subjects will eternally bear him. Confirmed in his decision by a posterity whose warm acclaim he can already imagine, he rises from his seat and hurriedly leaves his chambers. And such is the haste with which he departs that a handkerchief slips from his pocket and drops with a catkin swirl on to the floor.

The Duke's footsteps have long been muffled by the length of the far-off corridors when Alonzo decides that it is now safe to crawl out of the basket. He walks over to the handkerchief, picks it up, and examines the Chamberlain's ducal arms, finely embroidered at its centre. Unsure what to do with it, the dwarf nonetheless puts it in his pocket. It is a curious fact that, for a reason which he cannot grasp, the way out of the Duke's chamber appears to be more difficult to negotiate than the way in. However, after he has wriggled his rump like a rat's caught in a sewer, he manages to squeeze through the narrow frame of the antechamber's window and to climb back via the drainpipe into the circular staircase.

173

The plot which he has uncovered is so heinous that Alonzo realizes that it is crucial that his song be both memorable and exact. The first tune into which he tries to fit his words of warning is arch and the result consequently discordant. The second, a martial hymn, sounds better when altered yet he also rejects it in case a courtier discerns the transposition of its well-loved stanzas. After numerous attempts into the hours of the night, during which his guitar has echoed around his quarters, he finally settles on what seems to be a perfect musical vehicle, a little known tune devoted to the frisson of forbidden love. Picking his way through its lascivious lyrics, he subjects them to subtle changes. And when the song's reconstruction is at last complete, he prays that it will be able to convey the terrible danger facing the King.

"There was little time left. The Feast of the Assumption was to be celebrated in two days. And so I went to work immediately and, with good fortune, was able to fit new words to an old tune."

The Assumption of the Virgin Mary, one of the major apocryphal journeys, is, some say, only paralleled for dramatic power by the Prophet Elijah's in a chariot of fire. It is highly unlikely however that the carousing courtiers have their minds on either of these numinous events even though Murillo's somewhat banal depiction of the Virgin's rise has been specially erected for their edification on an easel close to the High Table. Their thoughts and their palates are more probably focused on the cress soup, the slices of pork, and the freshly-caught and finely-filleted fish bathing in the wine-laced sauces for which the Court cook is deservedly famous. And although it is true that certain scholars have detected in the impulsive decisions of potentates the eructations of the gustatory tract, the constricting pains of the hernia, the constipation that game produces, the diuretic quality of certain fruit, and the general indisposition that the badly or overfed gut may produce on the mental faculties, it is not our task to explore that particular avenue. For, as far as we are concerned, Palace revolutions and cabals are an inevitable by-product of the concentration of power in one hand, and the Chamberlain is thus no more guilty of unwitting impulse than of greed. Moreover, as this is a highly seminal scene, now is not the time to jeopardize the build-up of tension with treatises on the effects food may or may not have on a state's intestinal affairs. We should instead return to the banqueting hall and concentrate on how Alonzo, the one man privy to a perfidious possibility, is going to try to save his King.

It is a measure of the King's boundless grief for the ten-year-old loss of his wife that the chair at his left is always left empty on important feast days. On his right he has placed his trusted Chamberlain with, next to him, his gracious wife, the full-bosomed and dark-haired Lady Isabella whose love for her husband is a legend throughout the land. The Feast is proceeding at a goodly pace and everybody appears to be enjoying the event. Sole among its participants the King's minstrel, sitting at a nearby table with the other court retainers, seems to be detached and yet watches the principal actors with a vigilant eye.

The Feast is nearing its end and courtiers are already exchanging wisdom on the various *digestifs* which they favour to ease down their fare when, without any warning, Alonzo springs up, his guitar in his hand, and, bowing before the King, stands before the assembly and proceeds to sing a serenade. Not only is the tune obscure but the little melomanic interest it might have engendered in the early part of the feast has long since been drowned in wine. The entertainment is therefore greeted with considerably less enthusiasm than the servants' refilling of cups; and in spite of the minstrel's efforts conversations soon resume their usual vigorous pitch. A bonhomie that the Duke visibly does not share, for his face has become livid and his eyes seem incensed. The cause of his fury, Annabelle immediately realizes, is the minstrel's unexpected turn. For this ridiculous intervention seriously threatens his timing. And his hired hand is due to act any minute. When, O when, will this hobgoblin cease his dreadful singing?

"I had not been sure at first. Was this really, I wondered, the right moment to intervene? One glance at the Chamberlain's face, however, showed me that I was indeed acting in good time."

Fine. Point made, Annabelle comments, noting the scene's emphasis on one of the Marquis' cherished principles.

The King leans over his barely touched food and ponders the meaning of Alonzo's lyrics. The muscles in his face grow taut. Is this possible? He again listens to his minstrel's refrain. Corruption at the heart of his Kingdom! He downs his goblet. He is threatened from within! Worse! Not only is the traitor apparently supping with him tonight but he is also sitting – God forbid! – at his right hand!

While the dwarf's song rises and falls across the Great Hall, the Duke sits in a state of utter helplessness. How can he warn his hired hand to stay behind the curtains where he must even now be waiting, dagger in hand, and doubtful what to do?

The King discreetly turns to the Captain of his Guards and whispers a few words in his ear. The latter leaves the hall to return a few seconds later accompanied by three soldiers. Falling in behind the Chamberlain's chair, the armed party seizes the Duke and pins him down to prevent an escape which, from the expression of complete confusion which overwhelms him, was unlikely to have occurred. Alonzo rounds off his song and falls silent while the rest of the assembly, struck by the astonishing sight of the Duke being marched off by the Captain of the Guards, and the King, sombre and still, rising from the table and walking head erect towards his own apartments, remains hushed for a moment before exploding in a wave of shocked exclamations. Struck by the public ignominy of her husband's arrest, the Duchess Isabella slumps on the table and is led away by a group of compassionate ladies.

Along a warren of corridors and down a series of staircases loudly echoing with the sounds of arms clattering and of doors being locked and loosed, levelling off deep in the hollows of the Palace where the light of day never seeps and where the walls, if pressed, could tell stories as maleficent as the Prince of Darkness, the Duke is led by his armed escort to a cell where, in perpetuity, the brazier burns, the instruments are whetted, and the rack stands ready to panhandle from the babblings of the tormented the confessional nuggets needed to formalize guilt. And there he is subjected to treatment which it is not our intention to relate as we do not believe in indulging the dubious tastes of those who enjoy hearing of limbs being torn and of minds being drowned in the sea of their own fears. Nor do we intend to describe the many ways in which man's inventive barbarity has been encoded, justified, and given legal sanction by the dark side of the state. It should amply suffice, when we draw back the veil of propriety from this scene, to note that the Duke sits naked in an iron chair, that his face is bloody, his flesh wealed, and that in a corner of the room, as meticulously as if

176

itemizing the bushels of wheat to be paid to the Exchequer, a clerk is inscribing the details with which the Chamberlain cut short the horror that befell him in those dark, dank vaults.

A few days later, as is its seasonal wont, the cold winter wind is fretting at the Palace's keen-edged towers and at its crumbling crenellations. And as it skirts past ramparts and encircles turrets, it tilts at a newly-erected obstacle, the folds and flaps of a body swinging at the end of a taut rope.

It is perhaps to underline this grim image – which has almost made Annabelle retch – that Alonzo adds: "As a warning to others, the King ordered that the traitor be garotted and that his body hang on the castle ramparts until it drop."

To preserve the secrecy of his minstrel's role, the King chooses to reward Alonzo in one of his most private chambers. Having proclaimed the dwarf's sagacity and looked forward to many more years of faithful service, he places in his diminutive hand a small gold medal embossed with the regal image, a medal which catches the meagre light trickling down from a low candelabra.

On a cold and blustery day a horse-drawn carriage stands at the foot of the Palace walls. From the sight of the three children packed into its small shell, the amount of baggage piled high on top of the roof, and the scratched-out ducal crown on the carriage door, it is apparent that the disgraced Lady Isabella is about to leave the Palace with her tragically diminished family.

"Once he had stripped her of her husband's lands, as a mark of his boundless clemency, the King permitted the Duchess Isabella and her three children to retire to her country estate."

Is it a coincidence that Alonzo is the sole witness to this desolate scene in which a former high Lady of the Court creeps away in the wake of her husband's treachery? Hardly, thinks Annabelle, who is progressively discovering in the story the application of the Marquis' principles. Whatever the narrative's motive may be for placing him high on the Palace ramparts, Alonzo, wearing a large billowing cloak which completely engulfs him, is now staring down at the departing party. Fortunately the gibbet in the distant background stands empty. And the Duchess is about to enter her readied carriage when a detail in her appearance strikes Alonzo profoundly.

"As the Duchess crossed the Palace's courtyard to rejoin her children in her carriage," says Alonzo, his voice slightly quavering, "I thought how very pale she was. It was then that I noticed something else, something of which I had had no idea. By all the relics in God's Holy City! The Duchess' stomach was swollen! The Lady Isabella was with child! A shiver ran down my back. I could not take my eyes off the scene. For was there not something horribly familiar about this? Had I not seen it somewhere before? But if so, where? And when? . . . A few seconds of intense contemplation soon taught me that what I had earlier experienced had not been from the heights of a Palace. Nor had it been from the safety of its thick walls. No, the echo which I had heard had arisen from when I had myself lain secure deep in the watery depths of my mother's womb!"

The parallels, Annabelle has to admit, are telling. Two ladies leave the Court under circumstances hushed or disgraced. Both are heavy with child, both depart without their husbands. It is little wonder that a tremor of intuitive recognition should have burst upon Alonzo, a tremor so violent that in an instant it has changed his whole perspective. He turns his back on the windswept ramparts and on the distant silhouette of the Lady's departed carriage and rushes back to his quarters. There he paces about the room as if caged, then, with a cry of anguish, throws himself on to his bed. Unable to rest, his face etched by the acid of distress, he repeatedly beats his fists against the walls.

"I was in torment. The vision of that unborn child haunted me. I could not remain another day at Court. I had to see the Duchess. Yet how? For she had been sent into exile and I was convinced that she would not receive me."

On what pretext visit the Duchess? He barely knows her family. The part he has played in its destiny is one on which he prefers not to dwell. Round and round the room he wanders, punching at objects he has purloined, kicking at books he has never read. If only there were a way! If only . . . Suddenly he remembers. Of course! Why had he not thought of it before? Diving into the assortment of disguises he has often used to tease out truth, he soon comes across what he is searching for. The linen is admittedly crumpled, its colour a little stained, and the embroidery not as fresh as when he first found it. No matter. Here is the Duke's own handkerchief! The perfect fabric, thinks Alonzo, holding it high, on which to embroider my story.

Late afternoon's shadows have lengthened and the light has

taken on a deep amber glow when Alonzo, his horse and baggage, ride into the courtyard of the Duchess' hacienda. He jumps off his mount and tethers it to a generously flower-bedecked trough. Next he insistently rings the bell of the whitewashed villa until a white-haired and half blind servant, almost bent double with age, opens the door and informs him in an enfeebled voice that the Duchess no longer receives visitors. Alonzo, interrupting the majordomo with a curt wave of his hand, gives him the ducal handkerchief and orders him to take it forthwith to his mistress for what he has to say concerns her intimately.

In spite of the success of his braggadocio exercised on a creature whose doddery frame was most unlikely to have challenged it, Alonzo, waiting by an imposing wooden stairway in the hacienda's cool, dark hall, cannot conceal his nervousness. His bones creaking, his breath short and wheezy, the old servant comes tottering down the stairs and, with an exaggerated and strangely crapulous bow, bids the dwarf follow him to the upstairs salon where, he adds, his Mistress, the Duchess, is waiting.

Alonzo is ushered into a reception room in which the Duchess is installed on a large sofa, the handkerchief which he has brought plainly nestling on her lap, a couple of bone-gnawing spaniels at her feet. As the child that she is carrying has become in her mind a living memorial to her late husband, her fourth pregnancy has resulted in a glorious blossoming. Her dark hair she has piled up high, and her tall, languid body she has encased in folds of dark crimson silk becomingly offset with lace. The dwarf has hardly begun his introduction when the Duchess, cutting him short, informs him that, try as she might, she cannot conceive how an object as personal as her husband's handkerchief could now be in the possession of a Court entertainer. Nor can she recollect her husband ever mentioning him. She therefore insists that he tell her from where he procured it. And that done, will he also be good enough to name the reason for his untimely and – need she stress? – utterly unsolicited visit.

Alonzo, realizing with dismay that the interview is proving to be even more arduous than he had imagined, tries nonetheless to keep calm and to subdue the fear in his voice.

"That the Duke had never mentioned me, I answered her, was not, as she might suspect, a curiosity, but rather a matter of the highest confidentiality. It would indeed have been quite unthinkable for the late Duke to betray – even to his own dear wife – so vital a state secret. In the wake of his tragic death, however, I was at liberty to avow that I had been his trusted aide and that he had frequently assigned me to the most exacting tasks. As for the handkerchief, that too could be easily explained. Her husband had given it to me in recognition of a delicate operation I had brought to a successful conclusion. Regarding the matter of my presence here before her, I had hoped the Duchess might appreciate that I had come at the peril of incurring the King's wrath, and only to enquire after the wellbeing of my former master's wife."

On hearing out Alonzo's reworking of reality, the Duchess cannot prevent herself from betraying her emotions. Her tears start to flow and, without a moment's thought, she reaches for her husband's handkerchief and wipes her eyes with it. Quickly recomposing herself, she begs the dwarf to excuse her curtness. He must understand how lonely she has been. To be exiled from the Court is as desolate a fate as to wander blindly through a desert. And though she daily hungers to learn what is happening at the Palace, even that distant consolation has been denied her for the King has placed an embargo on all letters. Perhaps, she adds, Alonzo might look upon her invitation to spend a few days with her with a good eye? There is so much news with which she would like to catch up.

At first Alonzo makes a show of recalcitrance and plays up the dangers which would attend too prolonged an absence from the Court. He then again lets himself be entreated to stay. Once he has accepted, he basks in the radiance of her gratitude. In the days that follow, the delighted dwarf spends many an hour in the presence of the disgraced Duchess. And it is with poorly disguised fascination that he stares at the swelling in her stomach while she waters her flowers, upbraids her children, teases her spaniels, and, with never failing grace, manages her country affairs. There is indeed no activity of hers too high or low which he leaves unexplored, hovering outside her chambers during her afternoon rest, walking behind her while she inspects her vines, and willing to fetch whatever she might require at any time of day. Such subservience would no doubt seem inglorious were it not for the cool but genial manner with which she accepts his every effort.

"No, I was no dupe. A dwarf with a Duchess! Why, the idea was grotesque, disgraceful! And normally . . . But," adds Alonzo, drawing Annabelle a little deeper into the difficulties he had faced, "tell me what, if anything, was still normal in the Duchess' situation? Was she not in exile and in disgrace? Had her husband not been executed for treachery? Had his lands not been confiscated? While could I not boast of being one of the King's trusted courtiers and his favourite entertainer? So it came to pass that as I attended her, day in, day out, I became convinced that I deserved to win her love."

Apart from the solitary candle that burns close to the dressing table and the fire which has been lit to take the edge off the enveloping chill, the guest room lies in the dark. Showing all the care which the occasion demands, Alonzo, before a large oval mirror, adds make-up to his already unusual features. His moustache has been washed and waxed; his black hair glistens with pomade; his cheeks expose a shadow of rouge; his best velvet suit he has already donned. And, as a final flourish, to his lips he has given a light roseate sheen.

Alonzo, his stomach distended by a hearty repast – whose details we will for once not disclose – sits on a sofa opposite the Duchess in her upstairs salon and asks himself if the moment is right. How can he be sure? But as there is often no moment more propitious than the present, casting all caution aside he suddenly kneels before her and there and then declares his love. Unfortunately, as can occur when the empty shell of behaviour is paraded without an awareness of the causes and essences which initially gave it life, the dwarf has blurred the distinction between the heartfelt and the histrionic and is therefore unable to be, only play the part of, the artful lover. With his over-coloured lips pouting, his thickly-smeared cheeks puffed out, and his black-pencilled eyes rolling as if the Duchess were making him swoon, he breathes tender words of love each and every one of which he has culled from the songs he is wont to sing. It is only the wholly expected nature of his declaration – for what woman cannot predict when a suitor will expose the flames that consume him? – and the control she has on her composure which permit the Duchess to contain her amusement.

"And although I wooed her with all the charms I had learnt at Court," says Alonzo, "my efforts were to no avail."

The moment has arrived for Alonzo to throw his last card. He therefore decides to sing the Duchess a song. Is it tactlessness, a cruel desire to harp upon her most terrible moment, or some personal attachment to its theme which makes him intone the very song he had composed to warn the King? Whatever the depth, or the bravura, of his reasons, the melody promptly evokes for the Duchess the events which led to her husband's death. And strangely – for perversity knows no bounds – it also suggests to her that there is in Alonzo's passion something which, if she is fortunate, she might turn to her advantage. Well aware of the power that she has over her diminutive suitor, she decides to let him dig a little deeper the trap into which he is destined to fall.

"Once I had finished my song," says Alonzo, "I dared to ask the Duchess if I might live in hope."

Picking up the handkerchief which lies on her lap, the Duchess kisses it tenderly, a gesture which does not fail to exacerbate Alonzo's already sombre mood. When, a few seconds later, she turns her baleful eyes on him and answers no, it is in the knowledge that her refusal will cast him into the deepest pit of despair.

"Hope? she asked. No, I should entertain none. Unless . . . she whispered. Unless what? I cried, seeing a sliver of clarity in a world which I had seen strangled by darkness. Unless, she answered me, I was willing to undertake a special task. Without hesitating, I promised her that, whatever was her heart's desire, I would gladly do it. In that case, she said, I should ride back to the Court and there search for her husband's crown. His crown? I enquired. What did she want with it? Surely her husband's position was beyond repair. As for her own name . . . She put a finger on her mouth. I should ask her no questions, she said. Let her reasons remain a surprise. I should not however doubt the seriousness of her request for there was nothing that she wanted more for her yet unborn child than this sacred relic of her husband's life. She herself had not seen the crown since his arrest. But if I found it, and brought it back to her, then, yes, she would take me to her heart. Until that happy moment, she added, she and I would not meet again."

Neither the ravines through which he and his mount cut, nor the gullies over which they run, nor the plains whose dust mingles with his hair, nor even the appearance at the cusp of dawn of the Royal Seat towards which he has been racing through the night make any imprint on Alonzo's mind when compared to the joy of becoming the Duchess' most obedient Knight.

His clothes begrimed, his body worn out, his expression wild and haggard, Alonzo rides into the courtyard, stables his horse, and dashes through galleries and corridors until he reaches the King's antechamber. There, at a large desk, behind a wall of bold black tomes, he confronts the King's Secretary who is busy sealing State papers. Bowing low, Alonzo apologizes for the intemperate nature of his appearance and asks him if he might be granted an audience with the King.

"The King's Secretary informed me that I had chosen my moment poorly. His Majesty had not retired for the night but had been sitting up, meditating on the death of His wife. However, as I was adept at soothing His torpid humours, he would make an exception and allow me in."

Wearing an inconsolable expression, the King is seated at the far end of his Throne Room. Alonzo approaches the carpet-covered dais and, with all the reverence due to his Master, bows low. Painfully aware of how infrequently he has addressed the King directly – for since he received the King's letter has song not been his sole form of communication? – he quakes at the idea of having to make so particular a request. Yet with the image of the fair Isabella dancing before him, and the echo of her promise in his ears, and the expectation that all will be well once he has found the missing crown buttressing his fracturing confidence, Alonzo summons his courage and at last dares to greet the King. His voice quavering with trepidation, he asks if he might be granted a favour. Without so much as a passing enquiry what this might be, the King cuts Alonzo short and demands to be told why, when he has surely come to entertain Him, he has not brought his guitar?

"Was it the lengthy journey, or the lack of sleep, or my overexcited state? I shall never know. What I remember is that, as I stood before the King, I suddenly became tongue-tied and could no longer answer him with my customary fluency."

The briefest examination of Alonzo's shivering frame, drooping eyelids, and oneiric expression suggests to Annabelle that it was probably a combination of all three which took away his energy and left him stranded before the King.

"No, I stammered, I had not appeared before His Majesty to soothe Him with song. Rather I had come to beg for the Duke's crown. Might He know of its whereabouts? And if He did, might I, as a mark of His Royal favour towards me, be permitted to have it?"

Flying into a formidable rage, the King shouts at his minstrel that never has such insolence been paralleled. That a dwarf should dare ride so far above his station, a station which, as God has decreed, was meant to be ever lowly, is unspeakable! For this act of exorbitant presumption the King will teach him a lesson which will stay with him to his dying day.

"What! he screamed. The traitor's titles, the conspirator's lands! I, a pitiful creature, a stunted root, dared covet ducal robes! Just because I had distracted him on a few occasions and poured poison on His most trusted Minister, I now thought I might become a Grandee! Well, He would remind me of my base origins. Yes, a prolonged spell in the countryside would soon bring me back to my senses. And with those cruel words, He ordered His Guards to expel me forthwith from the Palace."

It is perhaps only fair that in a story in which metaphor has so far been predominant, building bridges between areas of artistry generally regarded as distinct, it should now be metonymy's turn to show off its particular prowess. Poor Alonzo! How could he have divined that the part which his inspiration ordered him to search for would be mistaken by the depressed Monarch for the whole so that the mere mention of the Duke's crown, far from focusing on an extravagant curve of metal emboldened with semi-precious stones, would instead evoke the whole train of ducal privileges, armorial symbols, and divinely-affirmed fiefdoms with which it is usually attended? One tiny semantic misunderstanding, one linguistic process mishandled, and Alonzo's privileged position at Court is utterly destroyed.

No sooner has the Monarch ordered the dwarf to be seized than two guards appear on either side of him, turn him around, and carry him out so fast that his feet do not even touch the ground. As the large oaken doors of the Royal Chamber slam shut on Alonzo's presence at Court, his voice, pleading to be heard, ricochets aimlessly down the wide granite corridors.

"Pity! I beseeched His Highness. He had misunderstood me. I had asked for the Duke's crown, not his title, nor his land, only his crown!"

Highly amused that the upstart should receive his just rewards, the guards toss Alonzo out of the Palace courtyard and watch him roll about in the dust. Bruised and soiled, he picks himself up and stares at the dark walls from whose heights, he mordantly recalls, he had not so long before witnessed another dramatic departure.

"With my mission an abject failure, my hopes were also dashed. As I had nowhere else to go, I made my slow and arduous way on foot to the Duchess' hacienda."

Dirty, dishevelled, and horseless, Alonzo arrives after a three-day walk at the door of the hacienda. Although he repeatedly rings the bell, nowhere is the Duchess' old servant to be seen. Unsure what to do, and no longer able to summon the cocksureness of his former behaviour, he waits quite some time before timidly trying to open the door. It is with surprise that he discovers that it is not locked. Even stranger, there seems to be no one about. Indeed, Alonzo observes, on venturing in and wandering through the whitewashed rooms, the hacienda's interior is quieter than an ossuary.

As his first attempts to ascertain why the hacienda should be deserted meet with no success, he heads up the main staircase and enters the salon. In its ample and modestly furnished acreage he confronts, to his astonishment, sitting all by herself, and without so much as her dogs to keep her company, the Duchess dressed in black. Overjoyed to see her in good health, if in a state of mourning for a reason he cannot divine, he casts himself at her feet and proceeds to describe to her the shocking events which have befallen him.

"Shamefaced and defeated, with tears in my eyes, I threw myself on the Duchess' mercy and confessed that I had returned empty-handed."

The moment she has digested the dwarf's story, the Duchess' heart fills with the rancour of failed expectations.

"Her face – I shall never forget it – was terrifying. She told me I was a paltry being, the dried-out remnants of a man. She, however, would also have to shoulder the blame for never should she have expected a mere minstrel to negotiate a matter as delicate as the recovery of her dear departed husband's crown. After so dismal a performance, there was nothing for it but to have me thrown out. Having reconsidered my pitiful fate, she was willing to relent. Even as great a fool as I must have noticed that the house was quiet and that she herself was dressed in mourning. While I had been at Court, mishandling the mission with which she had so unwisely entrusted me, her old servant, a man who had never, in all his years of service, let her down, had suddenly died. If I took on his duties immediately, she would give me one final chance to redeem myself. Well? she insisted before my speechless expression. Did I want the position or did I not?"

The Duchess stares at the dwarf whose bad fortune has reduced him to the lowliest status. And it is on that image of utter abjection that Alonzo winds his story down and calls on the merchant and his secretary to show him the compassion which he feels he deserves.

"Banished from the Court – and with nowhere else to go – what choice had I but to accept? And that is why, strangers, I have been here since, my every moment sheer torment, banned from so much as breathing a word of love to the Duchess while she, fierce and unapproachable grandee that she is, takes pleasure in treating me with the cruellest disdain. Yes, tell me! Am I not the most miserable man in the world, condemned by my own damnable hope to linger here for ever?"

Both the Marquis and Annabelle shift on their chairs – their stiff backs have given them cramp – and exchange knowing glances. From the vantage of the mahogany chest on which he is still perched, Alonzo stares at them. His expression is equivocal as if the disclosure has unburdened him of a great weight but has also left him feeling vulnerable.

"What a terrible tale!" the Marquis exclaims.

Can't he do any better? thinks Annabelle, quick to criticize the Marquis' response to the dwarf's story. It surely betrays a paucity of imagination to respond more or less in the same way to all three characters at the end of their story. But then, she admits, he has just narrated an unusually colourful story so to expect him to make brilliant ripostes consistently is not fair. For after all the episodes have also taught her that only so much energy is available at any given time and that consequently one has to choose with care on what one should lavish one's attention.

The Marquis pauses as if for effect, then adds: "Though now that we've heard the tragic circumstances that surrounded your birth, I'm convinced that we can help you. That's, of course, if you do us that small favour which we asked for."

"If I put myself to all that trouble and bring you some oil," Alonzo asks the Marquis, "what guarantees do I have that you'll fulfil your side of the bargain?"

"What a question, Alonzo! Why, look at Annabelle's face. Isn't beauty the reflection of an honest soul?"

"Ha!" the dwarf sneers. "Spare me your philosophy. Don't forget that it was beauty that ensnared me!"

"In that case, Alonzo," the Marquis answers, "if you won't found your trust on my companion's appearance, will an older man's word do?" He makes the sign of the cross. "I swear by all that's holy," he interjects, "that we'll abide by the bargain which we've made."

"Very well," Alonzo answers, his voice empty of conviction yet forced by the logic which confronts him to accept the terms of the exchange. Almost ponderously, he walks over to the four-poster bed, sits on it, shapes his hands into an arch, and closes his eyes.

Annabelle follows suit and can soon make out among the mists that greet her the poorly focused form of a steep cobweb-bound staircase. Leading to it, the seemingly interminable entrail of a narrow corridor. Only a meagre amount of light falls from the setting's sole aperture, a narrow iron-barred window. Little by little the scene pulls itself into sharper definition, permitting her to see that dust has gathered on the uneven floor in small grey mounds and undulating dunes. What is that noise in the background? Sounds like the low whistle of a draught skirting rough stones. At first hardly more than a gasp, then more and more powerfully, a cold gust begins to blow past her, whipping up the dust, swirling it about, and endowing it with flurrying forms and wraith-like shapes. Round and round this miniature maelstrom runs, sweeping grit into ever smaller particles until a cloud has formed so thick that it thoroughly obscures the stairs' rickety silhouette.

Basing her prediction on the manner in which the Marquis has repeated his narrative formula, Annabelle suspects that the next thing to appear out of the whirlpool will be the dwarf, who will be suffering no doubt from some disability, his shape cankered by God knows what problem. As all the other apparitions have occurred like that, recognizing the tendency for his stories to be predicated on the same principles, she is willing to bet that this episode will too. And, indeed, a faint form is growing in the eye of the whirlpool, a form which is gathering itself out of the infinitesimally small grains of sand which are still flying around. Then suddenly the gust collapses and leaves in the centre of the corridor a shape akin to a very grainy, grey sculpture. And yes, Annabelle has guessed rightly, for somehow out of the dust that lay on the ground Alonzo the dwarf has arisen.

An apparition which looks as if it is about to fall apart. With every move which it makes grains of dust fall off it, although it appears sufficiently stable to make its way down the steep staircase. The small amount of light which filters on to the scene makes it difficult for Annabelle to ascertain whether, as in the previously recreated incidents, it is the background which lacks colour or whether it is merely the murky and leaden atmosphere of the corridor which has bleached it of any brilliance.

Meanwhile Alonzo, his movements ponderous, his gestures awkward, surrounded on all sides by tiny cyclones berating the dust on the ground, makes his way down the circuitous corridor until he approaches a beam on which there hangs a lit lantern. He picks it up with difficulty and continues towards what Annabelle presumes is likely to be the hacienda's cellars. Down a jagged assembly of corridors he shuffles, the lantern casting its bashful rays from a glass-encased candle on to the grey surroundings.

It takes the Spaniard some time to reach his target for every so often his grainy figure fades in and then fades out as if memory were failing him and robbing him of the concentration which he requires to move. When is he going to get to his destination? Annabelle frets as yard after yard of the most tedious architectural tubing goes past her mind's eye, unalleviated by the slightest historical artefact which might amuse her while this pursuit takes place. After considerable shuffling, Alonzo's tremulous figure reaches a wooden door which stands at the end of a cobwebbed corridor. It proves to be difficult to open. As he struggles with it, dust falls from every part of his body. When it does at last come loose on its worn hinges, he enters a cramped and low-ceilinged cellar.

It is a cellar filled from its sandy floor to its whitewashed but severely mildewed ceiling with row upon row of wine casks.

Interspersed with these are ancient agricultural implements, mouse traps, wicker baskets, hubs of wheels, and sealed cases whose contents Annabelle has no opportunity to investigate as Alonzo has already moved to the far end of the room and has now stopped opposite a massive, sweaty vat of oil, squat on a semi-circular plinth. On a nail in the wall dangles a bat colony of upturned gourds. Alonzo takes one of them. Moving towards the fattest vat, he takes its cock and prises it open. There ensues a terrifying rattle. And, indeed, so violently is the vat racked by what appears to be a coughing fit that it thoroughly shakes its wooden base, a base which looks as if it will not long withstand the shock. Foul-tempered, the dwarf gives the vat a swift kick then another until the container, with a full gargle, lets slip a clear stream into the mouth of the gourd.

The dwarf refastens the vat and shuffles past the rich assortment of objects. Surprisingly the door is easier to close than it was to open and, once he has secured it, he drags himself up the stairs. At its head, a phalanx of loudly spinning typhoons wait ready to consume him. Throwing the lantern aside on to the ground where it clatters but does not extinguish, Alonzo holds the gourd tightly in his hand and walks fearlessly into the thick of them. In a few seconds, like a mill's wheel crunching the sap of corn, the typhoons have scattered across the corridor the dust from which the dwarf had coalesced.

Annabelle opens her eyes and examines the dwarf. Following his imaginative transformation, he sits completely still on the bed, then suddenly shudders. The Marquis rises from his chair and goes and stands in front of him. And in much the same way as he did in those other mysterious, empirically dubious yet presumably necessary transfers, he examines the ingredient which he has just managed to elicit. Taking the dusty gourd from the dwarf's hands, he uncorks it and sniffs its humid tip. Delighted with the oil's quality, he turns to his companion and signals to her to complete the agreed exchange.

Annabelle brings the cardboard crown from under her jacket and hands it to Alonzo. The moment the dwarf catches sight of its gilded shape, he trembles with joy.

"Tricks!" he cries. "I knew it! Magicians' tricks!" But for all that intemperate outburst, he still fondles the crown, apparently unconcerned that it is a cheap replica, that its serial number is printed on its underside, and that even in an age likely to regard the superficial brilliance of electrolysis as an impressive achievement, it still lacks the weight and texture of a genuine golden ornament. "Witches! Yes, I was sure you were witches! But I do not care now, no, I do not care!" he adds ecstatically.

Alonzo rushes around the room, grabs hold of a porcelain pot sitting on a mantelpiece, raises it above his head, and dashes it against the wall where it shatters with a crash. A gesture which is instantly met by an angry cry from the other side of the bedroom. Annabelle looks round and is astounded to see the Duchess Isabella standing in the doorway. And with her stomach prodigiously swollen and her breasts bulbous from lactation, she seems to be on the point of giving birth.

First the Duchess casts an imperious gaze at her menial before turning her scrutiny to the two strangers. Finally, raising herself to her full height, she exclaims in a fit of outrage: "What is the meaning of this madness, Alonzo? Answer me immediately! Who are these two strangely garbed people?"

"Mistress!" Alonzo cries, thunderstruck by the Duchess' unexpected appearance. In spite of her brazen expression and of the fear that she inspires in his heart, he shows considerable presence of mind and startling agility, seizes a chair, places it next to her, and climbs on to it. As if confounded by the speed with which her servant has acted, the Duchess remains motionless. Nor does she brush him away as he stands close to her on tiptoe and sets the cardboard crown on her head.

The Lady Isabella puts both hands to her head and feels the crown. Is this conceivable? Can this really be happening? Her husband's crown? The one object she has longed for above all else? Making no reference to the paradox that Alonzo has managed while in her employ to locate a crown when he had returned empty-handed from the Court; asking him for no explanation of his feat and thereby showing her close affinity with a world view which accepts the miraculous without subjecting its phenomena to the rhythms of rational causes, the Duchess, overjoyed that the golden symbol of her formerly elevated position should now be perched on her head, wraps her arms around the little man and lifts him effortlessly off the chair. They then sidle jerkily towards the four-poster bed upon whose soft and welcoming folds they collapse in a confusion of limbs.

Annabelle has now sufficiently relaxed to enjoy the grotesque performance. The events after all have taken place within safe ambits and have, except when flouted, led to nothing more serious than a certain amount of outrageous behaviour and the magical incarnation of gastronomic ingredients. Along with her increasing acceptance of the illusion, Annabelle sees no reason why she should subject the enormous discrepancy between Alonzo's earlier description of his aristocratic love and the comic appearance of this amour to criticism. For what would be the point of making fiction stand trial before the tribunal of naturalism or of any other positivistic criterion? None whatsoever. And as she is aware of the close links which the imagination has forged with every human activity, sending images of power into sectors as different as science and art, and fertilizing them with insights into their field, she is willing to concede that the strange images which she has experienced, which have haunted her, and which have confronted her with powerful processes – and a few vegetables and bulbs to boot! – may well lead her towards her own epiphanies. Enlivened by her new-found optimism, she smiles at the Marquis who, seemingly satisfied with the outcome of his most ambitious tale to date, smiles back at her.

In her moment of passion the Duchess makes complete abstraction of the two strangers gazing on the scene. To begin with she unpins the upper part of her dress and loosens her voluminous mammaries. She then takes Alonzo's passive head in her hands and presses him hard, as a mother would her child to her breasts. Without any embarrassment the dwarf, as if he had been waiting for this precious contact from the first occasion on which he had met the Duchess, falls on to the fuller of the two aureolae, and sucks it avidly.

Annabelle casts a last glance at the scene and ponders what she has learnt from this episode. She concludes that she now has a greater awareness of the Marquis' principles of creativity. Timing for instance: yes, the story lucidly emphasized its importance. As for methods, well, she has worked out a few: for instance, how to dispose of secondary characters; the lasting value of twists in the tale; how to orchestrate a narrative exchange; and the need for repetition. What about sympathy? That particular principle, she has to admit, she has yet to run to ground. However, the breakthrough which she has made into so many of the operations of the illusions suggests that it too will sooner or later fall into place.

"Isn't it time we left?" asks Annabelle.

Holding the gourd in his hand, the Marquis answers that it is. "But before we do, I think we should draw a veil over this scene," he says, going over to the bed and pulling its curtains to.

The travelling companions walk towards the secret wooden panel in the wall and proceed into its narrow confines. The Marquis tries to close it but has to exert himself to make it curve back to its former position. The moment it is fast, it cuts them off completely from the noises which were issuing from behind the brocaded curtains of the four-poster.

As the Marquis' lighter will not fire, there is no choice for them but to feel their way through the darkness, he in front, making sure, in a rare display of concern for Annabelle's wellbeing, that she is not trailing behind. After a few minutes of slow progress, his hands meet the wooden frame of a door. He grasps its handle and shakes it. It offers little resistance, releases a burst of fresh air into the corridor's dank atmosphere, and swings wide open.

The train is deserted. Not one passenger, not a single functionary traipsing down the corridor, nobody. Exhausted and glad to be back within the train's familiar folds, Annabelle takes refuge in the silence of her thoughts. The Marquis, gleaming with vigour – a phenomenon which she has noticed before and which, considering the energy he has just expended, she cannot explain – leans against the wall and, immersed in his own concerns, stares down the length of the train's gently swaying concourse.

CHAPTER ELEVEN

Their throats parched, their limbs weary, the time-travelling companions head for their favourite retreat. And it would be easy for a stranger to cast his eye on the tired pair sitting at an alcove table in the Bar Buffet and to note the bonds, if not of friendship then at least of complicity, which have grown between them. It is in these agreeable surroundings, the table linen reflecting its dimmed lights and the rhythmic movements of the train ruffling the pale surface of an excellent Gevrey-Chambertin '35, that the Marquis, nursing his glass, pursues the correspondences with which he has been regularly regaling his apprentice.

"Time to propose another toast, Annabelle," says the Marquis to his companion. "Let's raise our glasses to cooking and to storytelling. Yes, to imagination's fascinating twins!" He clinks his glass against hers.

Under a temporarily clarified horizon, the countryside reveals the gorges and inclines of an ashen landscape. The train is now cutting through a ravine from whose heights Annabelle can see a stream imprudently trailing its taffeta gown over rocks which have in no time reduced its fabric to a ghostly spume. She is just about to make some comment about the landscape's poetic quality when the setting suddenly switches back to darkness and there is nothing to see except beads of moisture trapped between the window's insulating sheets. Noting the Marquis' intense expression, she hazards that, knowing him, he would probably have dismissed her comment as being of no relevance to the subject under discussion.

"I'd like you to understand," says the Marquis, "the extent to which my hands were tied. However much I might have liked to tell you the full story when we met in the Brasserie, an invitation to a cooking course was really the only viable invitation I could have made. Imagine your reactions if I had offered to initiate you into the secrets of storytelling? You'd have written me off as a madman and probably dined off the story for months. No, that most certainly would not have convinced you to join me. What I needed was a hook – the hook of sympathy – with which to draw you in. And I admit that I was particularly fortunate to come across an event as perfectly timed as that ruined meal.

"Without an audience – face it – what are you? At best a bundle of specialized skills desperately seeking confirmation. I mean: what could be sadder, more pathetic than a cook concocting dishes for people who won't even bother to turn up? Or a storyteller who can't find an interested ear? That's why it's so imperative, Annabelle, that you learn how to catch and hold an audience.

"Every situation requires a specific approach. For someone you meet in a bar you must devise one type of invitation. For a woman sitting next to you in the transit lounge of an airport another. And if at some dinner party you find that you're placed next to someone you find *sympathique*, well, you just invent something suitable. It doesn't matter who they are or what they do: you can rest assured that something somewhere excites them. What that is it's up to you to discover and to then exploit. Let me tell you a secret about humanity in general: most people would love to be different. That's right: they're cankered by a terrible sense of loss, of failure. If you look as if you can show them the route to their particular fantasy, I promise you, you'll never lack people to work with.

"I've already stressed that there's no point being squeamish when preparing food. You can't afford it either when storytelling. It just doesn't pay to let scruples get in the way. You must adopt and apply one criterion, and that's reaching your goal. Which means that any trick's worth pursuing as long as it gets you the results which you're after." The Marquis pauses, studies his companion's slightly disapproving expression, then continues: "So the fundamental question which you need to answer is: how should you go about it?"

Having heard the Marquis state that the course is infinitely malleable and that one of its main targets is the hunger for fantasy supposedly lurking in the human heart, Annabelle is keen to hear him discuss practical aspects. For the limited vision and the insufficient details with which she has had to put up so far have been, to say the least, frustrating. Tired of grappling with odd pieces which never quite seem to fit together, she hankers to experience his vision in its full, if horrific, splendour.

"My aim has been to show you that gastronomy and the arts of narration have processes in common. Processes which take basic ingredients and which then turn them into powerful products. Nothing could be easier for a Master Chef than to transform a simple substance into an exotic dish. Consider the enormous distance which the potato travels to end up as a *crêpe vonnassienne*. Well, the storyteller is endowed with similar powers. Using the materials which he picks up – personal experiences, anecdotes overheard, general observations – he can manipulate them with equal versatility. Watch him take some humdrum detail – a shopworn habit maybe, or a tedious turn of phrase – place it in a telling context, lead you straight to the essence of a fictional personality, and thereby illuminate its innermost workings. Because what cooking and storytelling share," the Marquis summarizes, "is the peculiar ability to take basic ingredients and to then elevate them on to a much higher plane."

Nor is that the sole parallel which the Marquis would like Annabelle to discover. And it is with a never abating sense of wonder at the agility of his metaphor, at its apparently infinite pliancy, and at the threads which he tresses so elegantly between the two worlds that she leans back on the Bar Buffet's welcoming seat and continues to listen to him.

"In the main, heat is responsible," says the Marquis, playing with his half-filled glass, "for evoking an ingredient's full flavour. Heat also burns down fats, rarefies proteins and, in effect, does much of the stomach's work for it. You could say that heat facilitates the whole of the digestive process."

At around this point, Annabelle surmises, the Marquis is going to reveal to her that heat is also pivotal to storytelling.

It is with the pleasure of having accurately intuited the next step in the Marquis' argument that she hears him describe – without a trace of irony – the formative influence which heat is indeed supposed to have on the arts of storytelling. Partly to provoke him, and partly in reaction against such a ludicrous idea, she puts up a token resistance.

"Do let me finish!" retorts the Marquis, yet with none of the petulant highhandedness which he displayed at the beginning of the journey. "I'm not talking about a naked flame! I'm referring to the heat feelings generate. For it is emotions which are fundamentally responsible for transforming ordinary perception into the crystalline elements of art. Why don't you examine ordinary experience for a moment? Within the many and varied activities we get up to everyday, there are thousands of intricate patterns which most people neither have the time nor, for that matter, the inclination to seek out. But place them under the skilfully directed focus of an artist's emotions and they'll soon become highlighted within a framework within which their value can become plain to whoever looks at them. Just as food feeds the body and stimulates the palate, so you'll discover that a story can strengthen ordinary perception and deliver a telling message."

Without showing the slightest sign of exhaustion, the Marquis again and again throws his net of correspondences over his favourite subject. It has meanwhile dawned on Annabelle that her responses to his teachings are becoming increasingly ambiguous. On the one hand it is flattering, even alluring, to be inducted into a mystery, to sense that one is elect, and to be promised the reins of strange and wonderful powers. At the same time she cannot quite suppress the notion that his designs, for all their cunning and inventiveness, may ultimately be deranged. But if she adopts a reductive stance and dismisses him as, at best, a luminary, and at worst, a lunatic, where does that leave the experiences which she can hardly deny she has already had? And were she to downgrade the Marquis' theories, would she not also negate the evidence of her own senses? To acquiesce, on the other hand, is to remain dependent on his authority: which she is fast finding an increasingly unpleasant situation. It is with an inner sigh, part weariness, part pain, that she recognizes the little comfort which each option offers her.

*

A few glasses of the fragrant wine later, the Marquis introduces Annabelle to a further range of ideas.

"Some years ago, as I told you," says the Marquis, "I worked my way around the world as an assistant chef on a cruise ship. My duties were onerous, my hours long, and as for being imprisoned with a group of overrich and spoilt guests that, I assure you, was enough to tax a saint's patience. Anyway, early one autumn morning the ship docked in Madras. It was to stay there for a week. I used to close the kitchens down for the day, and while the passengers assembled on deck before traipsing off on some guided tour or other, I'd leave the ship and spend part of the morning before it became unbearably hot on one of the less polluted public beaches. Which is where, Annabelle, I came across the most remarkable cook I have ever met.

"His name was Sami Lalan and he and his two sons ran their small restaurant from a beach hut – to be honest it was hardly more than a few upright planks covered by a badly peeling tarred roof. And yet the *dhosas* and *bhel poories* which he produced on a small palm oil stove in that tiny kiosk were immaculate. I must have tasted his range of dishes half a dozen times when, curious to discover how he managed to prepare food so beautifully and in such modest circumstances, I went up to him, told him I too was a cook and began discussing the art which we both practised. He spoke French surprisingly well – I seem to remember that he had had dealings with merchants who exported pineapples from Pondicherry to Paris – and where my smattering of English and my gestures failed to make sense, he somehow bridged the gap in a charming mixture of *titi parisien* and Mediterranean argot. Now though undeniably a Master Chef, he could not have been more unassuming. Quite matter-of-factly he showed me the fresh ingredients which his sons bought every day at dawn from the local fish and fruit markets. He also revealed the composition of a few time-honoured recipes. But what really surprised me was that I could make out no mystery. It was all very down to earth, all very simple. What was the peculiar quality, what was the magic which lifted his food to such a peak of excellence? I asked him. Ah! he said, putting his hands together, if I was after supreme results then I should take great care what went through my mind when cooking. Thoughts of wisdom, he assured me, before I could betray my amazement, would add the subtlest savours to the simplest fare. He himself always recited the Vedas while working. No doubt I would find suitable holy texts from my own background. On the other hand, he warned me, malice and mean thoughts would turn food sour and, he raised his eyes to the sky, might even make it poisonous. As usual," adds the Marquis, a reticent smile suggesting the piquancy of that particular reminiscence, "I'm digressing. That particular example of the powers of sympathy is a subject which you can investigate for yourself, if you care to, one day. What's crucial now is for you to learn to trust your skills. Because if you put the principles which I've taught you into practice, your imagination will immediately triumph."

With the bottle three quarters empty, a roseate hue has appeared on Annabelle's cheeks while the Marquis' own mood has become increasingly genial. And in another of those rapidly developed and equally rapidly blurred vistas (which the land-scape through which the train is passing seems to have made into something of a speciality), Annabelle observes that the ever-unfolding countryside has now replaced romantic crags and fierce cliffs with arable plains dominated in the distance by the silhouette of what she suspects is Cézanne's ceaselessly redefined Mont St Victoire.

"Not that what you've told me hasn't been fascinating," interjects Annabelle, exasperated. "It has! But please, could you be more specific! I mean: going on and on about the magic of cooking and storytelling and the correspondences the two arts are supposed to have with each other hasn't helped me put it into effect, now, has it? I agree that I've picked up hints and that I've experienced a great deal since the course started, but in every other respect I feel that I've remained a passive spectator. I still haven't the first idea how to go about it!"

"How to go about it? Why that's simple. I've told you time and again: you do it by trusting the process. The problem is that you want me to spell it out. And there, I'm afraid, Annabelle, you're in for a disappointment. The last thing a chef does is give away his favourite recipes. On the contrary, having worked hard for them, he'll keep them a closely guarded secret. Of course he'll be pleased to prepare a meal for you in which he'll expose his favourite *pièces de résistance* but don't also ask him to scatter his learning to the four winds. Which is why I'll gladly show you what tools you need to create scenes. How to put them into effect however, that, *ma chère*, you'll have to discover for yourself."

At a signal from the Marquis, a second bottle of the excellent wine is brought by one of the *garçons*, a somewhat surly young man who, as he places the beautifully labelled object on the table, casts an impudent look at the travellers. Either because he has failed to notice this behaviour, or because he does not care to be interrupted a second longer than is strictly necessary, the Marquis sends the *garçon* on his way before the tiresome rigmarole – the slow decantation of the liquid, the expert appreciation of its bouquet, the serving of the guest before the paymaster's own glass is filled – can be enacted. Clearly put out to have had his minor moment of glory ruined, the *garçon* returns to his colleague's side and murmurs a few most probably disparaging words about the couple. Quite unconcerned by this display of petty pique, the Marquis proceeds to fill out a few more of the spaces which are still lying empty in the frame of his theoretical structure.

"Sharp knives, sound vessels, a constant source of heat: they're your culinary requisites. Now, what do you suppose you need, Annabelle, when preparing stories?"

Annabelle shrugs.

The Marquis takes out of his jacket pocket a sketchpad and a pencil and places both on the table. He turns the pad round so that Annabelle can view its well-thumbed pages. How well she knows it for having seen him studying it secretively before each episode! Now, in a surprising volte-face, he seems willing to divulge its contents to her. With the punctilio which an antiquarian might well display for some priceless object – a veneration which its dog-eared appearance signally fails to deserve – the Marquis flicks the pages of the notebook in front of her. Page after page, she can see, is covered with finely executed, monochrome drawings. Most are bound to the book; a few, however, are loose and folded. She examines their surfaces and recognizes many of their details. Surely, she asks the Marquis, she has come across them before?

"Indeed you have! You've already sympathized with quite a few of them," he answers her. "And they too, for that matter, have been through you."

Through her? Where has she heard that before? A strange image, as if the Marquis meant her to think that she had consumed the drawings, eaten them, somehow made them part of her. It takes her only a few seconds' concentration to locate this particular reference. Of course! The sounds in the train, the sounds which overwhelmed her, didn't the Marquis also describe them as having been through her?

Her companion turns back to the beginning of the pad where all the pages are headed by titles, and some are marked with short lists.

"When planning a meal, the first thing you should do is compile a list. What ingredients you'll need, what's missing from the larder, and so on and so forth. The same applies when organizing a story. Here, take a look at these!"

The Marquis' lists, Annabelle soon discovers, are as precise as the commission a rich merchant might hand a master painter. No sooner has she recalled this one aspect of the historical relationship between artist and patron than a scene rises in her mind. And so vivid and colourful are its details that for a moment she allows their seductive rhythm to take her over and to distance her from the Marquis' imperious demands . . . Covered in lustrous lowlands fabric, the velvet-hatted trader hands the tempera-stained craftsman his subject. A Nativity. Foreground in blue. Far spaces in green. To be used: so many ounces of ultramarine. The burgher wants his florins' worth of gold leaf. As for composition, set against the background of his farmstead in the olive tree-studded hills, he and his wife are to be caught in a clear Tuscan light kneeling on either side of the Virgin. Lifesized, naturally. While some in Flanders may still wish to belittle themselves before the Holy Mother, as the artist knows, here it is no longer the fashion for donators to quake like mannikins at Our Lady's feet. Their *raison d'être* in the picture's order? Good question! Let them be cognoscenti, people of means come to pay homage to the Holy Birth. No, the artist need not have the slightest reservations. Only last week, at a private dinner, Monsignor, Confessor to the Carmine, spoke of the importance which the Holy Father attaches to the production of new forms to grace the flowering of the Spirit. A word of warning in the artist's ear, however. This is not the first time that the merchant has sought to have this subject painted. Sadly not. The last man – he will not abase himself by mentioning that charlatan's name – who was honoured with the task failed to distinguish between the refreshing draughts of honest invention and the vile brew of barbarous fantasy. Indeed, he drew – no, the term is too kind – he scraped images of the most sacrilegious nature from the depths of his distempered imagination! So disgraceful were its content that, for the sake of propriety, the merchant had to have a canvas on which much had already been spent destroyed. For this particular work – to be hung in the private chapel His Reverence the Bishop consecrated but a month ago – the merchant insists, let space be rinsed in the august clarity which has made their city the world's envy! Let Nature reflect God's plan, not some devil's festering blueprint! Consigning this hastily evoked vignette to the gallery of her creativity, regretting the ease with which she was seduced from the Ecole des Beaux-Arts by Melanie Blanchard's promise of fame, wishing that she had not been taken in so easily by her conniving partner's blandishments – the pearl necklace, all those dinners in the Marais, visits to the inner sancta of famous couturiers – but had wandered instead for at least another year the length of the Louvre and made diligent copies of Old Masters, Annabelle, skipping through the Marquis' lists, concludes that they contain all the ingredients with which he skilfully constructed his episodes.

She selects a folded and crumpled piece of paper – one which the Marquis must have stuffed into his pocket before going into a cabin. Titled "The Leopard Woman", it is divided into two parts: Cast and Settings. Under Cast, Annabelle reads:

The Leopard Woman, An Artiste. As a 12 Year Old Girl; Her Parents and Brother.

The details under Settings are equally precise:

A Dressing Room; A Wood; A Cottage; A Lake.

The second list which she examines is firmly attached to the notebook and refers to one of the objects which she saw in the leather suitcase: 'The Silk Scarves'. Under its title, however, there is no Cast, no Settings. It must refer to some episode which, for reasons which Annabelle ruefully ascribes to that still mysterious quantum sympathy, the Marquis did not exploit. Leaving it aside, she searches through the other pieces of folded paper until she comes across the Egyptian episode. She scrutinizes its Cast list. Yes, there they all are:

The Young Architect, The Princess, A Soothsayer, A Maidservant.

The more she pores over these characters, which have been reduced to a Cast list, and places them neatly itemized under Settings, the more she comes to understand that they are not simply facts on a piece of paper. They are not just sterile, indistinct items. No, they've become part of her experience, they're shapes in her mind, forms she knows intimately! In fact so vividly does she recall them that, were she to go over them, she is sure she could evoke them in every detail. Fortunately, before this highly erroneous line of thought is permitted to go any further, she herself checks it. For, as her mind wanders on to areas with which she is more familiar, seeking to establish parallels in much the way that the Marquis is always doing, she soon concedes that were she, for instance, to try to recreate one of Coco Chanel's designs, she would fail. Why? Because since the time of the *grande couturière* of the Rue Cambon, cutting techniques have changed. Genuine cloths from that period are impossible to find. And improvements in sewing technique, however tiny, would inevitably intrude. Even if she did manage to engineer a superficially meticulous reproduction, it would still betray, at least to a purist's eye, its modern woof. Nor, for that matter, would that be the sole obstacle to authenticity. She would also have to take into account (as she well remembers from the art history lectures which that bitch Melanie made her give up) that often debated, much ridiculed yet obstinately resistant notion of *Zeitgeist*, the Spirit of the Age. A notion said by certain idealists to imbue every moment, every deed, every artefact with its mysterious imprint, and which thus make it impossible to recreate anything, reducing such efforts at best to a soulless simulacrum, to something as ridiculous as the train company furnishing its first-class carriages *à la belle époque*. As soon as Annabelle has turned this difficult notion over in her mind and realized that the Marquis is probably right, and that once a story is told it can never be retold, it can only be told again, she abandons that knotty ontological problem and resumes her examination of the remaining lists.

Alonzo, His Mother, Her Husband, The King.

Yes, there they are, along with the other cameos who featured in the Spanish melodrama's *dramatis figurae*. No waste. The Marquis has summarized everything and has put it all in its place. So it would seem that lists, very basic lists, lie at the source of it all. It is with an amazement not untinged with admiration that Annabelle concedes on what practical foundations the Marquis' inspiration appears to be grounded.

Not just lists either. For – without waiting for the Marquis to invite her to do so – Annabelle has skipped to the first pages of the notebook and has there confronted, precisely drawn in a hand which, if not professionally trained, is at least accurate, a number of drawings. Similarly to the lists, those which are crumpled and torn out have been used while the others are little more than titled doodles. Wasting no time on those which have failed to make the transition from the flux of fantasy to the constraints of fiction, she puts them to one side and unfurls the others.

Strangely, not once during her unauthorized exploration has the Marquis raised the slightest objection. He has merely dragged on his cigarette and pondered some private concern which, for good measure, he has shrouded in the inscrutability of a laconic smile.

Uncanny, muses Annabelle, just how close the Marquis' drawings are to his stories. They really are precise blueprints for everything that occurred out there, in the numbered compartments. Her artistic interest is further spurred by the discovery that they have all been executed in the dominant pictorial style of the historical period which they visited. The young architect's profile, for example, typical of Egypt's precise yet impersonal facture, bears no resemblance to Amonhotep but could denote any young delta male. Alonzo's renardine individuality on the other hand, with his thick beard, swaggering manner and eager eyes, shines through the Marquis' Renaissance line drawing. As for the looming and oppressive woodland scene and its naive adolescent, they are depicted in the crude and angular style favoured by agitprop artists. Although careful not to impose on the drawings a theory which might distort their nature, Annabelle cannot help suspecting that the Marquis must have created them as *aides-mémoire* to evoke atmosphere.

"Basically, Jean-Loup," Annabelle says at last, waving a hand at the pieces of paper on the table, each one visibly a key to the imaginative incidents which she has experienced, "you knew exactly what would happen within the various episodes."

"No," the Marquis answers adamantly. "I'm afraid you're mistaken there. It's true that I wrote down where events might happen and who to. But while I naturally did everything I could to influence events so that the key, the phial, and the crown would play central roles, what I couldn't possibly predict was the actual outcome of the stories. The fact is, Annabelle, there's always an element of risk in the undertaking. Many things can go wrong. You can run out of energy. You can lose the thread. And incidents outside your ken can suddenly interfere. Which is why it's so vital that you remain all the time in control and keep as strictly as possible to the creative principles which I've taught you."

Aware that Annabelle is casting a quizzical look at the other lists, divining the direction of her thoughts, the Marquis deals with her still unformulated question. "You're wondering, aren't you, why I devised more lists and drawings than we were likely to use? That's easily explained. As there's never any telling with which particular object you'll be in sympathy at any given period, you just have to spread the risk and be ready for any eventuality."

Allowing a few moments to pass before tackling the next layer of explanations, the Marquis studies his apprentice. As she appears to have followed his thoughts part with interest, part with disbelief, capitalizing on that rich and malleable mixture, he decides to provide her with a little more information. "You've understood by now, haven't you, that the key motive of the course is exchange? The reason the main characters we invent, discover, evoke – call it what you will – can get us the ingredient which we're after is because we project them into historical periods where it is easily available. We in turn, as you know, have in our possession the one object that'll solve their problem. An object which we must make sure plays a major part in their personal tragedy, otherwise," he waves his hand to connote emptiness, "we'd have nothing with which to bargain! There is however another important aspect to the course, perhaps the most important of all. If you manage to understand it, you'll have understood the very foundations of the imagination and will immediately become aware of the two paths down which its full activization can take you. I presume that you'd like me to tell you to what I'm referring?" asks the Marquis, then pauses, as if offering her the opportunity to say that, standing as she is on the very threshold of truth, she in fact prefers to step back and not to have revealed to her its most esoteric nucleus. Choosing to interpret her silence as assent rather than wordless trepidation, he continues: "Very well then. As this particular aspect of the course won't be of any use to you until much later, I shan't dwell on it too long but will let you draw your own conclusions." With the gravitas of an actor about to deliver a momentous speech he takes a sip from his glass, looks at her carefully, and says: "When you've mastered the principles of creative cooking, Annabelle, you'll be in a position to manipulate two particularly powerful processes. On the one hand you'll be able to gather from whatever sector of the imagination you care to delve into any ingredient you want – which, by the way, need not be a gastronomic ingredient but anything, anything at all. And, on the other, you'll be able to free any aspect of your imagination which has, for some reason or other, become blocked."

Annabelle finds the enormity of the Marquis' argument hard to digest. She therefore concentrates on the one process which he has never mentioned before. Herself no stranger to the drought which can periodically afflict the creator's mind and reduce the grasslands of inventiveness to a tundra, she listens with fascination as he reveals that her initiation into the secrets of creative cooking is not limited to shopping for far-flung gastronomic ingredients.

"Are you still with me?" asks the Marquis. Reassured by her nod of apparent comprehension, he presses forward with what sounds to Annabelle astonishingly like an affirmation of the existence of a philosopher's stone. "You're probably wondering how you can gauge whether your imagination is blocked or not. That's actually quite simple: you can't avoid the fact. The faculty itself makes it very plain. All of a sudden the dreams you have, the thoughts that roll through your mind, even the stories you narrate become invaded by situations in which obstacles, stalemates, problems of all shapes and sizes, abound. It is these repeated themes of obstruction which point to something being wrong. Now, if you confront these themes in yourself head on and, more importantly, if you know how to solve them, then, Annabelle, you'll have earned your freedom from all the pains or traumas which haunt you."

The landscape has suddenly taken on an almost baroque quality. Vast columns of clouds cut the moonlit horizon into unequal portions while below them the mass of an industrial estate throws spumes of reddened smoke into the sky. A vista which, depicting the visible world as a menacing panorama, seems to have conjured up a particularly telling counterpoint to the Marquis' comments.

"Let me be honest with you," the Marquis says, giving Annabelle a look of such ambiguity that she is not sure whether to take his recommendation at face value or, on the contrary, to regard it as a forewarning of trickery. "The characters which appeared in my stories, the characters we rescued, the young girl, the Egyptian, the dwarf, they all embodied problems, problems with which I have had to cope. Their quandary, the sad state in which we found them, represented creative blockages in a guise which I could recognize and with which I could deal. By promising then actually offering them the one object which guaranteed their freedom, I paid the price of expiation and thus freed myself from the spell which their stalemated situation represented. That is why, as you no doubt noticed," the Marquis adds with a complicitous wave of the hand, "the stories grew in scope and theme. The first was a simple affair. But the more I unloosed blockages in myself and harnessed creative powers which had been shackled, for reasons which are too personal to go into, the more I was able to develop the range and scope of my tales. Because, you see, the effect which arises from dissolving a problem is that you then have access to the creative energies which were bound up in it."

The orgasmic dénouement to the stories, the resolutions of stalemated situations, the vibrant, ecstatic eruptions which shook the mausoleum, which shimmered through the Leopard Woman, the bursts of energy which enlivened the Marquis after each episode, all these elements which, when encountered, she considered grotesque, theatrical, incomprehensible, Annabelle is now being asked to regard as representations of the liberation of creative forces! Metaphors shattering their manacles, loosening their energies which had been imprisoned! The first moments of freedom for emotions long stymied! The hidden world, the energetic substructure, the therapeutic theory whose existence the Marquis has just announced to her make her feel dizzy yet also braced by an almost feverish desire to continue the course. For if her imagination can really fetch anything, anything she wants from any sector she chooses, all her dreams, her most secret and fervent hopes, may soon fall within her range. And if at the same time her own neuroses, all the petty hindrances which her temperament has put in the way of her complete satisfaction, can actually be solved, what amazing results might she attain! But no! It is impossible! Surely the two most yearned-for goals of existence – untold riches and spiritual health – cannot have just been offered to her?

"If you know how to oil the wheels of exchange, not only will you rid yourself of creative blocks and gain control over your own energies but you'll also achieve everything to which you put your mind! Yes, and it'll be easy to sense that you're on the road to success. Indeed, it'll be quite unmistakeable. Your stories, your dreams, your thoughts, they'll all develop a special dynamic, they'll hum, they'll speed along! However," says the Marquis, inserting a footnote farced with his customary brand of reservation, "I wouldn't want you to think that it's a smooth process. There are pitfalls a-plenty – you've confronted a few already – and if you don't act with the greatest care, you can make disastrous mistakes, mistakes which could cost you dear, which could, in fact, cost you everything. The rewards of working productively with the imagination are countless but the penalties for misusing or, for that matter, for being misused by it are equally terrible. Were you, Annabelle, for instance, to fail to finish a story, do you realize that it could pursue you for ever and repeat its same intolerable, broken rhythms, to the point of driving you insane? I wonder if you have ever come across mental patients endlessly reciting the litany of their deranged achievements, lacking the satisfaction, the solace of a decent conclusion. It's a sad fact that asylums are full of people who inaugurated their own special story but who, for one reason or another – lack of will, illness, ambition unmatched by talent – were never able to complete what they had started. People who have since been thoroughly corroded by its enervating repetition. You remember the portholes in the corridor from which I dragged you? The ones which exerted such a hideous fascination over you? Well, they were classic examples of that very condition. O yes! Annabelle, don't, whatever you do, belittle the dangers involved. And among them, there's one in particular which you should never lose sight of: and that is that the characters you invent have purposes – minds isn't too strong a word for it – of their own. If you lose control of your creative rhythm, be it through misfortune or sheer clumsiness, they'll so pervert your narrative, it'll end up somewhere you never wished to go to!"

Although dearly tempted to ask the Marquis the question which she almost put to him at the time – how on earth did he know what scenes were playing when he did not even look through the portholes? – Annabelle in fact bursts out with: "For Heaven's sake, Jean-Loup! That doesn't make sense! Didn't you just tell me the stories were your own creation?"

"So are children, Annabelle, but that doesn't mean they can't make your life a misery, does it?" the Marquis answers. He drains his glass and beckons to the still-surly waiter to bring the bill. "However I rather think we've done enough philosophizing for the moment. And, anyway, reciting recipes is not the point of the course. It's high time you prepared your own concoctions. Yes," he adds, "I'll be interested to see how you get on."

No sooner has the waiter pocketed the note with which the Marquis settles the bill, found change, and placed the coins on a plate than he resumes his formerly aggressive behaviour and stares at Annabelle with what she takes to be naked effrontery. The fixity of his cat's eyes levelled at her seems to intimate that the reason she has been sipping wine with a bizarre character in the middle of the night when most honest citizens are fast asleep, and consequently looks exhausted, verges on the indecent. Annabelle, who has still not grasped the full significance of what the Marquis has been discussing nor the imminence of her own ordeal, finds it hard to swallow that, on top of everything else, this flunkey should now choose to be impudent. Realizing that she cannot shame him into ceasing his spiteful tactics, she adopts her most icy composure and cuts him right out of her field of vision. That done, she thanks the Marquis for moving her chair, rises, and turns her back on the wretch's insolence.

The Marquis escorts Annabelle out of the Bar Buffet's swing doors and lightly places his right hand on her shoulder. Perhaps because she has only just recovered from the waiter's petty attempt at embarrassing her, she instinctively stiffens. But then, compensating for her involuntary coldness, she directs a warm gaze at her companion.

Down the corridors of the smoothly progressing train they walk, exchanging pleasantries on the distance which the Mistral has put between itself and Paris, the various towns through which it has swiftly and anonymously passed, and at what hour it is likely to berth in Nice. But when, outside her own compartment, the Marquis hands Annabelle the sketchpad and asks her to take no more than an hour to devise her episode, she can no longer conceal her mounting apprehension at having to shine within the enchanted circle of this most capricious art.

CHAPTER TWELVE

His face flushed, his manner brusque, Jules Pinard leaves the English Lady's compartment and heads for his own cubicle. On reaching it, he unlocks it and slides in. His jacket he places neatly on a hanger while his posterior he seats on the folding chair before his table.

No visible improvement. Anatole has remained curled in his basket, his coat drab, his attitude despondent. Nor has he so much as touched the plateful of food which his master put out for him. Jules tidies away its foul-smelling substance into a drawer and, determined no matter the creature's mood, to share his adventures with him, begins to tell his latest news.

"You'll never guess why the Lady called me, Anatole. Her dog, yes, her little dog has gone! Pouff! Vanished! And do you know why? How could she be so stupid? Because she let it out of her compartment. Yes, into the corridor. What for? To let it do its business! What does she think the train is? A forest? An open field? And she, a Milady too! Now of course the bitch's nowhere to be found! When she told me what had happened, I thought: so? What does she expect of me? Does she want me to get down on my hands and knees? Go sniff it out through the train? No thank you! But then, Anatole, she looked at me with those eyes of hers, and I realized I couldn't leave her in her mess. Not her, Anatole, not Milady! Anyway, I had an idea and I said to her. 'Milady! Do not despair. I have a friend. And my friend, he has a nose, yes, a wonderful nose. If anyone can, he'll find your little dog.' Her response? Cold, but then that is her way. Cold and magnificent. So, *mon vieux!* You will help me, won't you? It can't have gone far. Could be in the kitchens. Could have poked its stupid nose in one of the compartments. It's possible. You will find her, eh? You want to know what she looks like? Er . . . well . . . About as big as that." Jules' hands gesticulate a poor approximation of the bitch's size. "She's got a fluffy coat and . . ." He suggests a variety of shapes, contradicts himself, wavers, until, unsure, his hands fall down in frustration. "Eh, Anatole! I almost forgot!" He slaps his head. "I can do better than that. Here! I've got just the thing! See, that'll do the trick."

Out of Jules' pocket comes a leather lead, its smooth, shiny and flexible length betraying its expense. He places it before Anatole's nose. The moment the ferret catches a whiff of its scent, he goes through a remarkable transformation. He uncurls, moves close to the lead, sniffs it with repeated avidity, and visibly perks up. Noting the acceleration in Anatole's breathing, and the intense beaconing of his small black eyes, the Steward is overjoyed to see him so fired up for the hunt.

"Careful, mind! Search for the dog, Anatole, that's all! I don't want you disappearing God knows where and then having to track you down too. And remember: everybody's asleep. So keep nice and quiet. When you've found the stupid animal, come back and tell me where the bloody thing is. I'll be waiting here for you. *Allez! Et bonne chance!*"

The Steward picks Anatole up by the neck. What a shiny coat! What intense eyes! And a nose second to none! He congratulates himself on the felicity with which he let the gypsy he caught without a ticket ride on without a fine in exchange for the ferret which he had been hiding in his grimy overcoat. Then, with a fond chuckle at his own inimitable cunning and at the *quid pro quo* which he should soon – if fortune smiles on him – be able to effect, he gives the ferret's frisky flanks a paternal stroke, drops it to the floor and, delighted with the animal's nervous readiness to leap, opens the door. A fast blur, little more than a grey trace on a slow exposure, and Anatole, utterly familiar with the train's every contour, and guided by the radar of his powerful olfactory sense, rounds the corner and disappears.

Jules straightens his necktie, gives his hair a hint of pomade, curls his moustache, takes from a locker a bottle of cologne and, sprinkling it all over his face, prepares himself for his next scene. An actor's sly smile, a beau's knowing manner, and a last-minute inspection of the apparition in the hand mirror convince him that he is ready. All he has to do is wait for his ferret to locate the dog, return the aggressive little thing to the Lady, and be rewarded for a heroic effort. And, indeed, so high are his expectations of his animal's unerring sense and of his own consequent triumph that for once he neither curses nor shows the slightest anger when a solitary attention-seeking flag falls, a flag which – as he is spruced for quite another type of service – he ignores with complete equanimity.

CHAPTER THIRTEEN

Stretched out on the bunk, eyes closed, the Marquis appears to be resting. But he is not asleep. Instead he is busy assessing how his stratagem has progressed so far and what obstacles remain to be hurdled. Everything appears to be in place: Annabelle learning her lessons, about to try her luck. Best not to be overconfident though. There is still so much to be done.

Although he would dearly like to bask in the warmth of his partial success, the Marquis cannot prevent his thoughts turning to sombre matters. What if Annabelle proves ineffectual, fails to rise to the occasion? What if, in spite of his recent warning, she aims too high, produces a story she cannot complete, and is doomed thereafter, in the depths of some asylum, to eternally repeat? In which case the accursed cycle into which the boy beguiled him will remain unbroken, and he will have no choice but to start the whole ghastly process again! The idea of unearthing yet another victim is too depressing, especially as Annabelle has shown all the right qualities. Never has he come so close to his aims before. She must – yes, she must – hold on!

His last effort, he admits, was dismal. Utterly dismal. It makes him shudder to think of it. It was of course a totally different scenario and a very different type of woman. He recalls her brittle features, her high-pitched voice, her gestures marked by a whippet-like intensity. Where did he meet her? Ah, yes! He was visiting one of the grander auction rooms. The sale had just got into full swing when he had noticed her pursuing some obscure daub by a lesser known devotee of the Barbizon school. He had correctly appraised her hunger and had decided to bid against her. Soon all other bidders had fallen away, leaving the two of them dancing to the intoxicating rhythm of fast spiralling figures. She had given him a cold glance, had clenched her teeth, and had refused to give up the chase. At around twice the painting's reserve, he had veered off, letting her swoop alone towards her fictive triumph. Proud of her purchase – a somewhat uninspired precursor of *pleinairisme* – she had walked over to the clerk to claim her canvas. He had then approached her and had congratulated her on the perspicacity of her taste. A fine example of the harsh quality of light on the plains of La Bière. How he would have loved to have secured it for himself. Sadly his funds had run out. Would she – a worthy opponent – make his loss a little sweeter by doing him the honour of dining with him? Her manuscript-thin skin flushed with victory, she had looked him up and down before finally accepting.

The Montparnasse restaurant to which he had taken her, a restaurant famous for its refusal to fall in with minimalist fads, and its commendable fidelity to the tenets of Boulestin and Escoffier, had served them well. And it had been over a brace of perfectly cooked *langoustines*, laced with a delightful Riesling, that he had made her a proposal. Might she be interested in a source of antique ceramics which he had good cause to believe was still untapped, unknown? Her eyes had examined him for a hidden condition, had met none, and then had leapt at the chance.

But when he drove her over to the little villa which he had specially hired for the occasion in a cramped sidestreet in the Yvelines, and they had settled down over a glass or two of Veuve Cliquot, and he had introduced her to the power of his creative illusions, showing her the objects he had brought and making her touch them, his plan had suddenly collapsed. For no sooner had the objects "talked" to her than she had screamed, fallen in a heap on the floor, and lain there very still. Nothing, not a slap across the cheeks, a dose of *sal volatile*, not even a tot of brandy had brought her round. He had had to drag her to the car and, afraid that some curious concierge might espy him and call the police, he had rushed her to a nearby hospital.

Had the lady been under stress? the unpleasantly inquisitorial doctors had asked him. Not as far as he knew, he had answered. Stress indeed! One look at her contorted face showed that what she had been through had provoked not stress but acute horror.

That frequenter of art rooms, that auction house devotee, that small-time dealer had been seduced right out of her depth and had had to face for the first time her own abysmal lack of imagination. Oh, yes! It was no doubt pleasant enough to feed on the faint emanation of artistic objects and to make money out of them. But to confront the pulsations of creativity head-on had been too much for her. Leaving her half comatose in the hands of the hospital staff, he had handed them a false name and address to avoid legal complications, and had vanished in the night. All in all a disaster. A whole week in which he had once again tried to secure his release, a whole week wasted. And there had been other occasions, all of them failures. As for the days they lost and the hopes they betrayed, he prefers not to dwell on them.

He keeps his eyes shut and listens to the wind scratching the smooth hull of the train. It is surprising but he now feels torn between excitement and fear. Excitement that Annabelle may at last be the right victim. Fear that something may go wrong. He wonders whether it was a mistake to reveal to her so much about the effects of storytelling. Not that he has lied: a tale well-told does release energies, can liberate neuroses and break the back of mindless repetitions. No, he consoles himself, no harm done. If all goes well, she will have to learn the process anyway. First things first, however: entrapping her is, and must remain, his main goal.

What a strain narrating proves to be! As for duplicity, it is no easy game to play. Fortunately he is almost sure that he has manoeuvred Annabelle into the right frame of mind, even if her occasional obstinacy has been hard to cope with. A situation for which he has had to pay a high price: no letting up at any time. Even a short and well-earned respite like this one has to be utilized to plan the next stage. And he has had to concentrate hard to stay steps ahead of any response she might make. Most he has predicted. Most, but not all. The memory of that near disastrous infinity room still reverberates through him, making him shake with anxiety. What that bitch has made him go through! On the other hand if she swallows the bait which he has put out for her and permits him to escape, then, yes, it'll all have been worth it!

As this is a story set against constant movement, the Marquis' slowly unfolding bouts of depression, expectation, hope and anguish cannot hold us any longer. And so, in search of further stimulation, we must leave the recumbent Marquis and wander into Annabelle's compartment where we find her poring over the sketchpad, her pen at the ready, her mind overcast by an imaginative void dogging her every attempt to devise a plot. She bites her lips. Her hand will not stop fidgeting. And if the way to evoke inspiration is via a formula, then it is clear that she has never learnt it.

Certainly, using the influence available to all omniscient and interfering narrators, it would be easy to intimate to her by what means other artists, faced by the dearth of invention, have primed their creative pumps; what role the rabbit's foot, the tall pulpit, the ritual cleaning of the desk, the sharpening of pencils, and the seclusion of the cork-lined room have played in literary histories; and by what propitiatory actions doleful minds have done their damnedest to beg from a capricious Muse a kiss. But whereas these held, stood before, exercised, or retired into have been known to produce the sought-after gush of images and progeny of words, it is not in fact the peculiar object, the obsessive practice, nor the hermetic loci themselves which have mattered, rather the evocative links they have had the power to generate. However, as Annabelle is rather more accustomed to filching visual ideas from her rivals, to parade before her the various devices by which literary deserts have been made to bloom is unlikely to do the trick; and would perhaps remind her too strongly – she who is so much the enemy of the copied article – of the role which borrowing plays in all creative activity. After a short bout of despair, during which she is very tempted to throw in her hand, she resorts to one of the oldest narrative techniques – when at a loss recapitulate – and runs through what of the course she has so far understood.

To begin with, there are the Marquis' injunctions: barter is the law of life; the essence of the course is exchange, and so on and so forth. Then there is his basic formula: ingredients, methods, sympathy. The important thing, as he would say, is first to find your ingredient. Very well. Hers are in her handbag. She picks through it until she comes across the silver locket with its mother-of-pearl inlay; a locket she remembers she ran down at the *Puces* at a rascally dealer's who, the moment she showed an interest in it, turned sweet on her and tried to push her onto a chesterfield in the back of his shop. A locket with which she fled without disbursing so much as a *sou*! Serve him right! And is that what she is to barter with? muses Annabelle, turning the attractive little object in her hand. While hardly overendowed with exciting memories, it'll just have to do.

Next, methods. If she has grasped the Marquis' meaning rightly, she has to plan her episode, draw it on the sketchpad, and rough out a Cast and Settings list. Which shouldn't be beyond her if only she had something to tell. And, finally, there's sympathy which, as far as she can make out, somehow comes into play when selecting the object to be traded, and with showing sensitivity to the historical period in which the ingredient is to be procured – that much she does recall the Marquis discussing. Whatever other function it may also have remains a mystery. Apart from these basic elements of groundwork, and a few intuitive notions picked up during the three other episodes, the subject, she has to admit, leaves her mind a blank.

What about that other astonishing ability which the Marquis promised may soon be hers: the ability to send her imagination to any epoch to fetch anything she fancies? For a few delightful seconds she meditates on a collection of royal jewels which she recently saw mocked up in paste at the Musée Carnavalet, jewels whose originals she is sure would look good on her and on the dresses which she would design to complement them. An exquisite if mercenary reverie which she is sadly forced to cut short. For, really, they are not at all what she is now supposed to be seeking, nor is this the moment to indulge in her fascination for baubles.

Somewhat depressed, Annabelle returns to the matter at hand: the need to conjure up a good story. So, she must place the locket in her episode and use it to secure the final gastronomic ingredient which they are pursuing: those are her goals. A process which, the Marquis has informed her, will not only help some character apparently bound up with her psyche to gain its freedom – a character she hasn't yet invented or, would it be fairer to say, discovered? – but will also loosen creative energies which, frankly, she did not even know were blocked. Having summarized the information which the Marquis has divulged to her, she feels that she might as well have recited some lesson learnt parrot-fashion for all the sense it makes. Yet time is running out and she has less than an hour to satisfy the Marquis' request for a well-crafted tale, a tale which she has not even begun!

She turns her head to the window and attempts to forget for

a moment the challenge which the Marquis has thrown her, cursing her folly in falling for the lure of the unknown, and in attempting to be something she is not, be it gastronome or all-purpose narrator. Of one thing she is sure: the events which she has been through in the last few hours have worn her down. So why go on? What keeps her chained to this manic pursuit of the magical? Curiosity? Greed? The challenge that whatever she is supposed to achieve she will? Or, rather more pointedly, might it be the Marquis' jibe that she may not have enough talent for the course still ringing in her ears? Yes, perhaps that's the reason she cannot hand him the easy victory of being proven right. If he can relate a story and reach his ridiculous ends, so can she! Why should she doubt her creative powers, at least until they've been tested? Hasn't the Marquis been counselling her *ad nauseam* to invest in trust? Very well then, she will! Applying her powers in an atmosphere as infinitely suggestible as the train's should not be beyond her. And, on top of all that, she reminds herself, if the course turns out genuine, not only will her efforts be rewarded by her mother having to concede the mastery of her daughter in the one field in which she has always held the high ground, but she might also reap untold riches culled from the depths of fabulous treasure troves! A delicious prospect, though one whose fulfilment, she balefully recognizes, still seems a long way off.

Dammit! She angrily scatters the sketchpad, the unused pencil, and the uninspiring locket, sending them flying to the floor. Enough! She can't bear it any more! Has she really been taken in by all this nonsense? Can she have fallen for so pathetic a fantasy? She'll go and tell the Marquis what he can do with his confounded course!

A few seconds later, contrite before the mindless destructiveness of her impulse, she picks the objects off the floor. Thankfully nothing broken: the pencil sharp, the sketchpad unruffled, the delicately ornamented silver frame still in one piece. Resignedly she places them on the table, takes the fashion magazine which sits at her elbow and, to calm her nerves, rifles through its pages.

What is there to be gained from perusing the magazine except putting off for a while the attempt to give birth creatively? It is without much enthusiasm that Annabelle flicks through its pages. Various advertisements for cosmetics, from guards against menstrual discharges to fragrances designed to help Mademoiselle Unetelle catch her man, are interlarded with items of topical banality. She is ambling through the wealth of material when a headline catches her eyes. Yes, here is something interesting, its subject unusually appropriate. Backing its case with a generous spread of photographs, the article which has seized her attention surveys the various methods by which food can be processed. The article's central thesis is easy to gauge. Dividing all food into two categories, it contrasts those injected with chemical preservatives with those produced in a more natural fashion. As for the tone of its copy, it is so shrill that it seems hell bent on making immediate converts to its dietary doctrine. Annabelle who, in spite of a firm grounding of common sense, long ago surrendered to the contemporary equation of sin with fat, and who ceaselessly scours newsprint for ways of keeping her waist close to the canons of high fashion, skims through the article which, if slight in information, is at least presented with enough brio to hold her. She soon concludes that, in spite of its overemotional treatment of the topic, the article is worth reading.

She is particularly struck by one photograph among the colourful array. This features a thin and bespectacled nutritionist in his laboratory, a serious savant surrounded by the retorts, alembics and bunsen burners of his profession. The photograph is a tribute to the didactic pose for in it the scientist has been made to hold high in his left hand a sorry loaf made with refined flour, while in his right the stylist has placed a fat one made from wholemeal. Quite a telling contrast, Annabelle concedes, sensing the beginnings of narrative potential within the loaves. The key questions, though, are: one, with what meaning can she invest her locket to release this reedy thinker from the love-based quandary into which he has become quagmired? And two, how will this act of liberation seduce him into handing her – what's the next ingredient which she's supposed to be procuring? – ah yes, parsley!

What about . . . muses Annabelle, grabbing the pad and applying the pen's sharp tip to its unindented paper. It is gratifying that her ability to compose sketches ad lib in a public place has at least not deserted her. And, indeed, her sketch soon develops a storyline which, if a little tenuous, is still quite pleasing. She has put the finishing touches to three small storyboards when she detects within them additional themes which she might usefully exploit. And so intrigued is she by their felicitous appearance that she almost forgets that she also has to devise Cast and Settings lists. A few minutes later, if somewhat scrappily, they too are done.

Has she, like some amateur dramatist creating an overrich blend of speaking parts, she wonders, made her Cast list too long? Headed by a male lead – the scientist – it is supported not only by a female assistant, a monkey and a mad professor, but also by a ten-person committee and, for good measure, a group of charitable ladies. Her sketch is a more modest affair, plagiarizing the photograph by portraying the white-coated scientist upright in his laboratory and surrounded by row upon row of chemicals stored in a range of translucent bottles.

A problem has arisen, however, and a rather knotty problem at that. Should her main character not be a woman? Would it not be wiser when telling a story first time round for her to focus on her own sex? On the other hand, Annabelle ponders, making abstraction of her mentor's greater experience in the field, the Marquis managed to convey the life of an adolescent girl so why shouldn't she that of a man? No, she resolves, once again gazing at the photograph, then at her own faithful reproduction of the scene, the original for her inspiration was a male so, if only on naturalistic grounds, she really cannot justify a last-minute change of sex.

Once she has subjected her handiwork to further assessment, she concludes that she has quite enough material to set the mechanism rolling. Mindful of the Marquis' advice, she decides to trust her imagination to come up with the rest. She leaves her compartment and, clutching her sheaf of notes covered with newly-created details, sets off towards compartment no 44.

The twin dice fly through the air, land on the Marquis' compartment table, and prance on their pointed corners before revealing their final score. A one and a two. Annabelle takes the locket out of her jacket pocket and says breezily: "That's settled then! Cabin number three it is and," she shows her companion the small silver object, "this little locket!"

The journey is predictably disorienting, a contradiction in terms which Annabelle has learnt to accept without difficulty. Is it not extraordinary, she muses, how many conceptual leaps she has made in such a short space of time? This either shows a basic resilience in her character – and one of which she was not previously aware – or, on a rather more general plane, that man is plastic by nature and, given the right force of coercive circumstances, can overturn age-old values with surprising agility.

Every so often the ordered calm of their movement through corridors which have lost nothing of their traditional character is violently punctuated by strident sounds like that of a jet engine, or waves crashing against the shore, or some powerful fast-revving machine grinding its gears. But when, rounding the next corner, they do not find themselves staring into the baying jaws of a fire-spitting reactor, nor peering through the vulva of an aquamarine cave at the murderous roar of the sea, nor, for that matter, perched on the edge of a Moloch of fiendishly spinning cogs, she accepts with philosophical detachment that they have just walked through a library of vagrant sounds which, for purposes proper to them, yet surely related to the stock of images she earlier caught sight of in the corridors, have simply been exercising themselves.

Annabelle is relieved at how easy compartment no 3 is to find. There it lies at the end of a nondescript corridor, its number plainly inscribed on the door. A little bashful, conscious of how difficult it is not to imitate the Marquis' every stance, yet determined to forge her own style even within so formulaic a routine, she takes her notes out of her pocket and reads them conscientiously, closing her eyes to recall their details.

When she has firmly committed her notes to memory, and placed them back in her pocket, she nods to the Marquis who, pleased with her progress, has been standing at a respectful distance from her. And it is with poorly disguised trepidation that she at last opens the door.

No sooner has she glanced into the chamber than, her face ashen, she abruptly shuts the door.

"Well?" asks the Marquis, surprised at this radical departure from laid-down procedure. "What's the matter?"

"I'm . . . I'm not at all sure," Annabelle answers nervously. "But for some reason your principles haven't worked for me."

Frowning, the Marquis goes up to the door and peers in.

Unlike all the other chambers in which they have pursued

their quest, this one, he notes, is immediately accessible past the door. Either Annabelle has not bothered to provide the episode with the distraction of an antechamber or, worse, has simply forgotten to do so. A small detail but one with whose basic and simple structure, he feels, she really should not have dispensed. That, however, is not the least of her shortcomings. For what now confronts him in the chamber is a truly terrible mess.

The chamber which she has created is large and has clearly been abandoned for years. Everything in it is topsy-turvy, every square inch is filled with more mismatched objects than even a demented antiquarian could ever have collected. In stunned silence the Marquis stares at it. It is quite a while before he can distinguish any kind of order. Eventually, under the shattered furniture, agricultural tools, autumn leaves, sycamore branches, packs of deodorants, holiday brochures, goblets and paintings covered in dust which have somehow ended up here, he can make out the remnants of a structure which, he hazards, might once have been that of a scientific laboratory. Yet so dilapidated is its equipment, so dirty its implements, so shabby its overall appearance that he is not sure to what branch of science it might have belonged. Having gazed on this sorry sight long enough, the Marquis closes the door firmly.

"Appalling!" he says, turning to his apprentice. "Grubbier than an *oubliette*. I've never seen anything like it. It has to be cleared up this instant, Annabelle!"

"I realize that!" Annabelle exclaims. "But how should we go about it?"

"We?" the Marquis emphasizes, as if Annabelle had just mouthed an obscenity. "Correction, Annabelle! How do *you* go about it? This is your episode! The fall-out in that junk heap of a room is your creation, and yours alone." He shakes his head. "You better start off by going over your lists and sketch again."

Annabelle examines her notes in bewilderment, looks around at the chamber then retorts: "I never sketched any of that!"

"Maybe not – but you still let it in. Don't you see? You have to control everything. Not just what you want in but what you want to exclude as well. You can't afford to let any old bric-à-brac creep in like that. No matter how big or small a set happens to be, you have to know where everything, but absolutely everything, is even if it seems secondary and doesn't serve the main aim of the story. Otherwise, your imagination will get the better of you and I hate to guess where you might end up. You have to study everything in detail," he adds, taking her notes from her hand in which they have been hanging limply, perusing them quickly and setting them before her. "There's nothing wrong with these sketches. So, close your eyes and visualize the scene exactly the way you want it. And don't go changing important structural details arbitrarily. The stories I told all had corridors between the door and the chamber – and for good reason!"

Choosing to leave unexplained why he constructed his sets in that particular fashion, and thus standing on an artist's inalienable right to keep the nature of his infrastructures secret, the Marquis nonetheless insists that, to ensure success, she should put tried and tested experience behind her.

This time, her eyes closed, manipulating ideal matter within the infinitely malleable sphere of her mind's eye, to the best of her ability she does what he has ordered her, and imagines each square inch of the stage on which she wants to set her scene, establishing its functional furniture, its various implements, and its working props. When she is sure that nothing short of an explosion could possibly budge her props – and ruefully admitting to herself that her first attempt was indeed sloppy and lacked the concentration which her own professional standards should have engendered – she opens her eyes, and, exhausted from the effort, leans against the side of the carriage.

Has she executed his advice to the letter? he asks her. She confirms that she has. With marked courtesy, he opens the door for her and lets her pass. And as this time she does not recoil from her newly-organized chamber, he follows her in.

Annabelle walks through the compartment door and passes through a rather rudimentary corridor, but one which, she hopes, will fulfil the Marquis' demands. Dank, gloomy, rather narrow and leading, via a slightly circuitous and disorientating route, to another door. This she pushes open and breathes a sigh of relief. For all irrelevant objects have vanished and the now completely cleared laboratory has faithfully replicated the one which she saw in the magazine. True to the mettle of her reawakened standards, her creative flair has taken the trouble to get details right. Even the pallor which descends from the fluorescent lights across a stalactite array of test tubes displays the very same lambency as in the article's photograph.

Just as he should be, the thin, bespectacled and white-coated scientist is busy at his varnished bench while next to him a bank of retorts bubbles away and a plantation of alembics releases thin wisps of yellowy spume into the air. Annabelle, delighted that the process seems to be working for her, and beginning to savour the feeling of being in charge, makes her way towards two stools which are standing near the main worktable. She grabs them and, placing them opposite the scientist, sits on one sidesaddle. She then invites the Marquis to take the other. Which, with a nod, he does.

"And a good day to you!" she says, addressing the scientist who has looked up from his experiments but who does not appear surprised to see the two visitors.

His gaunt features betray the hours which he must have spent cooped up in the laboratory. His face is sallow. As for his eyes, they are deeply-set behind lids heavy with sleeplessness. The scientist, turning towards Annabelle, answers her. "A good day?" His voice is as strained as a tremolo. "How can you say that when there's so much to do and so little time to do it in? No, don't tell me why you're here. You've come to interrupt me, haven't you? As if I didn't have enough problems as it is."

"There's no need to be abusive!" Annabelle retorts, somewhat taken aback that her own character should begin by berating her, its creator. Swiftly parrying his ill-tempered verbal volley, she adds: "Especially as we've come here to help you."

"All right! Don't rub my face in it!" the scientist exclaims with irate emphasis. "I know you've got me over a barrel and that if I don't meet my end of the bargain, you'll abandon me!" He scurries from behind the bench, revealing to the Marquis how inordinately thin his legs are, stick insects, encased in the loose folds of an old grey suit. Pacing up and down, a pained expression on his lips, he waves his arms around the laboratory, and adds: "And if there's one thing I just couldn't bear, it'd be to see all my years' work go to waste!"

Fascinating, those nervous tics scrambling like an army of grubs beneath the scientist's face, thinks the Marquis. Very probably a symptom of Annabelle's hesitant hand, the kind of tremor an apprentice puppeteer might well transmit to his figurine when first performing in public. A characteristic which should vanish the moment she settles down. Of greater significance is the quality of her storytelling technique. Or rather, as the Marquis is forced to mark, its seriously defective nature. For so far it has left him cold. Not only is her plot structure abrupt, it is also void of finesse. To take but one example: the flagrant absence of introductory material. There they are, having just arrived unannounced into her character's laboratory, and she has not even provided herself, nor him for that matter, with a decent identity. Instead they have been thrown *in medias res* with not the slightest background from which to make, if asked, an adequate reply. And how very crude to have got the scientist to blurt out that he has to fulfil a bargain. Whatever next? Why not make him confess that he is no more than a fictional being, that his words have been prepared for him long in advance, and that he has no intelligence except that of his preorganized text? And even if that were true, which he has already told Annabelle it is not, to have produced a tale so lacking in basic finery shows a distinct lack of respect for the considerable embroidering which he himself produced for his stories, and a disregard for the examples which he hoped she would follow. *Bon sang de bon Dieu!* There is an art to all this, an art his apprentice is flagrantly ignoring!

True, the Marquis adds, for all her defects, Annabelle is still being seduced. And true, she has still no idea of the extent of the toils into which she is to fall. That, however, does not mean that the process need be barbarous. Nor that it should ditch her at the end of the course with nothing but the taste of her own defeat. If only she would learn from him now, her later situation could become sweetly victorious, if at someone else's expense – that goes without saying. No, the Marquis has to admit, assessing the first minutes of Annabelle's performance, she has disappointed him. It is not as if he had never before come across plays which make their makeshift construction painfully plain during their exposition later to illumine, in a confessional fit in the third act, the reality of their being produced there and then, live, as it were. But, frankly, he has no reason to suppose that her dramatic debut is motivated by a desire to ironize common narrative processes, rather than by a profound lack of *savoir-faire*. And yet, for all her clumsiness, he has to concede, she has at least produced the bare bones of a story. That much ground has been gained. To what extent she intends to flesh them out he will have to wait and see.

His angular features stretched, his manner both raucous and hesitant, the scientist stares at the two travellers, then pleads fretfully: "You have brought it with you, haven't you? You have brought it?"

"Yes, yes, I have," Annabelle answers in her most soothing voice.

A hangdog expression permanently affixed to his face, the scientist rushes over to Annabelle and sniffs the air around her with distaste, a gesture to which she meekly, indeed with overt complicity, submits.

"And that's what you want me to get you?" he asks, lunging at her as if she were a difficult specimen under examination. "Parsley?"

The Marquis interprets the smile which Annabelle casts in his direction without any difficulty: she is smugly signalling that she too can organize expository material. To a limited extent, he nods his silent agreement. For the scientist has not sniffed him like a bloodhound on the scent, which presumably means that she has failed, or forgotten, to make him reek of parsley too. Not an easy task admittedly yet one which her imagination might have risen to had she made it do so! As for the scientist not asking her the reasons why she stinks, thinks the Marquis, determined to push his criticism further, that too is another serious oversight. Clearly he has to take some of the blame for her lapses: he has not inculcated the rules into her properly. And there are also a number of questions which he has to answer: these variations in the story, are they proof of her going her own way – a laudable if dangerous enterprise – or, much more worrying, do they signify that she has next to no control over her material?

"Yes, parsley's exactly what I'm after," Annabelle answers. "So the sooner you get on with it the better."

"I presume you know everything there is to know about me?" says the scientist. "The years I've dedicated to research, the benefits humanity would reap if I were successful, the dreadful conditions under which I have to work?" he adds, as if reciting the themes of an overplayed repertory piece.

No, he will not interfere. Although nauseated by her shameless use of narrative shorthand, and her insertion of techniques more suited to strip cartoon than to adult fantasy, the Marquis decides to bide his time. He consoles himself with the notion

226

that it really does not matter whether she dances, pirouettes, slouches or sashays towards the trap that he has set for her, as long as she is drawn into the imaginative process, and eventually falls into it.

"As it so happens," she says, "I do. I've studied your case in quite some depth. But as there's no substitute for a first-hand account, I'd be glad to hear your version and I'm sure my secretary would also gain greatly from it." She looks in the Marquis' direction. "Isn't that right, Jean-Loup?"

"Yes, indeed, Mademoiselle Fleury," answers the Marquis, refusing to be upset by being assigned a status as lowly as any he offered her. Instead, now that he has a role to play, he swiftly moulds his behaviour to suit it. "I would be most interested."

"Very well then," says the scientist, slipping on a pair of thin surgical gloves which have been sitting on top of the workbench. "It won't take a minute to get you your heart's desire so that's what I'll do first. Then I'll share with you some of the ordeals – I couldn't tell you all of them, there have been so many – that brought me here and the reasons why my research has been stymied and my health wrecked. And when I've done that, you'll let me have the little locket, now, won't you?"

"You've my word on that," answers Annabelle, slightly taken aback by this reversal of the usual procedure, and hoping that to be granted the sought-for ingredient before the scientist has told his story will have no adverse effect on its outcome. But then, she thinks to herself, why on earth should the pattern of a woman's narration slavishly follow a man's?

The scientist, his movements jerky, his manner single-minded, darts round the laboratory and picks up a jar of chemicals from a long glass shelf. He reaches for the white powder within it and puts some into a beaker. Then he turns on a number of gas burners and switches various electrical implements. And as he rushes round, the Marquis hears him mumble a ditty.

> If you choose your ingredients wisely,
> And pick your methods right,
> Never forget your timings,
> Sympathy'll look after itself.

A bit of this and a bit of that.
A touch of this and a touch of that.
A smidgeon of this and a smidgeon of that,
Sympathy'll look after itself.

What an excruciating song! thinks the Marquis, sure that he could have produced more passable verse. In an attempt to be charitable towards Annabelle's early effort, he decides to overlook her singularly poor ear. Indeed, he muses, it is little short of a miracle that lacking decent doggerel, hamstrung by a rickety structure, and threadbare of plot, her story should still be holding to its tracks.

Humming all the while, the scientist places a variety of chemicals and liquids into glass vessels upheld by tripods over the blue prongs of bunsen burners, and keeps a vigilant eye on them as they start to boil. For all his weird appearance and overnervous disposition, the Marquis concedes, the boffin does have an air of professional competence about him. What is he up to now? he wonders, as the thin-necked creature disappears for a few seconds behind a barrage of steaming apparatus. Ah, yes, there he is, dipping the long thin nose of a thermometer into a beaker, craning over its calibrations, and checking the liquid's temperature. Satisfied with the reading, the scientist pours the brew into yet another beaker, stirs it, then tips the green, viscous and elongated result into a crucible.

Annabelle is not at all unhappy at the role which precise methods and accurate readings have played in the scientist's concoction – without the slightest intervention from her. To gain a better view of the process, and to gauge exactly what the scientist is doing absorbed over the implements of his trade, she tilts her stool towards the wooden varnished workbench.

It would seem that he is busy pestling some greenish substance in an earthenware crucible. A little while later she can see that the substance has become pliant and that he is letting it stand. He walks over to the other side of the laboratory, rummages around in a cupboard, extracts a cast-iron mould, and carries it back to the workbench. He then gingerly lifts the thickened paste from the crucible and places it in the mould.

It is a heady experience to be aware of the intimate choreography of a scene – for in most of its details it has remained true to her sketch – yet to be constantly taken aback by the direction which her own character keeps taking. For instance, isn't there something incongruous about a nutritionist, a real food expert, going to so much trouble to produce a synthetic substance? Or could he perhaps be making a telling point about the execrable processes that are part of the manufacture of artificial products? Or has – much more disturbing – something gone wrong? She will not deny that her story has departed in a number of details from the patterns which she experienced under the Marquis' tutelage. Has she omitted something essential, an element whose absence has unbalanced the narrative mechanisms and prevented them from acting according to the formula? The curious thing, she avows, is that although she cannot figure out where the problem lies – if indeed there is one – this has not affected the excitement which she feels at what her creature, the scientist, is up to. It is as if his every gesture were the fulfilment of some secret desire. But of what desire? Difficult to tell. Witnessing the materialization of her own creative substance? Seeing the story which she herself invented unfolding before her eyes, even if in a form estranged and reshaped? Or might it have something to do with those other materialistic desires which the Marquis has revealed to her, desires so infectious, so alluring that, however hard she has tried to repress them, keep playing on the margins of her mind? Shaking off their images of luxury, and reminding herself that the Marquis has repeatedly chided her for her lack of trust, she decides not to interfere with the mysterious process regardless of her doubts.

A mysterious process which is not over yet. For the scientist is now palping the paste round the mould and forcing it to adopt its shape. That done, he takes the mould over to a small electric oven, puts it in, and switches the oven full on.

"This is just a secondary result of the main thrust of my work," says the scientist, looking up from his labours and giving Annabelle an uncharacteristic wink. "But I know you will be impressed."

Not only has the scientist now shrugged off his extreme nervousness, the Marquis remarks, and is getting down to the procedure in a no-nonsense manner, but he also appears to have developed some kind of rapport with Annabelle. A good sign.

What was that he just brought out of his white-coated top pocket? A stopwatch! Whatever for? the Marquis wonders.

Annabelle is also amused to see the scientist hunched over the timepiece, his lips counting like a child's the passing of every second. She is even more amused when she hears him on the other side of the workbench recite the very sequence of random numbers which she has devised in her own head. Astonishing the control she has! What unhoped-for power! Clearly she must be applying the Marquis' principles the way she should.

Little by little an atmosphere of such gravity descends on the chamber that even the Marquis is affected by it as he sits quietly on his narrow stool.

The cooking process is thankfully not very long. The scientist peers through the glass porthole of the oven. Having decided that the substance is properly baked, he dons protective mittens over the gloves which he is already wearing, and opens the oven door. A puffball of greyish smoke emerges out of the oven and rushes towards the ceiling where it is immediately absorbed by the chipboard with which it is covered. The scientist carries the mould over to the workbench and places it on a small silver tray. He then administers a number of sharp knocks to its bottom with a small hammer. At the third blow a long, green, matted and still steaming foliated object falls out of it.

So that's what he has been up to! the Marquis remarks, unwittingly repeating Annabelle's own phrase and thereby showing that control over one's thoughts does not necessarily entail control over the expressions one uses. No mistaking that gnarled mass, nor those green leaves! Of all the unlikely things, the scientist has just produced sprigs of synthetic parsley!

Before Annabelle has fully recovered from her shock, the scientist has rushed over to the liquid simmering all the while in its beaker and has turned the burner off. Next he has poured the liquid into a plastic pipette, walked back towards the steaming parsley on its silver tray, and sprinkled an aromatic dew all over it. His commission complete, he brings the tray over to his client and, with all the flourish of a proud creator, presents the finished product to her.

Annabelle stares at the proffered tray. So virulent is the parsley's aroma, so viscous its appearance, and so obviously is it the sum of a chemical process that it is ludicrous to equate it with anything that might have grown in soil.

"Isn't it beautiful?" the scientist asks Annabelle, his formerly tetchy expression now smoothed by pride in his achievement. "And – don't you agree? – quick to prepare too. Just you wait!

I've got so many things to show you once I get on with my work. You wouldn't believe what I can make here!"

Nor, frankly, does she ever want to find them out. Unsure what to do with the unattractive mass which is already curling on the tray, she waves it away. Surprised, the scientist puts it down on the side of the worktable and gazes at his two visitors apprehensively.

Annabelle wonders what her companion has made of this weird result. Will he congratulate her for achieving one of his prescribed effects – the unexpected? Show her how impressed he has been by her progress? True, the parsley is not fresh but at least it is related in appearance and aroma to the herb. That much she has produced. Not that she has been fully responsible for the construction, though the blueprint was hers. He himself knows that it is no easy task manoeuvring a fictional character towards a predetermined point. No, she really cannot explain how the scene took this route, and she hopes that he won't ask either. It just happened that way.

Not that the process is over yet. There is still the scientist's saga to orchestrate. His years of ardour, the terrible events through which he went trying to get his invention to work, and the manner in which she has ingeniously integrated – even if she does think so herself – the little locket, that should all be of interest, shouldn't it?

A glance in his direction proves that she has seriously overestimated his tolerance.

Without a word, the Marquis seizes the coiled mass of parsley from its tray, grabs Annabelle's arm, and whisks her roughly off her stool. Then without the slightest hesitation, he drags her towards the laboratory door. Taken aback, she has no choice whatsoever but to stumble behind him.

What is going on? Has fire broken out? Is the laboratory about to collapse? In that case why is the scientist, surely the first to sense danger if there was any, still standing by his workbench, staring at them as they retreat, his mouth wide open? Hanging on to a shred of optimism, Annabelle, dragged by the Marquis towards the laboratory door, attempts to interpret what is happening in a favourable light. A second later her pretence caves in. Not again! The Marquis is dealing her another blow! Treating her like a wayward child and – the humiliation of it all! – on her own set too!

"Wait!" she cries breathlessly. "What are you . . . ?"

But the Marquis is in no mood to quarrel. He reaches the door and tries to open it.

The scientist, realizing that he is about to be robbed of his due, shouts, "Hey! What are you up to, you two? Come back! Come back immediately! We had a bargain! I did what you wanted! For Heaven's sake, don't leave me! You said I could have the little locket! You promised!"

His arms flailing, his mouth agog, the scientist runs after the two visitors and grabs Annabelle's dress. Pulled in one direction by the scientist whose crazed and acrid breath she can smell, and in the other by the Marquis still fumbling with the door, she screams. His face twisted by the pain of betrayal, his eyes tearful behind his round metal-framed spectacles, the scientist hangs with a terrier's stubbornness on to her dress. The Marquis is stronger. With his one free hand he shoves the scientist away so powerfully that he sends him sprawling.

The scientist tumbles backwards and his glasses fly through the air. In a desperate effort to regain his balance, he grabs the worktable and scatters a number of bottled chemicals from their shelves. As these strike the floor in a terrible clatter and spill their vile liquids, the chemicals interreact and a cloud of dense, black fumes soon spreads its malodorous shadow throughout the laboratory. And while the scientist, coughing in the midst of the gases, searches without any success for his glasses, the Marquis, making full use of this distraction, at last loosens the obstinate door, thrusts his apprentice through it, and slams it shut.

Down the dark corridor he pushes her, so fast that she ricochets from one side to the other. Past the final door he propels her and into the train proper where, winded, baffled and angry, she is catapulted on to the hard edge of the plate glass window, and there collapses with a cry.

Annabelle picks herself up. No physical harm, even if frustration and anger are almost choking her. Unbelievable! Her inaugural effort ruined! Her creation betrayed! She turns on the Marquis: "You . . . you bastard!" she shouts. "You ruined my story – when it was going so well!"

"Going well!" he answers, his voice iced over with contempt.

"You've turned the course into a farce. And this," he waves the matted mass in her face, "is how you repay me for the time and trouble I've taken over you. A vile piece of synthetic parsley!"

"You're incredible!" Annabelle cries. "You told me I could do what I wanted. Then because I don't do it your way, you abort my episode. You didn't even let me develop the scientist's story."

"I prefer not to think about the ending you worked out. Seeing you ride roughshod over the spirit of the course was enough for me. So you got a few steps right – and I do mean a few. But, in every other instance, your story lacked all semblance of sympathy. It was an arid and soulless exercise."

"You haven't any idea what I might have achieved," Annabelle exclaims, screening her own ignorance of the story's finale with the fumes of her indignation.

"Really! A piece of gum sprayed with some foul-smelling chemical!" the Marquis retorts. "If that's the height of your creativity, then it doesn't augur too well! However, that's not all. A genuine mistake I could have forgiven. But perverting the course to suit your greedy ends is quite another matter!"

So gross and unexpected is the accusation that she has no response to it. Instead, tears welling up in her eyes, she stares at her tormentor. "What – what are you talking about . . . ?" she stammers.

"How do you explain this?" the Marquis asks, holding the tightly bound sprigs of parsley in one hand and ripping them open with the other; a gesture which to her startled gaze reveals the tiny, perfectly shaped and unmistakeable shimmer of a pearl.

"I . . . I don't know. How did it get there?"

"Through your inability to control your thoughts, that's how! Not satisfied with the rewards of narrating a story, you got that ridiculous caricature of a scientist to manufacture this pearl for you. I presume this is some jewel to which you took a fancy?"

"I . . . !" Lamed by the evidence held in the hollow of his hand, her voice trails away.

"Well, what's your explanation?" the Marquis questions her, his gaze stark and unwavering.

She remains silent.

"I've told you before: you should have only one aim in mind when cooking creatively! If you allow other thoughts to intrude,

I promise you, you'll wish you had never started. How often do I have to emphasize it? Working within the realm of the imagination is not a game. And it'll exact a high price from people stupid enough to treat it as if it were. You had a task. You didn't take it seriously . . ." The Marquis raises his hand to quell the objection which her expression of outrage shows she was about to make, "or not seriously enough. Result? Your story went wrong – very badly wrong – from the start. If I had let it run on, God knows where it would have ended. Quite possibly with you spending the rest of your days stuck in that ridiculous laboratory. Imagine being locked in your mind with that inane character singing his appalling song! That'd certainly have been fitting punishment!" He consults his watch. "I'm going to give you one last chance, Annabelle. You've half an hour in which to create an episode that'll get us what we're after or I'm writing you off as a hopeless case. And this time, for Heaven's sake," he adds, "work from the heart. Tell a story you know something about. Describe a world you understand, for which you have some feeling. Because if you use themes that are foreign to you, all you'll do is land up with another fiasco." He points at the door of the disgraced episode. "By the way, the object you were going to exchange – a locket, wasn't it? – can't be used again. It obviously didn't have enough power to evoke a satisfactory episode. Focus instead on the other one you brought. All right! I'll meet you back here. Normally we'd also have to search for another compartment but as you've hardly scratched this one's potential, erase from your mind what's left of the last episode, and start all over again."

The Marquis turns round and, with the enigmatic pearl rolling in the hollow of his left hand, curtails all further discussion by walking away.

Amazed to be told that the destruction of her story, far from being an act of wanton vandalism, might have been her salvation, and forced to admit that to have spent any longer than strictly necessary with the scientist would indeed have been excruciating, Annabelle realizes with dismay that she now has no firm ground on which to stand. Her episode is dead, a shambles. And she has nothing, absolutely nothing, to show for it. Nor, shamefully, can she hide from herself that the pearl did momentarily, yes, one lustrous object among a hoard of others, appear in her mind while she was in the laboratory.

Disconsolately, and with a profound sense of loss, she stares as the tall figure of her mentor disappears at the end of the corridor.

The Marquis has only just vanished when, to her surprise and delight, Annabelle feels her resilience rising. Quite against the odds, and in spite of the humiliation to which she has been subjected, she has a fervent curiosity to discover what lies behind the door of the compartment. Yes, in spite of two disastrous incidents – the red-earthed canyon which almost ate her alive and the pummelling which her mind received in the infinity room – her curiosity has not abated. Nor does the risk put her off. After all, why should she be afraid? Can matters get any worse? And, anyway, the Marquis will never find out. Not that she has to go into the compartment. No, all she'll do is peer in.

She waits while the train surges through a tunnel, shrieks, and reissues into the night, walks up to the compartment, and slowly opens its door.

It is with much the kind of disappointment which a child sneaking up to the rich velvet curtain at the foot of the auditorium, lifting its skirt and peeking at the screen behind it might well experience that Annabelle stares at an unformed, dully humming and utterly deserted grey chamber. Not the slightest telltale detail in it to reveal what mechanisms created the illusion in which she has just participated. Nothing. Every item has vanished. The demented scientist, the pulsating laboratory, its effervescent apparatus, not a trace of them. Only a vast empty chamber. Crestfallen she closes the door, shakes her head, and heads off to the left in the vague hope of finding the Bar Buffet or some other haven in which she might momentarily forget herself.

Given the present state of her luck in which she might have spent an hour looking for, yet never coming across, the little *estaminet*, a lack of punctuality which would have led to her foregoing her last chance of playing the Marquis' game and of proving herself skilled in it, it is fortunate that Annabelle lands outside the Bar Buffet remarkably quickly. She strides in and takes a corner table in order to be left in peace.

There is in fact little danger of her being disturbed, for the Bar

Buffet's sole customer is a middle-aged drunk at a nearby table who seems to be crying in his cups. Nor is the waiter who stared at her so impudently anywhere to be seen. He has either retired to the lavatory or is enjoying a break in his workshift, leaving his colleague to serve the few customers likely to frequent the locale in the early hours of the morning.

First she orders an espresso to bolster herself after the disturbing incidents which she has experienced. Then she places the sketchpad and the two objects in front of her. Impossible when she gazes at the sadly redundant locket not to think of its stillborn narrative possibilities. Nor can she stop mourning the death of her plot. For she still feels that she conceived an ingenious exchange value for the locket which should have resulted – if everything had gone according to plan – in the scientist's research being saved from oblivion and crowned with well-deserved success. Instead her plot is defunct, the locket is useless, and the only thing she has left to get her out of her mess is the mirror. And how on earth is it, she puzzles fretfully, to come to her rescue?

Her attention is suddenly seized by the drunk who, having decided to sober up with a bowl of soup, is now making a terrible fuss about a hair which, he insists, has landed in it. Leaving Annabelle to ponder the pressing problems which face her, it is perhaps worth noting that a hair in the soup can be regarded not simply as an affront to every code of civilized behaviour, nor as a betrayal of the trust that the client places in the restaurateur, but as a *cri de coeur* coming from those whose effort in the kitchens has been unnamed and unlauded too long. For just as it was once revolutionary, and is now *de rigueur*, for works of art to champion their facticity by parading the manipulations to which their materials are subject, the stammerings to which their production is prone, and the pressures and hiatuses which their fiction has to overcome to be enunciated, so a hair in the soup can also be viewed as the eruption of an interrogating presence in a history otherwise biased towards concealing the identity of the people who actually make the menu's exploration of the hard and the liquid, the spicy and the bland, possible. In the same light, a hair in the soup can be regarded as a salvo of liberty sent by the wage slave in the galley across a divide narrow – yet O so severely reinforced by the *maître d'hôtel* – towards his paymaster, the capitalist in the dining room. There is even a sense in which an offending follicle can be seen as standing firm against the occultation of the processes of gastronomic fabrication, and as defiantly calling out to those who still think that the ingredients which appear fully dressed on the table somehow arrive there without having passed through the processes of honest fabrication to deny once and for all their bad faith, repudiate their false consciousness, rip away the hoodwinks of their self-serving vision of reality, and denounce this refusal to admit the presence of the working factor in the creative process. For is *ars celare artem* not the idealist notion through which fine art derives its self-satisfaction by concealing its effort, vaunting its artifice, and never exposing its facture to the light of day except when bleached of the birthmarks of creation? Here surely is a situation which can no longer remain unthought-through, but one whose emasculating ideology needs to be challenged, foregrounded, revoked, and finally overthrown. So, while it may be true that, from a prosaic point of view, a hair in the soup, a chef's button in the trifle, or a false eyelash in the *ragoût* are simply slips of hygiene, there is also a level at which they can be heroically reinterpreted as a battle cry of radical intervention.

But as this far-seeing argument – transforming a sordid mistake into a freedom lance of conscious struggle – would not cut much ice with the waiter were the customer's alcohol-steeped brain even able to conjure it, we will leave it, an enlightening if inactive ferment, where it stands, and quickly return to Annabelle, still staring through the panoramic expanse of the Bar Buffet's plate glass windows.

From the few details which she can make out of the slowly dissipating landscape – monochrome prints on the contact sheet of the night – the train seems to be ambling through the forsaken sectors of a fluorescently-lit suburb. One after another, the smudged silhouettes of factories and of cyclops-eyed *marques* pass her by. Most probably the outskirts of Lyons, Annabelle surmises. While the metropolis pays out its silent satellites before her tired eyes, she sips her coffee and absentmindedly strokes the little mirror, letting her fingers slide over its narrow arm and the oval of its faded glass. What a long and exhausting destiny it has had! Once the cherished possession of an aunt she never met. Now to be placed pivotally in a story which she has not yet invented in exchange for sprigs of parsley for which she could not care less!

A blank, a dead end, a feeling of failure are the sensations which Annabelle experiences as she watches the lifeless cityscape proceed past the windows. This lacklustre vision, however, does not last long, for, as if a missing facet of a puzzle at which she had stared helplessly had suddenly become evident, not by the appearance of an actual piece but by an intuitive awareness of its nature, she is overwhelmed by a strange and powerful memory.

Yvonne! Tante Yvonne! *Bien sûr!* Why hadn't she thought of it before? No doubt about it: the Marquis' method would suit Yvonne's story to perfection. As for sympathy, *Ciel!* she exclaims, seeing its active application for the first time: if she can't feel sympathy for Tante Yvonne, for whom will she ever feel it? What facts did her mother tell her about Tante Yvonne's life? There was L'Epoque, the Fashion House, yes; Yvonne's close relationship with its owner, Jeanne Servay; the events leading up to her death. And the war. Yes, more than enough there to work on. And why not, while she's about it, give Melanie Blanchard a little role, nothing too prominent, but one with just enough potential to allow her to sharpen her claws on her ever demanding partner?

After surveying her near epiphanal find and the extraordinary richness of details which it has handed to her, Annabelle is left with the tortuous problem of how to interweave the mirror into the fabric of facts.

Hunched over the problem of how to integrate an object into a story which she has heard many times before, Annabelle has difficulty imagining how she can organize the exchange. For ingredient she has a mirror. With it she must conjure up sprigs of parsley. That much is clear. Moreover the mirror must also help resolve a love story which has somehow reached a point of despair. Aware that the slightest departure from the course's fixed precepts is likely to lead her into trouble, she decides to abide by the Marquis' storytelling structures as closely as possible.

Fortunately, in much the way that a particle of dust falling in a supersaturated solution provides a foundation for the invisible crystal within to materialize, Annabelle, drawing on her memories and benefiting from the process by which a network of connections once inaugurated can dig deep into the psyche until an almost ineluctable sense has emerged, discovers that she can visualize a strong blueprint and that the more she thinks about it, the more her intimate knowledge of Tante Yvonne's fate seems capable of furnishing her with the details which she needs to tell a good story. And as she continues to rummage among the reminiscences which her mother related to the wide-eyed and half forgetful child she once was, she is delighted to find within it a coffer-full of usable anecdotes.

She soon realizes that not only has her story a definite rhythm but also a clear-cut beginning, middle and ending. With skills not dissimilar to those which she uses to make cloths conform to the lines of her designs, she now shapes this new material, the stuff of her memory reworked on the dummy of her imagination, until stitching together anecdotes, raising the hem of incidents, and sewing in odd facts, she succeeds in designing a setting, an atmosphere and even, yes – she shudders with delight! – a definite moral. And as the story forms before her mind's eye, she tries to keep the motif of the mirror firmly in place to ensure that it will accommodate the Marquis' guidelines.

Rather than belabour the point that Annabelle's story is bound to borrow from other people's efforts and thus that her own dislike of copies is, at worst, disingenuous, at best, uninformed; preferring not to give away the tenor of a tale which she has culled from the most profound source of her memory and which she is now busy elaborating, we will describe the fervour with which her pen cuts across the pad, making precise and colourful notes and a particularly telling sketch, until all the details of her active imagination have fallen into place. In the knowledge that she is ready, that her Cast is manageable, and that her Settings are precise, she sits back, drains her coffee, and admires her work which she feels sure will this time supply her with the dynamics of a fruitful tale.

CHAPTER FOURTEEN

Annabelle's sketch depicts a woman trying out a full length evening dress in front of a changing room mirror. Her Cast list, in contrast to the troops she intended to deploy in her last story, is very simple: two protagonists with a small support of cameo roles. Most scenes she has placed in but a handful of Settings. And she is standing next to the door of the stricken episode, studying her notes to ensure that they will be described to perfection, when the Marquis arrives at her side and asks her whether she is ready. She signals to him that she is and, without further ado, they both walk into the compartment.

After he has passed through a half-lit corridor from which there hangs a row of dim and naked light bulbs, the Marquis, following closely behind Annabelle, crosses the threshold of a dingy room and enters what appears to be a dressmaker's cutting room.

It is a high-ceilinged room and would no doubt draw considerable clarity from a broad skylight had Annabelle not decided to set her scene at night. A dusty lamp, hooded by a green glass shade, hovers overhead, casting its weak rays across it. Everywhere is chock-a-block with the implements of the couturier's trade. Among these the Marquis sees a range of cloth-cutting tables littered with paper patterns, and a number of dark grey tailor's dummies. Also adorning the room with their loosely pinned fabrics, an array of finished and half-finished dresses reflecting sleek and daring lines dangles from a rail. But what seizes the Marquis' attention above all is the presence of an elegantly dressed woman slumped in a chair across one of the worktables, her face buried deep in her hands and her body quite motionless.

Startled by the travellers' arrival, the woman stirs from her position and looks up. Even in the poor light the Marquis can make out that her eyes, flecked with red, contrast starkly with the pale porcelain of her features. He also marks the prominence of her cheekbones, the thinness of her frame, and the brittleness of a face which betrays lack of sleep. Her age? Late thirties, he suspects. His interest heightening, the Marquis wonders about the reasons why this lone female should seem so depressed. Terminal disease? Pressing financial problems? Or is he gazing at yet another character who, like his own, is suffering from the pangs of unrequited love?

There being no immediate answer to be had, he casts his eye around the cutting room, surveying the decor which Annabelle has built at such short notice. The scene's period? Circa 1941, he hazards from a cursory examination of the posters on the walls, some of which exhort the population to buy reconstruction bonds, others to abide by rationing regulations. The circumstantial details seem to be about right. As for the furnishings, they too are more or less in keeping with the times even if the set bears the stamp of a rather too meticulous, polished reproduction about it. An understandable slip. For where could Annabelle have culled her images but from old films and photographs? Apart from those occasional lapses, there are, as far as he can tell, no outrageous anachronisms.

As for the atmosphere pervading the room, it is cold and gloomy. This might reflect the woman's mood, Annabelle using the admittedly *passé* device of pathetic fallacy to inflect the scene's development. Or, the Marquis muses, it could equally echo the year and the season in which the scene is set. The opprobrium of surrender, the shame of the Occupation, these sentiments together with the rout of a once confident army could well coalesce into a fit of collective depression. After meditating on these and other aspects of a world which he was old enough to live through but too young to comprehend, the Marquis takes a seat in a shadowy corner from which he means to judge how his apprentice handles the demands of her imaginative territory.

Her eyes distant, her face motionless, the elegant woman waits until Annabelle has herself taken a seat near her. Then, her voice strained and husky, she asks: "Who are you? What are you doing here? Weren't you told that the House is shut at this hour?"

"You don't know me," Annabelle answers.

"Then, please, go away!"

"You did however know my aunt."

"Your aunt?" Struck by this note of familiarity, the woman hesitates for a second before adding: "Who's she?"

"Her name was Yvonne. Surely you remember her?"

"Yvonne? Yvonne?" the woman whispers. "You mean you're Yvonne's . . . ?" She slumps back in her chair as if Annabelle's revelation had drained her of all energy.

"Yes, that's right: I'm Annabelle, her niece."

Her voice distant, the woman gazes at Annabelle and adds: "They took her away, they beat her . . . I haven't seen her since that . . . that terrible day." She opens her eyes wide. "Yvonne's niece?" she asks, as if still finding it difficult to grasp what has just been said. Taking hold of herself, she stares at Annabelle and, with greater firmness, says: "Come here, child."

Annabelle, betraying no trace of self-consciousness, and playing her part to perfection, leaves her chair, kneels next to her aunt's friend, and lets her stroke her hair. She holds Annabelle's face between her cupped hands then slowly kisses her brow.

"Yes, I can see it. You do have something of hers, the look, the eyes." She absentmindedly touches Annabelle's clothes. "Strange cut. This material . . . I've never met anything like it."

"I'm not surprised. Like you I too design clothes. This material's a new fabric. But we can talk about that some other time."

"And the smell?" the woman asks, perturbed by an odour which has wafted towards her. "Is it your *eau de toilette*? It's unusually strong."

"That! *Ciel!* No! That's nothing to do with perfume! However, let me explain. Jean-Loup, my travelling companion and I," she points to the Marquis in the cutting room's shadows, "have been ill for many months."

The Marquis is amused to hear that Annabelle has produced no better cause for the outbreak of the overpowering smell than to attribute it, just as he did, to disease. Perhaps now she can accept that it is no easy matter to imagine alternatives for each story. Indeed there are occasions when an old recipe cannot be improved on. Aware that he has just been shown his cue, the Marquis adds weight to Annabelle's introductory comment with a suitably long-suffering gesture.

"I'm very sorry to hear that," says the woman sympathetically.

"The fact is that we've caught a rare disease. That smell, dreadful as it is, is one of its less unpleasant symptoms. It's a disease, what's more, which almost nobody knows anything about. When we discovered that we had contracted it, we visited every specialist, every consultant, although that got us nowhere. Nowhere at all. We were steadily getting worse – Jean-Loup had gone to a clinic in Haute-Savoie for a rest and I was staying with my mother, spending most of my time in bed – when one day I chanced across a newspaper article. It was all about a herbalist who said that he could often effect cures where ordinary medicine had failed. I must have been desperate because I immediately cabled Jean-Loup and asked him to come back to Paris so that we could visit the man together. He turned out to be extraordinarily busy but agreed nonetheless to see us within a week. Well, the day came and we were ushered into the eminent practitioner's *cabinet*. He had given up traditional medicine to tend to the needs of patients which the rest of the medical world could or would not help. I was examined first and then retired to the waiting room. Once Jean-Loup had seen him too, I came back to the doctor's study. And there we both were before his desk to hear his diagnosis, when, matter-of-factly he looked up from his notes and told us that our condition was quite hopeless unless . . ."

Keen to receive confirmation of how ingenious her preamble is, Annabelle turns round and glances at the Marquis. He winks at her to show that he has indeed appreciated her expository performance.

"Unless . . . ?" the woman asks, succumbing to the needs of the narrative.

"Unless we followed his every instruction – and he meant his every instruction – to the letter. Realizing that we had nothing, but absolutely nothing, to lose, Jean-Loup and I said that we would. After all, no one else seemed able to help us. Anyway, the next thing was that the herbalist wrote out a lengthy and, to my mind, unbelievable prescription. Here were the details of a natural medicine, he said, handing us a piece of paper, which, if taken properly, might eventually lead us back to the road to health. There was however one requirement: if we wanted to get better, then we'd have to search for the ingredients of the medicine ourselves! That's right – ourselves!" Annabelle shrugs. The woman seems startled. "Yes! That's what we thought too: incredible! On the other hand, when your body's covered in sores, you can't sleep at night, and you're worried by the spectre of ever-mounting clinics' fees, you'll clutch at straws. Somehow the herbalist – don't ask me why – inspired confidence in us and so we put our trust in him. Ever since, we just haven't stopped travelling. We've been to Spain . . ."

At a loss for an adequate description of where the Leopard Woman episode took place, Annabelle looks enquiringly at the Marquis.

"To Central Europe," he says, briskly coming to her rescue.

"Er, yes. We've even been to Egypt."

"Really? You've travelled right round the world?" the woman asks, losing sight, if only for a moment, of her own sorrows.

"Not quite. Though I must say it has occasionally felt like it! But don't misunderstand me. I'm not complaining. Far from it. We've been very lucky. Almost each place we've visited, we've found the exact ingredient we were after." She looks over her shoulder at her companion, as if trying to include him in a conversation from which he has clearly separated himself. "Jean-Loup has a rather wild theory about it: he thinks that the search was part of the cure. As for me, I don't know. Maybe he's right. One thing's for sure: we both feel much better, even if, as that strong smell shows, we're not yet fully cured." She pauses. "I had to tell you where we stood. The point is that I remember my mother saying that Tante Yvonne had visited your country house, that you had a wonderful vegetable garden there, and so I thought . . ."

"You thought you'd come and visit me! Remarkable! You, Yvonne's niece!" the woman says, her voice sloughing off its lethargy. "I'm surprised she never said anything about you, although I do recall her telling me about her sister."

Annabelle holds her breath. Is her identity, so early in her narrative, about to be challenged? How could she explain that, strictly speaking, as far as the story's chronology goes, she was not even born?

"I'm very glad you did," the woman adds, taking Annabelle's hands, "even if you have come at a bad time, a particularly bad time, for me. But what has my vegetable garden to do with this?"

"As I was saying, so far we've located every ingredient – except for parsley. I thought I had it a little while back," she adds, casting an accusatory glance at the Marquis, her resentment at his aborting her story still unpurged. Visibly untouched by her attempts to make him feel guilt, the Marquis stares back at her with equal pugnacity. "It later transpired however that I had made a mistake."

"And that's what you want?" the woman enquires, her voice registering a hint of disbelief. "Parsley, from my garden?"

"I realize it must sound strange. But we're not after exotic ingredients. Not at all. The herbalist stressed that we should get them from the right place and from people for whom we felt a certain sympathy."

"What an extraordinary request! I've never heard anything like it. And, I can assure you, when you're in the business of clothing the rich, you do come across the most bizarre things. I've often thought clients mistake the quiet of the changing room for the solace of the confessional. As for your story, well . . ." She hesitates, as if unsure whether to humour this young woman calling herself her best friend's niece and her completely silent companion. "Still, if you insist that parsley's the herb you're after, I'll see what I can do."

"You will?" Annabelle exclaims. She looks over her shoulder towards the Marquis. "Isn't that wonderful, Jean-Loup?"

"Most fortunate," answers the Marquis, relieved that the process is under way. As for the excitement which she feels now that her character is fulfilling its function and becoming an articulate agent of her desires, of course he understands it: Annabelle is at last beginning to understand the meaning of sympathy and is riding with its persuasive rhythm.

"However, Tante Jeanne – may I call you that?"

"*Naturellement.*"

"There's something else – something quite crucial – which I have to add. When the herbalist handed us his prescription, he also made us swear that we'd never accept anything from anybody without at least trying to fulfil their heart's desire. Which means that if you're willing to help us, we in turn will do our best to provide you with whatever it is that you want." She puts her arms round her aunt's closest friend. "I couldn't help noticing how sad you are. Will you tell me why? If you like," she

245

adds, a smug expression on her face, "I'll ask Jean-Loup to leave us alone."

The cheek of it! thinks the Marquis. Hardly has he handed the little hoyden the recipe for cooking stories than she concocts a plot to exclude him! And on what foul premise? That women have things to say to each other a man shouldn't overhear! Prejudice of the worst sort! No matter. Whatever female secrets those two exchange can't possibly affect the outcome of the course. He'll make damn sure of that! He smiles at each woman in turn, as if only too happy to oblige their every whim.

"If you ladies would prefer to be by yourselves, I shall be glad to leave you in peace," says the Marquis.

"Please! There's no need!" Jeanne exclaims. "A friend of Yvonne's niece is a friend of mine."

The Marquis is relieved that Annabelle's plan has been foiled and that what might have developed into an unfortunate obsession – the creator's for her own creature – has not progressed any farther. For such narcissistic infatuation could end badly, blurring for his apprentice the difference between the texture of reality and the play of fantasy.

Jeanne, her red-rimmed eyes and sad complexion heightened by this refocusing on her own situation, pauses a while. There is hesitation, fear even, on her face. Are the memories which she is being asked to divulge that painful?

"Thank you for your offer, but no. You couldn't possibly understand."

"We've come across a great deal on our travels, you know," says Annabelle gravely, afraid that her character may remain immured in her sadness and refuse to divulge her story.

"Yes, yes, of course you have. I'm sorry." She agains pauses. "But since Yvonne's disappearance, I've had nobody to talk to. I've had to learn to live with the pain. Perhaps you're right: it will do me good to tell you. You must promise me, however," she adds, glancing nervously from Annabelle to her companion's shadowy figure, "that you'll keep what I tell you entirely to yourselves and never repeat it. It's a story that no one has ever heard before – no one, that is, except one person. Yes, that's right," she stares into Annabelle's eyes, "your Tante Yvonne. Nobody else."

The Marquis settles back in his chair and closes his eyes. And it is with the cautious abandon of a Master whose pupil is about to pilot for the first time the craft whose mercurial complexities he has been trying to teach her that he lets the situation take him over.

Although it would certainly solve some problems to abide by Jeanne's strict injunction and to keep the tale she has agreed to narrate to her best friend's niece forever hidden under the terms of her bond of secrecy – for we would then neither have to match nor surpass the other three stories, nor disclose whether Annabelle's artistic gifts have lived up to the Marquis' – to do so would be unfair to her own efforts which, now that she has entrusted herself to her creative powers, may well exceed her high hopes. And so, rather than pretending that we have no inkling of where her tale will lead, we will instead describe how she performed in the last part of the course in which her curiosity fatally inscribed her.

Surrounded by piles of materials – shot silks bending light along their undulating weave, lace lustrous with teasing arabesques – and hunched over pedal-powered machines fastidiously tracing out designs dispatched from drawing boards on the first floor, a roomful of young and not-so-young women toil over clothes on whose classical lines L'Epoque has made its sound, if uninspired, reputation. Among those diligent women slowly ruining their eyes for the sake of flowing necklines and sequinned trains, a young apprentice bends over her work and lays on the front of a full-length *moiré* dress a line of gilt buttons which, as she carefully sews them in, refract the pallor of her face. Not the slightest movement visible. A complete absence of colour. Silence all around. For this scene stems not from the flux of reality but from a monochrome photograph taken by a stringer for one of the Paris dailies, *France-Soir*, for a report on the capital's fashion houses, among which, rather more for its ancient lineage than for its skill at stimulating *tout-Paris* sartorial interest, L'Epoque has been included. "Nimble-fingered ladies in the Champs-Elysées' work room," so runs the caption, leaving in the shadows seminal questions such as work conditions and rates of pay and the degree to which unavowed and unsatisfied sapphism for the exquisitely long-limbed models wafting in and out of the sweatshop is the sole compensation some of these workers will ever receive for their poorly-paid labour.

But what, if any, is the link between the young, pale apprentice busy working in the photograph and the middle-aged woman, her face smeared with tears, slumped in a fitting room? As she leans back on her chair, Jeanne concentrates on the patterns of her story and weaves the threads with which she means to connect the two images.

"I presume that your mother must have told you that when I took over L'Epoque," says Jeanne, her voice growing in confidence as if the past held fewer fears than she had at first thought, "I turned it into the most influential fashion House in Paris. What she may not have told you is that I started at the bottom. No one did me any favours! The day my mother visited the proprietor, Mme Blanchard, and offered her a few hard-earned francs to take on an untrained girl of fourteen, I was in. From then on I was up at six every morning and in the workrooms by seven. I couldn't begin to count the number of hems and linings I had sewn on by the time I was twenty."

Annabelle holds her breath. So far so good. The question is: can she continue like this? Or will she be overwhelmed by the demands of the story? No, she must not panic. She must trust to the rhythm, the rhythm she can feel flowing through her, the rhythm dipping into her experience, extracting the details needed to elaborate this strange impassioned story. She must let Jeanne speak. Let her say what she is supposed to say. Yes, Jeanne will take care of everything.

Eventually, by dint of unstinting effort, the young seamstress earns her promotion and joins the cohort of immaculately spruced assistants who serve in L'Epoque's salon and tend to its clients' requirements.

No expense has been spared to ensure that L'Epoque's salon cultivates the slightly fustian atmosphere which will make its staple clientele, middle-aged ladies from the 16th arrondisse-ment, feel at home when purchasing the gala gowns and sumptuous stoles their social calendar demands. Be visible but not showy, the thin-lipped, censorious and always black-attired Mme Melanie Blanchard never ceases to admonish her em-ployees. Clients will pay for ostentation if it enrobes their shoulders, flatters their profiles, or engarlands their waists. They most certainly do not wish to see it paraded to greater effect on you! And after running through that and a thousand other suggestions, she rounds off her morning homily by reminding her girls to place mirrors as tactfully as possible around the salon so that corpulent ladies need not view themselves against the background of their own svelter bodies.

"Five years, five long years, that's the time it took Mme Blanchard to summon me to join her salon's staff," says Jeanne. "And after waiting such a long time to serve L'Epoque's clientele, what discovery do you suppose I made? That the heights of *haute couture* were rarefied? That the world of changing shapes was glamorous? Not at all! What I came across was how ghastly clients could be! Oh yes, they had millions in their pockets but *Dieu!* – they also had steel in their souls! Steel and, as I was to find out one day quite by chance, something else besides."

Wearing one of the House's less extravagant styles, a plain grey and impeccably cut *tailleur*, Jeanne is looking after a particularly fractious client in one of the salon's changing rooms. This middle-aged woman, her double chin encasing though not wholly obscuring the traces of her once striking features, loudly insists that the dress which Jeanne has brought her is quite unsuitable. Suppressing a spontaneous sigh, the young assistant gently helps her out of it.

With the curdling of her ovaries, this overplump female spends most of her days putting her husband's bank book through exorbitant paces. On that particular occasion her irritability is demonstrated by an almost formic-like inability to stand still. As if fascinated and disgusted by the degeneration to which her own flesh has been subjected, she flirts with then repels the advances of her own image in the large oval changing room mirror. Returning to the problem of her wardrobe, she stands in her shift and, with an imperious wave of the hand, orders Jeanne to have her other choices brought in.

Has Madame made up her mind? Jeanne asks as she wheels in a clothes horse on which hang seven dresses in a variety of unadventurous but beautifully cut cloths. Might Madame consider this one? she proposes, taking from its hanger a calico print whose pattern Deauville much admires. Its subtle tints, she hazards, would complement Madame's complexion to perfection.

No matter how hard she expatiates on the virtues of the dress, which the woman deigns to put on, Jeanne soon concludes that this item, like all the others which her client ordered weeks before, and for which she has already had numerous fittings, will never – regardless of her objections – suit her any better than it does now. Yet Madame remains adamant and will not settle for it. What on earth has befallen L'Epoque, she tartly remarks, that nothing should fit her any more? Not so long ago, she recalls, everything suited her. She will not mince her words: she is profoundly dissatisfied with what Jeanne has shown her.

Her client is disrobing and, in a highly agitated state, is muttering to herself when Jeanne, casting a glance into the mirror, notices something remarkable. Something so remarkable that had she not been on duty, and fully instilled with Mme Blanchard's strict rules on poise and decorum, she might have failed to contain her amazement.

"Not that there was anything special about this client, you understand. Tiresome, arrogant, very rich. I had served thousands like her. I had just finished showing her the clothes she had ordered – without any success – when, looking in the mirror at her face, I came across the most terrifying expression I have ever seen."

What confronts Jeanne, traced out on her client's reflected face, are vivid emotions, a churning mass of feelings. Even more bizarre, this transformation seems to have no existence beyond the looking glass frame. For on her client's actual face there is not even the smallest trace of the appalling apparition.

"That afternoon, for the very first time I felt what my client went through when she looked in the mirror. You mustn't think though that this experience was limited to my seeing it. Oh no! I also felt it, whatever it was, I also felt it working its foul course through me. How can I describe it except to say that it was a deep and all-pervasive self-loathing from which she couldn't hide and which had sunk its roots into her mind. One final detail. I know it will sound extraordinary and yet it is the truth: the way that dress hung on her made her feel worse; yes, it somehow accentuated her pains.

"You may not believe this," Jeanne adds, clearly out to engage her audience's sympathy, "but as I stood in the fitting room, stared into the mirror, and tried not to betray to my client that I had stumbled on to her guilty secret, something else happened, something to which I owe my whole career. I still don't understand what made me do it. All I can tell you is that the next minute there I was kneeling on the floor, with my hands flying, darting across the dress and her body while she stood there, speechless, staring down at me, until, with pins secured and folds in place, I had done it. Don't ask me how, but I had come up with a sartorial answer to her suffering. Nor was it just sartorial. Though, to be honest, I wouldn't discover that until much, much later."

The Marquis has noticed a slightly jarring disynchrony between Jeanne's narrative and the images which he himself is receiving. It would appear that Annabelle has not yet gained complete control over her storytelling. Sometimes the words introduce the action. On other occasions, it is the action which precedes her descriptions. Little more than a superstructural oversight, the Marquis concedes, and one which hardly detracts from the ease with which, at her second attempt, his pupil has slipped into her role. Soon, very soon, he congratulates himself, she should be finely fastened like a fish to the nets of her imagination.

As the Marquis has pointed out, the scene which he next witnesses has already been described by Jeanne in its disjointed aspects. Indeed, here she is in the changing room, driven by a hunch whose scope she had not yet fathomed. She takes the pins which she always carries about with her from their little wicker box and alters by subtle, almost imperceptible means the way in which the fabric hangs. Minor alterations which, however, have an immediate effect. The client admires herself in the mirror. Next she pavanes in a small circle around the dressing room. Then she appraises the new shape which has been created in the dress. And finally, a broad smile conquering the weight of her dewlaps and allowing, if only for a second, the vestiges of her joyful self to shine through, she grasps Jeanne by the hand.

The young assistant stands up. She is as astounded as her client. For while the slight alterations she has made to the dress have indeed ironed out minor imperfections, apart from that, why, she did nothing! Yet there, in the mirror, is the undeniable result: her client's bitter emotions have been soothed away and the expression in the mirror now possesses the same childlike radiance as the smile on her client's face. No longer any chasm between image and reality. Jeanne carefully smooths the fabric around the woman's ample shoulders and, parrying her profuse compliments with a shy expression, glances into the mirror, struck silent by the awesome power which she has unwittingly evoked.

"As soon as I had made alterations to all the other dresses, a task which she insisted I undertake, she bought them, yes, she went and bought them all!" Jeanne adds.

Jeanne's contented client makes her ceremonious way out of the salon, shakes her hand, and politely bids Mme Blanchard, presiding as always by the cash desk, good day. As her chauffeur, buckled under the weight of the seven dresses, trails behind her at a respectable distance, she marches out of L'Epoque and slumps on to the compliant leather of her awaiting limousine.

The vehicle has just crossed the avenue and become engulfed by the line of plane trees which lead toward the *Grand Palais* when the cold beam of the proprietor's gaze alights on Jeanne. With a nod she commands her employee to proceed to her office where a certain matter needs to be discussed in private. There, garbed in her customary black crêpe, her hair strictly dressed in a bun, her face devoid of all emotion, installed behind her sparsely decorated desk yet choosing not to put her subordinate at her ease, she asks Jeanne to explain how such an important sale to one of L'Epoque's most notoriously difficult clients was made. The young assistant, at a loss and most unwilling to discuss what she herself still does not comprehend, makes a small hand movement and, disclaiming responsibility, answers that as far as she can make out the lady bought the clothes on a whim. She informs her employer that she has no idea what brought about such a change of mood, but that if it ever happens again she will of course do her best to examine the factors behind such snap decisions. Registering that her assistant, for all her youth and inexperience, has adopted a commendably respectful attitude towards her position, and part placated by her reply, Mme Blanchard summarily dismisses her and decides to keep a close eye on her.

"Afterwards I convinced myself that it had been an accident, some freak event which could – no, which, I prayed, should – never happen again."

It is still going well. Annabelle has thoroughly enjoyed denigrating Melanie and has watched with fascination her partner ageing and being vilified. And it has all been so easy. She has had to do little except keep in mind, and adhere to, the patterns of her plan. She wonders what the Marquis is making of her effort. Has he been impressed by her recovery and the so far faultless application of her newly-learnt skills? Although she would dearly like to open her eyes and check his expression, afraid of disturbing the illusion she decides to forego that pleasure.

But the same event, with its question-provoking and answer-defying consequences, soon after recurs to push Jeanne a little further towards the fate that awaits her. The time: one afternoon a few days later. The place: another of L'Epoque's changing rooms. Not only is Jeanne's client markedly graceful, her blonde hair tied in a bow, her shapely legs encased in pale white silk, and the dress that she is wearing a fascinating example of what L'Epoque has never quite managed to create, simplicity and wit in black chiffon, but she is also – as none of the clients in the salon has failed to appreciate – very famous, having only returned a few days before from a protracted shooting session at Nice's Studios Victorine. At a loose end, and at the nether section of the Champs-Elysées, she has dived into the old-fashioned couturier for a quick browse. And there she is shown by Jeanne various cloths recently imported from Scotland which turned into a coat and matching evening wear would, in the assistant's opinion, create a sensation. While agreeing that the cloths are indeed magnificent and no doubt represent months of painstaking work, the actress nonetheless appears distracted and constantly casts glances into the mirror, her facial muscles occasionally trembling. To help her admire it, Jeanne drapes one of the Highland plaids around her client's finely sculpted shoulders, and immediately witnesses the sadness which the opulence of her clothes and the surface confidence of her manner cannot conceal.

"Unfortunately it did happen again – and the very next week! This time my client was not a regular customer but a famous actress who had dropped in to L'Epoque. I was trying to interest her in various cloths when, gazing at her face in the mirror, I saw it all: yes, I saw the unspeakable pain from which she was suffering and the mounting pressure of her fears."

With the same fluent gestures as before, here adding a red muslin scarf, there changing the curve of the neckline, and, as an afterthought, raising the hem of the actress' own dress, Jeanne, acting under the impulse of an ineffable instinct, quickly devises a means of reducing the actress' insecurity and of restoring, if only temporarily, the frayed corona of her brilliance. She gives no thought to whether she is right or wrong; pays no attention to the stunned expression on the actress' own face as her hands fly past her, adjusting, pleating, rearranging, but simply reacts to the overpowering urge which has taken hold of her.

When she has exhausted her efforts, she once more examines the actress in the mirror and observes that her reflected face has become somewhat calmer. That is at least something, she muses, even if she has no idea how she did it. And isn't it extraordinary, she adds to herself, tying the red scarf and draping it over the actress' shoulders, how she, an unknown shop assistant, a nobody, a mere speck in Paris' constellation, has somehow succoured this illustrious woman and cast a little light into the obscurity smothering her? How she, no more than a junior assistant in a famous fashion House, has brought comfort to a member of the *beau monde* whose name is on everybody's lips. Yes, how she has soothed someone the yellow press once intimated was a man who became, via various monkey gland extracts, androgynous. Not a shred of evidence for that, the young assistant is relieved to discover; for when the actress takes off her dress to let its hem be resewn, not only does she reveal the startling absence of any underclothes but the unmistakeable femininity of her body.

Although that cruel rumour has been exploded as the blatant lie it is, the truth which the changing room mirror unveils to Jeanne is far more sordid, is indeed so shocking that the only aspect which Jeanne is willing to intimate to her audience is that the actress' death from an overdose of chloral a month later – the one sure cure for what the quality press had discreetly called a wasting disease – had profoundly saddened but had in no way surprised her.

In his shadow-cloaked corner the Marquis fumes. What sleight of hand! To come so near to disclosing a tantalizing secret about a created character then to veer off without doing so! He cannot suppress his irritation at Annabelle's refusal to unveil what she has imagined, not because he is interested in the details permeating the private life of a fleetingly developed cameo part, but for the insight it might have offered him into his apprentice's sexual nature which she has so far steadfastly concealed. Admitting, in spite of his irritation, that it is not that critical an aspect of his overall strategy, he brushes it aside and concentrates on the story.

When the actress had first arrived in the changing room, Jeanne recounts, she had seemed irascible, not because of Jeanne, no, but with herself. She had curtly commented on the clothes which the assistant had somewhat shamefully shown her; clothes which, while the most exotic L'Epoque could hope to muster, were clearly too classical for a style such as hers. Instead she had leant against the wall of the changing room, her eyes glazed, her fingers playing with her hair, and had kept whispering almost manically, as if her self-control had been loosed and she no longer cared who heard her innermost thoughts: what did it matter what she wore, what did it matter any more? It was at that unnerving moment that Jeanne had looked into the mirror and had caught sight of the horror at the centre of the actress' life. Then, under the force of an irresistible urge, she had deftly altered her dress, added the long red scarf to her outfit, and had managed to quieten, however impermanently, the drumbeat of her tension.

"Oh, yes, the whole world thought she walked a golden path! But I can tell you what in the end broke her mind: exposure to the public's adoration. As for the minor solution which I found for her and which brought her a kind of peace, I knew it would only last a short time. You see, she had only a few weeks to live when I met her. And yet, it's strange but that afternoon I think I made her happier than she had been in years."

The Marquis cannot help admiring the self-satisfied manner with which Jeanne has congratulated herself for having let seep in, however narrowly, a fresh draught into the stifling and despair-racked chamber of the actress' life. No doubt, in her mind, Annabelle imagines herself capable of equal translucence. Fine! he muses: if all goes according to plan, she'll soon have more opportunities to exercise her benevolence than she'll know what to do with!

On her way out of the salon – and having purchased nothing except for the red scarf which she has strikingly wound around her neck – the actress embraces Jeanne and says that never have her own clothes fitted her so well. What an amazing transformation she has effected. *"Vous êtes un ange!"* she exclaims, twirling the dress. "I'm convinced you've got a secret," she adds teasingly, "but that you wouldn't dream of sharing it!" Just before crossing the salon's threshold, she turns round and blows the young assistant a kiss.

With a curt wave of the hand Mme Blanchard, who has witnessed the last part of this melodramatic departure, quells the ripples of spontaneous chatter which have broken out through the salon. And as she shoos away those of her younger employees still gaping through the windows at the famous actress, she concedes, if grudgingly, the speed with which her most recent recruit has picked up the rudiments of good sales-manship, and her possession, in unquestionable if not yet fully developed amounts, of the gift of divining clients' intimate wishes, a gift which, having herself never been blessed with, her envy has fully qualified her over the years to appreciate in others.

For all its rebarbative revelations and its unveiling of the shadowy side of certain ladies' character, Jeanne's talent becomes in a remarkably short period a common occurrence, her initial horror of its perverse powers giving way to her wary if accepting use of them. The Marquis is next invited to detect this subtle change in Jeanne's attitude in a series of time-lapsed sequences. Set against the backdrop of the salon, with only the day-to-day variations in her own dress to show the swift passing of the seasons (among which change of clothes her old grey *tailleur*, a thistle blue twin set, a black woollen skirt and white shirt adorned with a polka-dotted bohemian tie all feature), the Marquis sees Jeanne smile, ring up the till, and thank her many customers for being so kind. But as this carousel gathers pace, he observes the young assistant clenching her teeth, becoming more distant, regarding L'Epoque's more eccentric *habitués* as odious, praying that they never return, and even on occasion surprising herself by wishing the worst of them dead. That however does not sum up her attitude to her own transforma-tion for, not surprisingly, she is also flattered that people are openly discussing her flair, and that her reputation is slowly but surely being made by the grapevine of *thés dansants* and of salon chitchat. And the greatest accolade occurs when Mme Blanchard invites her one day to accompany her on the round of the enterprise she regularly makes, and among a host of professional matters shows her the big black tome in which all outstanding loans are inscribed, to whom and under what terms, a mark of trust which suggests to her senior staff that the old lady is grooming Jeanne for the succession.

Pleased with the flow of vignettes, and with the simple effect which they have had on her audience, Jeanne proposes a further cross-section, a series of farewells with which she means to illustrate the increasing eminence of her clientele.

"*A très bientôt, Madame,*" she says to a Dowager, whose Thursdays key members of society unfailingly attend, their widely diverging views finding common ground only in their abomination of their hostess.

"*Mademoiselle est trop bonne,*" she replies to the compliment of a diminutive woman universally known by her maiden name even though she has buried three husbands, rejected a Grand Duke's proposal of marriage, and recently confirmed her independence of spirit by placing funds in an exclusive bordello.

"*Milady sait qu'elle est toujours la bienvenue,*" she sweetly addresses a Lady of the British realm who six months of the year frequents sanatoria and the rest regales literary salons with belles-lettres none but vanity-publishing could expose to the light of day.

A cross-section which, the Marquis feels, owes rather too much to the influence of another storyteller's acidulous portrayal of the *gratin* of society. But as there exist few creative expressions which have not been touched in some way or another, tangentially or head-on, by earlier practitioners of the art, he decides to overlook Annabelle's flagrant plagiarism.

It is with a sense of dismay that Annabelle too has noticed that the form of her story, far from rising fresh and new from the foam of her imagination, has in fact borrowed considerably from a number of sources – and from some so openly that were it not for the change of sex and the difference of epoch she would feel quite shamed by it. Realizing, however, that the task of producing her narrative is quite arduous enough without her trying at the same time to conform to her old puristic canons, she resigns herself to the reality that, even though her material is in part autobiographical, the way in which it is being told owes a great deal to other practitioners.

The little wicker box now sits on a capacious walnut desk which dominates an office tastefully furnished in the florid convolutions and priapic fervour of Art Deco, a setting capped by a fine-stemmed Lalique vase filled with irises and a set of tulip-backed chairs commissioned from the workshops of Mackintosh. At her desk, L'Epoque's Chief Buyer is sorting through a pile of luxurious and newly-designed fabrics. Suddenly the telephone shimmers on its stand. Picking up its receiver, Mademoiselle Jeanne Servay immediately upbraids her interlocutor about the fabrics which her workshop ladies have rejected on the grounds of poor quality. No, she insists, she will not finalize the order. Her specifications, she ripostes to the objections which the tightening of her lips and the violent doodles which she is penning on a notepad clearly show are coming down the line, will have to be met to the letter. She will not be satisfied until each and every detail itemized has been put right.

The Marquis makes a mental note to tell Annabelle that over-evocative background details can have a double-edged effect. While they help to build atmosphere, they can also sap attention by slowing down a narrative's pace. He himself prefers to keep sensual beauty down to a minimum. Even when a complicated Spirit of Place is to be conjured up, he still prefers to moderate the effects which an excess of plastic values is bound to have on a story's rhythm. Admittedly her resorting to luxuriance may stem from a difference in sensitivity. She may for instance have provided her setting with a surfeit of period details to bolster her confidence in her ability to create a fictive world. And anyway, he pulls himself short: as her plot is coherent, he really should stop quibbling and let her get on with her story.

"Do you realize," adds Jeanne, "that in less than six months fashion-conscious Paris was flocking to our doors? And how do you suppose that had happened? Had the House altered its old lines? Developed a bold new style? Not in the least! Only one thing had changed. Not its clothes, nor its staff, but the quality of service it provided. Yes! The reason well-heeled *bourgeoises* patronized L'Epoque was because they discovered that I could ease their most secret pains."

With fame Jeanne has acquired the amulets of wealth. To evoke the stages of her social rise, she projects on to her captive audience a few key images from the period. First there is a photograph of her at the wheel of her white Bugatti, driving up the Champs-Elysées at dawn, Sascha her Dalmatian yawning in the passenger seat. Then her standing, arms outstretched, before the whitewashed expanse of the empty master bedroom of the mansion she has just purchased on the Avenue Foch, consigning decorative details to a designer weighed down with a flush of architectural plans. Next, a cover of *Vogue* on which she can be admired, poised and wistful, before a full bloom of azaleas. And a news item, distorted by the poor quality of its photogravure, taken on the day L'Epoque's new logo was erected in neon on the façade of its Rond-Point des Champs-Elysées headquarters. Another rather more intimate snap catches her ambling through the high-walled vegetable garden of the country house she has been refurbishing, discussing crops with the elderly and stooped figure of Jerome, her gardener. And, lastly, in a series of flash-illuminated stills which have caught her unawares, there she is in the Fashion House's dressing room, inspecting her models before one of her shows, the highly-charged atmosphere tellingly pinpointed in the fixity in her eyes.

"The next step was of course to design. I already knew that when I gave them my personal attention I could soothe my clients' souls. The question which came to obsess me was: what might I achieve on paper? One afternoon I decided to test myself out. I locked myself in my study and concentrated. Can you imagine my delight when within a few hours I had come up with countless ways to conceal my clients' pains from the world?"

Armed with figures which chart L'Epoque's dramatic increase in sales since her influence has made itself felt, and muscled by the astonishing designs which her talent has lately unveiled, Jeanne Servay stands in the proprietor of the Fashion House's office, and waits for the right moment. She patiently listens as the elderly lady tells her of the debt she owes Jeanne for the renewal of the House's reputation and of her fond hope that she will continue to take L'Epoque to new heights. It is exactly that debt, Jeanne interrupts, her voice void of emotion, which she has come to discuss. To put it succinctly, either Mme Blanchard sells L'Epoque at a price which Jeanne and her backers can afford, or she will leave, take her clients with her, and found another House. It is a sad statement to have to make but for too long L'Epoque has been run without a shred of inspiration. It is high time a new broom swept away the dust of a fallen age. Not to put too fine a point on it, she continues, watching with well-concealed pleasure the old lady hardly able to hold in her anger, the House under its present management has lost any flair – if it ever had it – for design. And as Mme Blanchard knows, without innovative design, it might as well be dead.

Yes, the old lady admits to herself, she has felt it. The world's changing contours have recently made less and less sense to her. And it was bound to happen: sooner or later her assistant's outstanding achievements would lay claim to power. Stiff in her seat, and feeling for the first time the horror of her own office, with the furnishings she chose with such care failing to uphold her authority, Mme Blanchard stares malignly at Jeanne and resorts to the sole defence her enfeebled position has left her: silence. Sensing the seeds of intransigence taking root in her elderly antagonist, and keen to extirpate them before they gnarl at her ambitions, Jeanne turns to go with the words that if the proprietor does not even have the House's future at heart, then there is nothing further to say. She is just about to open the office door when she is stopped by Mme Blanchard's abrupt capitulation. In principle, the proprietor says, her voice fluting under the strain, she agrees that design is L'Epoque's lifeblood and that her own style has perhaps become a little out of date. She will not waste her breath, she adds, staring at Jeanne with disgust, on the odious nature of her assistant's ingratitude: she has lived too long and seen too much to expect anything else. Nor will she sue for the best terms which, however justified, Jeanne and her so-called backers might not be prepared to pay. Rather, for the sake of the House's continuity, she will settle for a round sum and a life-long *rente*, and on that basis will hand Jeanne the reins. Dissimulating as best she can her joy before a triumph which a year before would have been beyond her wildest dreams, Jeanne pays tribute to Mme Blanchard's wisdom in heralding the new age and assures her that, if from a distance, she too will soon bask in the greatness for which the House is destined. And while her employer contemplates the crumbling remains of her formerly elevated position, Jeanne bows to her and departs.

Surprising, thinks the Marquis, that Annabelle should spend so much energy on making her main character humiliate her employer. Might this scene be veined with more than a trace of personal odium? Unable to trace its origins, yet sensitive to the fact that the fictive often provides for the timorous a privileged sphere for the settling of accounts, and that dominant and resented influences can there be belittled in almost total impunity, the Marquis does not try to intuit what in Annabelle's behaviour is, at best, only secretive and, at worst, cowardly. Of far greater significance, even if it does provoke in him another burst of irritation, is that her creativity in the field of narrative matches his own and that, having focused on a world with which she clearly has an intimate relationship, she has now shown up his own efforts as reasonably crafty but less than convincing projections of what he – for their distance in time – could only experience at second hand.

Caught under the constantly flashing Leicas of *paparazzi*, a clutch of her clients, scouts from her rivals, international buyers, and the usual coterie of society ladies have gathered at Jeanne's first fashion show. To the sounds of a string quartet playing Baroque on a podium in a corner of the room, models glide across the catwalk and parade Jeanne's creations. It will be with enthusiasm that the next day's society columns will signal a revelation, welcome the birth of an exotic collection, speak of a Rond-Point revolution, and hail the arrival of L'Epoque's new era. Some, still reeling from a show the like of which Paris had not seen in a decade, will rather cattily suggest that Mme Blanchard's two-year-old decayed corpse must have spun in her grave at the wizardry of the daring *couturière*'s designs.

Annabelle is delighted to have at last consigned Melanie to outer darkness. She is also amazed at how details which she thought were buried deep within her memory are making well-timed appearances in Jeanne's account. Of course she has frequented numerous fashion shows and could easily describe them. On the other hand she would most likely leave out the decorative details of the *grands salons* in which they usually take place to concentrate on the carousel of clothes. But for some reason – atmosphere perhaps, or a question of firmly establishing the setting – the story's background has been more than adequately sketched in so that she presumes that by now the Marquis, travelling along the swell of her fantasy, must be convinced that she can handle her material. The strange thing is that she actually has very little control over what is going on. She too is letting herself flow, letting Jeanne take what she wants from her experience. She is even coming across patterns in her mind's eye which she did not know she carried. The secret really does seem to lie in having a good ground plan and in allowing it to play itself out. If this is how the Marquis did it, then trust is indeed, as he has consistently maintained, a crucial attitude.

At the far end of the salon, in front of the hall door, the new *couturière* watches the procession of her girls and trades passing comments with a middle-aged fashion critic immaculately turned out in Prince of Wales check whose melodious mannerisms make no secret of his inversion.

"Wealth, success, acclaim, I had them all. But, as you yourselves know, everything in life has a price," Jeanne adds to her hushed audience. "And it is wise to have some notion of what that price will be before committing yourself to purchase. A piece of advice I'd have given to any young woman with too much money and not enough sense wandering through L'Epoque. Unfortunately, by the time the one person who could have warned me what that price would be had come into my life, it was already too late."

Within the bloom of success, the Marquis muses, festers the weevil of decay. A common literary theme. Could Annabelle, he wonders, have based her story on a proverb? But long before the ground plan which she has used for her story can be divined and the array of paragrams, founding images, musical phrases, felicitous correspondences and inspirational routes which the creative imagination may borrow to find form have been passed in review by the Marquis, Annabelle's story has taken yet another turn and he has to hurry to keep abreast with it.

Although surrounded by the applause of her partisans and her rivals' poisoned plaudits, Jeanne can think of nothing but the pain in her side. The conversation with the critic is far from demanding yet there comes a moment when even that inoffensive exercise in gossip becomes more than she can stand. She therefore touches him lightly on the shoulder, excuses herself, and, before he can enquire where she is going, she heads up the flight of stairs to her private washroom. There she manages just in time to lean over the bowl and to spatter it with bile. Still nauseous, she reaches over to the basin and rinses her face. When she has wiped clean the corners of her mouth, she scrutinizes herself in the mirror. Incredible! She cannot believe it. Why, she looks exactly the same! No difference. Not the slightest sign of her corroding despair. True, her features are drawn, there is tension at the corner of the eyes, and her mouth tastes of vomit. Otherwise, apart from an occasional pain pulsing through her stomach, nothing.

"It did not take me long to discover that the penalties which I had unconsciously contracted were very severe. But by then I was caught, yes, caught in a trap of my own making."

What? The Marquis senses a painful tightening around the chest. Has he heard Jeanne right? Did she just mention a trap? Could Annabelle have uncovered his stratagem, intuited what is to come? Surely not. Hasn't he manipulated everything with the utmost discretion, never letting anything slip? Or did she notice something during that accursed infinity room incident, something which has made her suspicious ever since? On the other hand, isn't it a little too much like the hammiest type of coincidence come to rescue a poorly planned story to have Jeanne, the main character in the story, suddenly refer to the theme of entrapment? For his part anyway the Marquis, fidgeting in his seat, regards it as at the very least unnerving. Still nurturing doubts, he tries hard to convince himself that Annabelle's apparent prescience is purely coincidental. Then, keeping his eyes closed so as not to disturb the fragile illusion which his pupil is weaving, to buffer the pangs of his suspicion and to console himself he rapidly recites the mantra of his entry in the Almanach de Gotha. And once Jean-Loup Aristide Stanislas Gilles de Lampadou, Chevalier de la Licorne, Marquis de St Lyre has run through the full diapason of his titles and has thus rebolstered and renewed his identity, he settles back in his chair to gauge the rest of his apprentice's story.

The *couturière* rinses her mouth, brushes her dress, and walks downstairs to ensure that the proceedings are going as planned and that her absence has not been noticed. The audience, which has been feasting on the display of finery over whose every detail Jeanne has slaved for months, has in fact not given a thought to her whereabouts. In the knowledge that the show is running well and that her models are exhibiting her clothes with the finesse she has inculcated in them, she takes the lift to her office, aims for one of the drawers in her desk, and seizes the little wicker box with its cache of pills. Hoping that the opiates will soon take effect, she immediately, and without the benefit of a drink, downs three. Anything to be rid of the pain.

Half-dressed, stripped down to her shift, Jeanne stares into space. She is exhausted. Although covered in a thin linen sheet, the couch on which she is lying feels clammy and cold. And it is with unflinching and almost malevolent intensity that the examining light peers down at her from the end of a long metal arm. On the other side of the surgery the doctor rinses his hands with care and, in the warm yet precise tone of voice with which he usually pacifies the neuroses of his richest clients, he informs her that she will be glad to hear that there is nothing wrong with her. She is admittedly slightly run down, hardly surprising when considering the enormous responsibilities she has recently taken on. Otherwise she is not suffering from anything that a good rest could not cure.

Jeanne rises from the couch. She cannot credit what the doctor has said. A clean bill of health? Ridiculous! Why, she should know how she feels! Surely, she asks in despair, the doctor has overlooked some detail, has made some error? From the height of his professional pique only slightly ruffled by this *arriviste*'s defiance of his diagnosis, the doctor informs her that she is of course entitled to a second opinion. However, he can inform her that she will be wasting her time as, apart from exhaustion, she is in excellent shape. Excellent shape, she echoes his words with disbelief, staring at his professionally charming yet impassive face, and unable to fathom how such a high-priced, oft recommended physician can have failed to detect the cause of her pains.

As a result of its renewed image and concomitant increase in sales, L'Epoque's salon has been – during the *creux* of the midsummer months – tastefully, some might say almost ascetically, refurnished. Clean lines and open spaces now distinguish its visual approach, a starkness only slightly offset by a series of Suprematist-inspired blocks of primary colours which have been artfully juxtaposed on the walls.

In a corner of her newly-appointed salon, Jeanne, busy at a white lacquered desk, pores over a pile of invoices and sales vouchers. One of her apprentice assistants, the youngest daughter of a very wealthy client, approaches her with a somewhat sombre woman in tow and says that, try as she might, she has not managed to select anything suitable for the lady. The client, half embarrassed at being a difficult case yet not unhappy that the famous designer should be about to deal personally with her tastes, makes herself as still as a tailor's dummy and waits. Looking up from her papers, the *couturière* asks the client to turn around, pens down a few notes, and hands them to her assistant with a batch of in-house numbers. Her docile demeanour poorly disguising how impressed she is by her employer's quicksilver solution, the assistant leads the client away to be fitted out in a discreetly concealed fitting room. A few minutes later the client comes back seeking the Head of the House's approval. And, indeed, the transformation has been successful, the dress and the accessories which she had long hoped for have materialized on her all too thin figure. Feeling worse by the minute, the *couturière* accepts her praise with polite indifference and, leaving her correspondence unanswered, returns to her upstairs study where she collapses on her sofa and cries at her never-ending downward spiral of pain.

"What was even more perplexing," says Jeanne, adding her comment to the scene which has just taken place, "was the fact that though the pains grew day by day, my secret skills seemed in no way affected."

To have to deal with the administrative matters which have piled up on her desk is a struggle for Jeanne. She fidgets with her pen and her gaze wanders down the avenue where the wind is fast stripping the last leaves from the plane trees. A moment later, unexpectedly, there is a soft knock at the door. Taken aback, she curtly tells the caller to come in.

Her visitor proves to be a tall, raven-haired and aquiline-nosed woman, her features striking, although far from beautiful. Jeanne casts her eye over her and recognizes that she and this new arrival are about the same age. Her clothes, Jeanne notices at a glance, even if chosen with care and arranged in tasteful contrast, have not been purchased at any of her rivals but were most probably made up by one of the thousands of semi-professional seamstresses who, for their modest bourgeois clients, mock up the fashion houses' seasonal offerings at a fraction of the price. In a quiet yet trenchant manner the woman introduces herself. Her name: Yvonne Lackmar, her profession: sales representative for a fabric house. Jeanne recalls the company's reputation for its quality goods of a worthy if somewhat *passé* nature. Without further ado, the sales representative places her book of samples on a side table and opens them up for Jeanne's scrutiny.

"One morning," Jeanne says, "a morning on which I remember I was feeling particularly bad – my eyes were hurting, my stomach was upset, my head seemed ready to explode – a sales representative burst into my private office. I had asked my secretary to make sure I was left undisturbed so I was both surprised and angry at the appearance of this unknown woman. What on earth did she want? I didn't remember agreeing to see her."

The representative has selected a few fabric samples and is about to present them to L'Epoque's Buyer when Jeanne erupts.

"Was it her cheerfulness, the glow of her hair, or the confident manner with which she carried herself, I'm still not sure. What I do know is that the moment your Tante Yvonne came in, I completely lost control."

The Marquis, who has been mulling over how to explain the distance between Annabelle's initial grotesque effort and the surprising fluency of this story, on hearing of the identity of the new character realizes that she has taken his advice to heart and has used material with which she is conversant to spin out her story. No doubt about it, he muses: once it has been rarefied, personal experience usually provides the best building blocks. At least, he sighs with relief, Annabelle's now named aunt isn't some pathetic straw figure like the laboratory scientist.

"This was quite intolerable, I said to her. I had expressly ordered my staff to make sure I would be left alone this morning. Apparently I might as well not have bothered. For, at the first opportunity, what had happened? Exactly what I had tried to avoid: an ill-timed, irritating disturbance. It was regrettable but there it was: I hadn't the first clue to her identity. As for the merchandise she had brought along, I had no interest in it. So if she'd be kind enough to leave and to take her bazaar with her, I'd be very grateful. There were thousands of doors on which she might go a-knocking, but mine certainly wasn't one of them."

In contrast to the vehemence and pent-up malice of this outburst, the Marquis notes, the sales representative watches Jeanne's composure fracture with complete, and indeed, unnerving detachment.

"I know I should never have spoken like that," says Jeanne, attempting to distance herself from her own behaviour. "If I hadn't been so ill, it would have been unforgivable. Mind you, the last thing I expected was the answer your Tante Yvonne then gave. *Dieu*! Did she stand her ground. In fact her reply cut so deeply into me that I realized I had met my match. Whoever this extraordinary woman was I had to see her again. Although, I admit, that wasn't the only surprise she had in store for me."

Now that the Head of L'Epoque has had her say, her voice resolute and calm, Yvonne answers her. To begin with, she says, she did not barge into the *couturière*'s office but made an appointment and had had it confirmed the day before. She does not regard being at the head of a large business an excuse for flagrant discourtesy. An appointment booked is an appointment kept. Secondly, in all the years she has acted as a representative, she has never allowed anyone to insult the goods she sells and she is not about to let anybody start now. These are fabrics of the finest quality, a fact which Mademoiselle Servay could have inspected for herself if she had only taken the trouble to do so. However, before she leaves, she does have one statement to make. Mademoiselle Servay should not imagine for a minute that she has fooled her. She is well aware of the seriousness of the *couturière*'s complaint. And, she adds, if she does not face up to her illness and receive proper treatment soon, one thing is definite: she will never get any better.

"I was overwhelmed. Not only had I not been spoken to like that for years but, dammit, she knew. She knew that I was ill. Yet how could she, a simple sales representative, a woman with, I presumed, no medical training, state so categorically that what doctors had failed to recognize she had detected straightaway? Thoroughly ashamed of my behaviour, I stammered an apology and told her how much her words meant to me. I hadn't meant to be rude but with no one to help me and no one to turn to, I had become obsessed, and, I confessed, insensitive. She was right. I was indeed suffering from a disease, and worse, a disease that no one could diagnose. Would she please, I begged her, dine with me? I so wanted to discuss the matter further with her."

Yvonne's face remains impassive while she hears out Jeanne's act of contrition. Then, cutting the supplication short, she accepts the invitation. Scribbling her private address on a piece of paper, the *couturière* hands it to Yvonne. Would seven o'clock do? Should she send a car round to her home – wherever it is? The sales representative takes the address and replies that no, that will not be necessary: she will make her own way there. Finally, giving the head of L'Epoque – much diminished behind the handtooled leather expanse of her desk – a sympathetic look, she leaves the room carrying her book of fabric samples.

Jeanne stares at the door through which, without any warning, a salutary figure has just withdrawn. Can that have been the solution for which she has so long prayed?

Marcel, the *couturière*'s silver-haired, liveried majordomo, appears at the threshold of the sitting room in which the two women are sitting, aperitifs in their hands, and announces that the meal is ready. Madame may go through whenever she wishes. And while she admires with a few well-chosen words Yvonne's white silk dress, sagaciously set off by a thin jet necklace, Jeanne leads her into her finely furnished dining room.

The Marquis, who has been listening with interest to the development of the narrative, has detected the occasional anachronism in Annabelle's tale. *France-Soir*, for instance, the evening daily in which L'Epoque supposedly features in an article, was not founded until 1941. Bugattis, on the other hand, had stopped being manufactured by the mid-thirties so Jeanne could hardly have bought a new one in '38. While actively brown-nosing into people's private affairs, *paparazzi*, an ever-present feature of high society, were not then known by that modern transmontane term. And, on a less factual note, is it forgetfulness on Annabelle's part, or tact on the majordomo's, which made him address Mademoiselle Servay as Madame? Slight inconsistencies for which a film art director would no doubt be reprimanded and the continuity girl upbraided. But, the Marquis reminds himself, Annabelle is not trying to get a period right in every detail nor is she keeping tabs on the convergence of eyelines or the match of backcloths. She is out to win her spurs as a creative cook, a task which, necessitating a feat of juggling between two separate areas of artistry, is rather more complicated. Nor is that all: the Marquis' earlier favourable impression of his apprentice's achievements has been steadily confirmed. Not only has she made the mysterious outbreak of a psychic disease more or less understandable, without explaining its causes or its ultimate results, but she has also, proof no doubt of her art history education, provided the story with vivid background details. Even if some are rather dubious. A Soviet-inspired decorative motif in the salon of a capitalist fashion house would seem to be an aesthetic solecism, although adorning the dining room wall with a full-sized Gobelins of a Velasquez depicting the mythic contest of an arrogant girl weaver failing to beat a goddess at her own game is a rather telling inescutcheoning of the attempt which Annabelle is herself making, initially in emulation of, but, as the Marquis has remarked, more and more as a challenge to his own artistry.

Continuing his inventory of the decor, the Marquis remarks that the crystal ware on the dining table looks genuine St Louis and that the cream-coloured lace tablecloth, through whose tracery the walnut of the highly polished table reflects the candlelight, could come from Quimper. In the meantime the two women are being served by a young and handsome footman who bears an uncanny resemblance to the insolent waiter in the Bar Buffet, for whose now servile manner Annabelle has found no greater role in her story than the ordered presentation of a three-act meal.

The first act is a gravity-defying performance by a *feuilleté de fruits de mer* in which this lightest of flaky pastries envelops within its thousand and one strata an artfully diced saraband of mussels, squid and scallops and is itself tenderly accompanied by the melody of a shallot-flecked bechamel.

In the second, the two tightly-trussed birds which compose the *ballotine de faisan au genièvre* swim in a white wine sauce, a tour de force valiantly backed by a mound of first marinated then grilled chestnut stuffing.

Almost replete, the two women decide to eschew the cheese platter on which a catholic selection is festering on a bed of vine leaves; which, as Marcel permits himself to say to his mistress, is a shame as only that afternoon Alphonse, the chef, visited the market and there picked out a *Saint-Marcellin* at the very height of its unctuous maturity. Wisely expanding the little space and appetite they have left with the well-timed *trou Normand* of a shot of calvados, they delect the third and final act, a *sorbet de cassis avec macarons*, which the well-trained and almost obsequious footman presents to them in tall crystal goblets around which lightly browned, almond-shaped biscuits have been peacock-fanned. Finally, with its fitting epilogue, a well-percolated *robusta* of considerable strength served in thin cups of English bone china, the curtain falls on their meal.

Conversation, in contrast to the rarity of the food and the confident unfurling of Alphonse's genius, has been somewhat lacklustre. Jeanne, in whom the desire to put her guest at her ease has been in conflict with the need to discover her secret as soon as possible, has been lost for words: while Yvonne, either awed by the well-rehearsed mechanism of her hostess' courtesy, or choosing to hide behind the formality of an unyielding gaze, has failed to add to the kind of passing topic which can prevent a social occasion filled with expectations from degenerating into pregnant pauses no one thereafter dares interrupt. Yet warmed by the fare and slightly intoxicated by the three wines which they have consumed, a procession which started with a perfectly potable Haut-Brion '29, chased midway with an anonymous *marc* sent to the lady of the house by a supplier in Rennes, and culminating in a particularly memorable Château-Yquem '21, Jeanne eventually broaches the topic for which the meal has been little more than the frame. How had her guest told at a glance that she had been ailing?

"Yvonne replied that she had seen it straightaway. Perhaps under normal circumstances she would have kept quiet and left me to my fate. But my outburst had convinced her how much I was in need of help. As you can imagine, I stared at her across the table, terrified of the one question tormenting me. Aware that I had nothing left to lose, I at last asked her to name the cause of what was wrong with me."

The sales representative seems taken aback by the question. Is it really possible that Mlle Servay has no clear picture of what has befallen her? Surely she must have considered the penalties which the position she has attained in the world, her enormous and influential clientele, and the fame and success which now attend her, would entail?

"I answered her that no: I had considered nothing. Everything had happened mysteriously. All I knew was that my rapid rise in society had been accompanied by illness and that none of the various doctors I had consulted had been able to diagnose anything. Moreover most of them had flown in the face of my entreaties and had tried to still me by insisting that I was as fit as I could expect to be."

Yvonne gazes at her hostess and answers her that, if she truly ignores the cause of her disease, it will not be simple to explain it. There is indeed only one method: she will have to give Jeanne a practical demonstration. A demonstration? Jeanne asks. Where and how? Why, in the drawing room and, if she would like, this very evening, her guest retorts. Would she please tell her servants to retire? Quiet and total concentration are what they must have above all. After which, if Jeanne will make herself comfortable, she will try to reveal what has occurred.

Perplexed, Jeanne acquiesces, rings for Marcel, and asks him to leave the table just as it is – it can be cleared on the morrow. As for the rest of the staff, would he inform them that they can have the night off. The house, she insists, must lie in complete silence. Marcel replies that he will see to it that they are not disturbed. Once the majordomo has enquired of his mistress if that will be all, and has been told that nothing else is required, he receives her reply with a bow and leaves the two women alone.

It is with a self-assuredness which her earlier apparent discomfiture in the dining room belied that Yvonne takes her hostess by the hand and leads her into the drawing room. She seizes a single hard-backed chair, places it in the centre of the room, and invites Jeanne to sit on it. One by one she turns off all the lights, apart from one tall standing lamp whose shade she so focuses that its beam shines in Jeanne's eyes. Taking a little mirror out of her handbag, she places it in her hostess' hands and tells her to stare deep into it. As Jeanne does so meekly, surprised by her guest's efficiency, yet also comforted by the clarity in her voice, Yvonne stands behind her and addresses her in a gentle and soothing voice.

So there it is! The Marquis exclaims, as the second object which Annabelle brought with her on the train makes its timely appearance.

"I sat down, I admit, frightened. Your Tante Yvonne put a little mirror in my hand, a little mirror which, she said, was an old friend she always carried about with her, and told me to look deep into it. Once I had stared into its surface and concentrated just as she asked me to do, she unveiled the whole, yes, the whole terrible truth to me."

A pause. Jeanne's voice stammers, hesitates, and suddenly fades away.

What has gone wrong, the Marquis wonders? The narrative thread seems to have snapped. Has the strain become too great for Annabelle? Is trying to control so many details, themes, subplots, motifs more than she can cope with? Keen to discover what has happened, he opens his eyes. It is not until he has examined the scene with some care that the Marquis realizes that it is not Annabelle who has collapsed but Jeanne, for the *couturière*, her face in her hands, is now sobbing.

Quick to recover from what the Marquis presumes to be an unexpected break in the performance, Annabelle takes a clean handkerchief from her sleeve and, telling Jeanne to use it, hands it to her. Distraught, her head shaking with shame, Jeanne blows her nose. No, no! the Marquis overhears her say to Annabelle, she can't, she really can't go on!

Rather an ingenious way of interrupting a storyline without openly admitting that she does not know what the next step is, thinks the Marquis, appreciating his apprentice's storytelling trick. Not a ploy he has ever tried himself. Yet one which, granting Annabelle time to breathe, he concedes is highly effective.

"You've nothing, nothing to fear," Annabelle says to Jeanne comfortingly. "Whatever your secret happens to be, I promise, it will be safe with us."

That she would need an interlude only became clear to her a few seconds before when she recognized that she was not sure what the mirror should reveal. Relieved that she had not given way to panic, she had put her mind to it and had come up with something which she thought might work. First she had interrupted the story. Then she had willed Jeanne to cry. To her delight, Jeanne, as if little more than a puppet, had done so. While engaged in the practical details of consoling her, she had quickly turned over all the alternatives which she could conjure up. Some were ridiculous: sure proof of the Marquis' warning that imagination is a dangerous and capricious faculty and that all kinds of aberrations will come seeking form if given the chance. The problem was a simple one: what did she want the mirror to do, to say? The interlude had afforded her exactly what she had been after. It had allowed her to see the plot in the round, reminded her of the motifs which she was building in and which had threatened to seep away, and to leave no trace of their influence. Thankfully it had not taken her long to work out a new angle from which to pursue the tale, a new angle which would tie up the loose strands which had almost stopped the story from reaching its conclusion. Finally she had insisted that Jeanne blow her nose, made her say that she was feeling better and, to make matters more lifelike, had forced out of her a few more tears. She had then made her adopt an apologetic expression and say to the Marquis that she was sorry for the interruption and that she thought she was now ready to resume her story.

The Marquis gazes for an instant at the two women, then closes his eyes to await the narrative's resumption.

It takes Annabelle only a few seconds to revivify the

structure of her tale and to make all relevant details fall into place.

As ordered, silence has been imposed on the mansion and its servants have hurried to their favourite bistros or retired for the night. The salon is dimmed. In its centre, Jeanne sits stiffly on a chair, her face raked by the slanting rays of the single shaded light, her body in the shadows. While she begins to search through the fog of Jeanne's memories, Yvonne speaks in a quiet incantatory tone. What were the causes of the extraordinary process by which a young and unknown shop assistant became the most lauded dress designer in Paris? That is the key question, the Marquis muses from the comfort of his dark recess, which his apprentice must answer.

"Can you remember the very first occasion?" Yvonne asks Jeanne who is staring at her own face in the little concave mirror. "I'm sure it must have happened very quickly. One moment weren't you looking at your client's reflection, the next staring deep, deep into her soul? Didn't the mirror suddenly swing open and reveal to you a world of fear and guilt? Poor Jeanne! Didn't you feel sympathy for those lost souls? And weren't you happy when the mirror cleared and they seemed free? Ah! If only you had known that by helping your clients, their darkest secrets would be sealed in you. For their fear and their guilt are now within you. They're eating into you and are destroying your health. Each time you felt sympathy for a client and were moved to help her, each time you confronted that forbidden world, you took on her burdens. Yes, Jeanne, the poisons of those wasted lives flowed into you."

Jeanne shivers. Her throat runs dry. Her legs weaken. What is this extraordinary woman telling her? If this is really her predicament, it is truly intolerable.

"You don't believe me?" asks Yvonne. "Then look in the mirror! There you'll see everything I've said, everything I've told you."

And, indeed, Jeanne, looking into the mirror, does see it all. For the mirror's narrow screen, which a second before reflected her own anxious features, now reveals, at first aqueously, then with more and more clarity, the old changing room at L'Epoque in which her first experience occurred. There it is, that fateful afternoon, unmistakeable, concrete. And there she is too with her grey suit. And there is her plump client about to take off her dress. Everything is sharp, precisely delineated. And she can remember those reactions – her amazement, her attempt to keep calm when she caught sight of the fear in her client's mirror-face. And . . . but what was that?

Staring with fascination into the little mirror, Jeanne is startled by a detail which she has never met before. A shadow. Yes, something like a black shadow has just emanated from her client's back and has slid on to hers. There it is, perched on her shoulders like some witch's familiar. Then, in an instant, as if her flesh were no more than water and it were some depth-seeking snake, it has dissolved into the fabric of her dress and vanished!

Whatever it was, she certainly was not aware of it. No, she was far too confused, frightened, disoriented by what she had just witnessed in the mirror. She had no idea that she was being – how is Yvonne describing it? – invaded, possessed. What a disgusting notion! And, all of it, over in a moment. Taking her by stealth. She had felt nothing, had noticed nothing. Damn it! How could she, who had just been stupefied by the vision in the mirror, suspect that anything else, beyond that already catastrophic appearance, was also taking place? Such a tiny, invisible event! And what is that word that Yvonne is using to describe it? A transfer?

Ingenious, thinks the Marquis. Through a psychic crack in a mirror Jeanne peers into her clients' private lives and takes on their guilt, becomes in effect a scapegoat! As he has already noted, he has met the plot before. Annabelle has replaced the London of the last century with Occupation Paris. And, another interesting difference: if he remembers rightly, the protagonist of that other tale of the horrifying truth lying behind a pristine social mask, was a man.

"No, I never discovered what powers your aunt Yvonne used on me," Jeanne adds. "It might have been hypnotism. It might have been autosuggestion. What I do recall is that she conjured up a vision in the mirror so that I could see before my very eyes every gesture, every incident which had occurred in the changing room. Yes, she showed me how, on that first occasion and on all the others too, I had quite unconsciously soothed the sickness in my clients' souls. And I had taken on so much more than I could have ever imagined. For the message in the mirror was inescapable: every time I had come face to face with the secrets in my clients' tortured souls and had felt sympathy for them, they had walked away free while I, poor idiot, had carried their illnesses locked inside me. No wonder I felt so sick!

"I had viewed this so-called transfer again and again and been nauseated by the sight of those strange shapes running off my clients' backs and crawling inside me when Yvonne told me there was something else she thought I should witness. *Dieu*! How I wish I hadn't looked! But she had said that there was no other way to a cure. And, she insisted, it was vital that I understood the full story and confronted the true condition of my face, yes, of my own secret face in the mirror. To steady me, Yvonne put her arms around my shoulders and told me to look deep into the little mirror. Then . . . No, no! I can't, I can't describe it . . . !"

The little mirror once again becomes opaque before shedding its misty quality and revealing a vista on the hidden side of Jeanne's reality. Nor is it surprising that Jeanne cannot bring herself to describe the vision. For with enduring horror she discovers that what she had in all innocence allowed into her has now become a monstrous growth, a growth which has invaded her every pore. She gasps and lets out a scream which is first dampened then muffled by the carpet's thick weave and the furniture's elaborate upholstery.

No, surely this can't be her! She stares at the image which has appeared on the mirror's surface. Can those delta-veined pebbles be her eyes? Have her cheeks really become lined with lizard skin? Are those her cheekbones jutting out so crudely? And is that her tongue slithering between the parched and blackened rocks of her mouth?

"Yes, Annabelle, that evening your aunt made me stare at the ravages which my true face had suffered. And how it had suffered! It had puffed out and become a vessel into which my clients' sins had flowed. But don't think that that was the only contribution your aunt made to me. She also saved my life and taught me what I should do to recover."

Striding out of her office at l'Epoque, neither acknowledging her secretary's frantic enquiry nor glancing at the various sales ladies waiting to see her, Jeanne heads across the main reception area towards an unmarked door. She knocks, does not wait for an answer, but walks straight in. Behind a large drawing board the newly-appointed Head of Fabrics pores over a mountain of samples. Yvonne Lackmar looks up warmly. The *couturière* goes round the desk and peers over her friend's shoulder. Lightly resting a hand on her hair, she examines the range of samples laid out across the desk. She picks through the most exquisite and listens with interest as Yvonne explains how their unit cost is still too high and suppliers' delivery dates have proved unsound. These and other related topics they discuss until, turning to go, Jeanne reminds her new colleague that they have planned a quiet evening together: no callers. Suits her perfectly, Yvonne replies. She looks forward to meeting at the mansion after work.

Jeanne is sprawled out on her bed in her pale silk nightdress. Yvonne, her dark blue dragon-motifed kimono draped over her back, kneels behind her. A lambent pallor cascades from the red-shaded lamp on the bedside table onto the coverlet. Jeanne caresses the mother-of-pearl mirror, turns it over in her hand, and then starts to speak, her voice calm and soft. And while she recites the day's events, emphasizing each detail, as if trying to remember a lesson, Yvonne grips the nape of her neck in a manner strangely reminiscent of . . .

Nice use of available material, the Marquis purrs, gratified to recognize the reflexological technique with which he himself massaged Annabelle's tensed sinews.

However much the women's physical closeness might lead one to suspect that they have already embarked on their private voyage to Cythera, there is in this scene, as in Watteau's own rendition, a chaste distance between the visible and the potential, between Yvonne's embrace and the gestures which might, but which are not actually seen to, follow. Nor can the red light suffusing the bedroom with an erotic glow provide us with sufficient information to ignite our imagination. Therefore, if we yearn to see the two women entwined, legs akimbo, each sunk in the other's parted petals, we will have to make looms of our desires and on them weave the patterns of our own lubricious fantasy. For in the dim bedroom the sole activity appears to be confessional, the *couturière* quietly gazing into the mirror while her friend, genial pilot, guides her past the worst reefs of her fears.

A tantalizing vision which leaves the Marquis still unsure of Annabelle's proclivities. Not that he is about to fall for the oversimplistic equation of regarding her fictional creation as an unmodified representation of her world view or, indeed, of her experiences. On the other hand he does not think himself mistaken in regarding these elements as betraying at least a penchant for the sapphic. It is anyway irritating to lack clear-cut, incriminating evidence: Annabelle has again flirted with the issue yet avoided committing herself.

Annabelle breathes a sigh of relief. Uncanny to have had her nights with Melanie so closely copied down to the actual positions in which they used to lie and the suggestive lighting which her lover preferred. It would only have needed a slight veering and their intricate involvement might have been revealed; Melanie hunched over her, forcing her to lie back, to plead, to kneel, making her . . . But then, thank goodness, the censorious voice took over, veiling the scene, preventing the worst from coming out, blocking a direct equation between her two fictive characters and her own nocturnal activities. Annabelle hopes that the Marquis has not adduced anything from it. Why should he anyway? He knows nothing, or next to nothing, about her. However as Jeanne's story is still going on, and Annabelle is afraid of staunching its flow, she abandons her fears and lets it proceed.

"Every night," says Jeanne, "before I fell asleep, Yvonne would come to my bedside and help me get rid of the pains which I had collected during the day. First she'd make me look into the little mirror. Then she'd insist I described who I had served that day, whether I had had a vision, and what I had seen. The strange thing is that it worked. Talking about it, admitting the horror of what I occasionally saw in my clients' eyes, even witnessing their ghostly re-enactment in the mirror helped. By the time I was ready to fall asleep, I was as well as I could hope to be. Yes, we had settled down to our new life – L'Epoque gaining in influence and popularity, yielding impressive sales, everything running just as it should be – when the war came and ruined everything."

The long ivory-handled knife hesitates then slits through the brown envelope, disgorging an official document from its interior. She had expected as much which is why she purposely left it till last. With the rest of her mail scattered around the floor like so many windblown leaves, Jeanne sits on a large grey sofa in her office, Sascha somnolent at her feet, and examines the document. On either side of the Ministry of the

Interior's letterhead, the tricolour and the swastika. Jeanne frowns. What do they want from her now? Haven't they taken her best men, a driver, two packers, a commissionaire, and expatriated them to work camps?

"One day," says Jeanne, her voice hushed as if by the sorrow of her memory, "I received an official letter. It was – I shall never forget it – the most obscene document I have ever seen."

Itemized and logical, its hatred validated by bureaucratic jargon, the document which Jeanne has had sent to her is the official translation of the Nuremberg Laws which France, a nominal partner in Axis policies, must implement. A brief guideline informs her that as an employer she will be held responsible for making sure that L'Epoque keeps no racially suspect nor overtly Semitic elements on the payroll. She is further notified that in a month her employment register will be subjected to a thorough inspection. Tagged to the back of the document, she comes across an addendum. The *couturière* turns its pages and examines a glossary of salient features – hooked noses, curled hair, Hashidic locks – and descriptions of general physiognomic details which have been included to aid the Aryan purity of the Frankish races rid itself of the spoors of the outlawed race. Jeanne throws the document to the other side of the room and shudders.

Of the two bottles of Gevrey-Chambertin '35 one has already been drained while the other is three quarters on its way. On the table the document lies in tatters. It is very late. Jeanne, a half-filled glass before her, is slumped across the table while Yvonne, her eyes glazed, hums a tune as famous on one side of the front line as on the other. She picks up another document from the table: an identity card with, on its inside page, a recent photograph of her. As good as if that *salaud* Laval had had it specially printed for her! she exclaims. Come on! she says to her inebriated and downcast companion, cheer up! They now have the confounded pass even if they did have to wait long and pay over the odds for it. There's no time to lose. They must get away from the filthy little mousetrap Paris has become. At least they'll be safe at Jeanne's country house and needn't return until the hateful atmosphere has cleared.

"As usual Yvonne was right. We had to act fast. Purchasing a forged identity card for her had been difficult enough and had set our departure from Paris back weeks. And there were rumours that the Germans were already rounding up Jews in the suburbs. It only needed one denunciation and Yvonne would be arrested. I therefore made all the necessary arrangements, put one of my senior staff in charge of the House, and told her I'd be gone for a while and that I'd send her instructions by post. That done, we decided we would head the next day for the safety of my country house in the demilitarized zone."

A footman pushes open the large wrought-iron doors of the mansion's courtyard, allowing Marcel, peaked-capped and in a sombre suit, to drive the Bugatti out. In the back of the limousine, the two women and the dog are comfortably ensconced on the leather seats. The car slips down the Bois de Boulogne and heads for the nearest gates of the city.

"There was nobody about: I remember that very clearly. True, we had left early but you could usually spot strollers promenading their dogs in the Bois even on a Sunday. That morning, though, the lanes were deserted. Everybody had stayed in as if they knew that this First Sunday in Lent wouldn't culminate in a joyful Easter."

The Bugatti has put the wide boulevards behind it and is fast threading past rows of red-tiled houses, their tiny gardens festooned with early blooming flowers, when suddenly, at the end of an avenue of plane trees which opens out on to their first sight of green fields, they confront what they had feared above all else, a Gestapo road block.

A cold sweat works its way through both women's pores. The Dalmatian growls between them. There is, however, no alternative but to drive in a slow and stately fashion towards the awaiting barrier. Next to the block a lorry has been stopped and searched while a group of civilians are standing in a forlorn huddle on the other side of the road. The moment the limousine reaches the military group, two soldiers, their hands raised, their weapons trained, march on to the road. Ordered out of the car, Marcel is thrown against its side and is frisked with a violence that takes no account of his age. With some respect shown to their sex and apparent wealth, the two women are escorted to a trestle table where a tall, dark-haired SS officer, so handsome that Jeanne is forced to admit that the devil seems sometimes to have the best tunes, presides over a number of confiscated personal effects. He orders them to present their identity papers, barely glances at Jeanne's yet lavishes considerable scrutiny on Yvonne's. Reaching for a big black tome, he spreads it wide and checks through its closely typed pages. It takes him only a few seconds to discover that her card's number does not tally with those authorized. Responding to a discreet hand signal, the soldiers, bloodhounds pining for their master's move, pounce on Yvonne, pin back her arms, and arrest her.

Perhaps to compensate for having had to delouse a dismal little suburb so early in the morning and for forfeiting a night with a torrid little mannequin – an act of horizontal collaboration for which at the end of the war she would have her hair shaved, her pudenda mustard-smeared, and a placard put round her neck by a mob incensed at her giving pleasure to an agent of pain – the *Obersturmführer* decides to make an example of this black-haired bitch. He strides up to her and slaps her across the face. Yvonne has hardly recoiled from the first blow when the officer deals her a second. He then demands that she tell him from where she has procured the forged pass. Shaken, a thin, spittle-filled rivulet of blood trickling down both sides of her mouth, Yvonne answers nothing. Goaded by her silence, the officer grabs her hair and stares into her eyes.

What a vicious turn her tale has taken! thinks the Marquis. Strange that Annabelle should have so much violence in her. Is it, he wonders, a displaced sense of self-hatred which has made her loosen sadistic impulses on a member of her own family, or is she simply trying to render her wartime episode more realistic? The Marquis has, however, no opportunity to dwell on the root causes of Annabelle's narrative treatment for Jeanne is already describing how she watched powerlessly while her friend, permitted but one suitcase, was thrown on to the back of an open lorry in which stood four other suspects, three men and a woman of singular gypsy appearance who suddenly struck up the *Internationale* until a rifle butt from a guard had sent her spinning to the floor. And how the SS officer, flinging the forged card on to the ground and trampling it with his feet, had sworn that where he was dispatching Yvonne she would have no need for it. Once this pathetic scene has taken place, Jeanne, her face pressed against the side pane, stares at the lorry ponderously rolling away, while Sascha, its ears twitching, its tail cowered, whimpers at her feet.

The lorry has become a fast diminishing speck at the end of the straight road when the staff car, the impassive officer stiffly seated at its back, drives off, its wheels scattering dust and pebbles on the group of listless bystanders. Among these an old man tries to comfort a middle-aged woman in a flowerprint dress who, in spite of his efforts, will not stop crying. Close by three children gaze at the fast vanishing vehicle neither understanding what has occurred nor why. The soldiers dismantle the road block. The crowd forms into small clumps then, like extras dismissed by the bark of an assistant film director, disperses. Only the badly torn fragments of Yvonne's pass, splayed in the gutter, remain to recall the scene. And there is something eerie about the photograph as it lies there, spine broken, pages ripped. For crushed under the Nazi's boot, Yvonne's face now appears as haggard and as puffed out as Jeanne's in the mirror.

"Never again," says Jeanne to her hushed audience. "No, I never saw your aunt again. In fact I have no idea whether she's alive or dead."

Ashen-faced and sickly, brought low by her disease, Jeanne is lying in the bedroom of her country house. Thickly drawn curtains shield the room against the light of day. At the end of her bed, forlorn and still, the dog, its head between its legs, has spread itself out. On a sidetable there is a tray on which sit a bowl of chicken consommé, its surface cold and oily, and an apple which has not been touched. As for Jeanne's eyes, they are fixed in a wide, expressionless stare.

"After Yvonne's arrest," says Jeanne, "Marcel drove me to my country house where I immediately collapsed. Because, you see, with her disappearance I had lost everything. Not just my closest friend but my healer as well."

It is a cold and blustery day. Across the avenue late summer leaves are being flung from porch to porch while from the top of Paris' cycling stadium Vichy's flags, alternating with the Fatherland's, rasp and crackle in a dusty wind. Wrapped in a black coat, Jeanne encircles the perimeter of the Vélodrome d'Hiver's high bulging walls and muses how easily a pleasure palace can become an obscenity.

"It took me a month to leave my sickbed. Two before I had made a full recovery. The moment I was fit to travel, I did everything I could to discover Yvonne's whereabouts. I paid the right people, promised favours to others, and eventually pieced together what had happened to her. She and a thousand others, it seems, had been rounded up like cattle and taken to the Winter Cycling Stadium. From there, after a short period of transit, she had been deported. Where to I have never found out."

Encased in long kid gloves, Jeanne's fingers ceaselessly intertwine. The setting into which she has been ushered, an office furnished in the distinctive ormolu and purplewoods of Louis-Quinze, is impressive. As for the official who presides over it, his voice, precise and insinuating, has within it an undertow of menace. Those are Jeanne's initial apperceptions as she stands opposite the almost caricatural image of a Prussian officer, his head shaved, his small moustache perfectly sculpted, his broad hands neatly folded on his desk.

The officer in charge of the Department of Political Detainees at the Ministry of the Interior invites the *couturière* to a seat, then addresses her in a gratingly guttural French. His message is stark and simple. If what Mlle Servay seeks is a quiet life, if she would like to remain in business, and unless she is particularly keen to visit the basements in which much of the Gestapo's specialized work is done, he advises her to forget the forger she so foolishly befriended and to reinvest her energies in work which will raise her country and its friends' morale. Yes, she should produce a collection like the one she brought out just before the *drôle de guerre*! Now that, the officer stresses, striking the front of his desk, had been what he calls a show!

Taken aback that a model of organized villainy, a functionary of darkness, should not only have a passing interest in fashion but should also be acquainted with one of the shows she put on at her salon, Jeanne concedes that some of these Germans, for all their barbarism, must have sensitive souls, and that if only . . . The vapidity of her idealism is however rapidly debunked when the officer, revealing the dominant streak in his character, orders her to stop mixing with vermin and never to disturb him again with requests for information on matters which do not concern her.

Her slim form has become wasted, her face is raked by the strain of despair. Standing before a mirror in her drawing room, Jeanne stares at herself. No doubt about it: she is getting worse. Nor will she last another season if her clients, indifferent to the raging of the war and never betraying the slightest shame at the collapse of their country, keep exhausting her, whiling away their days trying on her clothes.

"I no longer had the energy to continue yet what choice did I have? However depleted its staff might be, L'Epoque was still a going concern and my employees relied on me. So, my fruitless search for Yvonne at an end, I went back to work, screening myself as much as possible from my clients, terrified of the poison in their hearts, and hoping against hope that I'd one day hear from Yvonne again. But as the weeks went by, I realized she was gone, gone for good, and that without her, I couldn't survive."

At the end of the day, when her staff has gone and the House is encloaked in silence, Jeanne places her papers in a neat bundle and leaves a note in her office for her Chief of Sales. She then drags herself to the top of the building and collapses in a chair in the cutting room. In the greyish half-light which falls from the pelican-necked street lamps, the dummies seem even more grotesque than usual; while all around her half-finished garments hover like wraiths in the penumbra. No, she concedes, Yvonne will never reappear, will never hold her again, will never . . . No point carrying on. She contemplates the wicker box in her hand brimfilled with pills and wonders who will discover her body in the morning. Perhaps some young apprentice, starting like she had once at the bottom of the House, keen to experience the brightly-coloured fruits of fame, will find her slumped across the table, her limbs draped over the chair, the bitter savour of those same fruits suffusing her lips.

A chill has settled across the cutting room. In the distance the rumble of heavy tracks, perhaps of armoured vehicles, is making its way down the avenue. Pale and immobile, Jeanne rests her thin hands on the pattern-strewn table and, staring at her unexpected guests, adds a coda to her tale. "And that's the state you found me in – yes, at my wit's end. If you hadn't come in, I think I'd have gone through with it . . ."

Relieved that she has so timed her appearance as to prevent Jeanne ending her life, Annabelle goes over to her and holds her hand. "There's no need to despair, Tante Jeanne. You remember I said we would do something for you? Well, now that I've heard your story, I'm convinced we can help. Don't you agree, Jean-Loup?" She turns towards the Marquis who, from the shadows in which he has been sitting, backs her with a nod. "I

283

told you – didn't I?" she adds to the mournful *couturière*, "that we're looking for parsley with which we'll prepare a tincture which should hopefully rid us of our disease. I know you're tired and depressed and that what we're asking for will demand a tremendous effort from you. But please, will you get us a few sprigs? In the meantime, Jean-Loup and I'll think up a solution to your situation."

"A solution? What do you mean? . . ." Jeanne asks, her face seemingly blanched by the strain of telling her story. "Still," she adds resignedly, unable to make any inroads on the inordinate offer of the young lady calling herself her best friend's niece, "if parsley's what you really want . . ."

Then, like all the other characters, as if finely tuned to the procedure – which is hardly surprising as Annabelle has witnessed it on three separate occasions – the *couturière* leans back in her chair, cups her hand, and closes her eyes.

The beautifully laid out vegetable garden to which the Marquis is transported the moment he closes his eyes is surrounded by a high wall. At its cardinal points finials shaped like pineapples show off the Pondicherry background of the merchant whose cunning in the commerce of imported spice constructed the fake Renaissance château which Jeanne purchased for a song. Similar to the other scenes in which a character was asked to locate one of the ingredients which the travellers sought, this set is hazy and its colours are washed-out.

In a corner of the garden, next to a number of cracked glass jars and of broken-down horticultural implements, there stands a small pile of rocks. It is on this that the scene's focus comes to rest. It does not take the Marquis long to work out why. For among the various flints and pebbles which have ended up pell-mell on the pile, there is one, a fat, multi-veined and liver-shaped stone with a broad crack in its side. Out of this crack there begins to ooze a greyish mist, a mist which at first swirls shapelessly but which then gathers itself and becomes more and more solid until, at last, from within its mass the faded figure for which the Marquis has been looking out arises. The figure of Jeanne.

Wearily does this apparition from the heart of the stone journey across the garden, leaving heavy footsteps in the muddy path, as if each move were at the expense of enormous pain. Her hands are barely material, more like clouds somehow prevented from wafting away by some tenuous and ever diminishing spell. Jeanne's figure nonetheless continues along the path until she reaches a sector of the garden which is surrounded by a wooden lattice-fence. She opens its small gate and stoops to gather the herbs growing there in abundance.

The instant in which she lays a hand on a plant, the vegetable garden is punctuated by a terrible screech. Undeterred the gaseous being pulls even harder. Even more strident do the screams become until, surrendering to its fate, the plant is loosened from its bed and the stone figure shakes the mud from its wet strands. Half blind, the vaporous wraith then makes her way back towards the pile of stones. And there, in a thick cloudburst of dust which momentarily obscures the Marquis' view, her shape collapses and is scattered across the other pebbles on the pile.

Just as planned. Telekinesis, teletransportation, the miracle of metamorphosis enacted according to the principles laid down by the Marquis. Never once questioning its how or why, Annabelle takes the sprigs of parsley from the hollow of Jeanne's cupped hands covered in stone flakes and peppered with dust, and smells them. Admiring their full aroma, she passes them triumphantly to the Marquis. He in turn examines their colour and shows with a sign of the head that he appreciates their freshness.

"We've done it!" cries Annabelle, generously sharing the triumph of her spoils with her companion.

"We have indeed, Mademoiselle Fleury," says the Marquis, playing his subordinate's role to the hilt. "And now what we must do is hand Mademoiselle Servay the one thing which will bring life, colour and joy to her beautiful features," he adds to provoke an effect on Annabelle's creation. An effect which he immediately produces, for, taken aback by the sudden show of sympathy from the one person who seemed to have no interest in the proceedings, Jeanne stares in his shadow-soaked direction.

"Of course we must," Annabelle answers, faintly irritated by the Marquis' success in upstaging her and currying favour with Jeanne. "Here, Tante Jeanne," she says, taking the little mirror out of her pocket. "I'm sure you'll recognize this."

Jeanne catches sight of the mirror and gasps. She does not wait for Annabelle to give it to her but seizes it from her hands and clasps it to her breast. "Impossible!" she cries. "The mirror, Yvonne's little mirror!"

But this time it is the real object, not a simulacrum, nor a cheap substitute. Jeanne stares into its faded surface at her own tired, tear-soiled face, noting the lines of strain which despair has deepened. The mirror in her hand, she recalls the hours of solace which her closest friend helped her find in it.

The mirror's magic, it would appear, is far from spent. For, true to its ability to give form to the invisible, its surface becomes cloudy, as cloudy as the surface from which some deceitful djinn might arise in a fairy story. Yet it is not a djinn that appears, no. The features are unmistakeable. Are those not her brown eyes, her jet hair, and oh! her face so gaunt? Hardly daring to do so, Jeanne nonetheless calls out her friend's name. As if determined to prove that anything is possible as long as the imagination has cleared the ground and made all necessary adjustments, the face in the mirror answers back.

"Jeanne!" The voice is faint, little more than a whisper filtered through layers of the finest muslin.

"Is it really you, Yvonne?" Jeanne asks, gazing into the mirror, afraid that the apparition might vanish as enchantedly as it had risen.

"Promise me you'll be brave, Jeanne," the image in the mirror answers, "and I'll never leave you again."

"You don't mean that you're . . . that you're dead?" stammers Jeanne, forced to concede what she has suspected for so long.

Dismayed by the lacklustre dialogue which the ghost and the *couturière* have just inaugurated, the Marquis wonders why Annabelle is producing such dull stuff.

"Yes, I am." The voice crackles while the image, as if upheld by fragile, ebbing energies, disintegrates then reforms: "Believe me, Jeanne, I did everything I could to get the mirror to you. Everything. I had hoped my sister would send it on to you. Perhaps she tried. I'm glad my niece, Annabelle, eventually got it to you."

Aha! Self-reference, thinks the Marquis, recognizing the vanity that so often lies at the heart of all creation. The storyteller inserting herself into the limelight, seeking credentials for her efforts. So Annabelle wants to be reflected in her handiwork, does she? She has fallen for creativity's oldest ploy: the notion that the created object reflects its creator when more often the creation confuses the source and links it to a never-ending chain of self-admiration.

"Tell me what happened," asks Jeanne, her curiosity mounting. "I heard you had been taken to the Winter Stadium, but after that . . ."

Jeanne has made a wish. And like all wishes pronounced in the ever revolving, flux-filled atmosphere of the imagination, it comes true – or, at least, appears to. Once again the mirror offers its limpid surface for scrutiny and Annabelle beckons to the Marquis to watch over Jeanne's shoulder the next development in the story.

Around the internal perimeter of the Vélodrome d'Hiver, close to its racing track, a high electrified fence has been erected. Inside a great number of people have been herded, some standing clutching suitcases, others squatting on sacks of personal belongings. Like laboratory animals they stare at the searchlights as if trying to find some way out. This rapidly billeted compound – more accustomed to the cheers of cycling fanatics than the moans of prisoners still refusing to grasp that their nightmare is concrete and their abasement real – is not only cheek-by-jowl with able-bodied men but also has a full quota of women and children. Pacing up and down the stadium's outer track, their grey uniforms aping the conquering army's, French militiamen guard this mixed crowd from which humanity is slowly and deliberately being drained.

From the misery of those upturned faces, the focus shifts on to Yvonne. The Marquis catches sight of her, leaning against the wire fence, sitting on her sole piece of luggage. She closes her eyes and tries to fill the moment not with hope – for she knows all too well what ravages that virtue can wreak – but with the blank impetus of survival. How long does she remain there? She could not say as there are no chimes in this antechamber to hell. There comes a moment though when she does detect a change. A small, almost indistinct change. Someone, somewhere in the midst of the mass – she is sure of it – is staring at her.

She opens her eyes, blinks before the white haze, and surveys the multitude of dirty, fear-ridden faces around her. So lost in themselves have her fellow prisoners become that, as she casts her eye across them, they resemble nothing so much as a scarred slab of sculpted rock from which no sign, no response, can be scried. Out of this fearful range, it is easy to isolate the pinpoint beaconing her with such ferocity. And, indeed, as she soon makes out, a hundred feet away, a young, dark-haired militia-man's eyes are targeting her. To avoid the stark quality of his gaze, she turns and resumes her contemplation. Perhaps because his lack of years makes him insensitive to her desire to be left in peace, or because the temporary powers with which his uniform have endowed him have sharpened his will to combat her indifference, her self-absorption fails to deter him. A few minutes later, he is standing before her. She raises her head. He smiles, digs into the voluminous pockets of his overcoat, and offers her a cigarette. She rarely smokes yet afraid of alienating a potential ally she accepts his yellow-paper army-issue *caporale*. Somehow, in the hiatus created between the crowd's cowed state and the guards' distant vigilance, a conversation occurs. Without the slightest embarrassment, using the familiar form as if she were his older sister or his mother, the young militiaman relates to her a ragbag of personal facts: the backwoods from which he stems, the attraction of the city, the hand-to-mouth existence he eked out on first arriving in Paris to seek his fortune. Then how the defeat of the nation threw him into a uniform which he recognized was far from popular but which his former wayward existence prevents him despising. The pay is decent. He has some standing. He supposes he is happy.

Yvonne nods encouragingly at her gaoler's story and is rewarded with a piece of bread. As she chews its texture – is it fear or exhaustion which has made her mouth dry up? – she ruefully realizes that the young soldier has adopted her rather as he might a stray. Should she or should she not play the pet? Before she is coerced into a show of subordination, a strident call over the loudspeakers forces the young man to scurry towards another part of the fence, a vivid example of his low rank. Quite undeterred, he returns a little later and continues to confide in her.

At some late hour the lights are dimmed and senior guards bawl orders, sending orderlies fanning out around the fence to check for escape attempts. Before leaving her, the young militiaman slips Yvonne a half-filled pack of cigarettes and a box of matches and tells her that he will try to return on his second shift of guard duty. His voice sidling into a hesitant register, his eyes averting hers, he adds that he likes her very much.

Yvonne finds it extraordinary that she, who has never shown

great fondness for men, should have somehow – and at this particularly fraught time too – attracted a boy. As the featureless procession of hours passes her by and the arena becomes shrouded in early morning mist, she comes to recognize that the young soldier's extraordinary infatuation may have its uses. If only, before she is carted away, she could achieve what the suddenness of her arrest prevented her from doing: getting the little mirror to her friend, Jeanne.

After an interminable period, during which the sobs of neighbouring prisoners have eventually waned, the young militiaman reappears and presses a few slices of *saucisson* into Yvonne's hand. He does not have very long, he whispers; he will have to check the fence again any minute. Impetuously, as if he had made his confession but a few seconds before, he bends down towards her so that their faces almost touch and asks her whether she too likes him. Yvonne, who has been expecting the question, answers that yes, she does: he has been kind to her. Aware that this may be her last opportunity, she seizes it. Would he please, she asks him, do something for her? His eyes take on a wary look and he does not reply. Yvonne takes the mirror from her coat pocket and scribbles L'Epoque's address on a piece of scrap paper. Were he to take this object to this address, or to this one, she says, adding her sister's, he would make her very happy and could be sure of a reward. Unable, unwilling or too inexperienced to extract any advantage for granting this favour, the young militiaman stuffs the mirror into his trouser pocket and remains silent. A short moment passes in which the young man stares at Yvonne. Then he at last speaks and informs her that he has to leave. As his hands caress the mirror's cold surface, he swears that she need not fear: he will fulfil her request. His face flushed, he murmurs a final word, turns away, and resumes his rounds.

Have we perhaps judged the militiaman too harshly? For in a story in which every item has so far been exchanged for something else, this young man, dragged by circumstances on to a monumental fresco in which he will never be more than a bit player, may teach us a lesson about doing things for no greater reward than a smile or some even less tangible benefit. Compared to the objects which all the other characters have sought and been granted, this young man, however stained he may be by having donned a uniform designed not for his countrymen but for its invaders, has still shown a degree of selflessness which none of the other far more sophisticated and seemingly honourable creatures displayed.

"I shan't dwell on what happened next," says the ghostly face in the mirror. "There were mindless inspections, calls over the loudspeaker, and occasional glimpses of the Red Cross. Later – I can't say how much later because I lost all sense of time – we were packed into buses, taken to the freight depot of the Gare de l'Est, and from there shunted in cattle trucks. After a five-day journey during which we had neither food nor water, the doors of the trucks slid open on to a camp with a high fence. The details of my days after that, Jeanne, I prefer to spare you."

With those chilling words, Yvonne's face slowly vanishes from the mirror's silvered screen, leaving us to fill in the missing parts of the story: the soldier, taking the mirror first to L'Epoque, there to be told that Mlle Servay is indisposed, then to Yvonne's sister who presumably stocks it away somewhere among the family heirlooms from where it is brought out three decades later into the light of day and handed to her daughter.

While Annabelle and her companion withdraw into themselves, Jeanne, torn between her horror at her friend's fate and her joy at her return even if in truncated, two-dimensional form, sits very still in the chair and stares straight ahead. Just as she had suspected, Yvonne is dead. She looks into the mirror and places her lips on to it, and kisses it tenderly.

Without another word to her creation, Annabelle, holding on to the fresh parsley, and making a sign to the Marquis to join her, walks out of the dressmaking room. Before he follows her, the Marquis casts a last look at the set which she has so carefully crafted. The *couturière* seems to have relapsed into a quiescent state, not even the faint rustle of breathing interrupting her frozen features. Turning his back on the illusion, the Marquis closes the door behind him.

He is watching his companion fumbling through the one-bulbed corridor, trying to locate the exit, when suddenly there is a violent, wall-shaking sound: a sound like an old-fashioned, steam-driven siren letting out a cry, a cry so loud and felicitous that the Marquis ascribes it to the spirit of the train celebrating Annabelle's locating the fourth ingredient. And why shouldn't she have her success heralded? he ponders: she certainly deserves it. Her story, for a novice, was remarkably fluent.

Annabelle stands in front of a green door. Its paintwork is flecked with marks which, the Marquis suspects, have probably been notched by generations of tired hands searching for the exit after a hard day's sewing. As he comes up to her, she takes a deep breath, pushes the door open, and exits exhausted, if happy, into a corridor.

A first hairline crack of light has appeared on the far-off horizon, announcing the turning of the night.

It is happening. Yes, a delicious feeling is moving up her legs, through her groin, up her back, finally fanning out in a series of sensations the like of which she has never felt except here and there – when the Leopard Woman had her orgasm, when the Marquis massaged her neck – in such concentration, and those were anyway in much smaller doses. It is as if some weight, some blockage, some terrible feeling of guilt had been purged, yes, as if energies once stymied had at last been allowed free flow. Annabelle, experiencing this sudden onrush of energy, wishes that she had words of her own to describe the event coursing through her body instead of having to resort to the Marquis': liberation, blockage, release. She resents the fact that there seems to be nothing she can do which he has not already achieved and for which he has not coined some crafty explanation.

A second later, realizing that she is being ungrateful, that this is surely part of the therapy which the Marquis promised her all along, and that however exquisite and revivifying the nervous spasms were, they have ceased to ebb past her, she relaxes and beams at her companion.

"Congratulations! Annabelle," the Marquis says warmly as they make their way back towards their compartment. "I thought you staged that to perfection." Adopting a sombre expression, he adds: "Though there were times when I was worried."

Annabelle, proud of a performance which has only been marred by one small hitch, considers his reservation a form of criticism. "Oh? What about?"

"A question of logistics. You had organized the main brunt of the story and had almost concluded it and yet I couldn't see how you were going to explain your mother getting hold of the mirror. As it happens, the manner in which you tied up that particular loose end was both pleasing and elegant. Which goes to show,

Annabelle, that you're fast becoming a Master Cook – or should I say a Mistress? – in your own right."

"The strain was almost unbearable," Annabelle replies, concealing her pleasure at her companion's compliment. "Keeping those details running in my head really exhausted me." She smells the parsley and adds: "It seems to have all worked out rather well."

"It has indeed: very well. If you hand me the sprigs," says the Marquis de St Lyre. "I'll make sure they're kept fresh with the other ingredients."

In a show of affection, proof perhaps of the tenderness and bonhomie which comrades in arms are said to feel for each other, or, rather more macabrely, of the hunter's interest in his victim's compliancy, the Marquis takes Annabelle's arm. She in turn leans on his shoulder. Down the corridor they go, past innumerable compartments filled not with any belief-defying assortment of pilgrims, passers-by or perverts, but with the mix of travellers commonly found on long-distance trains engaged in the type of inoffensive exercise which the dulled mind produces to fill out the hours of its fretful transit. Past this soothingly simple sight they wander until they eventually come to a halt outside Annabelle's compartment.

While the Marquis hovers on the edge of his pupil's compartment and she gazes on him with the new-found warmth which her success has induced in her, a crucial question arises: what is to happen next?

Taking as many factors as possible into consideration, three options seem worth examining. The first points the story in a controversial direction. The second, reacting strongly against this, condemns it as a misreading of the travellers' relationship and itself looks to a much simpler conclusion to the scene. As for the third, it is so improbable that it is only mentioned here to illustrate the rare potions which can be cooked in the cauldron of fantasy.

But before the often-heard argument is wheeled on that for a story to parade its ambiguities is a betrayal of the trust which readers place in the narrator to lead them to a sure destination, and is thus an abdication of responsibility as shameful as would be, say, a sea captain's informing his passengers that faced by three compass points and nothing much to choose between them, why doesn't every jack tar put it to the vote whose hand should man the tiller? Yes, before that critical chestnut with its normative airs and graces is brought on, we should recall the dice which the Marquis and Annabelle used and whose main function was to unhinge the humdrum, break open the frame of the expected, and show the alternatives that circumscribe the arena of the possible. And it is with those dice in mind that the two most likely paths that the narrative could follow, together with one beyond the pale of probability, are here offered as curiosities.

It is evident that the Marquis de St Lyre and Mademoiselle Fleury have together tasted danger in the pursuit of a most unusual goal. Yet even that simple statement gives rise to opposing interpretations. For instance, those who say that there is no more potent combustible than the juxtaposition of bodies in a confined space and that the inevitable result of such promiscuity is for the protagonists to slip into each other's arms, may insist that the Marquis should now walk into Annabelle's compartment and manoeuvre her into a position for which the most pertinent epithets are possession, pliancy and penetration (although possession is a pitifully poor representation of reality for as everyone knows who has ever seen a recumbent and satisfied female smile after the act of love, man possesses nothing, is not triumphant, but is rather wasted, worn, and drained of his essence, while woman, filled with his flagellating substance, lies supinely victorious).

The second option could be bannered by any party that had noted the fact that not once in the story has there been the smallest indication of sexual attraction – Annabelle has been no *coquette*, nor has the Marquis behaved in any way other than as a gentleman – and that if seduction is to take place, then it should surely operate on a much subtler scale. To which it might add that as nothing is quite as fatal to certain types of relationships as coition, and that as the indices of each's homosexuality have been alluded to more than once, they hardly seem likely to bridge their mutually exclusive inversions.

As for the third option, it includes neither a bout of steamy love-making nor, for that matter, the chaste sequestration of the travellers in their own cabins, but has them instead pull the emergency cord in unison, thereby provoking a monstrous disarticulation of the train so that while the main body of the express rattles on, shaken but not derailed, their own carriage, by a fortuitous stroke of rerouting, is shunted towards a siding which speeds it at a brisk pace through what appears to be a faerie landscape within which they confront a volcanic pile belching sulphurous fumes, a tumbledown mansion veined with bulging conduits, a massive man-of-war atop a tiny pond, and other set pieces to which even a South American fabulist would find it difficult to ascribe common themes; until the carriage, slowing down, comes to a halt in front of a welcoming party made up of all the characters which the Marquis and Annabelle have incorporated in their stories who then proceed to make a great fuss of them and to lead them to a clearing where stands a large linen-draped table on which all manner of delicacies have been heaped and where, once they have partaken of a delicious collation, the young girl, the Mummy and the dwarf explain each in turn the aetiology of the blockage which they embodied in the Marquis' psyche and their boundless joy at his subsequent liberation, a dénouement which is capped by the *couturière* divulging to Annabelle what she symbolized in her story and along what great avenues of power she should soon – now that she has been freed – travel.

With the meal at an end, the travellers are escorted by the now rather more subdued party to their carriage which, the instant they board it, in defiance of the laws of inertia, rolls off through another scenic route. In no time at all this boasts a baffling carnival of images – whose luxuriance for the sake of brevity we will not here delineate. Debouching on to a track parallel to the one which the main body of the train took, and catching up with it in a little seaside station, with a boldness which would tax the most daring choreographer, it runs over coincidentally-readied points and slides smoothly into the empty space which is at that very instant being scrutinized by rail engineers desperate to discover how a single carriage could possibly have gone astray. There it takes up its proper place while the officials loudly maintain that never has such a move been seen before and are the railways not magnificent for permitting such graceful and unexpected synchronicities to occur out of the blue. To which they add that, frankly, once one has fallen in love with the silver banisters nothing, but nothing at all, can compete with them except perhaps the love of a good woman, and even that might pall, whereas the romance of the steam age, the plushness of the Pullmans, the technological wizardry that converts the power of

294

the diesel into the clean-as-a-whistle efficiency of electricity are, it should be admitted, a hard act to follow. And with everything back to normal – the missing carriage snug among its peers, the Marquis and Annabelle able to resume their journey – the engineers give the train a clean bill of health, the seaside station master (who here fortunately does not have to double as a substitute Steward) waves his flag and, with a monumental burst from its siren, the train sidles off to make up for the time which it has lost in its various peradventures.

With these three options sketched in, it is up to readers to decide whether they would like to picture the Marquis and Annabelle gyre, pivot and press in the intimacy of their reproduction *fin-de-siècle* bunkroom, projected into a hothouse atmosphere made out of wish-fulfilments and aberrant desires, or whether they much prefer the scene to come quietly to an end with the tired apprentice retiring to her compartment and her Master informing her that the train is due in Nice in a few hours and that he hopes she will join him for breakfast once she has had a rest, an invitation she courteously accepts before wishing him, not without a hint of irony, sweet dreams, and finally turning in. It is with the simple statement that no matter which rail route readers happen to choose, the outcome of the plot will remain exactly the same, that we take our leave of our protagonists, safe in the knowledge that when we return to them, they will be renewed and ready to fulfil their function in the final part of the story.

CHAPTER FIFTEEN

Not in the lavatory. Surveying its walls, canvas across which an army of felt penpushers have scribbled love notes, offered base pleasures, and warned of the viral dangers lurking on the seat; casting his eye over the usual bevy of jokes, nervous whispers, and messages as morally reprehensible as novels were once said to be, Jules sniffs around the tiny cramped quarters and curses. Miniature puddles, remnants of rapid if of inaccurate fire, have gathered in the corners of the cubicle while a few crumpled pieces of paper lie next to the bowl's mushroom-stem base. The contradictions of the system! Proud of its air-conditioning, publicizing the hours of road-jammed travel it can save, lauding its standards of comfort and style, yet still resorting to a flushing action that spreads waste on the soil of the tracks! But although Jules has always considered the disparity between the public and the private face of the train a scandal, he is not now rooting around the lavatory to lambast its primitive plumbing. Simply put, all he is after is his animal.

He darts out of the lavatory and searches further along the corridors, stopping at every recess, luggage space and empty first-class compartment until he arrives in the restaurant's kitchens, where the chef, mastodon-shaped beneath the wilting puff pastry of his hat, slouches at a table next to his *commis* who is dribbling the ash of a near-defunct cigarette over a tray of croissants. He awards them a perfunctory good morning, then asks them if they have seen his ferret. Concealing as best he can his impatience, he listens to their good-humoured response: sorry as they are that the little animal has disappeared, the little rascal can't have gone that far, they'll give him a shout the instant they catch sight of him, before adding the fond hope that he will soon come across it. Once he has heard out their well-meant but worthless homilies, he thanks them and rushes out.

Down one corridor after another Jules paces, minimizing the sound of his footfall so as not to wake the sleeping passengers, calling out every so often in a half whisper: "Anatole, where are you? Anatole, do come out!", and muttering to himself under his breath: "To think it was me who let that disgusting little animal out!" He trains his eyes on every possible hiding place, although discounting second-class compartments as the Mistral is overbooked and there are none lying empty within which Anatole might hide. "Eh, Anatole!" he says, increasingly unable to hide his irritation. "Come to Daddy, come to Jules!"

Jules' inability to locate his companion in the train's many enclaves makes him very bad-tempered. It is almost at the end of his tether that he steps into the last carriage, a carriage in which heavy articles of luggage and mail sacks have been stored behind a thick-set grille. He looks in. No lights. He searches around for a switch, finds one, and turns it on. To no avail. Bulb broken. He curses again. Just above a first-aid kit, in a corner cupboard through whose rusted lock he sends his passepartout foraging, Jules unearths a regulation torchlight, its batteries generating no more than a bashful beam. He is busy damning its dismal performance when he suddenly hears a sound from the massed disarray in the hold.

What was that? He swivels around and shines the beam in the general direction from which the noise came. No culpable form is caught in the dull net of his probe, only the misshapen lumps and looming figures of canvas bags bulging with letters. Perhaps it was only the rasping of a poorly-oiled wheel or the steam-driven brakes clenching their teeth or the palpitations of the carriage on its springs. He hesitates, listens again. Nothing.

Jules resumes his search and his mind is dwelling on a number of apocryphal incidents in which various objects have been discovered in the bowels of baggage compartments – rabid dogs, unclassifiable segments of dismembered corpses, clothes stained in the excesses of fornication – when he hears the noise again. No doubt about it: a yelp closely followed by the sound of paws scraping.

Amazed, Jules stands back from the grille and tries to gain a better vantage on the scene. As his torch will still not dispense more than an incontinent dribble, he cannot distinguish anything concrete among the jagged objects surrounding him. Searching for the entrance to the baggage hold which his passepartout is supposed to fit, he notices a hole at floor level in the wire mesh. He crouches down and examines it. Next to the hole his fingers feel a wad of fur. Most unwillingly, yet coerced by the very nature of his pursuit, he puts it to his nose and smells it. *Merde alors*! he exclaims, scraping away on the mesh the loose hairs which have adhered to his index finger. Is it possible that Anatole has ended up in there?

Fearful of what he might uncover among the luggage and the sacks, the Steward nonetheless advances towards the hold's metal door and endeavours to open it with his passepartout. Its lock unlatches but will not give. He presses hard against it: its resistance, however, easily matches his own. Then the sounds start again. Whatever has sought refuge here seems to have been roused by the noise. He pushes the door harder while the sounds, part hiss, part growl, with ever mounting ferocity echo round the hold.

"Anatole!" cries Jules, almost convinced of the noise's origins. "You're there, aren't you? Anatole! It's me, Jules. What the hell are you up to?"

But the sounds, far from abating, increase. Incensed, Jules give a concerted shove and finally forces the door to swing open.

Jules discovers that the reason why he could not have entered sooner is simple. Presumably overcome by the train's lurching, an immense wickerwork basket has tumbled over and has blocked the doorway. He drags it aside, pushes it back against the wall where it can do no more mischief, and is about to continue his search when he realizes he no longer knows in which direction to go for the noises by which he planned to orient himself have vanished.

His torch swerves across the room but is not bright enough to resolve the hold's dusty flank nor its shapes into clearly defined objects. From corner to corner Jules strides over sacks, gets his feet caught up in loose string, tumbles against indescribable things in the semi-darkness, and combats all the while his rising anger with the patience of his long Steward's training. How dare Anatole elude his Master! Hasn't he fed him, carried him about in the warmth of his pocket, tenderly cared for him? The cheek, the ingratitude, of it all! And he is about to threaten Anatole with the ultimate punishment, a starvation diet of several days, when he is forced to change his attitude. For digging in a corner of the room behind some sacks, his fingers meet a patch, a damp patch which, the moment that he has smelled it, he is sure is blood.

No! Anatole has hurt himself! Worse, the poor little thing has been savaged! Jules calls out to his ferret, urging him not to give up, not to let himself be done in, Jules is coming! A minute later, after he has scoured every inch of the overfilled luggage hold, and almost despaired of ever rescuing his companion, the only creature who understands him, the sole being to share his fretful existence, he knocks over a sack which, as it collapses, reveals the tensed and fur-bristling shape of the ferret crouched under a metal rack.

It is with a dreadful mix of emotions that Jules stares at what greets him: delight that the ferret is alive; wonder that his coat is so resplendent; pride that his manner is so warlike; and revulsion when he pieces together what has occurred. For Anatole has placed his bloody forepaws on the streaming ruins of the dog's ripped flanks and his snout he has buried deep in the coils of Cerby's entrails.

"What have you done?" cries the anguished Steward, unmoved by the poodle's destruction but shattered by the collapse of his amorous designs. "You've ruined everything! Everything! Now what am I going to say to her? When she learns about this she'll kill me!"

Exhausted after the excitement of his search and unable to bear the disappointment of his high hopes dashed into nothingness, Jules falls heavily on to a sack. And as the torch slips out of his hands and shines its pathetic beam on to the ceiling, the hapless Steward, with a heartfelt sob, puts his head in his lap.

CHAPTER SIXTEEN

The Marquis de St Lyre and Annabelle Fleury have changed, he into a light cream summer suit, she into a blue cotton dress. And once they have finished a light collation of croissants and of *café au lait* brought to them by the long-faced Steward, they turn their attention to the distinctive Provençal undulations which painters have so precisely caught with their palettes.

On this the last part of their journey through the pine-scented, cicada-filled and *mistral*-swept landscape, the Marquis is obliged by the still unfulfilled needs of narrative and by Annabelle's curiosity to reveal more of his past. He therefore relaxes on his compartment's well-upholstered bunk and agrees to elaborate on his work and origins. Selecting from a wealth of anecdotes, he relates to her the occasion when, apprenticed to an illustrious *faubourg* restaurant – whose first *patron* had been none other than the great Antoine Carême, and where it was inconceivable to get a table without booking three months in advance – he had concocted a *crème brûlée* so liberally laced with alcohol that on tasting it a portly client had collapsed. A story which, however farfetched, brings a smile to Annabelle's face – in itself a noteworthy occurrence in a story otherwise replete with sombre, bizarre and baffling episodes. And when he goes on to mention some of the outrageous ingredients which irreverent *souschefs* occasionally add to the dishes of customers they dislike, she cannot suppress a laugh. At last, unable to put the moment off any longer, and prodded by Annabelle's questions – why did he introduce her of all people to the course, and how did he discover the parallels between cooking and storytelling? – he settles back on the bunk, lights up a cigar, and begins to explain.

"I was wondering when you'd ask me that," says the Marquis, making sure that his Havana is well lit and that the airconditioning is circulating properly. "I'm also glad that you left it till now because having to produce elucidations at the wrong time can so easily ruin a story's rhythm." He sends out a puff of smoke towards the ceiling. "You'll recall that when we met yesterday I made a point of asking you to trust me. A request which you strongly resented. Come now, Annabelle!" the Marquis admonishes, amused by her refusal to admit the reality of her own resistances. "You're asking me to tell you the truth so you should be prepared to do so too. My reasons must be obvious to you: I had to make damn sure you didn't walk out on the initial part of the course. Because I was convinced that if you survived that far, your curiosity would keep you going thereafter. Your curiosity and, let us not overlook it, your pride. Am I right?"

"I certainly resented the way you tricked me into the course. And when you later implied that I might not have enough talent to pursue it to its end, well, that urged me on even more. I wasn't going to give you the satisfaction of being right about that – at least not without a fight!"

"Good! So I correctly pinpointed that aspect of your personality, that and, of course, your aggressive streak. Please!" says the Marquis, amused to see his pupil once again bridling. "Don't pretend that you've a sweet nature. I've ample proof of the opposite. Do remember, won't you, that I've just experienced your story so, really, I'm only exercising the right every reader has of inferring the storyteller's character from what has been related. However," the Marquis adds, who has enjoyed teasing Annabelle and who is now ready to adopt another tack, "we were discussing something else: whether you'd have stuck with the course if I hadn't imposed conditions on you, conditions that linked your pride to your potential success. You agree it'd have been a pity to have missed out on all our adventures. Though I must say when I consider how close you came to ruining the episodes with your petty expectations, I reckon you've been lucky."

Privately Annabelle concedes that the Marquis may be right and that had she managed to carry her prejudices into the stories' texture she might well have destroyed them.

"So, what would you like me to divulge? The glaring

anomalies within my stories? How come, say, in Alonzo's tale, the dwarf knew so much about his mother's behaviour when he had been rejected from her breast at infancy? How a poor Spanish boy brought up in the countryside could read and write? Why we never learnt what became of his legal father? Are those the kind of details you'd like me to pore over?"

Those particular discrepancies in the dwarf's story, Annabelle confesses, are not aspects to which she has given any thought. No, what she wants to discover is how the Marquis came to divine – if that is the right word – the principles of cooking, and how he realized that he could apply them to other artistic areas.

"Straight to the heart of the matter, eh, Annabelle? In that case," the Marquis says, stubbing out the smouldering remains of his cigar in a porcelain ashtray neatly inscribed with the state-run railway's insignia, "if you're to have a firm grasp on what happened, I'll have to take a leaf out of our characters' book and provide you with a certain amount of background history. We'll start, if you don't mind, with my title. You've wondered, haven't you, whether it was genuine or not? You've been too polite to ask but I'm sure it crossed your mind. After all, my at times outlandish propositions would have been that much easier to dismiss if I had turned out not to be what I pretended. The fact is that were you to thumb through the *Almanach de Gotha* and the *Encyclopaedia of National Biography*, you'd come across quite a number of us St Lyres. Yes, we've contributed a fair deal to France's history, if, I should add, rather more to its periphery than to its main arena! Among a clutch of notable eccentrics, I could name one medieval saint who – poor devil! – got boiled alive while on a mission to convert Madagascar savages. History doesn't relate whether this was punishment for interfering with their animistic traditions or whether the natives were simply unrepentant man-eaters! We've also produced a rich crop of soldiers, Matamores mostly who had a habit of hurling themselves into whatever madcap fray the Capetian Kings had devised to shore up their hold on the throne, fellows who, as a result, often as not left their bones a-bleaching on some long forgotten battlefield.

"The family seat, the romanesque Château de Lampadou, used to perch on a high crest overlooking the Dinard estuary. From its ramparts on a clear day you could make out the pennants flying on top of the Mont St Michel some twenty kilometres away. I said 'used to' because sadly the Château was ransacked during the Revolution and was reduced to a wreck. Fortunately the members of my immediate family, a prize target in those Jacobin days, managed to escape during the riot that razed the Château. Later that same night, disguised as tinkers, they made their way to St Malo where they boarded a caravelle which took them to the safety of their estates in the Antilles. They were among the few to survive: records show that over half Brittany's aristocracy fell under the guillotine. Others were drowned en masse in ships which the so-called forces of fraternity scuttled just outside the *Baie*. A grotesque end for a seafaring people, you will admit. My own branch of the family didn't return to France until the middle of the nineteenth century and then not to Brittany, of which it hardly had the warmest memories, but to Paris. So much for genealogy. As for me, I was born in the seventeenth arrondissement of the capital on the third floor of a spacious flat in the Place Malesherbes, barely a stone's throw from the Banque de France's gold reserves!

"An only child, I spent hours on my own. And yet, you may be surprised to hear, I was never lonely. Why? Because from the very first the kitchen exerted an extraordinary fascination over me. It seems that the transformations that take place in a cauldron's resonant belly, in a pot's englobing warmth, in an oven's controlled inferno have always held me in their thrall. Like yours, Annabelle, my mother was a fine cook. I think I must have graduated straight from her arms to watch her work her stove. Indeed my earliest memories are of her preparing every day – need I say with what care and attention? – the various *petits plats* which we would consume that same evening. I still vividly recall the aromatic harmonies she concocted. But, unlike you, Annabelle, I was not intimidated by her skills. Far from it: seeing her cooking made me want to join in. And although I was probably a great nuisance to begin with, I'm happy to say that she did all she could to encourage me.

"As you know, society as a whole tries to form children along set lines: boys get bought tin soldiers, girls are taught to fondle dolls, and so on and so forth. My parents, however, never once bought me a toy. Never. But if you contrast the cheap weaponry which a boy might get given with the armoury I had at my disposal – vast copper pans, the sharpest knives imaginable, long tin dishes in which a whole salmon could be broiled – you'll realize why I didn't feel done out. On the contrary. The moment the end of school bell rang I couldn't wait to rush home. Because my mother and I would then go shopping, for instance, to a local herb store where we'd comb through barrels overflowing with spices and sacks bursting with pulses and there search for condiments with which to heighten, say, the taste of a much-loved soup or a sauce which had perhaps grown a little too familiar.

"That's not all I did. I also spent hours in my bedroom, at my desk, writing out elaborate recipes in my neatest classroom longhand. There I devised giant menus for imaginary feasts to which I would then invite the Court's luminaries. Even after I had imbibed the lycée's history lessons and become like my classmates a fervent little republican, my fantasies did not change: only the composition of my guest lists did. It was no longer the King who would come to pass genial judgement on my more recherché dishes, but the President of the newly-founded Republic. As far as I was concerned, my dinner parties were culinary stations of the cross along which no self-respecting gastronome could fail to make a pilgrimage, shrines at which I would, of course, prepare every dish. *Fines bouches* with critical palates, literati postulating the latest trends, over-scented courtesans enrobed in ostrich feathers, not to forget the politicians who held the fate of the nation in the palms of their hands, would all troop to my house. Anyone who was anyone, people whose identities I had gleaned from charivari and society columns, were duly invited – when, that is, they were not fatally drawn! – to the wonders of my cooking. I must have spent half my adolescence daydreaming. Though, to be fair, not just daydreaming. For, Annabelle, by the age of five I could prepare an entire meal and not infrequently did so for my parents. You may think that a strange occupation for a child? My parents didn't. Far from it: they were delighted. Indeed my father, who, in his spare time, had published a delightful monograph on Creole cooking, kept buying me a selection of the best culinary books. Brillat-Savarin's *La Physiologie du Goût* I read from cover to cover by the age of ten. In my teens, I perused Magny's literary dinners and passed their menus in review. And once, just for fun, I tried my hand at some of the dishes Petronius describes for Trimalchio's feast and invited my parents to sample them. They very kindly tasted my effort – then left the rest of the somewhat over-piquant mix!

"In contrast to home's easy-going informality, life at the lycée was sheer horror. A horror I naively compounded one day when I informed a school comrade how I spent my spare time. Thereafter, as you can imagine, the teasing never stopped. I must have had every variation thrown at me: cook scullion, ship's boy, *saucier* and *la plonge*! But that's by-the-by. Once I had passed my *baccalauréat* the question of what career I should choose came up. I could have gone in a number of directions. My father was in shipping: I could have followed him and traded with my distant cousins in the colonies. Or gone to the Bourse where an uncle was a *courtier*. However, after much soul searching, during which I was asked again and again whether I was really sure I knew what I wanted to do, my parents finally agreed. If it was Jean-Loup's destiny to be a great cook, so be it. At the earliest opportunity – I had only just turned nineteen – they arranged for me to be apprenticed in the kitchens of the famous *faubourg* restaurant, *Le Sortilège de la Motte*.

"Unfortunately, within less than a year, my enthusiasm had reached a low ebb and I was bored. Why? Quite simply because my apprenticeship consisted solely of endlessly preparing roasts and desserts but never being allowed to experiment with sauces – which, as you may know, has always been and always will be the Master Cook's preserve. One evening, as I told you earlier, on a whim I suppose, I blended an unholy mixture of syrup of figs with marsala and created a dessert so potent it brought one of the restaurant's sweet-toothed clients to his knees! Not surprisingly I was sacked on the spot – and without references which, in those far-off days, I can tell you, was a very serious stigma.

"My parents were mortified. To be thrown out like a ruffian and from the great Carême's spiritual home too! Nor could they understand why I wouldn't immediately purge my wickedness through hard work and search for another position. But I couldn't: I was disillusioned. I had lost my way. I no longer wanted to be stuck in the kitchen's steam-ridden world for the rest of my life, getting up too early to see the sun shine, leaving too late and exhausted to notice whether the stars were shining. I had had my fill of that underpaid limbo existence. Nonetheless, if only to get some peace at home and to have a few francs to play with, I drifted in and out of various menial jobs, avoiding catering like the plague, seeming not to care that I was letting my hard-earned skills go to pot. Well, I had carried on like this for about a year to my parents' utter misery when – I must have been about twenty-two – I made a startling and totally unexpected discovery.

"It occurred, as epiphanies often do, in a deceptively simple fashion. I was at home one afternoon between odd jobs, helping my mother in the kitchen, when she made a careless move and spilled a pan of hot oil all over my hands. I was very badly scalded. Indeed the pain was so intense that I fainted. My mother had to call in a neighbour and together they carried me to hospital in a taxi. There I lay in bed with third-degree burns for over a month, heavily bandaged and in torment. Three weeks later – it was in the middle of the night and I was wide awake for having run up a temperature and slept it off during the day – out of the blue an extraordinary thought struck me. What if the arts obeyed the same rules as gastronomy? It was the kind of idea that fever gives birth to, an idea that should have been dismissed there and then. Though, to be fair, that night it did the trick: it excited me so much I was soon fast asleep.

"But when I awoke the next morning, the idea hadn't vanished. On the contrary: it was still very much with me. I couldn't get it out of my mind. I kept thinking: if cooking could really forge me a key to all artistic activities, then with what I had already gleaned, I'd soon be an expert in all the other arts!

"You're probably aware, Annabelle, that there's not much you can do when stuck in a hospital bed apart, that is, from eye the nurses, rib the patients, and wish the pain away. You've certainly more than enough time for an obsession to sink its roots into you. Over the next few days, I must have looked at this bizarre idea from every conceivable angle. And this glimpse I had had of what you might call the philosopher's stone grew so powerful that I somehow convinced myself that my love of cooking, far from being an end in itself was rather a departure point. The curiosity which had led me to experiment at home with bizarre ingredients and unusual sauces, and which was the main reason I had grown so disenchanted with a restaurant which had never let me try my hand at anything creative, was the force which was compelling me towards these other areas. Yes, the very same curiosity was making me search for a master key to locks which other people in their ignorance regarded as individually fastened.

"Well, the more this idea germinated in my head, the more I grew restless at the length of my convalescence. When would I get out? When would I be able to act on my hunches? I then did something which I can only describe as very foolish: I didn't keep my intuition to myself. The result was that I very quickly discovered that a hospital is hardly the place to give vent to wild ideas. Because, Annabelle, the nurses either think that you've become hyperactive and lace your food with bromides, or they decide that you've gone mad. In my case they plumped for the latter and acted in consequence. Early one morning the curtains were drawn round my bed and I was confronted by a cold-eyed consultant from the psychiatric wing who asked me all kinds of impertinent questions. That taught me to keep quiet. The last thing I needed was to exchange the green sheets of the epidermal ward for the white of mental cases! So I stopped berating the nurses, became a model patient, and set myself a secret task. If there was the slightest connection between the principles of cooking and those which underpinned the other creative arts, I'd make it my business to find it out.

"I rather suspect, Annabelle, that patients becoming prone to flights of fancy is not that uncommon a feature of convalescence. After all, for an unnatural number of hours per day one's body is fixed to a hospital bed. And it could be that one of the ways in which the mind combats the lassitude of the experience is by letting the imagination work overtime. A fairly innocuous way of spending the hours while waiting to get better. That could have been my case. But it wasn't. Instead my fantasy turned into an all-consuming passion. A passion which I've fortunately managed to prove to my, and to a few other people's, satisfaction. You've asked me how I did it. It wasn't easy. I did it by tinkering with odd notions. By working on the premise that if there were parallels between the arts, it was up to me to track them down. And, finally, most importantly, by believing in them long before I had the slightest evidence of their existence. Eventually by researching in just about every human activity, I had amassed enough evidence to be able to prove that there is only a narrow divide between man's various creative enterprises. It doesn't matter whether it's painting, sculpture, or the decorative arts, they're all founded on the same principles. To put it simply, you could say that they're different reflections of the imagination's guiding light. Which means that they obey the same rules and that, with the right techniques and the confidence to apply them, you can switch from the one to the other without difficulty. A process to which you, Annabelle, are now no stranger.

"It was in the Brasserie, wasn't it, that I first intimated to you the existence of the principles of gastronomy? Later, when we visited the Mistral's enchanted compartments, I demonstrated how, by using these principles as our theoretical base, we'd be able to slip into the realms of storytelling. Which we then did by manipulating the circumstances that surrounded us, by seeking out the alternatives ambient within every situation, and by veering towards them. But I'm jumping far ahead. Because the notion which I encountered in hospital was rough ore compared to the refined metal which you and I have encountered. How everything interrelated – and how I evolved a theory to back it – I wouldn't work out till my early thirties.

"When I came to be discharged, my hands partially healed if still painful, I knew more or less what I had to do. I'd research, yes, I'd research until I had found out the truth. To have had an intuition was all very well. Now I had to discover whether it had been right and whether the idea that the arts were interlinked had any substance to it.

"As I want to keep this preamble short, I shan't mention all the avenues down which I pursued my convictions. It took persistence, I'll say that much. I went up impasses, followed nonsensical leads, and misconstrued evidence. More than once I had to confront, admit and, indeed, overcome my own shortfalls. It was the devil of a task and it took years. One of the first problems I faced was my own stupidity. Because, you see, Annabelle, I had deluded myself into thinking I was an expert on cooking when, really, I didn't even understand its basics, let alone the principles we've been applying. Yet there I was, steeped in my own ignorance, and arrogant enough to suppose that I could become an expert in every other creative area.

"To make ends meet, and to keep my hand in, I went back to catering. You should have seen some of the kitchens I worked in, Annabelle! They were an education in themselves. Not that all were bad. Some were what I imagine Renaissance workshops to have been like: the Master gracing with a final flourish the concoctions over which his *commis* had slaved for hours. Others, on the other hand, were dives in which it was a miracle that customers didn't catch doses of salmonella poisoning! As for the tyrants lording it over their steam-filled kingdoms, I tell you, a primadonna couldn't have upstaged them! Anyway, I hired myself out to the highest bidder. I did stints as a pastry cook and as an assistant chef. I filled in for exhausted kitchen staff at weekends. And for a year I was the manager of the second-class restaurant of a luxury liner. A monotonous job though, to be fair, it did take me round the world and brought me into contact with some of the unusual recipes which I mentioned to you earlier.

"If my parents were mortified when I was thrown out of the *Sortilège*, they were appalled at the poor terms of employment which I seemed happy to accept. Not surprising when you consider that they had sacrificed their hopes for me of a good middle-class profession on the altar of an illustrious culinary career, a career which I had abandoned and which I now seemed bent on devaluing by hiring myself out to second-rate establishments. I, on the other hand, knew what I was doing. It didn't matter that I was often badly paid. It didn't matter in the slightest because, you see, all the while I was collating evidence, trying out new ideas, and looking at a variety of luminous and occasionally less than inspired hypotheses. In other words I was experimenting. Thank God, Annabelle, that my intuition was eventually vindicated, otherwise I'd have no doubt ended up in some asylum!

"It took time, five years all told, then one day things fell into place. Yes, they at last made sense. The pattern which I had predicted did exist. I could recognize the process of cooking at work in every human activity. Or rather, I should say, I discovered that the processes which I had learnt in the kitchen were universal. Its laws, its principles, were true across the board. It really did seem as if the search for the right ingredients and the precise application of correct methods were also keys to the production of artistic effects.

"The next thing I had to do was to confirm my theoretical findings in practice. Now, although I had always wanted to draw, I had never completed so much as a sketch, let alone a painting, in my life. This seemed as good a starting point as any. I bought a sketchpad, some charcoals, and began drawing. I have to admit that my early efforts were far from wonderful. And yet I could tell that there was something at work in their crude, tentative lines. A week of persistent experimentation later, the drawings had lost their rugged nature and the forms of a primitive perspective could be seen in them. I was astounded, Annabelle. This was incredible. I could draw, I really could draw! Exhilarated, I turned to another form which had always fascinated me: clay modelling. With much the same results. You can imagine how ecstatic I was. At least I was for a while. Because once I had got over the initial thrill, I discovered that I faced a problem. A very serious problem. In the sketches and the clay figurines which I had produced, something was missing. Although they were fair representations of the models which I had chosen, they were also lifeless. Was it perhaps, I wondered, a question of my inexperience, of my lack of style? To gain confidence, I visited museums, bought pattern books, and copied masters. That made no great difference. You've guessed of course, Annabelle, what was wrong. You too fell into the same trap. The story you set in the laboratory: what did it lack? Heart. Feeling. Well, I had made the same mistake. No amount of fancy techniques or of unending practice could get round that. True, I had uncovered the basic rules, but I had also missed out on one crucial aspect. For that, only a change of attitude could help. And that meant that I had to discover the meaning of sympathy for myself.

"Yes, sympathy: that particular ability to get under the skin of your material, to blend with it, to incorporate it into a thematic blueprint – that was what had been missing. Again it took time and effort before I had intuitively understood what was wrong. After all, unlike you, I had no guidelines to lead me towards a definite answer. But once I had latched on to the importance of sympathy through trial and error, my drawings, my sculpture, began to be imbued with spirit, an element of truth, a life force, call it what you will. Not that what I produced were master-pieces but at least they were inspired, profound, soulful. You yourself eventually discovered a rhythm which had the power to generate a story so you realize that while a change in attitude is a serious, even a painful issue, it is quite easy to effect. Fundamentally, the moment you make the connection in yourself with the necessary harmony, everything adopts its contours and operates within its controlling limits, isn't that so?

Jeanne – your *couturière* – belonged to her world. She was part of a sympathetic whole which genuinely reflected her concerns. And it was because she imposed her order on that whole, and because her values echoed through it that your story was convincing. However, to return to my own story, once I had discovered the missing part of the puzzle on which I had been working for years and had completed the task which I had set myself in hospital, what do you then suppose I did, Annabelle?"

Although Annabelle has enjoyed hearing about the Marquis' journey towards truth, she has no idea how much credence to lend it. As for what his next step might have been, why, he could have hired the Salle Pleyel for all she knows, and there delivered a lecture on the magic of creative cooking!

"That's just the kind of crass action I might have taken," the Marquis answers. "As it so happens, and rather more prosaically, my first thought was to share what I had discovered with those close to me: my long-suffering family, my disabused friends, my lover. In so doing you might well ask what I was after? What anybody who has been on a long spiritual journey which nobody else understands hankers for: confirmation, flattery, comfort. My lover was kind but, having shouldered my burdens for over a year and endured my bouts of depression, the moment I had reached my goal, and the struggle with which she had identified was over, she did what so many do when they sense the end of a particular phase: she upped and left me. My parents heard me out then dismissed my conclusions out of hand. For them this was the last straw. I had betrayed their hopes. It was now obvious that their son would never throne over the Grand Vefour or the Tour d'Argent, wouldn't be spoken of in the same reverential tones as Point, Escoffier, or Troisgros. It was a terrible blow. As for my friends, they showed no more sensitivity. To begin with they thought I was joking. When I insisted, they laughed in my face. An *idée fixe* about a girl they could entertain but this all-consuming creative theory of mine had become a joke. What on earth had happened to Jean-Loup, their old drinking companion? Yes, it was a difficult period for me, especially as I was determined to get my message across.

"Sitting in the Flore one afternoon, and feeling very low, I got talking to a journalist. A glass or two of *anisette* must have loosened my inhibitions because I was soon entrusting myself to this stranger. Clever lot, journalists. They can extract a secret from the most recalcitrant shell. Although, to be fair, I wasn't that much of a recalcitrant shell. Fascinating, he said. My story sounded fascinating. Why didn't he write an article about it? A week, two, three went by and I still hadn't received the copy he had promised to send me. It was then that I realized that the advance I had given him to check out my story had been converted to liquid! After that particular setback even an enthusiasm as misguided as mine couldn't hide from the truth that I was making no headway. No one cared. No one would listen, let alone assess the validity of what I was saying. So I made a decision, a hard decision: I decided that I'd do nothing. Absolutely nothing. I'd keep it all to myself. Do you think that was wrong? Do you think I should have persevered, put my head in the pillory, and listened to idiots making cheap insults about my findings? You should have heard some of the comments I had to put up with. I remember one man in whom I had confided looking me up and down, shaking his head, and saying that maybe I should go a bit easier on the *eau de vie*! For five long years I had struggled in the dark. I had then succeeded in proving that the idea across which I had stumbled, and which had changed my life, was correct. But dammit! Instead of paying at least a modicum of attention to me, no one seemed in the slightest interested. What choice had I but to face facts and to learn to live with the world's indifference?

"It took me some months to settle on that course of action. Disillusion can take a while to seep through. Once it had, I saw that I had nothing better to do than to rejoin the scattered traces of my career. My parents and I, I'm glad to say, were reconciled. One day in a catering periodical I came across an advertisement for a substitute cook for a restaurant in Nîmes. Its regular chef had fallen ill. I wrote off and got the post. It didn't take the owner long to work out who was the better craftsman. He told his chef not to bother to come back and I remained in charge. I stayed there five years until I was able to put a deposit down on my own place. I unearthed a run-down farmhouse in the hills behind Nice, bought it, converted it, took it on with a partner, Marius de la Garde, and there established La Fantaisie. As for the principles of creativity, I've shared them whenever I've come across someone I thought might benefit from them. Which is how, Annabelle, you and I came to meet.

"You may recall that earlier tonight I told you that cooking and storytelling were twins. It suited my argument to say so at the time but really, there are no twins, no privileged rapport. There is rather a family of creative relationships. For all arts are equal and derive their power from the same source. Which means that gastronomy ranks with storytelling and that the fabulist is on exactly the same level as the sculptor. I'm not denying that different societies ascribe a wide range of values to various creative activities. That's a documented fact. But what that range reflects above all is that choices made at any given time, in any given place, are arbitrary, that preferences are contingent, and that trends are local. Yes, what those variations prove above all is that no art possesses inherent superiority over any other. And attitudes change. Think of the overblown status which successful actors enjoy today and then compare it to poor Molière's family having to bribe a priest so that the actor-manager could have a decent Christian burial. Societies are fickle, their values mercurial. Don't misunderstand me, Annabelle: I don't invalidate personal preferences. Not at all. I'm personally very fond of stories and will use them – as you saw – to locate the right ingredients. By the way, you may be interested to learn that stories are not the only method by which one can get them," says the Marquis tantalizingly yet refusing to elaborate on this suddenly revealed vista on to new possibilities. "In the end though I always come back to my first love, gastronomy. Call it the prejudice of a Master Chef, if you like. I'm sure you too have a favourite artistic activity. Painting? Design maybe? It's of no import. I myself lost interest in superficial differences long ago to concentrate on the ground which they all have in common.

"I apologize if you've found my argument vague," says the Marquis, noticing that Annabelle's eyes are fidgeting towards the red escarpment of the unfolding countryside and the whitewashed façades of villas close-cropped within it. "That's what comes of trying to condense years of an often blind struggle into a few continuous phases. Perhaps it may help you to understand my argument if I provide you with a simple example," the Marquis adds, attempting to prevent his companion from drifting away. "You've tasted lobster?" Prompted by his question, Annabelle nods and meets his gaze. "Of course you have. Memorable flesh, don't you think? What about roast scarab?" He laughs. "No? I'm sure you won't be surprised to hear that there's a tribe in Borneo which cooks the most delicious scarab *beignets*. A dish which I suspect doesn't appeal to your palate. You're probably also wondering in what way it is related to the lobster. Well, although each creature occupies its own well-defined habitat, the one scurrying across the seabed, the other furtive on dry land, as the biologist will tell you, both belong to the same species, yes, both are classed as arthropods. I realize that it's a crude example, but do you see what I'm getting at? The thermidor and the Borneon *beignets* are, as it were, two culinary methods of dealing with the same family. To reach the heart of the matter – your goal, if I'm not mistaken – and to assess a situation properly, you must be willing to put aside superficial differences and to scour away the barnacles of cultural viewpoints. For, like those two creatures, under their often wildly variegated skins the arts are the same. Yes, Annabelle, all are moulded and motivated by the spirit of the imagination. I do hope," the Marquis adds, "that that has helped answer your question."

Throughout the Marquis' enthusiastic delivery of his favourite subject, Annabelle has chosen not to interrupt. Nor has she felt inclined to pick holes in his argument which, like most belief-based systems, she much prefers to understand rather than to deflate. She has, however, been fascinated by his allusion to other methods by which ingredients might be found. If storytelling is not the sole method, what are the others? Should she ask him to elaborate? She hesitates. Might it not mean hours of further lecturing or – God forbid! – another journey through even more arduous climes? She therefore decides to steer towards safety, certain that in her present exhausted condition she would not survive any detour from the main route of the course until she has had a proper rest.

"I accept that the shift to storytelling must have seemed confusing to you when what I had initially proposed was a limited if ambitious course: how to become a Master Cook. I chose to introduce you to the practical parallels of the principles via storytelling. But, as I said a little earlier, we could have reached our ends via any art," the Marquis adds, reading in the narrowing of her pupils and the slight bending of her head signs that her appetite has been whetted by his reference to another method. "It would have made no odds which we used. On the other hand, I thought it would be pleasant to resort to that old tradition. You know: travellers passing the time exchanging stories. Given the logistical restrictions which we faced – we could hardly have set up easels on the train! – storytelling was by far the most appropriate medium." The Marquis pauses. As Annabelle appears to be following his explanations without difficulty, he continues: "You now have the skills to gather any ingredient you choose. As for the principles of creativity, which through your mother's considerable talent were, as I told you, already lying dormant in your blood, they too have become fully active in you. Your own performance has amply confirmed them. Soon you'll be able to see for yourself just how versatile the course to which I've inducted you can be. For the moment you apply the principles of cooking to storytelling, you'll discover that you've in fact mastered both arts: in becoming a Master Raconteur you've also learnt how to cook. When we reach La Fantaisie, you'll be drawing on gastronomic skills which, *ma chère*, you didn't even know you had.

"True, Annabelle: I did trick you. But only so that you could learn to stir the cooking pots of your imagination any way you chose. From now on, the aromas that'll rise to its surface will be up to you. You've the tools, the methods, and you realize that the imagination is the mainspring of creative life. As long as you don't ever use them without sympathy – as you did in that absurd laboratory episode! – but produce tales like the *couturière*'s, I can confidently predict that everything you undertake will be marked by complete success."

"And what's that to be?" Annabelle asks, breaking from behind the mask of her apparent docility to reveal her exasperation. "Luring people on to trains is hardly my idea of a productive achievement! What am I supposed to do once I've acquired these amazing tricks?"

"Patience! The course isn't over yet. There's one thing though that should already be very apparent: no one can resist a good tale. If you know how to spin them well, Annabelle, I tell you men's hearts and souls will be yours for the taking." The Marquis raises his eyebrows. "Mmm . . ," he mutters, gazing out of the window as the train coils agilely round the corniche, "we should be in Nice in less than an hour. But before we head off for La Fantaisie, there are one or two things which I'd like to mention about your new-found skills."

While the Mistral swerves round the red-earthed pine forests and aims towards the Mediterranean's startling azure, the Marquis stimulates Annabelle with a number of scenarios which, he insists, will presently be hers for the picking. Some of the options which he discusses are so remarkable that she seriously questions whether he can ever be as good as his word. Will she really be able to give her desire full rein? And teach her mother a good lesson? And, as he keeps insisting, will that really be the least of her accomplishments? And yet, in spite of misgivings, and under the Marquis' seductive suggestions, Annabelle lets herself muse on the delights of wish-fulfilment which, like so many of the notions which derive their power from their apparent ability to join dream and reality, have in no time at all intoxicated her.

Once the Marquis has put the finishing touches to his tale and has pondered the extent to which its highly fictive nature has taken in his apprentice, and whether he has diverted her attention from its many inconsistencies, he too settles on his bunk and loses himself in the blur of the unfurling landscape. And as Annabelle meditates on the romantic routes which her companion has opened up for her, and as passengers throughout the train shake the dust of enforced promiscuity from their clothes and secure their luggage for the next stage of their journey, the rays of the rising sun revivify the chilled countryside and subtly adjust the scene and its various props to suit the final chapters of this story.

CHAPTER SEVENTEEN

With a glass of *vin de pays* cradled in his hand, the Mistral safely berthed, and the stark Mediterranean light cascading into his cubicle, Jules can at last relax. A whole languid day stretches out before him, yes, hours of rest before the train rushes tail-long towards Paris and who knows what adventures! In the meantime he will enjoy his wine, stroke his animal contentedly curled up in his wicker basket, and recount to him what happened when he visited the English Milady.

" 'Never lie, Jules,' my mother used to say to me. 'With a face like yours, no one'll believe you anyway.' It's funny, Anatole, but as I headed for Milady's cabin I kept hearing my mother saying that. Though, to be fair, if I couldn't lie, what was I going to say to Milady?"

The arts of dissimulation and the ability to pull the wool over the reader's eyes have always been part of the storyteller's stock-in-trade, so that their participation in the tale's thematic structure should come as no surprise. In quite a different league from the lies which the Marquis has purveyed to his companion, however, are those which secondary characters have spun to themselves and to others. In quite a different league, even if they do partake of the same nature, for lies, no matter their range and subtlety, have but one aim: to reinterpret truth in the light of expediency. When dealing with the crude adventures of the Steward, of his pet rodent, and of the English Milady, we have often had difficulty assessing their value in the scheme of things. It has often been a question of adopting the right attitude. But which one that should be has also proved to be a problem. Should we treat them with enthusiasm? Would indifference be better fitted to cope with their role? Or should we regard their peregrinations as minor items in a subplot and thus of very little consequence to the rest of the story? One way to handle their two-dimensionality might be to examine them as would say, a pathologist a colony of coli residing in a corpse's bowels: with the purity of scientific detachment. For apart from being spared the effort and strain of lending them any credibility, we might also learn from analysing their sickly states about the ordinary workings of narrative.

Leaving aside these difficult options, let us quickly return to the Steward's cubicle where Jules, forlorn, hopes dashed, and beaten by the play of circumstances, is forced to report the sudden death of a dog, a task which he is quite convinced will destroy whatever amorous designs he may once have entertained on its imperious mistress.

Guilt etched across his face, Jules knocks on the door of the Lady's cabin. No answer. He knocks again. Still no reply. As there is no one about, he slips his passepartout out of his jacket pocket, inserts it into the lock, and turns it. After he has looked warily to left and right, he creeps in.

Once he has entered the compartment and closed the door softly behind him, Jules discovers that the English Milady has fallen asleep with the main light on. Is she afraid of something which the darkness might force her to confront? Or has she simply been overwhelmed by sleep and not had a chance to turn it off? Unable to hazard what the reason might be, Jules – an inveterate materialist – focuses on what he can unmistakeably see: the lace festoons of her silk negligée generously frothing over the top of the sheets. Careful not to disturb Milady, he approaches her bunk on tiptoe. Her mouth hangs deliciously open and from its gold-flecked chasm he breathes in an aroma so rich that before he can check himself he has knelt by her side and has surrendered to its sweetness in deep, long draughts. How he would love to remain in this position for ever! But recalling the dreadful task which he must carry out, he returns to the bitter reality of his immediate duties.

Something else terrifies him: the distance which separates this prone, vulnerable, heavenly sight from the harridan he must summon from the vales of sleep. If only once awake she would remain warm and magnanimous! If only! All too well aware however that when alert she is most unlikely to greet him with a

318

tender gaze, he braces himself and at last gently shakes her shoulders.

Slowly rising from her bunk, the English Milady lifts her arms in a gesture so filled with abandon that it almost makes the Steward swoon to imagine himself embraced in those soft fat limbs. She yawns, puts a distracted hand through her full, dark hair, and at last opens her eyes.

"Milady! Milady!" Jules cries, showing no sensitivity to the pain which the shrillness of his voice is inflicting on her first conscious moments. "A terrible thing . . . a terrible thing has happened!"

"Calm down, man!" the English Milady exclaims, stilling the Steward's self-induced excitement with an icy stare. "What are you trying to say?"

"Your little dog!"

"Is that why you've woken me? To tell me you've found Cerby! Couldn't it have waited? Oh, very well, then: take her to the kennels and let her cool her heels there. That'll teach her. You do have kennels on this confounded train, don't you?"

"Milady does not understand . . ." whines the Steward, discovering that his task has been made impossibly difficult by her misplaced confidence in the success of his mission.

"All right, all right!" she says, propping herself on her pillow and accepting that the Steward will not be shaken off that easily. "Well, out with it, man! Where is she?"

"A tragedy! The little thing – how can I tell you? – the little thing is dead."

While fully prepared to be browbeaten, while armed against objects being hurled at him, and while even willing to forswear his mother's moral injunction and to spin a thousand tales to explain away the cur's disappearance, the one eventuality against which Jules has not steeled himself is that commonly deployed female strategy, the frame a-shiver and the face burrowed within the bedclothes, a performance capped in this case by loud and seemingly uncontrollable bellowing. The Steward, poorly equipped to deal with this deluge of decibels, nonetheless bends over the sweet-smelling bunk to try to console the Lady for the loss of her companion. And with a self-serving indelicacy which only panic could have generated, he adds whether it would not be wonderful if she could find a true buttress in this her hour of need.

These and other equally heartfelt commiserations fail to have any effect whatsoever on the stricken Milady.

"Milady, please do not cry! I promise you, the little animal never felt any pain," Jules whispers shamelessly.

Of course the question is: how can Jules have been so mistaken? A fundamental lack of insight into female psychology? An uncontrollable urge to be loved? Whatever the cause, the instant the English Milady re-emerges from under the bed-clothes, the Steward witnesses to what an appalling degree he has misread reality. For those are not cries of sorrow he hears nor tears of grief he sees! No, the Milady's reactions are quite against the grain of the Anglo-Saxon, animal-loving, creature-coddling archetype.

"I'll be damned, Anatole! First she stares at me with a crazed look on her face. Then she bursts into laughter. That's it, I thought: the dog's death has pushed her off her perch!"

As nothing in the small, state-compiled handbook of set procedure, through which he rarely thumbs, has programmed him to deal with the behaviour of a woman apparently on the margins of sense, it is with complete amazement that Jules gazes at the now-laughing Milady.

"Don't get yourself in this state, Milady!" says Jules flounder-ingly. "I quite understand that grief is difficult to cope with."

"Grief!" the English Milady cries. "Grief for that ghastly little mutt! Nonsense, man! Don't you realize that it's been torture, sheer torture, having Cerby by my side. Ever since my husband died, I have had to have her by me day and night! All because the bastard made me keep her in his will!"

"The bastard? You surely don't mean that your husband . . . you hated him?" Jules asks.

"Of course I hated him! And with good cause!" the Milady exclaims, examining the depth of his confusion, recognizing in it a certain usefulness, and deciding to exploit it. "However you, Monsieur le Steward, may be able to help me. That's if you'd like to," she adds.

As uxoriousness has been one of the themes controlling the course of this story, we have already experienced with what rapidity male characters can prostrate themselves at a woman's feet. It is therefore quite in keeping with precedent that, triggered by the suggestion of sexual satiety, the little function-ary should now throw himself on the English Milady's mercy.

"In that case, Monsieur le Steward," the Lady continues, delighted with his unconditional fervour, "I have a task for you. First, though, I'd better tell you the rest of my story. You see that leather-bound vanity case in the rack above my bed?" she asks. "Bring it over here, would you?"

So threadbare has the Steward's tale become that it is using every device found elsewhere to advance its aims, among which the unveiling of mysteries contained in a leather case.

Jules stares at the vanity case in the rack but fails to move.

"Well, go on!" the Lady hisses. "It won't eat you."

Whipped into action by the Lady's impatient wave of the hand, Jules obeys and fetches the case. He then places it on the compartment table and opens it. Inside he comes across, swaddled in a linen napkin, an unusual object. As large as a pineapple. Made out of bronze. On either side two handles. In appearance an osier casket bearing an armorial design.

"Look at it carefully, Monsieur le Steward, for that is the sole reason you see me on this train. You think that little bitch is a nuisance? You should have met her master! He, I tell you," the Lady says, a finger of contempt directed at the bronze casket, "was a thousand times worse."

A funerary cask! Containing her late husband's ashes! So that's what the casket is about, Jules realizes.

The English Milady takes out of her handbag a well-thumbed and slightly creased legal document and proceeds to unfold it. "Very keen on the small print, my late husband was," she says. "Listen to this: 'It is my last desire that my dear wife scatter my ashes along the Promenade des Anglais along whose concourse I spent some of my happiest hours.' The cheek of it! Shall I tell you how that dandiprat occupied his time in Nice? Not a stroke before midday. A leisurely breakfast in bed. Then saunter down to the Casino in the afternoon to squander a fortune on chemin de fer. And, to cap it all, most nights he could be found bouncing between *cocottes'* thighs. Cerby probably sleeping at the foot of the bed while he enjoyed his so-called happiest hours. And what does he leave me in his goddamn will? you might well ask. A pittance, and on one condition." She turns over two pages. "This should be an education for you, Monsieur le Steward! Listen!" She proceeds to read more of the will. "I give, devise and bequeath all my real and personal property to my good and faithful dog, Cerby, and to my wife the guardianship of my

321

estate during my beloved animal's life.' Oh, yes, nicely worked out! A pretty way to humiliate me," she adds, grabbing the casket and shaking it so violently that Jules hears sediment rattling within it. "And those are the terms by which I'm to stand if I want to keep the contents of his will. So, Monsieur le Steward, when you barge in on me in the middle of the night and inform me that Cerby's gone, don't expect me to shed any tears for that ghastly little cur!"

Now that he has been shown the dog in a new light, not just as an ugly little beast but as the very symbol of a fall from grace, the desecration of a marriage, and the humiliation of the Lady whose every gesture he finds intoxicating, Jules readily agrees with Milady that the dog's death was indeed a blessing. Spurred by a desire to repay the clemency from which he has unexpectedly benefitted by being true to his mother's injunction, he asks Milady whether she would like to hear just how her ward died.

"That's the very last thing I need to know!" she answers, quick to disabuse his proposal. "Keep it to yourself! If I heard it, my husband's lawyers might accuse us of collusion. However, Monsieur le Steward, if I understand right, you're now as involved in the dog's affairs as I am! So unless you'd like me to file a charge against your irresponsible attitude which caused loss of life, I suggest you listen very carefully to what I have to say. And, if you're a good boy and do what you're told, you can rest assured that I'll look after you."

As her words meet no more than the Steward's speechless assent, she proceeds to unfold her plan.

"The moment we arrive in Nice, you're to go to the nearest notary and there make out a sworn statement. Nothing too complicated, mind: all you have to say is how I asked you to look after Cerby, how you put her in the kennels, and how she vanished. I leave the details of her disappearance to you. Just enough to get me in the clear. Once that's done, come to my room at the Palace. There you and I will plan a little weekend somewhere nice and quiet."

No, it has never been easy to suspend disbelief in Jules' stories. As for this last explanation, it has surely gone too far. Not only are we now being asked to accept that the *grande dame* has been tied to a ridiculous clause in her late husband's will but that Jules has also managed quite by chance to work her release from the bondage of the bitch's year-round company. It is of course in the nature of first-person narratives that they can never be directly contradicted or, at least, only by other, and probably equally perfidious, first-hand accounts. But as the Steward's probity is of no great significance to the outcome of the story – his mythomania having served to illustrate various ways by which the imagination can elaborate upon the smallest details and use them to satisfy the most yearned-for aspects of existence – and as his ability to embroider has already been well documented, we need not concern ourselves unduly with the improbabilities which persistently pullulate his narrative.

Next, according to the version of events which Jules Pinard is hawking to his ferret, the English Milady puts her finger to his mouth and whispers: "'Why don't you do what you should have thought of long ago, Monsieur le Steward? Get me a bottle of champagne – nicely chilled, mind. And be a little daring and make it two glasses.'

"Then, Anatole, while she fiddles with the buttons of my uniform, she says: 'You will join me in a little celebration, won't you?'"

The glasses are visibly shaking and, as if from an inexhaustible supply, a steady stream of bubbles is let loose through the amber liquid. Can they too be on a voyage of discovery? Or are they about to be overwhelmed by oblivion? What sensations attend gaseous spheres moving from a pressurized through to the unsteady atmosphere of the open air? Now while it might be amusing to pursue this conceit further – tempting as it is to try to avoid relating the Steward's tawdry reality – and to consider these and other ambient details, contrasting their physical occurrences with the metaphysical properties which they might embody, we really cannot spend any more time meditating on the experiences carbon dioxide secreted in a bottle of champagne might encounter as it swims from the shallows of a crystal glass to the vastness of the world beyond. If we are that concerned with cause and effect, we would be better employed asking why the two long-stemmed glasses standing next to each other by the side of a railway carriage window are moving when, in the background, Nice Centrale's nondescript, provincial end station is stock still. For the Mistral is indeed fixed to its buffers and its passengers have long ago left their cabins. So what is the nature of the energy which is transferring its rocking motion to the champagne-filled glasses?

323

Were we to move back and to adjust the focus on the scene, it would soon become apparent just how this gentle swaying motion is being imparted. However, the standards of decency to which we have always tried to subscribe will not allow us to dwell too long on the thin shanks and the spasmodically jerking hips of the Steward, nor to show the disarray into which the English Milady has fallen as she submits to the pummelling which the French functionary is nervously administering. And although some might well say that to celebrate a poodle's sudden and bloody death by fornicating in a deserted train is highly unorthodox behaviour, others will point out that such outbursts of sensuality, while outrageous in the context, are not that dissimilar to the rites of far-off peoples in which life and death, sexual fervour and decay, are regarded as two sides of the same phenomenon rather than as discrete events never impinging the one upon the other. Nor, it should be admitted, is the scene of ardour such an infelicitous way of leaving two characters whose principal function has been to be wheeled in between the main acts of the story to provide comic relief – with no doubt varying degrees of success – and who, now that the ample English aristocrat grasps the gaunt Steward by the shoulders and senses the spray of his manhood within her, can at last be sent on their way.

To view the antics of those two characters for the last time is bound to remind us of the locomotive driver in his glass-spanned cockpit, unsung hero of adventures which we chose not to explore, lonely figure at the train's cutting edge where the wind is keenest, the landscape most blurred, and the definition of time and space closest to the fracture of their constituent parts.

His feet perched on the side of the small table on which Anatole is curled snug in his basket, Jules puts the final touches to his very own version of events.

"So we down a few more glasses and round them off with . . . But that's none of your business, Anatole. This, on the other hand," Jules says, extracting from a small tin on the table a morsel of bloodied meat, "should remind you – shouldn't it? – of another little incident, eh!"

It is with excitement that the ferret twists round his wicker basket to get a better purchase on the meat, biting with gusto on what little is left of Cerby's bloodied paw.

"*Eh bien*, Anatole!" says Jules, a broad smile on his gaunt face. "Looks like we both got our appetites back!"

Frayed by a thousand fidgety tracings, soiled by humidity and constant badgering, teased by the flickering light of the overhead fluorescent bar, the map of France's hexagon seems to have cast its spell over Jules once again. Down the route which the Mistral took his finger now runs: so many cities unexplored, so many kilometres of the tracks passed in silence, leaving little but a trail of possibilities through the air. From where it is skewered on a pin, the snapshot of a redheaded *Niçoise* stares down at him. Aware that sleep is calling to him, Jules stretches out his arms. Then with a dismissal all the more delicious for being so rarely exercised, he says: "Do you know what, Anatole? I don't think I'll look Minnie up. Not on this run anyway."

But what of the shady deal which Jules made with the English Milady? What of the affidavit he was supposed to sign? And what of the rich rewards she offered him?

In a story in which every episode has been provided with a neat if occasionally improbable conclusion, it is a serious disappointment to come across one whose loose ends will not, indeed cannot, ever be tied up. And yet perhaps it should not come as such a shock, that, having been so unconvincing from its very inception, this episode should now fail to match whatever small hopes had been invested in it. For no doubt every batch has its duds and no matter how well one calibrates one's quality controls, some are bound to get through and to show the others up. However, as there is no method of telling how good or bad, profound or shallow a story will turn out to be until it has been told, this sequence's flagrant shortcomings, its bathetic ending, and its lack of a pleasing payoff, will just have to be put down to the risks inherent in creation.

CHAPTER EIGHTEEN

The taxi winds up a series of steep terraces, veers into a narrow drive, and motors for a hundred metres through a shadow-flecked and resinous canopy of trees. When this cool curtain parts, it reveals a grassy expanse raked by a strong clear light. The road then takes the travellers past borders of flowering jacaranda and up a sandy track until the taxi's wheels come to a halt on the freshly-raked gravel of a semicircular courtyard before which stands La Fantaisie. The Marquis pays the fare and exchanges a few perfunctory words with the driver while Annabelle, rising from the dust-streaked limousine, appraises the setting.

Though part blinded by the sun's ferocity, Annabelle manages to pick out the restaurant's salient features.

La Fantaisie sits on a raised ledge overlooking on its south side a well-tended lawn which recedes towards a dense line of cork trees. As for its north prospect, up which the travellers have just climbed, it remains in a barbed and untamed state. It must have once been some smallholder's farm, Annabelle presumes, a two-storey *mas* which has been carefully converted, its basic shape respected, its rusticated stone facing and flat roof untampered with. She also admires the yellow stone fountain surrounded by terracotta pots in full flower which fronts the terrace. As for the linen-draped tables punctuated by the steel rods of parasols, they clearly provide the perfect site for open-air meals.

The taxi driver takes the travellers' suitcases from the boot and lays them on the gravel. Once his efforts have been rewarded with a large tip, he gets back into his vehicle and drives it away.

Hardly has the sound of its diesel engine faded away and the smell of its exhaust been blown far and wide by a suddenly roused breeze than a rubicund man dressed in a chef's crisply starched outfit steps out of the restaurant. With a roar of delight he strides down the few steps and embraces the Marquis.

"*Bienvenue, Maître,*" the chef says in a broad Provençal accent. "You're remarkably early."

"The Mistral was, I'm glad to say, its usual punctual self, Marius. But tell me," adds the Marquis, a frown creeping across his face, his hand waving towards the welcoming vista of freshly-bedecked tables, "isn't the restaurant supposed to be closed today?"

"Of course it is, *Maître.* Just as you requested I gave the staff the day off. I laid out these tables to welcome you. No one, I assure you, will disturb your privacy."

"Good," answers the Marquis, clearly relieved. He turns towards his companion who is still shielding her eyes from the sun. "Annabelle, I'd like to introduce you to one of my oldest friends, Marius de la Garde, chef and guiding genius of La Fantaisie."

"*Enchantée,*" replies Annabelle, her eyes pained by the brilliance thrown off from the restaurant's stone facing.

"*Tout le plaisir est pour moi,* Mademoiselle," says Marius, grasping her hand in a massive grip.

"Marius, *mon vieux,* meet Annabelle Fleury, my most talented apprentice," says the Marquis, completing the formalities. "You'll be glad to hear she has almost completed the course. And, so far, with flying colours."

"Congratulations, Mademoiselle!" Marius exclaims, bowing to her. "So Jean-Loup has been sharing his little secrets with you, has he? You are certainly most fortunate if you have managed to make head or tail of them!" A remark which he follows by bursting into laughter yet one which provokes, Annabelle observes with surprise, not the slightest reaction, neither disapproval nor reproof, from the Marquis. "But you mustn't mind me," the chef adds, "I'm only teasing. You and I both know that Jean-Loup is an exceptional teacher." He walks over to the travellers' bags, grabs them, and heads for the restaurant. "Please, Mademoiselle," he adds, "do come out of the sun! After a long night on the Mistral you must be exhausted."

"Thank you," answers Annabelle, slowly warming to Marius'

meridional charm. "You're quite right. I could do with a rest. The journey was fascinating but we didn't get much sleep."

"Yes, travelling with Jean-Loup has always been – how shall I put it? – demanding."

The Marquis again makes no response to his partner's innuendo, either taking Marius' rough humour for granted or preferring to leave the comment to fade away.

"Good suggestion, Marius. We'll go in now," he says, walking into the restaurant's marble-cool foyer. "Would you be kind and show Annabelle one of our guest rooms? I see there's a lot of mail which I'd better deal with," he adds, scanning a wad of neatly-tied papers lying on top of the reception desk. "I'll catch a few hours' sleep later. I suggest that you have a rest, Annabelle, and come down to the terrace at around one where Marius will make you one of his special apéritifs. Afterwards you and I will visit the kitchens and put the finishing touches to the course."

Annabelle assents to the Marquis' arrangement, leaves him rifling through his papers, and follows the wide-girthed Marius who is walking up the stairs with her bag.

Like those convenient little *baises-en-ville* which pepper the Marais and to which moneyed provincials come once a fortnight to bed their Parisian mistresses, La Fantaisie, although strictly speaking a restaurant, has a few rooms tucked away to which habitués – who have effected the age-old exchange of a night of pleasure for a good meal – can repair at a moment's notice. It is to one of these, decorated in the sparsest manner, its shutters tightly closed against the heat of the sun, that Marius now leads Annabelle. He places her hand luggage on the floor, makes sure that all amenities are at hand, then with a cheery "*A tout à l'heure*," leaves her to inspect her commodious quarters.

Glad to discard her clothes which have already been stained by the sweat and dust of the taxi journey, Annabelle disrobes and walks straight under a cold shower. She is amazed how much grime the long journey has left on her: in no time at all the sandalwood-scented soapsuds have turned a grimy yellow and the froth that vanishes down the bath hole is filthy. Still dripping, she pads over to the windows in a long white towel monogrammed with La Fantaisie's logo and peers through the slats at the cork and cypress-filled landscape slipping away towards a clear horizon. Once she is dry, she darts between sheets of the most delicious linen she can recall close to her skin.

What a relief to be shot of the train and to have put all those unbelievable events behind her.

She has mulled over the sensations which have coursed through her in less than thirty six hours, wondered what is to happen to her next, and how much she should trust the Marquis when sleep sidles up to her and drags her down into the fluid depths from which she hopes not to emerge until it is time to rejoin her genial hosts.

The Marquis de St Lyre has furnished his suite of rooms in a bare, almost monastic style. On either side of a low single bed sit two bedside tables in walnut; an olive chest squats on the rich rust of glazed quarry tiles; and on the walls a series of sepia-tinted prints represents choice perspectives of the Baie des Anges. Decorations which he has carefully chosen so that when lying on the bed, with the shutters wide open and the door muffling the sounds of the house, nothing can detract from the locust-lulled landscape with whose mercurial character – pastel at dawn, crystalline at noon, and muffled at dusk – he so long ago fell in love.

Relaxed, the Marquis floats in his bath-salts-scented water and considers his guest's condition. After some deliberation he concludes that everything is in good order. The trap laid, the approach to it unhindered and, as far as he can ascertain, Annabelle set to take the next crucial step. Keen to ensure that nothing has been overlooked, he once again surveys the lie of the land over which his apprentice is to tread. That done, almost convinced that he will not have to resort to last-minute stratagems, he stretches full out in the softened water and basks in the consoling thought that for all his mistakes, Annabelle will never discover the way in which, nor the reasons why, he was caught. For if all goes to plan, his fatal indiscretion should soon be redeemed and she be none the wiser.

He plays with the taps, adds a few extra centimetres of scalding water to the bath, and muses on the time and energy which he has had to expend to break his chains. The hours of inventiveness needed to lay baits! And the frustration of waiting for the right candidate! Can Annabelle, he wonders, be so naive as to imagine that their meeting was mere chance and that he had never before sat in the Brasserie? A startling thought then crosses his mind. Should he let her go? He contemplates the notion for a second. After all the work he has put into her! No! True, he has grown fond of her. For all her false starts and petty interruptions, she has proved to be an unsuspectedly accomplished storyteller. But that does not mean that he will be sorry to see her trapped. Too much – far too much – is at stake. He has exhausted himself to get others – and her, dammit – in his sights. So this is hardly the moment to start dispensing compassion!

Anyway, is she not to blame for falling for his toils? He invited her along, he did not twist her arm! Her curiosity did the rest, her curiosity and – he recalls her sly manufacture of the pearl – her greed. Yes, it will do her no lasting harm to experience how tedious constant invention can be. Let her find out about the endless preparations that attend a scenario's construction! Let her discover what it is like to stand by while a potential victim, who could have set you free, just walks away! If she only knew the number of times she will have to spin a narrative web with no guarantee of catching a fly! If she only knew how often she'd have to ditch a complex tale and invent another to earn her escape. No doubt the feast of the imagination seems alluring until you have to prepare it each and every day.

Relieved to be within sight of his goal, the Marquis rises from his bath, wraps a towel round his waist, and falls heavily on to the bed. No, he has no regrets. His lies, his subterfuge, the whole paraphernalia of deceit, have all been directed at one aim, surely the only aim worth having – his freedom. A freedom he lost so easily. Was it madness which made him wander so late at night down those Marseilles backstreets? He is still not sure. Or a feverish desire to experience more than he had ever dared? Was it concupiscence which made him such an easy prey for the boy? Should he have been less gullible before those urchin features, those wide beguiling eyes? It is with a tremor that he remembers with what ease he fell for the youth's tears and followed him to his lodgings.

Yes, he had gone down those dingy alleyways and had headed for the tenement with its blistered façade, its windows smeared, its railings twisted and half missing. Yes, he had climbed up those dark stairs and had heard the unshackled cries, the blows, and the broken bottles tintinnabulating down the corridors. And even when the smell that reeked from every corner of the building had assailed him, he had not turned tail. Nor when the boy had ushered him into his room had he needed any encouragement to sit on that shabby bed. From behind a crumpled box the boy had brought out a bottle of absinthe, had poured him a shot, then, as if it were the most natural thing in the world, had started to tell his story. A story with which the Marquis had first sympathized before submitting to its rhythm and allowing it to seduce him. And when the story was over and the alcohol was seeping through his brain, he had lain back and had shown no resistance as those silky, unbelievably expert hands had explored his skin and sunk their long, abnormally long, nails into him. Soon, all too soon he had become less a victim, more a depredator, astounding himself by the violence of his own appetites and by the precision of desires which he thought he had long locked up in the most deeply recessed room of his imagination. To each new position the boy had complied. To each act of daring he had wordlessly conceded. Even when blood had been shed, and the boy had cried out, and the Marquis had licked it off the boy's thighs, he had still not stopped but had pushed their mutual torment, their common joy, further into the night. A night concentrated into numberless periods of pleasure, pleasure to which he had surrendered, pleasure that had released him from years of neglect, pleasure which he could never have dreamt would cost him so dear!

But the next morning, as he had stared at the soiled sheets, and at the bloodied blankets, and at the expression of delight on the boy's face, he had had to confront the horror of what could only have been agreed in a moment of unthinking ecstasy. Yet there it lay on the dirt-encrusted floor, the document signed in his own blood, and the boy refusing any payment, except for his agreement that he would in turn search for a victim and thus pursue the unending cycle of doom.

Although it may well be fascinating to travel once again down those narrow sidestreets cloaked in the crepuscular folds of night-time, only occasionally lit, and then dimly so, by one-eyed streetlamps, and to track the Marquis to the boy's deliquescent den, and there to wide-angle witness his varied couplings and the fatal price which his passion cost him, the ins and outs of how he fell into a homoerotic trap are not, strictly speaking, within this story's ambit, revealing him, as they inevitably would, not in a seducer's enviable colours but in a punter's more tawdry light. And as keeping concealed the reasons why he had so far failed to lure various women to their doom does not invalidate them, we prefer to leave in the shadows how St Lyre's lust led him to a *giton*'s lap and why there, after being told a story which cannot be divulged for the terrible hold it has always had on all who have heard it, he was forced to honour a commitment made in a moment of madness and submit to the boy's demands. Rather than belabour details which would work against those aspects of the Marquis' character which have already been exposed, we prefer to conclude this interlude by recalling that the way in which the fox in the famous fable escaped from the pit into which he had fallen was by enticing the bear to take his place. And on that note loudly echoing with the theme of exchange, we will let the exhausted and contented Marquis tumble into the maw of sleep.

On one of the tables nearest the house, Marius has set a large crystal pitcher filled with a liquid in which fruits slightly out of season, nectarines and prickly pears, are bathing next to sprigs of aromatic herbs. An aperitif both piquant and sweet in which Annabelle is sure she can detect the presence of angostura. But however much she tries to extract the recipe from Marius, he goodhumouredly refuses to divulge it, insisting that a chef is only as good as his stock of secrets, and that as he hardly knows her he really cannot entrust it.

The sun is out, its searing edge blunted by a wind that ruffles the parasols, sending those of nearby tables spinning, yet bizarrely leaving theirs untouched. Annabelle is fascinated by Marius' gastronomic banter. For with enviable familiarity he digs up from his memory the most abstruse shards of culinary archaeology, delighting her with the composition of the fetid fish sauce with which the Romans flavoured their meals, how eels were frequently fattened on the live flesh of slaves, and remarking on the insouciance with which the first French Emperor frisked from dish to dish. With such charm does he deliver these anecdotes that for a moment Annabelle quite forgets why she is sipping an exquisite cocktail in his company, and even imagines herself on holiday. This pleasant reverie is however soon shattered by the appearance on the restaurant's threshold of the Marquis, garbed in a well-starched chef's outfit. With a wave, he calls her to join him in the kitchen where they can conclude the course.

La Fantaisie's kitchen – unlike less dedicated locales in which paraphernalia such as copper pots, fish dishes and jelly moulds are prettily placed around the walls and reduced to a decorative function – is fundamentally a laboratory in which, the Marquis informs Annabelle, he has spent many years trying to encourage the four elements to join in perfect palatal harmony. While he carries on conversing in this farfetched and somewhat orotund manner, Annabelle surveys the dazzling array of cooking accessories, all immaculate and at the ready. For a while she even luxuriates in the kitchen's no-nonsense design as if the instruments surrounding her offered her a welcome palliative against the illusions which she encountered in the train.

Her contemplation is suddenly interrupted when she catches sight of them. For the four ingredients are now neatly laid out on nickeled plates on a large aluminium-topped table; while next to them sits the ubiquitous wicker basket within which the Marquis stored them.

"There they are!" the Marquis exclaims, "the ingredients for which we strove so hard. You do know what your task is, don't you, Annabelle? To put to shame once and for all the disgraceful meal which you were served in the Brasserie."

"Are you ready?" asks Marius who has just come in behind them. He ambles round the room and switches on a number of discreetly camouflaged fans which soon fill the kitchen with their low vibrant hum. Once he has checked the apparatus, laid out a place for one on a simple wooden table, and informed the Marquis that he will now leave them to their labours, he wishes Annabelle good luck and, without further formality, walks out.

The Marquis fetches from a nearby metal cupboard two long wooden-sleeved chopping knives, three stainless steel serving dishes, a hand towel and a box of matches. He puts them on the aluminium table top and collects from a corner a stool on which to sit. Settling close to the table, he uncorks a local rosé, and with the finesse and superciliousness of a true *tastevin*, pours himself a small glass. He does not offer her one but rather signals her to start.

Each ingredient lies in the hollow of its own metal plate, each ingredient for which, Annabelle reminds herself, she has sacrificed a whole night's sleep and endured countless humiliations. To reap what? she wonders. But just as the question is about to overwhelm her with a set of conflicting answers, she

333

casts it aside and concentrates instead on the herbs and vegetables lying before her.

Annabelle finds it interesting that the long journey should have taken nothing away from the ingredients' essential freshness. The *cèpes* still have on their muddy brown surfaces drops of the forest's dew. Through the tracing paper of their faintly veined, roseate skins, the three cloves of garlic release a full, pungent aroma. The parsley, its roots still gummed with gobbets of kitchen garden soil, is almost phosphorescently green. As for the grey dusty gourd, flaccid yet half full of oil, Annabelle notices that it does not look unlike a man's sac waiting to be made taut by a lover's telling touch.

How should she start? What should she do? So many steps to get wrong! What if she peels the garlic against the grain, or harms the mushrooms' gills, or bludgeons the subtle fragrance out of the herb, or uses too much oil? What if . . . ? Annabelle, who has been upbraided more than once in her mother's kitchen for clumsiness, knows only too well the bewildering number of rules and procedures by which she should abide. She can even dimly remember some key injunctions. Is it cucumber which should never be cut with steel? Tomatoes which should be skinned under a naked flame? Lemon juice, not *vinaigrette*, the proper accompaniment to *pisse-en-lit*? The field of potential pitfalls before her makes her falter for a few seconds. She also feels intimidated by the Marquis' vigilant eye. His inscrutable expression, however, shows all too vividly that he does not intend to help her. No, she can tell that it is up to her and to her alone.

Alone she may be but that does not mean helpless. Caressing the *cèpes*' white skin, she senses the minute particles of dust with which they are coated and decides that she will start off simply by rinsing them.

A colander-like attachment straddles the stainless steel sink. Annabelle arranges the *cèpes* on the attachment's narrow grid, sets it under the tap, and lets the water play over them. Is it the delicacy of the *cèpes*' purple-brown ruffs which makes her suspect that they are the most finely flavoured parts of the fungus, and should thus be treated very gently?

She watches as grains of dust, barely denting the liquid's fast flowing surface, rush across the bottom of the basin towards the sink's orifice. She is absentmindedly tracking their journey and going over in her mind what her next step should be when she suddenly cannot prevent herself staring. For an extraordinary sight has just seized her attention.

Far from becoming clearer as it washes away the dirt on the mushrooms, the water has turned a rich tone of red. Was the earth in the forest that colour? Annabelle cannot recall. She again examines the now tinted water splashing on to the steel basin and decides that the red substance has nothing of the humus-steeped, worm-digested smell of soil. No, it is imbued with quite another smell, a powerful, full-bodied presence, the smell of decay, not an ancient musty decay but one that betrays a recent living origin.

Determined to overcome her rising repugnance and not to call the Marquis over to help her – for even if he were willing to listen, would enlisting him not be tantamount to admitting failure and to proving her lack of resourcefulness? – Annabelle dips a finger into the flow and tastes it. It is most decidedly not soil. No, it is blood! Reacting with poorly disguised disgust, she steps back and brushes aside the colander which rattles against the sides of the sink then collapses.

"Careful, Annabelle!" the Marquis exclaims from his distant vantage on the stool. "Don't go harming the mushrooms' texture. They're fragile and can easily lose their flavour."

Annabelle, irritated at having provided the Marquis with a reason to reprove her, picks up the colander, repositions it properly, and returns the unharmed fungi to its hollow. She then continues to rinse the mushrooms and does not even stop when the smell rising towards her makes her gag. Nor does she stop at the sight of the inexhaustible supply of blood which the mushrooms seem to contain. Indeed the more she smells it, and the more she sees it running through the water, the more she comes to suspect that the ruby-red liquid is intimately linked with the Leopard Woman. Yes, with her blood, her menses! A vile thought which she attempts to put out of her mind but fails. For, far from being suppressed, the image of flowing blood escapes her control and conjures up a set of incidents from the Leopard Woman's story. She remembers the blood that trickled from the mushrooms' severed stems. She remembers blood irradiating like a dye from the purple flower on the surface of the lake. Then, with a fascination which barely masks nausea, she meets another image in her mind's eye. She sees blood seeping from under the young girl's dress and running down her legs while her brother, a prurient grin on his face, stares at the red rivulet dripping on to the muddy ground . . .

Enough!

By focusing hard on the flow of water rolling across the mushrooms, she manages bit by bit to dispel the images.

The mushrooms' surface is now externally clean. Realizing that however much she rinses them, the bloody supply will not cease, she takes them over to the table and puts them back on their plate. Her face emotionless, behaving as if nothing out of the ordinary had occurred, she stares at the other ingredients, determined to keep her reactions hidden from the Marquis.

Step by step. That's it. One at a time. Think only of the task at hand. After what she has been through, surely the actual process of cooking can't be that hard. A question of common sense. No, she must not let the Marquis find out. Nor will she give him the satisfaction of witnessing her discomfiture.

The first garlic clove which she seizes from the plate yields to her knife's downward thrust and becomes two unequal hemispheres. She feels a certain simple satisfaction at the neatness of its execution, although there is something about it which also makes her uneasy. Could it be the particularly strong smell which comes from it? Convinced, without knowing why, that that is how they should be prepared, she very carefully dices the cloves. Then, out of curiosity, she puts a sliver into her mouth.

A peculiar taste. And one which she cannot pinpoint with accuracy. As for the images which rise up in her mind as she stands before the table, they too are hazy. What was that? . . . A candle flickering back and forth? Scouring across . . . what? Slowly, as if answering her bewilderment, the images gain in definition. In her mind's eye she next catches sight of a tall and imposing hand-painted wall. Is that a diminutive Egyptian figure painted on it, and why is he holding a golden vessel high? To catch what? With a shudder, she distantly recalls the reason. The image fades to be replaced by another scene. This time the focus is on a marble floor on which fresh marks like elongated teardrops indicate that a small amount of liquid has just been spilled. Annabelle, who has guessed towards what point these images are pressing her, now perceives the series of lithographs depicting the young lady being led step by step towards a climax

which will leave her confused at how fast she fell into the
seducer's trap.

Not that again!

Yet it is not the flux of images which makes Annabelle retch,
rush over to the sink, turn on the tap, and rinse her mouth out. It
is the flavour of the tiny piece of garlic which has suddenly taken
on a flavour a thousand times more evocative, yes, the quintes-
sential flavour of the male!

She dashes the water from one side to the other of her mouth
and spits it out. She then goes back to the aluminium table,
reaches for the knife and, hardly knowing why, again and again
plunges it into the cloves of garlic lying below her.

Impossible! How could they? Yet they are! The ghastly little
things are wriggling, yes, they're trying to get off the plate,
they're trying to escape!

Annabelle screams.

"Quick! Hold on to them!" cries the Marquis who has rushed
over to her side. "Stab them! That's right! Don't let them get
away!" Almost beside herself with horror yet held in check by
the Marquis' authority, Annabelle isolates the cloves and spears
them one by one. After a nervous flutter, the cloves at last cease
to move.

"I don't . . . I don't believe it!" she stutters, taking a step back
from the table on which the quiescent cloves lie. "The bloody
things are alive!"

"Or to be more precise, Annabelle, they were. Before you put
them out of their agony. Quite a death blow you administered!"
He gazes at her. Her face is so pale that he is afraid that she might
faint. "What an expression! And yet you know perfectly well
that we're dealing with the raw materials of experience, not with
some tasteless, freeze-dried food." He gently leads her back to
the work table. "Careful now. You're doing well. Don't, whatever
you do, lose your rhythm." He points to a large copper frying pan
hanging from the metal gantry overhead. "Here! This one'll do."

Annabelle, admitting by her silence the defeat of her reason
before the grotesque performance which she has just witnessed,
turns her back on the unpredictable vegetables on the table and
refuses to consider what caused them to jump like fish from a
poisoned stream. Burying her horror in a series of simple
gestures, she fetches the pan, walks over to the hob, and
switches on the gas which fires immediately.

Something about the haze rising from the pan's brushed surface tells her – she still cannot say why – that it is now hot enough. She takes the pan off the flame, goes back to the table, picks up the gourd, and pours a few drops of the liquid into the pan. The oil spreads across its black surface and a strong aroma wafts towards her.

What extraordinary ingredients these are! she muses. It is as if they were possessed of a spirit, as if they were somehow alive and sentient. Is this oil, she wonders, imbued with Alonzo's nature? Bizarre how the little man could not stop ferreting where he had no business to be. Sad too that he should have been brought so low by culpable love. She wonders where he is now and what he is up to.

The next moment – in total defiance of radical theories which insist that characters have no reality except their literary context, and that any attempt to substantiate their fictive beings beyond the page is a fetishistic activity – from the centre of the pan there comes a terrifying sizzle, an overwhelming and nauseating smell of mother's milk, followed by the eruption of a vast sheet of blue flame in which Annabelle glimpses, if only for a few vivid seconds, the dwarf sucking greedily on a vast, distended breast!

"A – ah!" Annabelle screams and jumps back to avoid the leaping flames.

The Marquis once again runs to her rescue, turns down the gas, and moves the pan off the burner. Then, with a marked show of sympathy, he puts his arm around her and asks her: "You're not burnt, are you?"

Thankfully the flames have left no traces on her, nor has her dress been carbonized. She is at worst shaken but unharmed.

"Make no mistake, Annabelle! These are very dangerous materials which you must treat with the greatest care. And don't be surprised if they show a fierce resistance to being cooked. They too want to hold on to life and, like you, aren't keen to see their stories come to an end!"

Speechless, Annabelle stands by the hob and accepts that this is as logical an explanation as any she is likely to get. Is there really no limit to the Marquis' tricks? "I know I should be used to it, Jean-Loup," she exclaims," but I wish the course were more simple."

"Simplicity, Annabelle, I reserve for epitaphs. In life I prefer surprise and sophistication," says the Marquis, flagrantly contradicting his earlier dictum that simplicity is a keynote to creative cooking. "You haven't found the course easy, have you? But now you've almost completed it, I'd like to ask you whether you've derived any enjoyment from it?"

The question seems ludicrous. Surely the sensations she has just been through are beyond mere enjoyment? A passage through fire, a trial by ordeal, a violent tempering, those are more appropriate descriptions. "Enjoyed it? I can't say I have. It's been too painful. Not that I've a right to complain: my curiosity brought me here and, I have to admit, it has been more than adequately whetted!"

"Yes, your curiosity has been whetted and, in a few minutes, so shall your taste buds. For this is a dish which will more than satisfy your every wish," says the Marquis, as if reciting from a fairy tale. "Once your imagination is unlocked, you'll find you can turn any situation to your advantage. Never forget though that each situation deserves its own recipe, and that each encounter needs it own special flavouring." The Marquis turns towards the work table and leads her to it. "I presume you've come across dishes specially created to celebrate some grand occasion or famous personage. You know what I mean: a dessert named after a prima donna, a chicken dish cooked at the scene of a battle, a romantic composer lending his name to a steak. In the same vein, each time you entice somebody into the world of your fantasy, you too must invent a new delight perfectly suited to their tastes, yes, you must create something that's appropriate to whoever you meet. The secret of sympathy – without which cooking is not a creative art but is reduced to a set of lifeless procedures – lies in intuiting, to the smallest instance, what the context you're in requires. You think I'm being needlessly complicated? I'm not, Annabelle. Just reminding you of the course's ground rules."

While unable to grant them full weight, Annabelle takes care to store his words away, preferring not to dismiss them in case they prove to be, like so much he has said, infuriatingly exact.

"Everything has occurred so quickly," the Marquis exclaims as Annabelle, confident that the oil is hot enough, lessens the heat, and walks over to the table on which the vegetables are lying. "Why, only yesterday you were telling me that you had no interest in cooking. And here you are, initiating yourself into the practice of imaginative cooking!"

339

"With no idea what to do with it," she adds, almost sulkily.

"Nonsense. Instinctively you know exactly what to do. By the way, how do you intend to prepare these delicious fruits of the night?" the Marquis asks, pointing to the mushrooms marinating in a small pool of blood.

Annabelle is pleased at the ease with which she answers his question without even thinking about it. "Oh, I'll cut them into strips . . ."

Afraid that the *cèpes* might scream, change shape, or partake of some equally outrageous act, Annabelle is pleasantly surprised at how compliant they are. Perhaps because they too have exhausted their imaginative potential, they submit to having their soft fibrous flesh sliced without resistance.

"And into the pan," she adds.

She hovers over the hob and places the slivers of mushroom into the pan. She fries them for a while, turns them over, then leaves them to grow dark and mellow.

Might he be of help, the Marquis asks? He could bring the chopped garlic over, she replies.

"Famous for its curative powers," he says, tending her the plate of finely diced cloves. "Some also say," he adds, "for its kindling of the fires of love."

Annabelle takes the cloves and, nerving herself for some aberrant reaction, scatters them across the sides of the pan. At first a bitter, musty smell reaches her. Just as the cloves are turning brown under the heat, she glimpses the Mummy's face in the midst of the rising fumes and hears a shriek. Then nothing. It is all over so fast that she has no idea whether her expectations supplied the illusion or whether she really saw the Mummy. A problem not confined to Annabelle's perception but which has haunted the whole of this narrative and to which we can supply no answer, as it is impossible to make a distinction between what we project onto the world, with what the world informs us, and the extent to which independent events simply obtrude on the narrow filter of consciousness from a wholly different and still uncharted sphere. And as this subject is too vast even for a story which has attempted, whenever it has had the opportunity, to deal with the contradiction inherent in its representations, we prefer to leave that fraught topic alone.

"*Dieu!* Did you see, did you hear anything?" Annabelle asks her companion, desperate to have her fleeting sensation confirmed.

"Nothing to worry about. It was only the garlic giving up the ghost," the Marquis answers, handing out yet another of his obscure explanations which, while impossible to comprehend, do at least fill in the unnerving hiatus between doubt and affirmation.

With almost all the ingredients sizzling together in the pan, a highly evocative aroma emanates from it, an aroma to which Annabelle, in spite of herself, unwittingly succumbs. It is indeed so powerful that it unnerves her sense of balance. She is soon swaying and has to hold on to the Marquis to prevent herself from falling. He grips her with one hand and with the other rapidly switches the heat down.

"It's ready," she whispers as the Marquis leads her to the wooden table and there sits her down. Overcome by the aroma, she rests her head on one side.

The Marquis returns to the hob and ascertains that Annabelle has cooked the mushrooms to perfection. He takes the steaming pan and walks over to the wooden table.

Her mind spinning, her head tucked into her elbow, Annabelle watches as out of some dark indistinct space the characters issue one by one. She ruefully accepts that it would have truly been astonishing if, in a world ruled by repetition and formula, they had not made their bow sooner or later. Certainly their sense of timing is impeccable, even if the medium through which they hazeously materialize is in its usual poor condition.

First the Leopard Woman, a leer on her face, mouthing words which Annabelle cannot decipher, beckons to her, as if determined to make her do something. Long before she has conveyed her meaning, however, she fades away to be replaced by the Mummy. His face reveals beneath the unwinding swathes of bandages the crackly surface of his skin. He stretches out his arms as if inviting her to come nearer, nearer. She shudders and is almost relieved when Alonzo tries to lure her with snatches of a garbled song. If there is any sense to these scenes, Annabelle cannot discern it. Next it is Jeanne's turn to rise out of the darkness. Her face is different. Unlike the others who smiled grotesquely and who urged her on, her hands point away and seem to be entreating her, yes, to be warning her to go away. But what should she flee from and where should she go to?

"Eh!" cries the Marquis, aware that Annabelle is losing her concentration and approaching her with the magnificently cooked dish in his hand. "I realize its aroma is evocative but that's no reason to faint!" He places the pan on the table, raises her head, and helps her sit up.

Annabelle, although light-headed, can still see straight. She gazes at the food. The mushrooms look enticing. Remarkably her appetite has not been dimmed by her short fit. Indeed the food's presence on the plate before her seems to have revived her.

The Marquis uses a large wooden spatula and, making sure that he does not harm the dish's golden brown décolleté, transfers it in one expert move onto Annabelle's plate.

She is just about to begin when the Marquis asks her whether she has not forgotten something. He is flattered that she should give his own ingredients preferential treatment but what about her own contribution? Her contribution? What contribution? What is he going on about? He looks down at her plate. She follows his gesture. Of course! Now she realizes what is missing. The ingredient which she fetched, the sprigs of parsley!

Strictly speaking, the Marquis adds, she should herself prepare the herb. But as she is still weak, he will do it for her. So, how would she like it? Finely chopped, she answers, again without any hesitation.

He brings over to the table a chopping board which was hanging from the side of a corner cupboard wall. Then with the graceful if staccato gestures of the consummate gastronome, he swiftly reduces the parsley to a fine hash and sprinkles a small amount over the steaming meal.

Could it be her desire to have this last ingredient – the one she herself evoked – play its full part, or a real and concrete occurrence which makes her imagine that she hears a long-drawn-out sigh as the chopped parsley lands on the hot dish, yes, a lonely, desperate sigh? A sensation which is then joined by the musk of intimate secretions. This odour immediately evokes in Annabelle's mind a vision of Jeanne. Yes, there she is, her face close to the little mirror, her lips parted, and her tongue licking with a fierce, despairing concentration the dew that has gathered at the corners of the reflecting surface.

"Go on! Enjoy it before it gets cold," the Marquis exclaims, deliberately making no comment on the amazement which has spread over his apprentice's face. "You've done it at last!" he adds, watching her put her fork to the crisp, aromatic mass, "*champignons à la provençale* the way they're supposed to be. Well, Annabelle, what else can I wish you but *bon appétit?*"

Famished – for, apart from breakfast, what has she had since she boarded the train? – Annabelle seizes the silver cutlery which Marius has put out for her and begins to savour her meal. The first mouthful proves to be a revelation. Never, no, never has she tasted anything as good. The mushrooms, for all their aberrant origins and their bloody exudations – perhaps because of these very characteristics – are tart, their texture smoothed out and strengthened by being cooked. The garlic has released a subtle sourness throughout the dish yet on Annabelle's tongue is perfectly assimilated to the mushrooms' delicacy of texture. The oil has lost none of its body in the heat nor has its rich flavour swamped the other ingredients. As for the parsley, it too has added its own memorable bouquet of freshness to the meal.

With each mouthful, Annabelle's appetite grows. Were it not that she wants to taste every morsel of the meal and to allow each perfectly balanced flavour its own time, she knows that she could easily have finished the plateful in a few greedy seconds.

Annabelle has tasted a few mouthfuls when, her fork in mid-air, she suddenly stops eating. Breathless, she stares straight ahead, pushes her plate away, and scatters the remnants of the meal on to the floor. Her eyes are wild, her body shakes, her face is radiant with an inner light. Her hands grip the table and rock it violently.

It has worked! His apprentice has swallowed the bait. As for the effects which the mushrooms *à la provençale* are creating, why, thinks the Marquis, scrutinizing his apprentice, they're sublime! He refills his glass with rosé d'Anjou and confronts his victim. "With your premission, *chère* Annabelle," he says to her, "I raise my glass to the tales you'll have to spin on your return to Paris. May they bring you the freedom for which you will have to strain!" In a neat and delighted gesture he drains his glass.

Annabelle writhes under the powerful surge of the ingredients now entering her bloodstream. In the throes of a process she can neither stop nor understand, the kitchen becomes incandescent, looms into angular shapes, declines into obscurity, before coming back into full view. Then she sees them again.

Yes, there they all are appearing one by one in her mind's eye. Is that delight on the Leopard Woman's face? Why is the Mummy's long finger pointing at her? What does Alonzo mean by his obscure song? But when it is Jeanne's turn to come out of the surrounding darkness, her face is so sad that Annabelle cannot even bear to look into it.

Overwhelmed by the pains coursing through her stomach and by the characters' timely apparition, Annabelle clutches at her throat and collapses on to the table. And as she lies there powerlessly, the last image which she catches before the dark rushes in is that of the Marquis, his face distorted by laughter, dangling before her the dim but unmistakeable pallor of a pearl.

CHAPTER NINETEEN

At around the time that Paris' traffic pauses before renewing its
assault on its circuit of sidestreets and avenues; at around the
time that Latin Quarter cinemas are showing nitrate prints to
bleary-eyed buffs at specially discounted prices and that ladies
of the night are gratifying their pimps with tricks no punter will
ever taste; and at around the time that armies of green buses are
letting hordes of dark-haired people loose on to the Sainte-
Chapelle to package it into shiny rectangles, a character dressed
in a large swirling cape, a black fedora, and a cane is walking
briskly down the Boulevard St Germain. Without any hesitation, indeed cutting a neat and deliberate swathe through the
throng, this figure stops outside a Brasserie with which we are
well acquainted for having spent some time there when the
story was just going through its first paces. Eyeing the customers, of which there are but a few, through its ample windows,
noting the constant presence of its blue-spectacled patroness
and of her corps of sultry waiters, the character goes in, finds a
table, and takes advantage of the excellent view which that
position affords.

Everything tires in this world. There is only so much energy
available in any given period. If the sets introduced in the early
days of this narrative have therefore begun to pale, show signs
of sagging, or have lost some of the fervour with which they
were initially endowed, this is as inevitable an outcome as the
entropic downcurve to which all matter is subject.

The figure whom we have followed down the Boulevard and
into La Fortune is of course none other than Annabelle Fleury,
wearing the same costume as the one which the Marquis

presumably bequeathed her and in whose fashionably altered fit, she, if we have grasped anything at all of the cyclic nature of exchange and the transfer of curses, now means to ply her duplicitous trade.

Leaning against her chair – its wickerwork sagging under the weight of the clients who have daily pressed against it – she beckons to the waiter who, she remembers, served her her first fateful meal. When he arrives, she gives him her order.

"A calva and a black coffee – and make it strong."

Is that a sign of recognition which has moved across his pallid features?

"Immediately, Mademoiselle," the waiter replies, moving with perhaps more than habitual vigour towards the counter. There he fondles a few bottles and chooses one unmarked before pouring a sizeable portion into a brandy glass, as if to make amends for an incident which he may still vividly recall.

As lunch time is long past only a few clients remain in the Brasserie. One, his maize-paper *caporale* hanging from his beak, is hunched over a radical newspaper whose banner headline exhorts the populace to inoculate itself against the bacillus of petit-bourgeois cretinism and to gather its destiny in its hands. Another, presumably in the last throes of that very virus, fingers the pages of a magazine colourfully devoted to hagiographies of the crowned heads of Europe. Annabelle's survey of the scene might have been more detailed had her attention not been interrupted by the waiter returning with her drinks. He sets the cup of coffee and the glass of calva down on to her table.

She thanks him, lifts the glass, and slowly sips the spirit.

She has already decided who most interests her in the Brasserie when the waiter pushes open the kitchen swing doors, walks up to the young man whom she has been examining, and places a steaming dish in front of him. Hardly moving from behind the dark glasses which he has donned not so much to shield his eyes from the natural light, of which little filters from a grey and overcast day through into the Brasserie, but to hide the gaze which he might level at his prey, he seizes a fork and attacks the contents of the plate. Annabelle is at too great a distance from his table to see what it is exactly that he is eating. Unfortunately, whatever the fare happens to be, he does not spit it out in disgust, nor does he call the waiter over and upbraid him there and then, as his urbane and well-heeled appearance suggests he would have done had the meal been below standard. Instead, with muted but unmistakeable gusto, he repeatedly plunges his fork into the food.

This is irksome. Either the quality of the food has improved or the young man's taste buds have a higher threshold of tolerance than hers had. More likely the chef is back in charge of the kitchens and the idiotic *commis* has been thrown out into the streets or reduced to menial tasks which even his hamfistedness cannot endanger. No matter for what reasons the food has now become palatable, Annabelle is forced to concede the collapse of her opening ploy.

She soon puts her disappointment to flight, admitting that it was a serious mistake to depend on fate's willingness to reproduce for her the one scenario with which she is intimate. A mistake and an act of laziness. For, to be fair, she clearly remembers the Marquis insisting that every situation deserves its own recipe. It is therefore imperative that she attempts to grace this instance with a new one.

She calls over the waiter who has been hopping from table to table picking up tips.

"Mademoiselle?"

She takes a piece of paper from her handbag. "Would you please take this . . . ?" she asks, scribbling on to it.

"Yes, Mademoiselle?"

"And hand it to the gentleman." She nods in the young man's direction who, if he has glimpsed her gesture, is too worldly-wise to betray it.

"Immediately, Mademoiselle," the waiter replies. He takes the note to the other side of the room and hands it to the young man.

The latter appears mildly surprised, looks up from his food at the waiter, and mutters a few words. In reply the waiter points towards Annabelle. Taking off his sunglasses, the young man gazes in her direction, purses his lips, and unfolds the piece of paper.

As soon as he has studied her message, he again directs his attention at her masculine costume, at the black felt of her fedora, and at the pearl so alluringly set on it. Although the tenor of her written invitation has yet to be confirmed by any gesture on her part and he is well aware that he might be walking into a feminine trap, he rises from his chair and walks

347

slowly towards the mysterious young lady who has already, if only by her imaginative brashness, invigorated his afternoon, and from whom he can at least expect a few amusing sallies, and perhaps, if fortunate, a visit to one of those discreet hotels which offer the unattached the opportunity to discover the tastes they have in common.